Edgar Cayce's
Atlantis

Edgar Cayce's
Atlantis

**Gregory L. Little, Ed.D.,
Lora Little, Ed.D.,
and John Van Auken**

ARE
PRESS

ASSOCIATION FOR
RESEARCH AND
ENLIGHTENMENT

A.R.E. Press • Virginia Beach • Virginia

A.R.E. Press
215 67th Street
Virginia Beach, VA 23451-2061

Library of Congress Cataloguing-in-Publication Data
Little, Gregory L.
    Edgar Cayce's Atlantis: / by Gregory L. Little, Lora Little, and John Van Auken
        p.   cm.
    ISBN 0-87604-512-3
    1. Atlantis. 2. Cayce, Edgar, 1877-1945. I. Little, Lora. II. Van Auken, John. III. Title.
    GN751.L52 2006
    001.94—dc22

                                    2006002728

Cover design by Richard Boyle

Contents

1

The First Account of a Lost Civilization: Plato's Atlantis

> Atlantis—next to God the most written about, debated, abused and ridiculed concepts on our planet.
> Andrew Collins (2002) *Gateway to Atlantis*

ATLANTIS — it's a legendary tale that has provided one of the most intriguing and enduring mysteries of all time while simultaneously provoking hostility from many archaeologists and philosophers. It's been stated that more books have been written about Atlantis than any other topic except the Bible. The first written account of this lost land was produced 2,360 years ago, and from that brief story, countless researchers have claimed to have found ruins from Atlantis virtually everywhere around the world. But no speculations about Atlantis have sparked the imaginations of millions of people as have the psychic readings given by America's famous "Sleeping Prophet," Edgar Cayce. Cayce's psychic readings include details from the day-to-day lives of the people of Atlantis and the actual dates of significant events that took place in that legendary land from its beginning to its fateful end. Cayce's depiction of Atlantis as a highly technological maritime civilization shatters accepted archaeological timetables. It reveals the locations of important places related to Atlantis and even provides an account of the end of the Atlantean empire detailing where groups of Atlanteans fled to escape the final destruction. Cayce's claim that Atlanteans carried out a plan to preserve records of their history and technology in three separate locations has spurred what many people consider to be the greatest archaeological hunt of all time—the search for the three Halls of Records. This search—at Giza in Egypt, near Bimini and Andros in the Bahamas, and at Piedras Negras in Guatemala—has been an ongoing quest from the moment Cayce first mentioned them in the 1930s. While many archaeologists scoff at Cayce's history of Atlantis, the evidence that many of Cayce's visions of the ancient world were correct has now accumulated to a level that is astonishing. This book presents Edgar Cayce's story of Atlantis and examines the research that has been done to prove—or disprove—the details Cayce provided. But before we examine Cayce's story of Atlantis and the evidence supporting it, the background of the story must be presented. That background is in the first two chapters of this book and summarizes what Plato and others believed about Atlantis.

Plato's Atlantis

When Plato wrote the first known account of Atlantis, *circa* 355 B.C., it's doubtful that he could have known the long-lasting effect of the story. Nor could he have predicted the controversy and intense interest in the story that would endure for the next 2360 years. Many modern philosophers assert that the story of Atlantis was a complete fiction, which Plato devised to impart moral lessons for the Greeks, but countless others—including archaeologists, scholars, and researchers—are convinced that Atlantis actually existed.

Plato was born around 428 B.C. in Athens. After his father died, Plato's mother remarried a politically influential man who urged Plato to enter Greek politics. But Plato instead joined his two older brothers and became a student of Socrates. Plato, considered a moralist, was deeply concerned with precise understandings and definitions in both science and philosophy. Eight years after Socrates' death, Plato founded a school in Athens, the *Academy*, which was the forerunner of modern universities. He directed the school and lectured frequently in science, math-

Plato. Source—*Ridpath's History of the World* (1894).

ematics, astronomy, and philosophy. Unfortunately, the vast majority of Plato's lectures were never documented. What does survive serves as a very valuable contribution to our understanding of the ancient world. For example, most of what we know about Socrates, who died in 399 B.C., was recorded in Plato's *Dialogues*. While many philosophers believe that Plato's accounts of Socrates are perhaps slanted toward making Socrates a more admirable person, no one believes that the dialogues about Socrates were a complete fiction. Most of his other dialogues use situations involving actual people to relate moral values and truth. The style Plato used in his *Dialogues* was one that followed Socrates' idea that thought should not be frozen in writing. Rather, Socrates believed that questioning others about situations was the route to truth. Thus, in his *Dialogues*, Plato never mentions himself or his own ideas. This writing style is one reason that many philosophers believe Plato's story of Atlantis was fictional. Other philosophers speculate wildly that Plato was so distraught over Socrates' political death, that he concocted the Atlantis story fully 34 years later to show the Athenian powers their fate. But the Atlantis story contains only one primary moral—how greed and the quest for military domination violated the link between humanity and divinity—leading to the destruction of Atlantis. And the details of this aspect are the sketchiest in the entire story. In addition, Athens and Greece are the heroes of the story. In truth, the only compelling reason that the Atlantis story is considered to be fictional is that conclusive archaeological evidence for its existence hasn't been found. But Plato himself related that the story was true and that he took great care to report the story exactly as it was told to him.

Plato included the story of Atlantis in two of his later dialogues, *Timaeus* and *Critias*. Written not long before his death in 348 B.C., both books are considered to be unfinished works. Despite the fact that many philosophers argue the Atlantis narrative was a complete fiction, Plato's account did involve actual historical figures and contained other accurate historical elements as well. Thus, the story cannot be a complete fiction. The main characters in Plato's Atlantis story, all of which actually lived, were Socrates, Critias (Plato's great grandfather), Hermocrates (a soldier/statesman of Syracuse), Dropides (Critias' great grandfather), and another Critias (the son of Dropides—not Plato's relative also named Critias). The key individual in the story of Atlantis was Solon, a well-known Athenian who traveled widely, wrote laws, and poetry. It is known that Solon actually visited Sais in Egypt, where Plato said the story was told to Solon. In addition, the names of historical Egyptian rulers and actual temples in Egypt were used.

Solon dictating laws. Source—*Ridpath's History of the World* (1894).

Plato's story of Atlantis comes from the tradition of orally handing down an important story from one generation to the next. Skeptics argue that since the story was told so many times, it could not have been recorded by Plato in its original form. But the details of his account are so precise and relate so many accurate facts that no one in Plato's time supposedly knew, that the idea the story is completely fictional seems highly unlikely. Plato himself emphatically stated that the story was not only true, but he was giving a careful account of it exactly as it had been told to him.

In *Timaeus*, Plato related that the tale of Atlantis was told to him by Critias, his great grandfather. Critias, as recorded in *Timaeus*, was told the story of Atlantis by his elderly grandfather (also named Critias), who heard it from his father Dropides. Dropides heard the story from Solon, who, in turn, heard it from Egyptian priests at Sais. The verbal passing of the story from one person to the next is complicated, but given the oral traditions is certainly reasonable. In *Timaeus*, Plato introduced Atlantis by asserting that the known history of the world was far from complete and that periodic cataclysmic destructions had wiped the memory of countless events from human knowledge. In addition, he stated that these cataclysms were caused by the shifting of physical bodies that move through the heavens:

✳ ✳ ✳

There have been and there will be many and diverse destructions of mankind, of which the greatest are by fire and water, and lesser ones by countless other means . . . but the truth of it lies in the occurrence of a shifting of the bodies of the heavens which move round the earth, and a destruction of the things of the earth by fierce fire, which recurs at long intervals. (*Timaeus* 22 C-D)

Plato's statement that "bodies of the heavens which move around the earth" can cause recurrent destructions on earth has long been considered ridiculous and is another reason "scholars" considered the tale to be fictional. Yet those words, written 2360 years ago, have proven to be frighteningly accurate. Until quite recently, scholars scoffed at the idea that cataclysmic events in ancient times could have destroyed entire civilizations. In fact, the idea that catastrophic events, such as earth strikes by comets or asteroids precipitating tsunamis, massive earthquakes, volcanic eruptions, and shifts in the earth's crust, have caused massive destruction in the distant past has only come to be accepted during the past 25 years. Prior to that time, geologists believed that changes to the earth were gradual, taking place over vast periods of time. With the recent verification of literally thousands of ancient craters marking the earth's surface, it is known that sudden, violent events do occur with surprising regularity. And with the December 2004 tsunami that completely devastated many South Pacific coastal areas, it's fully imprinted on our consciousness that maritime cultures can literally be wiped off the face of the earth in mere minutes—and completely without warning. In comparison to the devastation that Plato described as the end of Atlantis, the recent tsunami was very, very small. Precisely how Plato could have known that bodies in the heavens could cause catastrophic events—by both fire and water—is not mentioned by those who assert the story is fictional. It represents an important clue pointing to a level of sophisticated knowledge once existing in the ancient world that was somehow lost.

Regarding the physical existence of ancient Egyptian records documenting these events, Plato related what the Egyptian priests told Solon, "All such events are recorded from of old and preserved here in our temples . . . " (*Timaeus* 23 A) According to the Greek writer Plutarch (*circa* 50–120 A.D.), the Egyptian priest who related the tale to Solon was Senchis at the Temple of Minerva at Sais. The story of Atlantis was said to have been inscribed on pillars at the temple, but modern attempts to find the inscriptions at the ruins have failed to reveal them. However, the first commentator on Plato's works, Crantor, visited Sais around 280 B.C. to validate Plato's Atlantis story and related that the story was completely accurate. It has also been widely believed that the story of Atlantis was inscribed on scrolls kept at the Library of Alexandria, which was burned in 48 B.C. Half a million manuscripts are believed to have been destroyed in the library.

Depiction of a section of the Library at Alexandria. Source—*Ridpath's History of the World* (1894).

Plato's Dating of Atlantis

While countless theorists have proposed a host of dates for the destruction of Atlantis, Plato was quite specific about the timeframe. He gave the same date for this event three separate times. In *Timaeus* (23 E) Plato introduced the events surrounding the demise of Atlantis by telling how the Greeks successfully resisted an invasion by forces from Atlantis: "Of the citizens, then, who lived 9000 years ago, I will declare to you briefly certain of their laws and the noblest of deeds they performed . . . " In *Critias* (108 E) he started by reminding listeners about the date of the conclusion of the invasion by the Atlanteans: "Now first of all we must recall the fact that 9,000 is the sum of years since the war occurred, as is recorded, between the dwellers beyond the pillars of Heracles (the Straits of Gibraltar) and all that dwelt within them . . . " Finally, Plato again emphasized the 9000-year ago date in *Critias* (111 A): "Consequently, since many great convulsions took place during the 9000 years—for such was the number of years from that time to this . . . "

Before pinning down the date a bit more precisely, it's necessary to remind readers that Plato said he was retelling the story exactly as it had been related to him, going back in time to Solon. Thus, the timeframe of "9000 years ago" was actually 9000 years *before* Solon first heard the tale. In *Timaeus*, Plato said the original story Solon was told by the Egyptian priests in Sais was during the reign of King Amasis, who was best known as Aahmes II, whose reign began in 570 B.C. Thus, Platonic "purists," those who have applied a literal interpretation to the date, believe that the destruction of Plato's Atlantis occurred *circa* 9600 B.C.

Plato's Location of Atlantis

So much has been written about the possible location of Atlantis that it seems to be an almost fruitless task to present what Plato actually said. The problem is that various writers have placed Atlantis on every continent in the world as well as on every known island in the world. Many people have speculated that Atlantis must have been in the Mediterranean and assert that when Plato wrote that Atlantis was *beyond* the Straits of Gibraltar in the Atlantic Ocean he must have meant *inside* the Straits *within* the Mediterranean. Other fanciful speculations assert that his given location was just wrong or that he was referring to the Mediterranean as the "real ocean." These speculations are simply wrong— they are not supported by any of the interpretations of Plato's writings. A few people have claimed to make "new" translations of Plato where the word "beyond" really meant *well into the Mediterranean*, for example, in the Aegean Sea. A few clever people have written that "the pillars of Heracles" was really a reference to the narrow strait into the Black Sea from the Mediterranean. The Black Sea would then be what Plato called the Atlantic Ocean. But no accepted translations support these views. The Pillars of Heracles was the Straits of Gibraltar leading from the Mediterranean to the Atlantic Ocean.

The most telling descriptions of the location of Atlantis are scattered in several places in *Timaeus* and *Critias*. The location of the most important portion of Atlantis was provided early in *Timaeus*: "For it is related in our [Egyptian temple] records how once upon a time your State [Greece] stayed the course of a mighty host, which starting from a distant point in the Atlantic ocean, was insolently advancing to attack the whole of Europe, and Asia to boot." (*Timaeus* 24 E)

The small phrase, "starting from a point distant in the Atlantic ocean," is often ignored, especially by those who assert that Mediterranean islands or European areas were the location of Atlantis. But the phrase confirms that the war machine from Atlantis was not based in the Mediterranean, on the coast of Spain, or on a small island that was once just outside Gibraltar (see appendix). The center of the main political influence of Atlantis was at "a point distant in the Atlantic Ocean." Precisely "how distant" into the Atlantic remains the critical question.

Timaeus (24 E; 25 A) also leaves no doubt that Atlantis was located in the Atlantic Ocean:

✳ ✳ ✳

For the ocean there was at that time navigable; for in the mouth of what which you Greeks call, as you say, "the pillars of Heracles," there lay an island which was larger than Libya and Asia together; and it was possible, for travellers of that time to cross from it to the other islands, and from the islands to the whole of the continent over against them which encompasses that veritable ocean. For all that we have here, lying within the mouth of which we speak, is evidently a haven having a narrow entrance; but that yonder is a real ocean . . .

There should be no doubt that the location of Atlantis, as related by Plato, was some distance into the Atlantic Ocean. But the size and extent of Atlantis are more unclear. On the one hand, Plato reveals that the center of the Atlantis war empire was located at a distant point in the Atlantic. This may well imply that the capital of Atlantis was a considerable distance from the mouth of the Mediterranean. On the other hand, he speaks of multiple islands that can be hopped—island-to-island—until an enigmatic "opposite continent" is reached. These facts have led many to conclude that Plato was speaking of an island empire of many islands and that the chain of islands reached to the Americas. As with many of the revelations in Plato's story of Atlantis, those who assert that the tale is fictional have no suitable explanation for Plato's knowledge about an opposite continent.

Atlantis as an Island Empire

In Plato's description of Atlantis, he identified the size of the "island" in several different places. These descriptions are somewhat incompatible with each other, especially if one only thinks of Atlantis as being a single, huge island. But Plato stressed that Atlantis was an "empire" comprised of many islands. And the influence of the Atlantis empire extended from a host of islands in the Atlantic to areas in the Mediterranean, including Egypt and Tuscany.

The major stumbling block in deciphering the size of Plato's Atlantis comes in *Timaeus* (24 E), wherein he says, "in the mouth of . . . the pillars of Heracles . . . there lay an island which was larger than Libya and Asia together . . . " Historians note that in Plato's time Libya was the area of North Africa west of Egypt and Asia stretched from Egypt to India. In his classic book, *Gateway to Atlantis*, British scholar Andrew Collins pointed out that the island described by Plato in Timaeus would be larger than all of North America—an impossibly big island for the Atlantic. There is evidence that a small island once did exist in the "mouth of the Pillars of Heracles" (Gibraltar), but it was far too small to fulfill Plato's descriptions. The solution to this seemingly impossible massive island comes in Plato's other descriptions of Atlantis.

First, in several passages, Plato mentioned that Atlantis ruled many islands far into the Atlantic Ocean. As mentioned in the previous section, Plato related that the "opposite continent" could be reached by hopping from island to island. According to Plato, these islands were each governed by one of Poseidon's five pairs of twin sons. "So all these, themselves and their descendants, dwelt for many generations bearing rule over many other islands throughout the sea . . . " (*Critias* 114 C) The eldest son, Atlas, who became the first king of Atlantis, was named after Atlantis and the Atlantic Ocean. Atlas' twin brother was named Gaderius and was given reign over the portion of Atlantis just outside the Strait of Gibraltar. Plato also described how the empire of Atlantis, a confederation of kings each holding power over different portions of the main island and numerous other islands, came together during the war to conquer the entire Mediterranean. *(Timaeus* 25 A, B) The solution to the impossibly large island Plato described in the Atlantic has been presented by Collins and many others. Plato had to be referring to the vast extent of the island empire as it stretched across the Atlantic. Since he gave great details concerning the rulers of the many islands of Atlantis, this idea is clearly the most logical. Those who have suggested that Atlantis was simply a small island near the European coast or a small portion of Spain simply ignore the portions of Plato's texts discussing many islands and the idea that an "opposite continent" could be reached from the islands.

Regarding the physical size of the main island of Atlantis, Plato went into great detail, and the size he gives for that island is quite small in comparison to what would be "Libya and Asia" combined. Plato's measurements were given in *stadia*, the supposed length of the first foot race in the Olympiad. One stade is believed by most scholars to be about 618 feet. He began by describing a circular city, located on the southern side of the main island, near the sea. This city was, according to Plato, about two miles in diameter. But the size of the island on which the center city was situated is described in detail:

✳✳✳

. . . the part about the city was all a smooth plain, enclosing it round about, and being itself encircled by mountains which stretched as far as to the sea; and this plain had a level surface and was a rectangle in shape, being 3000 stades long on either side and 2000 stades wide at its centre, reckoning upwards from the sea.   (*Critias* 118 A, B)

Based on this description in *Critias*, the main island which held the Center City was somewhere around 340 miles long and 225 miles wide. This is a large island, but nowhere near the size of Libya and Asia combined. Since the island empire of Atlantis began at the mouth of the Straits of Gibraltar, there are only a few conclusions that are possible. First, if an island that was roughly 340 miles by 225 miles in extent did

exist just outside Gibraltar and extending into the Atlantic Ocean, then
the mystery would be solved except for the statements regarding many
other islands leading to the opposite continent. As mentioned earlier,
an island, named *Spartel*, did exist there at the height of the last Ice Age,
about 18,000 years ago. But it was only nine miles long and three miles
wide. And by 12,000 B.C., it was well under water.

Andrew Collins and others assert that Plato's claim in *Timaeus* of
Atlantis being the size of Libya and Asia combined, refers to the full
extent of the Atlantis empire. This idea is completely supported by other
details from Plato's story. It would explain why he mentioned many
other islands being ruled by Atlantean kings as well as why he made
the enigmatic reference to "the opposite continent" on the other side of
the Atlantic. This is a fact that no one in Plato's time supposedly knew.
Finally, if we accept the date Plato gave for the destruction of Atlantis
(9600 B.C.), other details in his story would preclude the area around
Gibraltar, Spain, the British Isles, or even the islands in the Mediterranean as being the main island. The reasons for this are quite simple. In
brief, Plato carefully described the climate of Atlantis as tropical. In 9600
B.C., the last Ice Age was nearing its end. But all the European and
Mediterranean areas were still cold, in fact, some areas were still covered by ice sheets. If Plato's dating of Atlantis is accepted, then the climate of these areas makes them impossible locations for Atlantis prior
to 9600 B.C.

In sum, Plato's description of the location of Atlantis clearly identifies
it as a vast island empire starting just outside Gibraltar and extending
across the Atlantic Ocean nearly to an "opposite continent." The main
island, where the fabled center city of Poseidon was located, was about
340 miles long and 225 miles wide.

The Beginning of Atlantis

Plato provided an intriguing story that described how Atlantis began, but he gave no dates for the beginning—only the date of its destruction. In *Critias* (108 B-C; 113 C-E) Plato related that the gods of
legend divided up portions of the earth for each to rule:

✳✳✳

> Once upon a time the gods were taking over by lot
> the whole earth according to its regions . . . So by just
> allotments they received each one his own, and they
> settled their countries . . . so Poseidon took for his
> allotment the island of Atlantis and settled therein
> the children whom he had begotten of a mortal
> woman . . .   (*Critias* 108B-C, 113C-E)

According to the story, the mortal woman was named Cleito, the daughter of Evenor and Leucippe. These individuals are described by Plato as "natives originally sprung from the earth." Following the death of her parents, Cleito and Poseidon married and Poseidon began constructing a circular city on the "low mountain" where Cleito lived. This hill was in the midst of a vast plain that had a mountain range to its north protecting the plain from winds and cold. To make the hill "impregnable," Poseidon constructed three circular canals around the hill interspersed with two bands of land. On the center hill, Poseidon brought "up from beneath the earth two springs of water"—one with hot water and the other cold water. According to Plato, the hill in the very center of the city, enclosed by the three canals, was just over one-half mile wide.

**Depiction of Poseidon and Athena at Nashville's
Parthenon reconstruction. Photo—*Lora Little*.**

After Poseidon and Cleito had their five sets of twin sons, the Center City of Atlantis was further enhanced by each generation: " . . . and as each king received it from his predecessors, he added to its adornment and did all he could to surpass the king before him, until finally they made of it an abode amazing to behold . . . " (*Critias* 115 D) Plato left no clues about the period of time that transpired from the beginning of Atlantis to the time it reached its height, but he related that many generations passed.

**The Center City of Atlantis.
Illustration—Dee Turman.**

Poseidon's Center City of Atlantis

By the time it reached its pinnacle, the Center City had a great palace on its central hill (now called the "Acropolis") with roads leading across four bridges over the three canals. At the center of the Acropolis stood the "Royal Palace," a huge temple 600 by 300 feet in size. It was a "holy ground" where Poseidon and Cleito conceived the "ten royal lines" derived from the five pairs of twins. A "wall of gold" encircled this area and the exterior of the temple was covered in silver with gold pinnacles. The interior of the temple was covered with gold, silver, and a mysterious metal Plato called "orichalcum." Plato wrote that orichalcum "sparkled like fire." A massive golden statue of "God" on a chariot pulled by six winged horses was the focal point of the temple. Surrounding this impressive figure were golden statues of 100 Nereids (sea nymphs), each riding a dolphin. Circling the temple's exterior were golden statues of all the princes of Atlantis and their wives, including the offspring of the original ten kings.

From the mountain range far to the north of the city a uniform series of canals were made that eventually led to the city. These canals were used to irrigate the fertile plain surrounding the city. Another wide, deep canal was dug from the city to the south where it emptied into the ocean, nearly six miles away. Harbors and docks were built in the circular canals and extensive maritime shipping of fruits and vegetables is described by Plato as taking place in the city.

Over time, high stonewalls were erected on the circular bands of land along the canals. The high walls allowed bridges to be constructed over all the canals linking the rings of land to the Acropolis. These were, according to Plato, so high that the largest ships could pass underneath them. Stone towers and gates were built on all sides of the bridges and along the canal leading to the sea. The stone for the projects was quarried on the island and was red, black, and white. The outermost stonewall, enclosing the entire city, was covered with brass. The second wall was coated with tin. The wall encircling the Acropolis was coated with orichalcum.

The temple of Poseidon located on the Acropolis—the focal point of the Center City of Atlantis—would have been similar in appearance to Poseidon's Temple at Paestum, Greece. The Paestum temple, much smaller than that described by Plato, lies in partial ruins today, but this reconstruction is believed to be accurate. Source—*Wonders of the Past* (1923).

On the two bands of land formed by the three canals, buildings were interspersed with plantations of trees and water reservoirs. Numerous other temples were erected in these areas for the other gods along with gardens, dwellings for important people, and barracks for soldiers and guards. A horse track was made around the entire circumference of the inner band of land and many people lived inside the far outer wall of the city in modest dwellings.

Plato's descriptions of the Center City are so detailed and grand that it's difficult to conceive what it actually would have looked like. The amount of gold, silver, and the mysterious metal orichalcum utilized in the various constructions is staggering. Many researchers have sought to find this incredible lost city. But the search is truly similar to looking for a needle in a very large haystack. Despite all the grandeur and splendor recorded in Plato's meticulous description of the city, one point needs to be stressed. The center city, the part of Atlantis that most people identify *as* Atlantis, was a mere two miles in diameter and it was located on an island that extended 340 by 225 miles.

Plato's Description of the Island and Its People

According to Plato the remainder of the large island was inhabited by "villages of country folk," streams and lakes, abundant timber, and animals of all kinds including many elephants. Timber was transported from the mountains to the city via the vast complex of canals. There were two growing seasons on the tropical island and farms grew a vast array of fruits and vegetables as well as providing rich pastures for animal herds. Metals of various kinds were extracted on many mines on the island.

The military of Atlantis was apparently composed of at least 100,000 horse-drawn chariots, about 600,000 men, and 1200 ships. Shields, spears, archers, and slingers (stone-throwing weapons) are all described as part of the military.

Religion and Government

✳✳✳

Each of the ten kings ruled over the men and most of the laws in his own particular portion and throughout his own city, punishing and putting to death whomsoever he willed. But their authority over one another and their mutual relations were governed by the precepts of Poseidon, as handed down to them by the law and by the records inscribed by the first princes on a pillar of orichalcum, which was placed within the temple of Poseidon in the center of the island. (*Critias* 119 C-D)

According to Plato, the rules pertaining to temple sacrifices and governing practices were written on the sacred pillar and it was there that the ten kings assembled periodically to council about public affairs. The meetings were alternatively held every fifth and sixth year. The ten kings began with a prayer and then hunted for a sacrificial bull outside the city with only staves and nooses. After capturing the bull, it was brought to the temple where its throat was cut on the orichalcum pillar. Wine was mixed with the blood and after swearing to obey the laws and punish transgressors, each king drank with the remainder of the liquid poured into a sacred fire. They then conferred through the night settling disagreements and rendering judgments, writing their decisions on a golden tablet. Plato cited their most important laws as these: They would not take up arms against each other; all kings would aid any other king who was in danger; no king could put another to death without consent of more than half of the ten; and the royal branch of Atlas was the acknowledged leader of the empire.

While many writers have described Plato's Atlantis as a sacrificial bull cult, it is important to understand that in any eleven-year period, only two bulls would be sacrificed.

The War Against the Mediterranean and the Demise of Atlantis

Plato asserted that Atlantis existed for a vast time period covering many generations. The people of Atlantis were noble and gentle, and maintained a link to their divine nature almost until the end:

✳ ✳ ✳

. . . the inherited nature of God remained strong in them, they were submissive to the laws and kindly disposed to their divine kindred. For the intents of their hearts were true and in all ways noble, and they showed gentleness joined with wisdom in dealing with the changes and chances of life and in their dealings with one another.   (*Critias*, 120 D)

Plato doesn't specify precisely how the Atlanteans fell from their noble and gentle ways, but greed and the desire for more possessions and power were involved. Over time, as their wealth and power grew, "the portion of divinity within them was now becoming faint and weak . . ." As they gradually expanded their influence, the Atlanteans eventually began a war to take over the entire Mediterranean. Plato is silent on when this war began or on other details of it. But he related that the Greeks played a key role in resisting the Atlantean war machine. Plato ended his tale of Atlantis by saying that Zeus decided to punish the Atlanteans for this unforgivable transgression and their fall from divinity. But Plato never finished *Critias*, and the tale is ended immediately after Zeus gathered the other gods to tell them of his decision. The final three words of Critias, ending his tale of Atlantis, are: "he spake thus: . . ."

The actual destruction of Atlantis is detailed by Plato in *Timaeus*. As mentioned previously, Plato hinted that an object from the heavens was involved in the destruction. That idea fits the statement that Zeus had decided to punish Atlantis for its "evil plight." There is no detail in the story hinting if the destruction came immediately after the war, sometime later, or might have served as a final blow to end the war. But in 9600 B.C., some time after the defeat of Atlantis by the Greeks,

✳ ✳ ✳

. . . there occurred portentous earthquakes and floods, and on one grievous day and night befell them, when the whole body of your warriors was swallowed up by the earth, and the island of Atlantis in like manner was swallowed up by the sea and vanished; wherefore also the ocean at that spot has now become impassible and unsearchable, being blocked by the shoal mud which the island created as it settled down.   (*Timaeus* 25 D)

2

From Plato to the Americas–
Atlantis Discovered?

Brasseur de Bourbourg held that Atlantis was an extension of America, which stretched from Central America and Mexico, far into the Atlantic, the Canaries, Madeiras and Azores being the only remnants, which were not submerged.

Lewis Spence (1920) *The Encyclopedia of the Occult*

Speculations and debate on Plato's Atlantis commenced the moment he first related the tale. As others retold the intriguing story, again and again, virtually everyone who was educated in ancient Greece became aware of it. The story was especially controversial because the Greeks' knowledge of world history and geography was very limited and mostly inaccurate. This fact led to two distinct positions on the authenticity of the story—a situation that persists to this day.

Aristotle, Plato's influential student, believed that the Atlantis story was fictional, but Aristotle also stated that Troy was completely fictional. Crantor, the first commentator on Plato, visited Sais around 280 B.C. and confirmed that the story was completely accurate. The Greek biographer Plutarch also wrote that the story was true. While the ancients debated the reality of Atlantis without the ability to assess the vast range of information that was available from various cultures, modern researchers have been able to examine nearly every ancient text for clues about Atlantis. Modern scholars have made extensive studies of ancient records and have concluded that there are literally hundreds of hints about Atlantis and other significant details from Plato's story that can be found in numerous texts and records.

One of the very best sources for these ancient records is the meticulous research presented by Andrew Collins in his 436-page book, *Gateway to Atlantis*. Collins found that the existence of Atlantis was "openly debated during the third century A.D. among the philosophers in the Platonic Academy attached to . . . Alexandria." Collins also discovered many references to ancient voyages that seemed to have been made to the Americas and unknown islands even before Plato lived. A few of these will be summarized here.

In 425 B.C. a Carthaginian named Hanno made a voyage down the Atlantic coast of Africa with 60 ships. Hanno reported that a temple of Poseidon was found on an island off the coast of Africa. Around 8 B.C. the Greek historian Diodorus Siculus wrote about mysterious islands called the *Atlantides* and mentioned that one of the sons (Atlas) of a Titan god ruled those islands. Siculus wrote of islands located well into the Atlantic Ocean, mentioning one "large and fruitful island" located "many" days sail from Africa. Siculus also chronicled an incident in which Phoenician mariners were pushed across the ocean by a storm and after many days landed on the "large, fruitful island." Another Greek historian, Hellanicus, wrote about the Atlantides in a work he titled *Atlantis*, sometime around 400 B.C. Plutarch also mentioned the accidental discovery of islands across the Atlantic around 80 B.C. There are many other similar references in ancient texts and readers are referred to Collins' book.

Despite consistent reports of strange islands lying well into the Atlantic Ocean, the people of the ancient world found the idea of Atlantis without definitive support. From the time of Plato to the 1500s, speculation on Atlantis was limited and was eclipsed by more important issues. The rise of Christianity, the fall of the Roman Empire, the struggles in Europe, plagues, and the ensuing dark ages plunged the world into a knowledge vacuum that persisted for centuries until the Renaissance.

Then, with the "discovery" of the Americas, the idea that Atlantis might really have existed became an intriguing topic because many people believed Atlantis had been discovered!

The Americas and Atlantis

When Christopher Columbus returned to Spain in March of 1493 after his first voyage to the Americas, his news of a "New World" was electrifying. Yet Columbus had only visited the Bahamas, Cuba, and Hispaniola on this first trip. It wasn't until his third voyage in 1498 that he made landfall in South America. He didn't reach Central America until his fourth and final voyage in 1502. Although others (such as the Norse) had visited North America far earlier, this "new" landmass was only first widely reported in Europe by John Cabot in 1497. After the civilizations in Central and South America were conquered and the mound builder culture in North America was discovered, a new problem arose. Who were these natives that occupied this strange new world and where did they come from?

Plato's story of Atlantis suddenly seemed to provide the solution. For example in the 1570s, the famous London–born astrologer and mathematician, Dr. John Dee, informed Queen Elizabeth I that the Americas had been Atlantis.

After Columbus' discovery, rumors began spreading that he had taken several ancient maps with him. The maps showed large islands far into the Atlantic. The Bennicasa Map of 1482, for example, is one that many researchers believe Columbus used. This map depicts an island called *Antilia* to the far southwest of Gibraltar. Antilia was named by early Carthaginian explorers who claimed that it was a large island in the western Atlantic, but it has gone by several names and spelling variations. According to Andrew Collins, a 1367 chart depicted Antilia near the Azores, in the mid–Atlantic. But the island on the map is far too large to be the Azores and later maps placed Antilia much further to the southwest. Early Spanish explorers identified the West Indies as Antilia, and the similarity of the name to Atlantis has long been obvious to many people. The islands of the Caribbean, consisting of over 7,000 small and large islands including Cuba, Puerto Rico, the Bahamas, and

Hispaniola, comprise the West Indies. But the most convincing link between that region and Atlantis was made during the exploration and excavations of the Maya and Aztec civilizations.

Excited by tales of travel in the Yucatan that were being widely published, in the 1860s a French monk, Charles Étinne Brasseur de Bourbourg, went to Guatemala. Brasseur soon discovered the *Popol Vuh*, a sacred history of the Mayan people, and subsequently published the first translation of it. Brasseur also came into possession of a native document called the *Troano Codex*, which had been removed from Central America by Cortez. As he translated the *Troano Codex*, Brasseur was stunned to learn that a cataclysm had taken place in Central America in 9937 B.C. Later in Mexico City, Brasseur found another native document, the *Chimalpopoca Codex*, which described a series of four natural disasters that took place in the region around 10,500 B.C. From his translation of the text, Brasseur surmised that the disasters were related to a shift in the earth's axis. Because of the similarity of these events to Plato's story of Atlantis, Brasseur reasoned that the people of the New World were descendants of survivors of Atlantis, and the advanced cultures of the Americas were remnants of Plato's lost Atlantis. Brasseur's Atlantis speculations were aided by a partnership with Augustus LePlongeon, who also traveled throughout the Yucatan.

Another Frenchman, Desiré Charnay, became obsessed with excavating Mexican and Yucatan ruins after arriving there in the late 1860s. Charnay found massive basalt statues at Tula that looked almost otherworldly. Reasoning they were from Atlantis, he called the huge figures "Atlantean," a term that is used to describe them even today. Charnay then visited Palenque where he became intrigued by the story of Votan,

"Atlantean" figures at Tula, Mexico. Photo— Greg Little, 1979.

allegedly a bearded white man who came to the area after a disaster destroyed his island homeland to the east. Votan, it was said, began the Maya civilization. Today, most scholars believe that the legends of the Maya god Votan (also called Kukulcan), the Aztec and Toltec god Quetzalcóatal, and the Incas' Viracocha (also called Thunupa) are all variations of the same story. These legends parallel some Native American tribal lore of their ancestors coming from the east after fleeing a disastrous flood that hit their island.

In *Gateway to Atlantis*, Collins traced the story of Votan back to Cuba, which he asserts was the main island of Atlantis. Collins also noted that Votan traveled up the Yucatan coastline and when he reached the first large river, turned inland. He then established a major city, which has long been thought to be Palenque. In a 2004 interview on the video documentary *The Yucatan Hall of Records*, Collins said he now believes that the river Votan traveled was the Usumacinta and that the present day Mayan ruins at Piedras Negras, Guatemala, may well mark the place where his city was established. As stated in Chapter 1, Piedras Negras is believed to be the site where one of the Atlantean Halls of Records was hidden.

Ignatius Donnelly's Atlantis

In his two books, *Atlantis: The Antediluvian World* (1882) and *Ragnarok: The Age of Fire and Gravel* (1883), Ignatius Donnelly forever linked the Mid-Atlantic and the Americas to Atlantis. Donnelly was educated as a lawyer and, from 1863–1869 served in the U.S. House of Representatives for Minnesota. When he lost the 1870 reelection, he became a newspaper editor and was later elected to the state legislature. Between 1878 and 1880, Donnelly completed the *Atlantis* manuscript, working from notes and information he gathered from the Library of Congress. It was an immediate best-seller and became the definitive book on the subject.

Donnelly's book was widely praised and even skeptical archaeologists admit that his research was scholarly despite containing what they consider to be fundamental errors. The highly skeptical archaeologist Stephen Williams wrote in his 1991 textbook, *Fantastic Archaeology*, that he "cannot help but feel a special kinship with this remarkable man." Explaining the popularity of Donnelly's book, Williams wrote, "First, it is a well-written and convincing tale explaining the past in forthright manner and with just enough specific evidence to make it very plausible. Second, the author quickly, and without boring the reader, establishes that he has done his homework . . . It is all pretty convincing."

Donnelly carefully presented myths and legends from Native American tribes, pottery and artifacts found in the Americas, the advanced civilizations in Central and South America, the sudden rise of the Egyptian civilization—all as evidence of the destruction of an advanced civilization lying between the Americas and the "Old World." Donnelly came to believe that the Mid-Atlantic Ridge, a long, massive underwater mountain range running nearly the entire length of the Atlantic, had once been Atlantis and that the Azores were the highest mountain peaks of the massive island. His second book, *Ragnarok*, was less popular, but it detailed what Donnelly felt was substantial geological evidence showing that the Mid-Atlantic Ridge had been above the sea level in ancient times.

Theosophical Speculations on Atlantis

As Edgar Evans Cayce (Edgar Cayce's youngest son) and his coauthors related in *Mysteries of Atlantis Revisited* (1988), the Atlantis speculations of Donnelly and the early explorers of the New World were based on first-hand observations, scholarship, and science. Beginning in the 1800s, however, a completely unique set of Atlantis ideas emerged from a tradition of obtaining occult—or hidden—knowledge through clairvoyance. The most influential of these came from a system of philosophy and teachings known as *theosophy*.

The word *theosophy* is derived from a combination of two Greek words, *theos* (god) and *sophia* (wisdom). The roots of the organization stretch back to a secret society begun in the 1400s and later formally established in London in 1510. The American Theosophical Society officially began in 1875 after Helena Petrovna Blavatsky met Henry Steele Olcott in America. The spiritualist movement was then at its height, and attempts to contact the dead and higher powers through séances were commonplace. The tenets of theosophy are beyond the scope of this book, but they contain some parallels to—and substantial differences from—the ideas expressed in the Cayce readings.

Theosophy and Blavatsky's Atlantis

Madame Blavatsky, as she is typically called, was born in Russia in 1831. Her family was related to Russian royalty and at age 17 she married a government official who was in his early 40s. The marriage lasted only three months and she subsequently began a series of travels that led her to Tibet, Egypt, India, Mexico, Canada, and America. During her childhood she was tormented with what is described as "spirit possession," but she displayed several remarkable abilities and an obsessive interest in ancient cultures. At the age of 42, she came to New York City, where she quickly married a young Russian immigrant. Although Madame Blavatsky never divorced her second husband, she became deeply enmeshed in a relationship with Henry Olcott that began from the moment she met him in 1875. In 1877 her first book, *Isis Unveiled*, was published and sold out within a week, running through the modest initial printing of 2000 copies. Shortly thereafter, Blavatsky and Olcott traveled to India, where they hoped to contact certain "Masters" who Blavatsky believed had been sending her psychic messages. After six years in India, the couple relocated to England, where legal problems ensued. Olcott soon returned to India, but Blavatsky moved around Europe, eventually moving back to London.

Blavatsky's Atlantis speculations are primarily described in *The Secret Doctrine*, first published in 1888. Much of the material in the book is attributed to her translation of a Tibetan manuscript called the *Stanzas of Dzyan*. In *The Secret Doctrine* Blavatsky reveals that seven "Root Races" are destined to evolve on earth during the "fourth round" of seven cycles. Each of the root races supposedly has a separate continent, however this is a puzzling point since the word *continent* to theosophists denotes not separate bodies of land, but rather means all the dry landmass on the earth during the appearance of each root race.

Like Plato, Blavatsky wrote that civilizations are periodically destroyed by cataclysms that result in changes in the earth's surface, but she added that each new root race springs forth from the destruction. The various root races overlap each other in terms of both timeframe and the land they occupied to such a degree that attempts to distinguish one race's development from another quickly becomes fraught with confusion.

The first continent and the first root race began near the North Pole. Blavatsky wrote that this area was not actually destroyed, and four years before *The Secret Doctrine* was published, suggested that the earth was hollow and that an opening at the pole was somehow related to the emergence of the first root race. This race, according to Blavatsky, was the first entry of spirit into physical matter. The destruction of the first root race occurred when Northern Asia was cut off from the North Pole and waters first divided the region from Asia. A shift in the earth's axis is given as the cause of the change.

The second root race she called *Hyperborean* and it also emerged near the North Pole extending into Greenland, Scandinavia, and parts of Asia. It too was destroyed by a shift in the earth's axis, but she related that nearly all people of the second root race died during the destruction.

The third root race was called *Lemuria* and it began some 18 million years ago in the Indian and Pacific Oceans. Lemuria was said to incorporate most of Asia extending around South Africa into the North Atlantic and Europe. According to Blavatsky, the major remains of Lemuria today are Australia, the islands of the Pacific, and portions of California. But because Lemuria also included the islands in the Atlantic and the

European coast, it is often referred to as *Lemuro-Atlantis*, creating even more confusion. The development of the fourth root race (Atlantis) greatly overlapped with the Lemurians, and Blavatsky related that a major destruction of Lemuria occurred 4.25 million years ago, "at the midpoint of the fourth root race and very end of the third." The last major islands of Lemuria supposedly sank over a 150,000-year period—from 850,000–700,000 years ago.

The Atlantean root race (the fourth) began in "the Atlantic portion of Lemuria," around 8 million years ago. The focal point of the emerging new race occurred in the center of the Atlantic. Eventually, that land became known as mainland Atlantis. Blavatsky related that Atlantis was once a large continent but it was gradually broken into seven "peninsulas and islands." As Atlantis began sinking, many people migrated to the Americas, Africa, Asia, Europe, and the British Isles. Before the final destruction of Atlantis, which is related in Theosophical literature to have been in 9564 B.C., there was one remaining island. Called *Poseidonis*, it was located in the Mid–Atlantic Ridge at the Azores, and was about the size of Ireland. Interestingly referred to by Blavatsky as "Plato's little island," it was destroyed by earthquakes and tidal waves.

According to Blavatsky, the fifth root race (the current one) developed in the Americas starting some four to five million years ago, overlapping the Atlantean period during the entire period. There were early migrations of these people to central Asia. A future cataclysm is predicted to occur that will destroy most of Europe and affect the Americas, ushering in the sixth root race, which will also center in America. A seventh root race will eventually develop on the ancient lands of Lemuria and Atlantis, which will rise from the seas when the sixth race is destroyed.

It should be noted that Cayce also used the term "root race" a few times in his readings. However, Cayce's depiction of root race is very different from that in theosophy.

Theosophy and W. Scott-Elliot's Atlantis

In 1896, the London Lodge of the Theosophical Society published a book-length article by William Scott-Elliot in their journal *Transactions*.

Initially titled, *Atlantis: A Geographical, Historical, and Ethnological Sketch*, it was immediately reissued as a book and retitled *The Story of Atlantis*. Relatively few people are aware that the psychics Annie Besant and Charles W. Leadbeater provided many of the details that Scott-Elliot included in the book. In 1925, Scott-Elliot published an expanded version of the work as *The Story of Atlantis and the Lost Lemuria*. The Preface to the 1896 book attributed its contents to both advances in scientific understanding and the utilization of clairvoyance techniques to gain access to memories of the past—thus revealing what occurred in Atlantis and the earlier Lemuria. The book contains scattered references to scientific findings of the time that support its assertions.

Scott-Elliot began by revealing that our current fifth root race is the Great Aryan race and that we are of *Teutonic stock*. Later he calls the Aryan race the more "noble one." With this assertion, we must take a brief but bizarre sidetrack.

In recent years it has become well known that Adolph Hitler and key leaders of the S.S. took an interest in the idea of a Great Aryan race and actually came to believe that Germany was destined to establish an idealized society based on his rather twisted vision of Atlantis. Hitler saw the "pure" Germanic peoples as the descendants of Atlantis. He ordered German archaeologists to work in the Yucatan at ruins as well as mounting a search for Atlantis in various locations. It is also known that Hitler dictated a follow-up book to *Mein Kamph* after he assumed power in Germany. The unpublished manuscript contains Hitler's plan to conquer the world with the United States cited as the necessary final conquest. Scholars believe that the book was stored in a safe—and never published—because it not only contained Hitler's step-by-step plans for war, but also his reasoning for the wars that were about to occur. Hitler asserted the German people had both the right and the destiny to rule the world because of their racial purity. He used the terms *Teutonic* and *Aryan* in descriptions of the master race, and linked the lineage of the Germanic Teutonic race to Atlantis. Scholars believe he was influenced by theosophical writings as well as a few other early writers. While some others had suggested that the superior Atlantean race was "White" well before Scott-Elliot used the term *Aryan* to describe the current root race, the idea that Atlanteans were white became more firmly en-

trenched with Scott-Elliot's works. Before going into more detail it needs
to be made clear that many of Edgar Cayce's visions of Atlantis are quite
different from the Atlantis described in theosophy. While these differences will become obvious in later chapters, one major—and significant—difference is that Cayce asserted that the Atlanteans were a "Red
Race," many of whom migrated to North America where they merged
with Native American Tribes. Cayce specifically mentioned the Iroquois
as a tribal group composed of many Atlantean descendants. Of course,
Cayce's timeframe for Atlantis also is at variance with that given in
theosophical writings.

Like Blavatsky, Scott-Elliot claimed that four major catastrophic
events took place over a vast time period resulting in the destruction of
Atlantis. The first three took place 800,000, 200,000, and 80,000 years ago.
(These dates are also very different from Cayce.) The final destruction
took place in 9564 B.C. Scott-Elliot presented a map of the world at the
time Atlantis was at its height, about one million years ago, as well as
other maps showing the earth at various times after the destructions
took place. He maintained that the fourth root race, the Atlantean, actually was comprised of seven sub-races. The details of these races are
somewhat complicated and are not of real relevance to this book. However, most of the descriptions that Scott-Elliot provides are quite different from Cayce's, so a few details will be summarized.

The first of the seven sub-races Scott-Elliot refers to as the *Rmoahal.*
They had "dark faces" and were 10- to 12-feet tall. The second sub-race
was the *Tlavatil,* a red-brown colored people who developed on a small
island off Atlantis. The *Toltec* race came next followed by the *Turanian*
race. The *Original Semite* race followed, developing in what is today the
British Isles. They are described as a "turbulent, discontented" people
always at war. The *Akkadian* race then developed just east of Atlantis.
These people were at constant war with the Semites and were a major
maritime people. The final sub-race was the *Mongolians,* who Scott-Elliot
stated had no contact whatsoever with the mainland of Atlantis.

Scott-Elliot reveals that after a 100,000-year "Golden Age," the people
of Atlantis became selfish and malevolent and began engaging in sorcery. A battle resulted between the forces of the "White Emperor," who
ruled from the "City of Golden Gates," and the followers of the "black

arts." The White Emperor was driven from the city and took refuge in friendly Tlavatil lands. Eventually, everyone betrayed the White Emperor and the practice of sorcery became rampant over all earth, allowing a "Black Emperor" to take power. These events took place 850,000 years ago. After 50,000 more years of evil, a "retribution" occurred in the form of a terrifying cataclysm. Massive tidal waves swept over all the lands of Atlantis destroying the City of Golden Gates, sweeping nearly all the land clean, and killing everyone except a few survivors scattered in various places. This destruction took place 800,000 years ago.

On a small Toltec island, called Ruta, survivors soon began a new dynasty, which was, unfortunately, "addicted to the black craft." At the same time, priests who survived the disaster elected a new "white king" to serve the "good law." Thus, as revealed in his book, Scott–Elliot says that the never–ending battle between good and evil was again initiated and the subsequent destructions (200,000, 80,000, and 11,564 years ago) took place as "retributions."

Scott–Elliot's *The Story of Atlantis* also claims that 210,000 years ago, the "Occult Lodge" of Atlantis formed the first "Divine Dynasty of Egypt," and began to teach the aboriginal peoples who already lived there. Just before 200,000 B.C., they erected the first two great pyramids at Giza as halls of initiation and a treasure house and shrine. The destruction that happened just after the pyramids were built submerged Egypt under water for a long time period. In addition, both of the later destructions (80,000 and 11,564 years ago) resulted in Egypt being inundated by water.

In addition, according to Scott–Elliot, Stonehenge was erected 100,000 years ago as a protest against the "over–decoration of the existing temples of Atlantis." All of these assertions differ drastically from Cayce's Atlantis.

It is interesting to note that Scott–Elliot's descriptions of the City of Golden Gates generally fit Plato's outline of the Center City. It had a central hill with a great palace surrounded by three concentric canals in the midst of a large rectangular plain. Flying ships made of wood and metal are also described with electric welding used for their construction. In the beginning the airships used mechanical power generated by the people onboard, but later they utilized an electrical power generated by devices similar to "which Keely in America used . . . " Using this electrical power, the airships traveled 100 miles per hour.

James Lewis Spence

Spence (1874–1955) was a respected Scottish mythologist who served as vice-president of the Scottish Anthropological and Folklore Society. He was fluent in numerous languages and studied hundreds of ancient texts from nearly everywhere around the world. His interest in the occult led him to publish the definitive *Encyclopedia of the Occult* in 1920. Spence took great interest in the legends of Central and South America and came to believe that traditions of the occult around the world were so similar that they had to have a single origin. Spence eventually published over 40 books, most of them on Atlantis and the occult. He concluded that Atlantis was the solution to this mystery and that the Americas were the key to understanding what happened to the Atlantis Empire. He published a series of books on Atlantis linking the lost land to the advanced civilizations found in the Americas. Strangely, Spence dropped all research on Atlantis after publishing *The Occult Sciences in Atlantis* in 1943 and he reportedly refused to discuss the topic again.

Wilshar S. Cerve

Cerve was the pen name of Harvey Spencer Lewis, founder of the Rosicrucian order of California. Cerve reportedly provided a synopsis from ancient Chinese manuscripts that were brought to California in his 1931 book, *Lemuria*. The book contains some references to Atlantis and a map showing Atlantis in the Mid–Atlantic.

Edgerton Sykes

Sykes (1894–1983) was a member of both the British diplomatic service and the Royal Geographic Society. He published two journals, *New World Antiquity* and *Atlantis*, for several decades and amassed a vast library of books, periodicals, and short articles on Atlantis published in nearly every world language. Sykes came to believe that the Americas were related to Atlantis and even focused on the idea that Cuba was Atlantis just before his death. Sykes collection of books and other materials was acquired by the Edgar Cayce Foundation and are housed at

the Association For Research and Enlightenment Library in Virginia
Beach, Virginia.

Phylos

In the summer of 1883, a teenager named Frederich Spencer Oliver
was helping survey a mining claim near Mt. Shasta for his father. His
task was to pound wooden stakes into the ground, number them, and
then make a written note on the number and location of each stake. As
he worked through the day he realized that his writing hand was trem-
bling. Inexplicably, he grabbed the pencil and pad he was using, and to
his astonishment, found that his hand began writing seemingly as if by
its own free will. As the tale goes, over the next three years Oliver completed an amazing story that was published in 1894 under the title, *A
Dweller on Two Planets.* The book is supposedly a historical account of
Atlantis told to Oliver through automatic writing by the Tibetan master
Phylos. Phylos' story was based on recollections he (Phylos) had of past
lives on Atlantis.

The book reads, at times, like a daily journal relating tedious, mundane details. At other times, the book is mystifying. It goes into depth
about the Atlantean government (even occasionally quoting labor laws)
and describes various portions of Atlantis. One of Phylos' past lives was
given as occurring in 11,160 B.C. According to Phylos, the ancient
Atlanteans established colonies in North and South America, Eastern
Europe, and portions of Asia and Africa. Phylos mentioned that souls
have "sojourns," but in a curious section, he flatly refused to answer the
question of whether life existed on other planets, although he added
that we would eventually know the answer.

Phylos' Atlanteans used electricity and had both airships and sub-
marines. The airships were called *vailx* and were of varying sizes. Curiously, the electricity on Atlantis was said to be created by capturing the
motions of the tides.

The location of Atlantis, was from the West Indies to Gibraltar—a
single landmass basically encompassing the current Atlantic Ocean.
Phylos claimed that Atlantis went through three days and nights of
natural disasters before a final blow ended the continent's existence.
After a brief tremble, the entire island continent sank "like a stone" to a

depth of about one mile. He also reported that a 1300-foot-high wall of water was created by the disaster. This massive tsunami destroyed almost everything as it circled the world.

Some aspects related in the book have similarities to Cayce's Atlantis. For example, the ideas that souls are able to travel in the astral plane and communicate with physical beings have parallels in the Cayce readings. Phylos, like Cayce, also maintained that a record of each individual's earthly existence was imprinted on the astral plane and that the souls of Atlanteans were now incarnating in America. Phylos is particularly relevant to the Cayce story since in 1933 (reading 282-5) the sleeping Cayce was asked, "Is the book 'A Dweller on Two Planets' by Phylos the Tibetan based on truth . . . ?" Cayce replied, "As viewed by an entity separated from the whole, yes. As TRUTH, that may be implied by one that looks only to the Lamb, to the Son as a leader, no. Choose thou."

Countless others have formulated both scholarly and expedition-based theories of Atlantis and in recent years, a virtual avalanche of new Atlantis speculations have been made. In a later chapter, these will be summarized along with research that has been done on Cayce's specific statements on the lost land. But this chapter has sought to provide a background of the early scientific speculations on Atlantis as well as summarize the psychic information that various people have presented. As we show in the next chapters, Cayce's visions of Atlantis are fully in line with the story Plato related but have major differences with other psychically derived material.

3

Edgar Cayce's Story: How the Father of American Holistic Medicine Envisioned Atlantis

> Conditions, thoughts, activities of men in every clime are things; as thoughts are things. They make their impressions upon the skein of time and space ... They become as records that may be read by those in accord or attuned to such a condition.
> Edgar Cayce explaining the Akashic Record (1936)
> Reading 3976-16

Cayce's story of Atlantis has entranced countless people, starting in the 1920s, when the first of his psychic readings on Atlantis took place. His story of Atlantis is quite different from the material of other psychics as well as from Atlantis theorists. For example, Cayce was quite specific about one area: *where* a portion of Atlantis would be found and even *when* it would be found—the Bahamas, in 1968 or 1969. As we shall see in a later chapter, that prediction may well have been realized. Another important reason Cayce's story is so different is the nature of his psychic readings wherein the Atlantis material was detailed. Most of the Atlantis readings were not about Atlantis per se. They concerned the past lives of specific people who came to Cayce for help in understanding their present lives.

There is one other fundamental difference between Cayce and the many others who have speculated about Atlantis. Cayce was, of course, a psychic. But he was unlike all the other psychics who have lived, and he was quite different from the other psychics who had visions of Atlantis, in this important way: Virtually *everything* Cayce said during his psychic readings was written down. Cayce's complete readings have been made available for researchers on a searchable CD–ROM and are also available on the Internet for members of the A.R.E. Thus all of Cayce's psychic statements are amenable to validation. What other psychics—or skeptics—can make the same claim?

Cayce's Life

Edgar Cayce (pronounced, KAY–see) was born on a farm near Hopkinsville, Kentucky, on March 18, 1877. As a child, he displayed unusual powers of perception. At the age of six, he told his parents that he could see and talk with "visions," sometimes of relatives who had recently died, and even angels. He could also sleep with his head on his schoolbooks and awake with a photographic recall of their contents, even visualizing the pages of books. However, after completing the seventh grade, he left school—which was not unusual for boys at that time. But because of his unusual abilities, the young Cayce became well-known in the Hopkinsville area.

Edgar Cayce.
Source—*Edgar*
Cayce Foundation.

When Edgar was twenty-one years old, he developed a paralysis of the throat muscles, which caused him to lose his voice. He was a clerk in a small bookstore in Hopkinsville at the time, and the problem threatened his job. Doctors were unable to find a physical cause or a remedy for Cayce's condition, and one night he found himself at a demonstration by a stage hypnotist performing in Hopkinsville. The hypnotist asked for volunteers and, because he was a local celebrity, the young Cayce was urged by the crowd to go to the stage. Under hypnosis, Edgar could speak, but after he emerged from the trance, the paralysis returned.

After hearing from friends that he had talked during the trance, Edgar turned to Al Layne, a Hopkinsville hypnotist and osteopath. Cayce asked Layne to hypnotize him and then, during the trance, suggest to Cayce that he could diagnose the problem and perhaps even suggest a remedy. Layne complied with Edgar's request. The entranced Cayce detailed a circulation problem in his throat area and asked Layne to suggest that the blood flow to Edgar's throat area be increased. When the suggestion was given, Cayce's throat quickly turned bright red. Then, while still under hypnosis, Cayce recommended specific medication and manipulative therapy, which eventually aided in restoring his voice completely.

Layne was astonished by the results. Realizing the potential of Edgar's ability, Layne suggested that Edgar try the same hypnotic method to help others. Layne's own stomach problems were the focus of Edgar's first health reading for others. Following the suggestions outlined in this reading, Layne's decade–long stomach problems disappeared. Doctors around Hopkinsville and Bowling Green, Kentucky, quickly took notice of Cayce and began testing him by having the entranced Cayce diagnose their own patients. They soon discovered that all Cayce needed was the name and address of a patient to "tune in" telepathically to that individual's mind and body. The patient didn't have to be near Cayce, he could tune-in to them wherever they were. The physicians were stunned to find that Cayce's ability to accurately diagnose physical problems and recommend a treatment was remarkably effective.

When one of the young doctors working with Cayce submitted a report on his strange abilities to a clinical research society in Boston, the reactions were amazing. On October 9, 1910, *The New York Times* carried two pages of headlines and pictures. From then on, people from all over the country sought out the "Sleeping Prophet," as he was to become known.

Cayce established a set routine for entering his hypnotic state. He would first loosen his tie and collar and then untie his shoes. Next, he would recline on his back on his couch and fold his hands on his solar plexus. After a few moments of deep breathing, his eyelids would flutter and his breathing would become deep and rhythmical. This was a signal to the conductor of the session (usually his wife, Gertrude) to make contact with his subconscious by giving a suggestion. Unless this procedure was timed to synchronize with his breathing, Cayce would move beyond the trance state and simply fall asleep. However, once the suggestion was made, Cayce would proceed to describe the patient as though he or she was sitting right next to him.

Cayce usually began by locating the individual, stating, "Yes, we have the body." Then he would scan the patient's body, similar to an x-ray scanner, seeing into every organ. He verbally described the results of this scan emphasizing the problems that were seen. When he was finished, he would say, "Ready for questions." However, in many cases his mind anticipated the patient's questions, answering them during the main session. Eventually, he would say, "We are through for the present," whereupon the conductor would give the suggestion to return to normal consciousness.

If this procedure were in any way violated, Cayce would be in serious personal danger. On one occasion, he remained in a trance state for three days and had actually been given up for dead by the attending doctors. In addition, Cayce had no recollection of what had transpired during the hypnotic session after he wakened. This fact necessitated that everything he stated during the trance state be written down. At each session, a stenographer (usually Gladys Davis Turner, his personal secretary) would record—word for word—everything Cayce said. Oddly, during a trance session, Cayce would even occasionally correct the stenographer's spelling. It was as though his mind were in touch with everything around him and beyond.

All individuals who had a reading were identified with a number to keep their names private. For example, the hypnotic material for Edgar

Cayce himself is filed under the number 294. His first "reading," as they were called, would be numbered 294-1, and each subsequent reading would increase the dash number (294-2, 294-3, and so on). Some numbers refer to groups of people, such as the Study Group, 262; and some numbers refer to specific research or guidance readings, such as the 254 series, containing the Work readings dealing with the overall work of the organization that grew up around him. Because of the great interest in Cayce's story of Atlantis, a series of special readings were conducted on the topic. These were assigned the numbers 364 and 996.

Cayce gave health readings to literally thousands of individuals, from famous people to ordinary citizens, even including President Woodrow Wilson. Cayce was secretly taken to the White House for this reading not too long before Wilson's death, and it has only been in recent years that Wilson's library released that fact.

When he died on January 3, 1945, in Virginia Beach, Cayce left 14,306 documented stenographic records of the telepathic–clairvoyant readings he had given for more than 6,000 different people over a period of forty–three years. The readings consist of 49,135 typewritten pages. The readings constitute one of the largest and most impressive records of psychic perception ever compiled. Together with their relevant records, correspondence and reports, they have been cross–indexed under thousands of subject headings and placed at the disposal of doctors, psychologists, students, writers, and investigators who still come to the A.R.E. to examine them. Of course, they are also available to the general public in books or complete volumes of the readings, as well as on CD-ROM.

While many people believe that Cayce's income came from the readings, the truth is that Edgar was a professional photographer for the majority of his adult life. He won several national awards for his photographic work and never charged for a reading. His hobbies reflected the things he most loved in life. He was an avid gardener, loved to fish with family members, and enjoyed carpentry. He also taught Sunday school throughout his life.

Accuracy of Cayce's Health Readings

Edgar Cayce is widely acknowledged as the "father of the holistic health movement," because of the accuracy of his health readings and the effectiveness of the remedies he suggested. As such, Cayce's health suggestions are given a great deal of credibility by medical science, and this recognition has actually been increasing in recent years. For example in 2005, a popular physician who writes a syndicated daily newspaper column, Dr. Peter Gott, began recommending the use of castor oil for arthritis in the manner Cayce outlined.

Substantial anecdotal reports and follow-up letters from individuals given health readings by Cayce have indicated that the majority of those receiving health readings endorsed his accuracy. In a biography of Cayce, Sidney Kirkpatrick reviewed research that assessed Cayce's health advice. Kirkpatrick reported that 14 of the 15 physicians who had treated patients who received readings (as surveyed by journalist Sherwood Eddy) gave Cayce a near perfect score. Even the one physician who was cautious had to acknowledge that the psychic's powers were "extraordinary." A 1971 study of Cayce's health readings published by Hugh Lynn Cayce and Edgar Evans Cayce found an overall 86 percent accuracy rate.

1923—The Atlantis Material
Unexpectedly Emerges

It could be rightfully argued that the emergence of Atlantis in the Cayce readings came as a complete surprise. In 1923, a wealthy businessman in Dayton, Ohio, Arthur Lammers, convinced Cayce to come to Dayton to conduct readings. Cayce gave numerous readings in a Dayton hotel with most of them health readings for several individuals. Lammers was deeply interested in psychic phenomena and he reportedly had discussions with Cayce on a host of psychic topics between the health readings. On October 8, 1923, Lammers decided to ask the sleeping Cayce a list of questions regarding the source of his information as well as on psychic phenomena in general (reading 3744-2). This was the first time that anyone thought to pose questions to Cayce in areas outside of health issues. The first definite reference to reincarnation in the

Cayce readings emerged on October 11, 1923 (5717-1). The first reference to Atlantis came on November 20, 1923 (288-1). In that reading, Cayce related that a particular female had a past incarnation "in that fair country of Alta, or Poseidia proper . . . "

The emergence of reincarnation in the readings shocked and challenged Cayce and his family. They were deeply religious people, doing this work to help others because that's what their Christian faith taught. As a child, Cayce began to read the Bible from front to back, and did so for every year of his life. Reincarnation was not part of the Cayce family's reality. After deeply reflecting on the issue, the family came to a decision. It was very clear that many people had been helped by the health readings. While the "new" information emerging in the readings was unusual, it also appeared to be helpful to individuals. So they decided to continue the readings until and unless anyone reported that they were hurt by them. This never happened, so Cayce continued to perform readings until his death in 1945.

Ultimately, the Cayces began to accept the new ideas, though not as "reincarnation," per se. Edgar Cayce preferred to call it, "The Continuity of Life." He felt that the Bible did contain much evidence that life, the true life in the Spirit, is continual. Many readings explained why there were repeated incarnations as well as how Cayce was able to access information from the past. The readings explained that everything that has ever happened, all that was done, and even things that were thought about were recorded on the Akashic Record. Many readings explained that the Akashic recording process was similar to a film of time and space. Some of these readings describe what can be interpreted as electromagnetic waves forming the record. In Cayce's trance state, his consciousness was able to access these records and interpret them.

Eventually, Edgar Cayce, following advice from his own readings, moved to Virginia Beach, Virginia, and set up a hospital where he continued to conduct his "Physical Readings" for the health of others. But he also continued this new line of readings, which were called "Life Readings." From 1925 through 1944, he conducted some 2,500 of these Life Readings, describing the past lives of individuals as casually as if everyone understood reincarnation was a reality. Such subjects as deep-seated fears, mental blocks, vocational talents, innate urges and abili-

ties, marriage difficulties, child training, etc., were examined in the light
of what the readings called the "karmic patterns" resulting from previous lives experienced by the individual's soul on the earth plane. The
bulk of Cayce's story of Atlantis is derived by piecing together pieces of
information from these Life Readings as well as two series of readings
conducted to specifically address the Atlantis story.

Problems Interpreting the Cayce Readings

Edgar Cayce's readings present some difficulties in interpretation and
understanding—especially when an individual initially tries to read
them. First, they are somewhat difficult to read, mostly due to their
syntax and the presence of archaic or biblical terms and style. They are
written records of a *verbal* presentation, a process that occasionally does
not carry the full intent that was expressed, and punctuation can significantly change the meaning or intent of the voiced statement. Also,
most of the readings were given to specific people with uniquely personal perspectives and prejudices on the topics being discussed. Therefore, the responses in the readings were often slanted to fit the seeker's
perspective and needs. For example, in a reading for one person, Cayce
recommends one marriage for life, to another he recommends never
getting married, and to a third he encourages him to marry at least
twice. In the few cases where a reading was purposefully done for a
broader presentation to many people the "sleeping" Cayce was still
somewhat at the mercy and wisdom of those directing the session and
asking the questions. Nevertheless, Cayce and his wife Gertrude and
their assistant Gladys were very conscientious people, always seeking
to be exact and true to the original intent of the reading. As mentioned
earlier, the "sleeping" Cayce would occasionally stop his direct discourse
to give an aside to Gladys about the way she was recording the material, correcting spelling or giving a clarifying explanation of something
he had just said. Finally, because some of Cayce's readings cover so
many points or issues within the text, it can be difficult to determine
which one he is referring to when the paragraphs are so complex. Despite all of this, with practice, one can become familiar enough with the
syntax, archaic terms ("thys," "thees," and "thous"); a repetitive use of the

word "that," and the complex thought pattern, that one can eventually learn to read and understand the Cayce readings fairly easily.

Edgar Evans Cayce's Analysis of the Atlantis Readings

Edgar Cayce's youngest son, Edgar Evans, was an engineer by profession who decided to evaluate his father's material on Atlantis. His best-selling books, *Edgar Cayce on Atlantis* (1968) and *Mysteries of Atlantis Revisited* (1988), with coauthors Gail Cayce Schwartzer and Douglas Richards, contained a numerical summary of the Atlantis readings. Of Cayce's 14,306 documented readings, 700, or 4.9 percent, contained some reference to Atlantis. According to their analysis, 21 readings concerned events related to the "First Destruction" of Atlantis, which occurred around 50,000 B.C. A total of 52 readings were associated with the "Second Destruction," which took place around 28,000 B.C. Another 352 readings detailed events related to the "Final Destruction," which happened *circa* 10,000 B.C. Atlantis was mentioned in 275 other readings, but the dates of the events detailed in these readings are indeterminate.

In 1923 only two readings mentioned Atlantis. In 1924, only 7 readings mentioned Atlantis. The years 1939 and 1940 had the most Atlantis references: 66 in each year. Over the 21 years that some of Cayce's readings mentioned Atlantis (1923–1944), the yearly average of readings mentioning Atlantis was 33. By contrast, during these same years, Cayce averaged a total of 332 readings per year. The implication of this is that even during the time period when Atlantis became a topic in the readings, the health readings remained the most important. Many Cayce readings emphasized that service to others and living life in a correct way were far more important than knowledge about the past.

Overview of Cayce's Atlantis

In this book, we have attempted to be as accurate as possible in presenting Cayce's story of Atlantis. But it has to be acknowledged that a few readings could be viewed as inconsistent or, at the least, open to alternative interpretations. These are discussed in subsequent chapters.

In this section our goal is to provide a thumbnail sketch of Cayce's Atlantis.

The readings actually introduce Atlantis by discussing the first appearance of human consciousness on earth. However, according to Cayce, these "people" were more like thought forms projected into primitive life than the human beings we know today. The readings indicate that a portion of southwest America was occupied over 10 million years ago, a time when the earth's land surface differed greatly from that of today. The land of Lemuria, or Mu, was located to the west of the Americas long before the island of Atlantis was occupied. The destruction of Mu occurred sometime around 50,000 B.C. (Cayce's information on Atlantis is far more detailed than that he provided on Mu.) But this 50,000 B. C. destruction was directly linked to what is called the first destruction of Atlantis.

Atlantis, located in the area of the Atlantic Ocean stretching from Gibraltar to the Gulf of Mexico, was first occupied by an advanced race of humans in 210,000 B.C. By 50,000 B.C., the country had developed an advanced culture with strange technology. Cayce's Atlantis was a maritime culture throughout its entire existence, trading with nearly all of the other lands of the world. Plentiful natural resources existed on the temperate islands, and the Atlanteans used stone skillfully and were adept at various forms of metalworking. Temples were constructed in the cities, and numerous canals were used for irrigation and navigation.

Perhaps the most public fascination with Cayce's Atlantis concerns a mysterious crystal, which has long been interpreted to imply a laser-like device. But the use of the crystal started rather simply and gradually became a focal point of a struggle between two factions in Atlantis. In the beginning, the Atlanteans were a spiritual people ruled by a peaceful group Cayce termed the *Law of One*. But gradually, the Belial (self-aggrandizement) influence began to manifest. An ongoing spiritual and material battle was waged between these two groups. The Sons of Belial worshiped self-aggrandizement, sought power over others, and practiced human sacrifice. Cayce stated that they had no standard of morality, no sense of right and wrong. In contrast, the Children of the Law of One worshiped one God, sought spiritual and physical attunement with the Creator, and espoused the ideal of treating others as oneself in their day-to-day lives.

But the Belial group consistently waged war and sought domination over others in their relentless pursuit of material wealth. While these actions appear to reflect Plato's descriptions of the Atlantis Empire as warlike, there is something more implied in Cayce's version of the story. In brief, according to Cayce, there was a more etheric or spiritual component in the Belial group's conflicts, which led to ill-defined destructive forces entering the earth. These destructive forces were, in part, responsible for the series of catastrophic events that befell Atlantis.

Cayce's story of how the destructive forces were unleashed is entwined with the mysterious crystal. The story begins with the "White Stone," a stone "in the form of a six-sided figure", which was also referred to as the "Tuaoi stone." Initially, this stone was used for communication with the divine, in a way that appears similar to how Native American shaman utilize crystals. A priestess of the Law of One would gather together a group and concentrate on the stone, eventually entering an altered state of consciousness. From the stone would come a form of speech interpreted by the priestess. The speech came from what Cayce referred to as the "saint realm," which imparted "understanding and knowledge" to the group.

As the Sons of Belial came to realize the unlimited power inherent in the stone, they began using it for selfish purposes. Gradually, the stone was set as a crystal, and the lights emanating from it were focused and utilized. The Atlanteans developed a system to collect and focus the rays of the sun, with the crystal housed in a domed building atop a multitiered structure. Cayce related that the focused energy was used to create heat to generate gases. These gases were employed in the turning of multi-geared wheels (to perform a variety of tasks) and also to fill what are described as hot air balloons and large, Zeppelin-like aircraft. In fact, when asked to describe aircraft at the height of Atlantean civilization, Cayce stated that the skins of elephants and other animals were sewn together to form the outer surface of these craft. He added that the gases were sometimes also used to propel these craft. Other readings refer to the Atlanteans using hot air balloons for transportation around the world. But the Atlanteans also had ships that could move under water.

The uses of this crystal were many and included a form of communication, which could be seen as similar to modern radio and television. But the Cayce readings on utilization of the crystal as a communication device can also be interpreted as meaning that the Atlanteans could project reflected beams of light into the air. This could be utilized for communication, but the exact meaning of these mysterious readings is not yet completely understood.

Whatever may be the correct interpretation of this aspect of Cayce's readings, the first destruction appears to have resulted from volcanic activity, which was stimulated by utilizing the crystal's energy as a weapon. According to Cayce, in 50,722 B.C., a meeting was held of the world's leaders to discuss how to cope with large herds of huge animals that were overrunning entire regions. A plan was made to use the rays of the crystal to produce explosions that would destroy the animals. The focused rays of the crystal were turned toward the earth and caused huge gas pockets to be released in the area of the Sargasso Sea. These gases apparently exploded causing a domino–effect series of catastrophic events eventually breaking Atlantis into five major islands. Cayce related that the catastrophic events included a buildup of ice and a shift in the earth's poles that resulted not only in the destruction of a large portion of Atlantis, but also in the destruction of most of the large islands. During this time period, many Atlanteans fled the disasters by migrating to other places around the world.

By 28,000 B. C. Atlantis had not only regained its technology but actually surpassed it. Machinery, electrical devices, and power transmission sources utilizing crystals are described. But the conflicts between the Sons of Belial and the Children of the Law of One not only resurfaced, they worsened. The continual feuds between the groups caused many Atlanteans to flee to the Americas, the Pyrenees Mountains, and Egypt. The Tuaoi Stone, once a conduit to God, had now become a "terrible crystal" or a "firestone"—an energy source that could be easily utilized as a powerful weapon. Cayce relates that Atlantis had several crystals set up into power stations located at various places. For unclear reasons, the crystals were accidentally tuned too high, causing a violent destruction. The eruptions left Atlantis with three large islands and several smaller ones. Most people accept 28,000 B. C. as the date for this event, but there is one reading that could point to the year 22,000 B.C. As occurred with the first destruction, Atlanteans migrated to various places following this event.

After the second destruction, Atlantis again faced rebuilding itself. But the much smaller islands apparently never saw a full return to the height of technology reached just before the second destruction in 28,000 B.C. During this final phase of Atlantis, the Sons of Belial seemed to have become the dominant political force oppressing all those who opposed them. Cayce does not discuss a war with the people living inside the Straits of Gibraltar, but this time period corresponds to the Atlantis described by Plato. Curiously, Cayce relates that an Atlantean priest became aware that an inevitable cataclysmic event was going to result in the near total destruction of all the remaining lands of Atlantis. This awareness came from contacts with a higher intelligence that could be interpreted as either extraterrestrial or psychic in nature and occurred sometime between 11,000 B.C. to 10,500 B.C. This source also revealed to the priest a plan to preserve records of Atlantis in three different locations. The priesthood of Atlantis subsequently made three identical sets of records and sent out groups to establish these identical "Halls of Records" at three locations. One of these was placed in the Bahamas, another at Giza near the Sphinx, and the third in the Yucatan peninsula. Shortly before the final destruction, more Atlanteans migrated to various places around the world. Cayce never gave an exact date for the final destruction of Atlantis. However, Cayce scholars generally agree that it was around 10,000 B.C. The cause of this destructive event is obscure, but Cayce related that the last destruction was ultimately brought about because of war between the Children of the Law of One and the Sons of Belial. As to the source of the destructive act, Cayce quoted scripture: "They that turn their face far from me, I will blot them out." In so doing, Cayce may have given us a clue about the source of the final catastrophe—it may well have been caused by a heavenly body striking the earth, the same cause implied by Plato.

[handwritten annotation: chesapeake Bay / carolinas region(s)]

4

Cayce's Dates, Geography, and Descriptions of Atlantis

Edgar Cayce's psychic readings on Atlantis do not contradict Plato . . . the Cayce readings seem to complement Plato's story while expanding detail.
Greg and Lora Little (2003) *The A.R.E.'s Search for Atlantis*

Cayce's story of Atlantis actually begins well before Atlantis existed. In the beginning, individualized "thought forms"—or consciousness—became intrigued with physical matter and physical life forms. Many of these thought forms projected their consciousness into primitive life forms. The process of this projection is termed *involution*. Cayce related that the first involution was in an ancient land called *Mu* or *Lemuria*, sometime prior to 10.5 million years ago. This first descent into matter was supposed to be a simple look–see visit motivated by curiosity. The descending entities were formless, energy beings attempting to discover how it felt to be manifest in form and matter. Since there were no human bodies on the planet at that time, these early visitors pushed their minds and spirits into whatever matter already existed.

It is said that Lemuria originally got its name from those isolated creatures found only in the Indian Ocean on Madagascar, called *lemurs*. These little creatures may have been among the first bodies to experience possession by these early human minds attempting to feel and experience this world through the physical senses. But the readings tell us that these early souls "pushed" or projected themselves into all variations of matter: from animals to elements. However, *lemur* is not just the name for an animal, it also means "ghost." Lemuria may have gotten its name not from the animals but from the many ghosts that were possessing matter in those lands. In one sense, Lemuria was indeed a land of discarnate ghosts. This also allows us to move the location of Lemuria from the Indian Ocean to the Pacific Ocean, where Cayce's readings of the Akashic Records placed it.

The next great influx of souls was 10 million years ago. This time the incoming souls were not just curious, they had decided to get deeply involved in the third dimension. They attempted to create physical bodies for themselves, but Cayce's readings say that their bodies were not the "perfected bodies" that were to come during the age of Atlantis. In one description of these post-10 million–years–ago creatures, Cayce stated that some were very small, like midgets and others were essentially gigantic, up to 10 or 12–feet tall (E.C. 364-11).

The third influx of souls is the focus of this book. According to Edgar Cayce's reading of the Akashic Records, Atlantis was a new land on earth and a new attempt by human souls to find meaning and understanding in this strange world of matter. It was, according to Cayce's readings, the third and most significant involution of human spirits

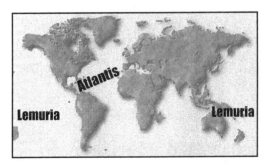

**Map showing general locations of Atlantis
and Lemuria according to Cayce's readings.
Illustration—*Greg Little.***

into matter. It began in 210,000 B.C. and went through many changes until it ended with the final destruction of Atlantis *circa* 10,000 B.C. However, Atlanteans continued to have profound impact on earth for many thousands of years after the last lands of Atlantis sank, because they had established a large number of outposts around the Atlantic Ocean and beyond. In addition, some Atlanteans migrated to specific places to escape the destructions. These Atlanteans often merged with the indigenous populations and exerted an influence in many areas. For example, America's Mound Builder culture was influenced by several groups of Atlanteans as well as others.

In addition to the beginning of Atlantis in 210,000 B.C., key dates in the history of Atlantis are 106,000 B.C., when Amilius and Lilith begin a new era of enlightenment and gender-separated bodies. 50,722 B.C. was the approximate date of the first major destruction of Atlantis, which broke the massive continent into five island regions. The second destruction of Atlantis began in 28,000 B.C. and seems to have occurred in several stages, ending in 22,006 B.C. The end point of the second great destruction of Atlantis was, according to Cayce, the historical Great Flood of the Bible. One reading dates this event to 22,006 B.C. (E.C. 364-6). After this second destruction only three major islands remained: Poseidia, Og, and Aryan. At each of these destructions, massive migrations to other lands occurred, taking Atlantean influence far beyond its shores.

Another key date in the history of Atlantis is linked to the purposeful division of humankind into five distinct parts. Five divisions of humanity were chosen because it is "the natural number of incarnate man." The date for this event is slightly problematical, but it probably occurred before the 50,722 B.C. destruction. W.H. Church's book, *Story of the Soul*, concluded that the five races developed in 12,000 B.C. by calculating back in time using biblical chronology of Adam and his descendants. But two Cayce readings (364-13; 5748-1) indicate that the division of the races happened before 50,722 B.C. Thus, we conclude the correct date for the appearance of the five races was likely before 50,000 B.C. The reason that the division of humanity occurred was because the souls of the incarnate beings had become so enmeshed and entwined with the physical matter experience that "escape" from the physical world required perfected bodies that focused on specific sensory problems.

A Mayan legend may well be addressing this exact event. The legend tells how the Lords of the Underworld had so confused and brought down the Children of God, that the Children entered into the "Seven Caves" for a pow-wow. At this meeting the Children acknowledged for the first time that they were not going to get out of this third dimension of form easily because they had become trapped in matter and were now caught up in the evolution of matter. This was to be a long and difficult journey, filled with struggle and suffering. Cayce called this "the journey up through selfishness." To help share the challenges, the one soul group of descended human souls decided to separate into five groups, each taking on some of the challenges of celestial spirits trapped in terrestrial matter, of cosmic, formless minds encased in finite physical form. Prior to 50,000 B.C. the one group of incarnating souls separated into the five "races" of humanity that we know today (yellow, red, black, brown, white), and into the five initial nations, at five initial locations: Gobi for the yellow race, Atlantis for the red race, Nubia (Africa) for the black race, western Lemurian highlands of the Andes mountains for the brown race, and the Caucasus and Carpathian mountains for the white race. Each race took on one of the five senses as their special burden to optimize while subduing the sense's negative aspects. The yellow race took hearing, brown smell, black taste, red touch, and white sight. More on these later. In addition to the five senses, five races, and five nations, Cayce's readings mention five reasons, five spheres, and five developments, but the readings do not explain these further.

The final key date in Atlantis' long history is 10,000 B.C. This is the approximate date that Cayce gives for Atlantis' final and complete destruction.

The Glory Days of Atlantis

According to Cayce's readings, the glorious period for Atlantis depends on what one considers to be the highest good: high-technology, physical comforts, and power or celestial attunement, psychic abilities, harmony with Nature, and consideration of others. He breaks these

glory days into two periods, but does not give exact dates. We can sur-
mise from his many comments that the high–attunement, relatively low-
tech period was from it's beginnings in 210,000 B.C., through the period
in which Amilius ruled, beginning in 106,000 B.C. and ending with the
rise of warrior energies and a leader named *Esai.*

ESAI

Esai and his kind sought personal pleasure, high technology, and
physical power. They devoted the Atlantean resources to the development of high–tech devices and weaponry. They introduced blood sacrifice and sought guidance from discarnates, mostly ancestors who had
passed on. They developed hierarchies and formed armies and slaves to
do their unpleasant work. Though it is not clear when Esai began his
reign, it was before the first destruction, in 50,722 B.C., because one of
the causes for this destruction was a result of Esai's edicts that allowed
the Temple crystals to be recalibrated for warfare.

Cayce said that the Atlanteans were originally a "peaceful peoples"
whose development in physical form and physical power grew rapidly.
He explained that this was because: "They recognized themselves to be
a part of that about them. Hence, as to the supplying of that as necessary to sustain physical life as known today, in apparel, or supplying of
the bodily needs, these were supplied through the natural elements."

Due to their oneness with the Natural Forces, the Atlanteans quickly
developed those abilities that "would be termed the aerial age, or the
electrical age, and supplying then the modes and manners of 'transpo-
sition' by that ability lying within each to be *transposed in thought* as in
body." They could travel in their minds as well as travel in their bodies.
Amazingly, this was not simply in the earth realms! Cayce said that they
were able "to transpose them bodily from one portion of the universe
to the other"! However, as time passed and materiality took greater hold
on the Atlanteans, many lost these psychic abilities. They therefore began developing the famous high–tech Atlantean devices for air, water,
and space flight.

Initially, their technology was not motivated by desires for power
but by need. For example, the need arose for particular individuals to
travel fairly quickly over vast distances. This led to the development of
lighter–than–air ships. When asked to describe Atlantean airships, Cayce
gave different answers depending upon which period in Atlantis' his-

tory was being discussed. In a reading for the early periods of Atlantis, he described a flying ship that used low-tech pachyderm skins that were sewn together. The airship was filled with gases for lifting the device and simple panels were used to convert the sun's rays into heat or electricity for impelling the device to move by turning a propeller.

However, he said that the metals used were a result of a lost art for making very light metals that could be used as both conductors and nonconductors. The nonconductors were used to construct the framing and the conductive metals were used to harness and direct the electricity. These metals, he said, were made through a lost method for *"tempering* brass, aluminum and uranium, with the fluxes from those of combined elements of the iron carbonized with those other fluxes."* This process made for the lightest metals and they could be used as nonconductors or conductors of electricity.

Later in Atlantis' history, Cayce describes powerful, high-tech flying devices that were run from a centralized crystal or cluster of crystals, which were refocusing the rays from the Sun and the star Arcturus. Crystals became powerful tools in Atlantis sometime after 106,000 B.C. and were in full force by the first destruction, 50,722 B.C. Prior to the 106,000 B.C. date Cayce mentioned a specific crystal used as a tool to make contact with divine forces. The crystal was initially called the "White Stone" and gradually became known as the "Tuaoi Stone." The crystal was used in a group ceremonial ritual where meditation was employed. A priestess who devoted herself to attunement to the divine would receive messages from the stone and interpret the messages. In addition, the stone was employed as a healing tool.

During the early golden age, the Sons of God, also identified by Cayce as the Children of the Law of One, lived and worked in harmony with the forces of Nature and the Cosmic Forces. They used innate psychic powers rather than high-tech machines. But after 106,000 B.C., the crystal began to be utilized for power and then for destruction.

Original Location and Modern Remnants

According to Cayce, the landmass of the continent of Atlantis was enormous. The continent was "between the Gulf of Mexico on the one hand and the Mediterranean upon the other." In these discourses he identified the great Sargasso Sea in the middle of the Atlantic Ocean as a significant portion of Atlantis and the very location into which Poseidia —"the Eden of the World" and one of the five great regions of Atlantis—sank beneath the sea (E.C. 1159-1). The Sargasso Sea is still part of the North Atlantic Ocean today, lying roughly between the islands of the Caribbean and the Azores islands, 900 miles off Portugal's coast. The Sargasso Sea is so named because there is a kind of seaweed, which lazily floats over its entire expanse called *sargassum*. Catching sight of these huge mats of seaweed has always marked the perimeter of this peculiar sea. Columbus himself made note of it. Thinking land was nearby, he fathomed the sea, only to find no bottom. In fact, the bottom is over 3 miles below on the Nares Abyssal Plain. The Sargasso Sea occupies that part of the Atlantic between 20 to 35 degrees North and 30 to 70 West (known as the Horse Latitudes). It is in complete contrast to the ocean around it. Its surface is usually calm yet the area is surrounded by some of the strongest sea currents in the world.

Cayce said that there are some "protruding portions" that "must have at one time or another been a portion of this great continent. The British West Indies or the Bahamas, and a portion of same that may be seen in the present. If the geological survey would be made in some of these, especially, or notably, in Bimini and in the Gulf Stream through this vicinity, these may be even yet determined."

However, when pointing to where one may find evidence of the Atlantean culture, Cayce directed us to look at areas where the migrating civilization went to escape destruction and death as their homeland sank. Cayce said that on the one hand "evidences of this lost civilization are to be found in the Pyrenees [the mountains between Spain and France] and Morocco [northern Africa—roughly 9 miles across the Mediterranean Sea from Gibraltar and Spain]," and on the other hand, in "British Honduras, Yucatan, and America." One reading (E.C. 1159-1) mentions the Canary Islands relating that Phoenicians ventured there and to the Sargasso Sea into the heart of the Atlantean land. Other islands in the Atlantic, such as the Azores, are not mentioned.

Cayce also pointed to North America when speaking of the royal Iroquois (E.C. 1219-1): "The entity then was among the people, the Indians, of the Iroquois; those of noble birth, those that were of the pure descendants of the Atlanteans, those that held to the ritualistic influences from Nature itself." The original Iroquois were comprised of the Mohawk, Oneida, Onondaga, Cayuga, and Seneca tribes. These peoples comprise one of the oldest living participatory democracies on earth. Governance was truly based on the consent of the governed. On June 11, 1776, while the question of colonial independence was being debated, visiting Iroquois chiefs were formally invited into the meeting hall of the Continental Congress. Both Ben Franklin and Thomas Jefferson borrowed from the Iroquois Constitution in developing the U.S. Constitution.

Interestingly, the Iroquois were matriarchal. Women held powerful positions. They owned the longhouses, controlled the land, and chose the chief. Children belonged to their mother's clan. When a man married, he lived with his wife's clan. This is interesting because Cayce said that prior to the legendary global Great Flood, the feminine was dominant throughout the ancient world. "Naturally so," he said. After the destructions in those ancient times, masculine became dominant. Soon, these two aspects of humanity's duality (Yin and Yang) will join into a united power sharing, as it should be.

A key point to note here is that the Atlanteans were the red race. Cayce described how they were originally "thought forms, able to push out of themselves, much in the same manner as the amoeba would in the waters of a stagnant bay in the present. As they took more physical form, they became hardened or set, much in the form of the existent human body of the day, with that of color as partook of its surroundings, much in the manner as the chameleon in the present. Hence coming into that form as the red, or mixture peoples or colors; known later by the associations as the red race."

A Typical Atlantean City

Cayce described a large city called Poseida. His readings are not clear on this, but it appears that Poseida is the main city in the land of Poseidia. In many ways his description of it is similar to what Plato described as the Center City of Atlantis. Cayce said that the city was on a hill that overlooked the waters of Parfa. These waters were a combination of natural rivers and walls that created pools from the river water. These pools had large canals, which brought water to homes and lands. These pools were kept constantly in motion over stone because the natural forces would purify the water within twenty feet of flowing over the stones. The buildings were built in tiers, one upon another, excepting the temples. The temples, he said, were where the sacred fires were maintained. The temples were built of large, semi-circular columns of onyx and topaz, inlaid with beryl, amethyst, and stones that caught the rays of the sun.

"These, as to the manner of the buildings, were of the outer court—or where groups or masses might collect. The inner, those that were of a select group, or those of the second chambers. Those of the inner court, or shrine about the altar, were only for the elect, or the chosen few. Those in the temple ruled, rather than those who held official political positions."

In this temple the sacred fires burned, and there were "the rising of the intermittent fires that came and went, that were later worshipped by some that brought on much of the destruction, because they waited long at the period before the destructions came. These were those places where there became eventually the necessity of offering human sacrifices, which when put into fires became the ashes that were cast upon the waters for the drinking of same by those that were made prisoners from portions of other lands."

Amilius and Lilith

Around 106,000 B.C., a new physical body was created on Atlantis. This body would help souls better incarnate in matter and three-dimensions. It was actually two bodies, one male and one female. Cayce called it the "third root race body." The Mayan legends called it the "Blue Maze" body, noting that it was perfect in every way. There will be more detail on body-types in another chapter.

This new body was conceived by two Atlantean souls named Amilius and Lilith. Yes, Cayce's reading of the Akashic Records identifies the legendary Lilith as the first true incarnate female. She was the first Eve, as classical Hebrew writings have always held. These two were twins of one soul, the yin and yang of one consciousness. They came to help souls better deal with the challenges and needs of incarnating into physical form. Initially, Amilius and Lilith were united in one over-soul. They were not your ordinary soul, however, because this was God's attempt to help the lost Children of God. Amilius and Lilith were the first incarnation of the Logos, or Christ—Cayce said there "never was a time when there wasn't a Christ."

Soon after entering this world and the third dimension, Amilius and Lilith realized how the duality of this dimension was forcing the twin aspects of the soul to separate into individual yin and yang forms. Cayce said that it took 86 years for Amilius and Lilith to perfectly divide their masculine and feminine qualities into specialized bodies for the male and female aspects of a soul. After this achievement, most of the other souls began using gender-specific bodies. The result was better comfort and companionship in this world. In the spirit or energy realms of life, companionship was ever-present because of the natural oneness of those realms. Everyone felt a part of a greater whole. But when encased in an individual physical body, the sense of aloneness was too great. Having the feminine and masculine bodies to comfort one another proved to be a better arrangement while in earth. Of course, as Jesus noted, "in heaven they neither marry nor are given in marriage." In the heavenly realms oneness brings with it a natural companionship.

The correlating story in the Bible is when God noticed that Adam was lonely in this new world, and among all the creatures of this world, no companion could be found for him. To change this, God cast a deep sleep over Adam and drew out the feminine side, separating it from the masculine side. Now they could be companions and "helpmeets" one to another.

According to Cayce, Amilius continued to create and improve the physical conditions and forms so that souls could incarnate with more of their higher consciousness present and usable in physicality. Temples were built to maintain and teach the importance of oneness with the Cosmos, with the Creative Forces, and with one another. These were glorious times in Atlantis.

Tragically, many incarnate souls, called by Cayce the "Sons of Belial,"

(500000 BC?)
TO THE 4TH RR
ADAMIC BODY

sought more and more their own self-interests and gratification with
less and less concern for the wholeness and cooperation needed for
oneness with Life and Life's creations. Moral decadence, power mad-
ness, loss of respect for Nature, disregard for oneness with the Cosmic
Forces, and a growing sense of hierarchy among themselves and superiority over others brought Atlantis and its people into turmoil. As much
as the spiritually oriented Children of the Law of One tried to call attention to this, the influences of the Sons of Belial took Atlantis into an era
of destructive activity and thought. The leadership of Amilius was replaced with that of Esai. The once peaceful vibrations now attracted
large, dangerous beasts—entering the Atlantean continent for the first
time (sabertooth tigers, short-faced bears, dire wolves, mastodons,
woolly mammoths, etc.). Now weapons were needed to protect the
people.

Once peaceful, healing devices were turned into killing machines.
Cayce says of the Tuaoi stone, later called the Firestone, that "man eventually turned this into that channel for destructive forces." The rejuve-
nating stone became, what Cayce called, a "Death Ray."

The subsequent loss of attunement and high consciousness resulted
in the crystals being out of tune, and the power devices being used to
kill rather than to enliven and regenerate body and mind. Out-of-tune
crystals caused enormous disharmony with the force fields in and
around the earth. The powerful Death Ray not only killed enemies, it
disturbed the environs of the planet in such a way that the planet rose
up against these vibrations and the first destruction occurred, Cayce
explained.

Cayce marked the reign of Esai as a turning point in Atlantis' history.
"With this reign, with these destructive forces, we find the first turning
of the altar fires into that of sacrifice of those that were taken, and
human sacrifice began. With this also came the first egress of peoples to
that of the Pyrenees first, [then] into Og [South America], or those
peoples that later became the beginning of the Inca, [then] those of the
mound dwellers [North America]."

Cayce explained that such activity "made in nature and natural form
the first of the eruptions that awoke from the depth of the slow cooling
earth, and that portion now near what would be termed the Sargasso

EDEN in ATLANTIS (?)

Sea first went into the depths." Sadly, Cayce noted that the destruction not only took the lives of many negative souls, it carried "with them ALL those forms of Amilius that he gained . . . in that great development in this, the Eden of the world." These violent eruptions broke the great continent into five islands. The first Eden, as Cayce called it, was no more. But not all Atlanteans were destroyed in the cataclysm and the struggle between the two groups continued. This destruction occurred in 50,722 B.C. and was linked to a meeting held at that time to discuss the problem of the animals. This is detailed in the next section.

Despite the violent reaction of the planet, the Sons of Belial continued to wrestle control away from Children of the Law of One. The problem was complex. If the Children stayed, they had to fight with Belial; this brought out attitudes and energies that the Children did not want to develop. Many chose instead to migrate to other lands and continue their oneness with the Creative Forces, sharing with and teaching anyone who would listen. Those who remained behind struggled against the darkness of Belial, Baal, Baalila, and even Beelzebub, Cayce stated! Eventually, the ruling council of Atlantis came under the complete control of the negative energies and desires. Cayce's readings actually describe how some well-meaning and highly-attuned Atlantean priests and priestesses tried to accommodate the Sons of Belial, believing that cooperation might help them come around to the truth, but accommodators eventually found themselves tainted by Baal and sinking into darkness and despair. *(BATTLE & HITLER)*

Beasts, Councils, and Nature—
Cause of the First Destruction

According to Cayce's reading of the Akashic Records, in the ancient times of Atlantis, the planet was overrun by gigantic animals that made it nearly impossible for the growing human population to survive. Of course, the huge animals Cayce mentioned were not the dinosaurs, because they were long gone by the time that human souls began entering the earth. As we have seen, Cayce said that human souls began entering about 10.5 million years ago, with a second wave entering around 10 million years ago. Atlantis, which Cayce said began about

210,000 years ago, was the period when a third wave of souls entered earth's realms.

With these dates in mind, we are obviously dealing with the large beasts that survived the end of the dinosaur age and those that evolved long after the dinosaurs. During this period the planet was home to sabertoothed cats, giant ground sloth, giant short-faced bear, dire wolves, mastodons, mammoths, and the like. According to current archaeological timetables, these animals became completely extinct about 11,000 years ago. Their extinction was so abrupt that some frozen mammoth carcasses have been found with grass still in their mouths, indicating that they died so quickly that they didn't even have time to swallow! Mainstream archaeology now attributes the disappearance of these large animals to some sort of disastrous environmental event combined with efficient hunting techniques. But Cayce asserted that the huge animals threatening human populations were destroyed far earlier—around 50,000 B.C. The readings do not state that the animals were made extinct at that early date, but those threatening the human populations were killed. Interestingly, Australia is the one area where it has been found that the dangerous large animals there (carnivorous kangaroos, 25 ft. lizards, and giant snakes) became extinct suddenly around 50,000 B.C. Again, scientists are at a loss to explain the reason, but believe that environmental change is the most likely cause.

Russian Mammoth—Actual specimen of a mammoth discovered frozen in the Siberian tundra with food in its mouth, on display at Leningrad Museum in the 1920s. The chapter in the textbook describing the frozen mammoths states, "It is clear that the Asiatic continent must have extended at one time much farther towards the pole than it does today." Mammoths are genetically similar to Indian elephants and not much larger than African elephants. Source—Wonders of the Past (1923).

From the Akashic Records Cayce gave a strange explanation for the abrupt changes that led to the quick death of the animals. He said that when God, or what he called the Creative Forces and the Universal Consciousness, became aware that the Sons of God (remember, their gender qualities are united, male and female in one soul) wanted to experience this world, God prepared the planet to accommodate incarnating human souls.

Before you get uncomfortable with a God that would kill animals to make room for humans, you have to keep in mind that according to Cayce's readings, there is no real death, only a change from matter to energy, or from form to formlessness. The animals, and all their glory, remain alive in the infinite, never-ending mind of God. They are no longer manifesting physically in matter on this planet, but they live. Many humans, after experiencing matter, may now prefer life in the infinite, formless spirit to that in the flesh of matter.

Before God acted to prepare the earth, Cayce's readings tell that human souls met in a council to discuss how they, the humans, might rid the earth of these dangerous animals. You recall that the Atlanteans had actually turned their life–giving ray into a death ray to use against these animals. But a better method was necessary if the planet was to become a human planet.

In his readings Cayce appears to give us two major council meetings. The first meeting occurred 10.5 million years ago and may have been in the mental dimension, not the physical, or in a quasi–physical form rather than in physical bodies like we have today. It was a gathering of minds to consider all the ramifications of godlings descending into matter and beginning a long journey through material evolution.

The second meeting was at the time of the first destruction of Atlantis, 50,722 B.C. It was held in the land of Egypt, but priests, soothsayers, and astrologers came from as far away as Tibet to join in the conclave. The gathering lasted "many moons," according to Cayce's readings. He states that the meetings were composed of key souls from around the world and from the five major nations that were on the earth in those times, each nation corresponding to the five major races (yellow, red, black, brown, white) and five major locations (Gobi, Atlantis, Africa, Lemurian Andes, Caucasus mountains). Interestingly, Cayce said that in the beginning, there were only 133 million souls on the earth, compared to the 6.4 billion today!

Here's what he said about the topics covered in the meeting:

"The first laws, then, partook of that of the study of self, the division of mind, the division of the solar systems, the division of man in the various spheres of existence through the earth plane and through the earth's solar system. The *Book of the Dead*, then, being the first of those that were written as the inscribed conditions necessary for the development in earth or in spirit planes. These, as we see, covered many various phases. About these were set many different ones to give the interpretation of same to the peoples in the various spheres that the individuals dwelled in that came together. Hence the difference in the manner of approaching the same sacrificial conditions in the various spheres, yet all using the Sun, the Moon, the Stars, as the emblems of the conditions necessary for the knowledge of those elements as enter in." (E.C. 5748-2)

Since both the Tibetan and the Egyptian teachers were present, perhaps Cayce's citing of the *Book of the Dead* is an indication that a basic manual was developed during the conclave and was later used as the basis for the eventual publication of both the Egyptian and the Tibetan books of the dead.

The Cayce readings specifically identify the leader of this gathering as one named "Tim" from the region of Poseidia, Atlantis. But the readings gave much more information about another participant in this conclave, an Atlantean named Asapha, from the city of Alta, also in the region of Poseidia. A fascinating aspect of this individual is that he was the male aspect of an androgynous body that also contained its feminine aspect. His feminine half was known as Affa. This androgynous entity ruled Alta for 199 years and played an unusual role at this meeting.

Asapha advised the participants of the conclave, including his fellow Atlanteans, to avoid using weapons and destructive forces (such as poisons) against the beasts, even though they threatened human existence. According to the readings, most members did not agree with Asapha, preferring swift and violent action. Here's a portion of one reading on Asapha's high-road approach to the problem:

"Then, as these were gathered from the five nations, we find the subjects of those pertaining to manifestations of the development of man and man's ability to cope with the conditions [giant beasts roaming freely], and the forces wherein men were given their supremacy over the other conditions in the earth's plane. And the first as was given by the ruler [Asapha] was, then, that the force that gives man, in his weak state, the ability to subdue and overcome the great beasts that inhabit the plane of man's existence must come from a higher source. Hence the first law of self-preservation in the physical plane [was] attributed to Divine or Higher Forces." (E.C. 5748–3)

Asapha wanted to find a way to coordinate human efforts to solve the problem with the Higher Forces. As it turned out, the Higher Forces did indeed clear the earth of these animals, following the misguided attempt by the Atlanteans. Here's another reading that describes what happened:

"The entity was among those who were of the Children of the Law of One in the Atlantean period. The entity was the timekeeper for those who were called *things*, or the servants, or the workers of the peoples. The entity then was among those who were of that group who gathered to rid the earth of the enormous animals which overran the earth, but ice, the entity found, *nature*, God, changed the poles and the animals were destroyed, though man attempted it in that activity at the meetings." (E.C. 5249–1) The Cayce readings explain that the Atlanteans decided upon using explosives created by the focused rays of the crystal, to kill the large animals. The explosions released natural gases, apparently from the ocean bottom, that created a catastrophic series of events. These events may have led to a shift in the earth's poles and what appears to be a sudden ice age.

The question that comes to mind is, if the pole shift and resulting freeze swiftly killed most of the giant animals, how did it not kill the humans too? Well, the Cayce readings indicate that most humans lived in areas that did not have high populations of large animals and were not as dramatically affected by the temperature change as the regions in which these large beasts lived. So, while the disastrous events broke Atlantis into five main islands and killed the beasts threatening human population centers, many Atlanteans survived.

Interestingly, Asapha and Affa left the earth for a time (died to physi-

17,000 BC

cality) and reincarnated 38,000 years later as the Ice Age was ending and Atlantis was in decline. Again, they incarnated in one body, containing both the feminine and masculine aspects of their whole soul. Their names were now Aczine and Asule. It was around 12,800 B.C. Unlike the previous incarnation in which Asapha was dominant, this time, the feminine aspect was dominant. Asule, the feminine side, was in the projected consciousness, while Aczine was in the subconscious, inner mind. They incarnated in Poseidia, Atlantis, in the city of Alta, at a time when this portion of Atlantis was nearing its final destruction and sinking beneath the Sargasso Sea. It was not a good incarnation for them. Asule succumbed to aberrant sexual temptations with animal-like beings. The Cayce reading implies that she was not completely at fault here but was so naive that the evil Sons of Belial and their distorted views of what life was for—pleasure-seeking and self-gratification—led her into the situations. As a result of the beastly encounters, the feminine portion became so disoriented by the experience that the reading says: "karma exercised in coma." She fell into a comatose state from which she could not easily extricate herself. This also resulted in the complete separation of the feminine and masculine portions of this one soul, causing the two of them to incarnate separately. They did, however, have many incarnations at the same time and helped one another along the way. The readings also state that they will unite in one body again when they reincarnate in the year 2158 A.D.

The Second Destruction

The beginning of the second destruction of Atlantis occurred in 28,000 B.C. But it is apparent from the readings that some Atlanteans were aware that a disturbance was about to occur. For example, Cayce told an individual that he had been involved in an effort "that was for the preservation of the peoples; and the entity—with others—migrated to what is known as the Peruvian, or later known as the Incal land" (E.C. 470–22). By the time the second destruction began, the technology of the Atlantean empire had apparently surpassed the earlier, lower technological development. Cayce revealed details in various readings that machinery of various types had been developed, electrical power transmission was used, and agricultural methods producing higher yields were employed. Air, ship, and submarine travel was developed, although it may not have been precisely as people today visualize. The source of the power for these devices came from power stations that employed crystals to focus the rays of the sun. The craft were also guided by transmissions from the crystal, and a form of communication described as similar to "radio vibrations" was utilized.

During the period between the first and second destruction, the conflicts between the two factions increased. Some Atlanteans left to find a better life elsewhere, and the Belial influence dominated. Cayce described the cause of the second destruction, relating that the crystals producing power were incorrectly tuned and a disaster occurred. But a series of long-term events seems to have been involved, culminating with a flood in 22,006 B.C.—the biblical flood of Noah. The destruction left Atlantis with three main islands and smaller ones scattered around. As these events transpired, some Atlanteans managed to escape to North America, South America, and the Mediterranean.

The Final Destruction

Prior to the final destruction of Atlantis *circa* 10,000 B.C., Cayce related that all the Atlanteans were "exceptional" to the extremes. "They either yield woe or great development" (E.C. 1744–1). The antagonism between the Sons of Belial and Children of the Law of One had reached a peak. Cayce related that a class of humans, called "laborers," were employed to work as slaves, greatly disturbing the Law of One followers. They were being treated like objects rather than human beings. Indications from the readings are that Atlantis lost some of its technological knowledge. But this was the time period of Plato's Atlantis, and according to Cayce, Atlantis was now an island empire with a strong maritime trade. Cayce does not mention a war with the people of the Mediterranean but does relate that the Atlanteans strove to rule over other areas.

A few hundred years before the final destruction took place, Cayce related details about a priest, "one who was the keeper of the portals as well as the messages that were received from the visitation of those from the outer spheres . . . " (E.C. 1681–1). The priest "received the mes-

ILTAR ?

sage as to the needs for dividing of the children of the Law of One and for the preservation of the truths of same in other lands. Hence, we find the entity was among those who were the directors of those expeditions, or the leaving for the many varied lands just before the breaking up of the Atlantean land." A plan was made to establish three sets of records and send out groups to preserve the records. Migrations of some Atlanteans took place to varied places including Egypt, South and Central America, eastern North America, the Gobi, and elsewhere. The final destructive event took place around 10,000 B.C. The cause was, according to Cayce, the result of the ongoing struggle between the two warring factions. The precise event that took place isn't mentioned, but an act of God is attributed to it, just as Plato related. As mentioned in a previous chapter, Cayce related, "They that turn their face far from me, I will blot them out."

5

Cayce's Story of the People of Atlantis

There were giants (nephilim) in the earth in those days, and also after that, when the sons of God came unto the daughters of men, and they bare children to them; the same were the mighty men that were of old, the men of renown.

Genesis Ch. 6

Before People There Were Thought Forms!

When Edgar Cayce was asked to describe the people of Atlantis, he did not begin with the people but by stating that individuals in the beginning were more "thought forms" than individual bodies with personalities as seen in the present. He explained that, in the early eons of life, they were minds with free will, not bodies with personalities. Their Creator had imbued them with a powerful impetus to be creative, to go out from the one, collective mind and to be fruitful and multiply their gifts using their own individual minds. And they did just that. They came out of the one, universal consciousness of the Creator and the Creative Forces (those forces that set all life in motion) to experience and to learn. Over and over Cayce stated that these many little minds—within the one, collective mind—were free to experience and to create,

67

and by so doing to become conscious companions to their Creator.

Among these many minds were those who would eventually become the Atlanteans. Not all of the primordial minds were attracted to the earth and the realms of form and matter, but those that were became a part of materiality. Their minds, once formless and infinite, *molded* to fit the requirements of the physical world. Yet, being cosmic minds, they had the ability to use the material forces in ways that seemed good or pleasing to them. Their minds constructed patterns that fit well within the structures and forces natural to this world, but they also modified the structures and forces of the world to better accommodate their celestial nature.

The Threefold Body

In one of his readings on Atlantis, Cayce said that the little minds developed projected layers of consciousness. He suggested that we use a star to graphically display the movement from the oneness in the center of the star to the individualized points out at the tips of the starlight. In the center of the star, nearest the original oneness, was the layer of the superconscious mind; the subconscious mind was an individualizing layer moving outward like a projecting arm of the star, and the conscious mind was the far tip of the star's projection. This reflects the layering of consciousness that the original godlings did in order to experience individualness in the midst of universalness, finite life in the midst of infinite life.

Because Cayce did not want us to think of these projected layers as separate things, Cayce labeled them the "threefold or three-ply body." It was important to Cayce that, even though they have become distinct parts of us (superconscious, subconscious, and conscious), they are more layers of oneself than separate selves or separate bodies.

He compared these layers to the classical Hindu terms of astral body, etheric body, and causal body. In one reading, Cayce identified this world as "the causal world." From Cayce's perspective the astral is a thought-form, the etheric body is a fluid form, and the carnal body is physical matter influenced by the forces of cause and effect. Cayce compared these bodies with the three conditions of water: vaporous, cloud-like form was the astral/superconscious; liquid, watery form was the etheric/subconscious; and hard, icy form was the physical/conscious layer.

What we call the conscious mind is ideal for physicality, and is the mind of the physical body. The subconscious he identified as the mind of the soul and the etheric or ghost body. The superconscious mind is the mind of the astral body, and is the most expansive level of mind, before one slips completely back into infinite consciousness.

Duality and the Human Body

In addition to the threefold body, there was another characteristic of this new world that had to be dealt with in primordial times, that of the natural duality of this realm. As we saw in chapter four, the incoming children of the Creator were finding this world difficult because, as Genesis records, they were "lonely." Incarnating in individually separate bodies isolated souls from the oneness they had known in the Collective Mind. As it is recorded in Genesis, the Creator eventually helped the young minds coming into this world to divide their yin and yang qualities into separate forms, distinctly female and male forms. These two qualities would then be able to be companions and helpers to one another, giving some comfort to individualized manifestation.

Cayce said that the first one hundred thousand years of Atlantis was an age in which both feminine and masculine qualities were together in one projected body. These early Atlanteans could reproduce like androgynous plants. From within themselves they conceived a new body, gestated it, and gave birth to it. From among their soul group, a specific soul would incarnate in such a body.

In the second hundred thousand years, Cayce says that these androgynous bodies were divided and projected into separate feminine and masculine bodies, which would each carry a portion of creative forces needed to create new bodies. They would then come together physically in the outer world to procreate.

Mixed Animal and Human Bodies

Another aspect of the Cayce story of early Atlanteans and Lemurians has to do with what we today know as possession, a condition in which a physical body is possessed by a spirit that has not incarnated properly into that body. In Cayce's tale of these early ages in the physical world, possession was very common, and in most cases, it was human souls possessing animal bodies. There were also cases of multiple human souls possessing one human body. But for Cayce, the possession of animals bodies was a most egregious mistake made by early incarnating souls—not just because of how bad it was for the animal, but for how contaminated the mind of the possessor became as a result of such a contact. The first three waves of human souls entering earth from the spirit or energy realms saw many abuses of the power these early children of God had been given.

However, in the midst of this abuse, there were outstanding uses of power by many well-intended souls. In a strange series of comments, Cayce related how some Atlanteans were so able to maintain their balance between physicality and spirituality that they could "harken back" to their oneness with the Creative Forces and the Creator while remaining incarnate in matter. Amazingly, these Atlanteans remained so conscious of the "essence" of Life that they did not masticate food for their bodily nourishment but were nourished by the élan vital, the life forces flowing through them.

On the other hand, other Atlanteans were becoming so "hardened" (Cayce's term) in physicality that they needed to assimilate the elements of matter in order to sustain themselves. Strangely, Cayce indicated that in so doing, they also assimilated the germs in physicality and became subject to diseases. Here's an example from his readings. It's a rather difficult reading, but you'll get the gist of it. The parenthetical comment is Cayce's. Also, when Cayce's speaking volume would rise, his stenographer would type the whole word or words in uppercase: "Sure they are germs! For each are as atoms of power. From what? That source from which it has drawn its essence upon what it feeds. Is one feeding, then, its soul? or is one feeding its body? or is one feeding that interbetween (its mental body) to its own undoing, or to those foolishnesses of the simple things of life? Being able, then, to partake of the physical but not be a part of same—but more and more feeding upon those sources from which it emanates itself, or of the SPIRITUAL life, so that the physical body, the mental body, are attuned TO its soul forces, or its soul source, its Creator, its Maker, in such a way and manner, as it develops."

Here's another example, and the lengthy parenthetical comment is Cayce's: "A developing of the abilities within each individual that has not lost its relation to its Creator, to live upon . . . its life source that there may be brought into being that which gives more knowledge of the source from which the entity's *essence* (Isn't a good word, but signifies that intended to be expressed; not elements, not rudiments, but of the entity itself, its spirit and soul—its spirit being its portion of the Creator, its soul that of its entity itself, making itself an individual, separate entity, that may be one *with* the Creative Force from which it comes—or which it is! of which it is made up, in its atomic forces, or in its very essence itself!) emanates; and the more this may be manifest, the greater becomes the occult force."

Thus, those who lost their relationship with the Creative Forces and the Universal Consciousness, became more earthly and aggressive. They began to create all manner of trouble. Here's one example from Cayce's readings of the Akashic Record for one Atlantean soul who reincarnated during Cayce's lifetime and got one of his famous readings: "Some brought about monstrosities, as those of this entity's association by its projection and its association with beasts of various characters. Hence those of the styx, satyr, and the like; those of the sea, or mermaid; those of the unicorn, and those of the various forms." Cayce often commented on how possessed the possessor became by the forms he or she mingled with. Even after leaving the body of an animal, the mind of the possessor was not able to easily remove the animal's nature, vibrations, and form from its mind.

The Perfected Bodies

This is where the two great divisions of incarnating people are more clearly identified by Cayce. The first group, called by Cayce, "the Sons of Belial" were those who "pushed their way into form to SATISFY,

GRATIFY, that of the desire of that known as carnal forces of the SENSES." Later, this group also contained those who initially came with higher intentions but lost their conscious relationship with their Creator and the Creative Forces. The Sons of Belial created destructive forces and promoted distorted perspectives of the truth. Cayce noted that a half-truth is more deadly than a whole lie, because it deceives even the soul.

The other group Cayce called "the Children of the Law of One." These were those that initially came into form motivated by what Cayce called "the first cause," which he identified as becoming companionable to the Creator. As stated earlier, souls were to go out from the Creator's womb and use their free wills to discover, learn, and grow toward becoming conscious companions with the Creator. Members of this group endeavored to maintain their relationship with the underlying oneness among all life and the truth of who they were and what their mission was.

The Sons of Belial constantly challenged the Children of Oneness, even to the point of making war against them. The Sons of Belial claimed that there was no central oneness to which all life belonged or from which all life originated. Multiplicity was the natural order of things. The strong should obviously dominate the weak. Survival of the fittest was the law of the land. All beings were not created equal; therefore, hierarchies were the natural order. The more powerful beings should rule the weaker. The Children of Oneness believed and promoted the opposite view.

In the midst of these struggles, the Children of the Law of One realized the need for an ideal physical body for incarnating human minds/souls, one that was unique to their needs and separate from the animal kingdom forms. The Children were able to develop the first of what Cayce called "perfected bodies." Into these bodies the minds of the Children of Oneness incarnated. Eventually, these bodies were modified to accommodate separate feminine and masculine qualities, allowing incarnating souls to project only one aspect of their nature while in these realms of duality.

As we learned in chapter four, Cayce's readings identify the renowned Lilith of classical tales as the first perfected feminine body and the little-known Amilius as the first perfected masculine body. Both of these were

Atlanteans and achieved this feat around 106,000 B.C. Lilith is described in more detail in the next chapter.

Cayce says that many of the Children devoted themselves to helping the lost souls rid their minds of animal influences and forms. Specific temples were created to lead a "contaminated" mind through a process that would release the hold that "animal magnetism" (Cayce's term) had on them. This helped their minds to reincarnate into one of the perfect bodies better suited to the human soul. These perfect bodies were being reproduced rapidly, often in temple-supervised breeding programs. Occasionally, even the priests and priestesses would fall victim to sensual pleasures while attempting to breed more bodies for incoming souls. But they could go through a cleansing and attunement process that would strengthen them again to their higher calling, higher consciousness. Spirit and flesh were always in a tug-of-war to capture the soul's attention in these times.

How did these temples release their patients' minds from animal magnetism? Cayce said: "Through that of CRUCIFYING, NULLIFYING, the carnal mind and opening the mental in such a manner that the Spirit of Truth may flow in its psychic sense, or occult force, into the very being, that you may be one with that from which you came!" In other readings he elaborated on this, identifying music, art, dance, and even surgery as part of the cleansing process. He stated that such a cleansing could not be accomplished in one incarnation but took several before the individual was freed of feathers, scales, horns, tails, hooves, and the like. These features were thought forms that became physical forms whenever the individual's mind incarnated. Cayce explained that the genetic process of creating a human body was influenced by the incarnating mind, causing the forming body to morph into the ideal held by the incarnating mind. If that mind contained contaminating images of animal forms, then skin did not develop properly, causing fur or feathers or scales to appear. One with such features could go to the temple and enter a program of cleansing that would help him begin the process of removing such thought forms from his mind.

Here is an interesting question-and-answer series on this topic in Cayce's readings:

"Q: How much transformation from the animal to the
human could be completed in a life-time?
"A: Little, save in the offspring—by the change of
thought, diet, and the operative forces [surgery]. In
the third or fourth generation it was completed.
"Q: Are there other books and material I can get to
help on these transformations?
"A: These would necessarily be in the form of the
older books written rather as legendary tales, see?"

E.C. 2067-6

Soulless Bodies—Zombies and Automatons

One of the strangest parts of Cayce's story is how Atlanteans were
able to project new physical bodies from within themselves, not to contain souls but to simply do the mundane work of physical life. Cayce
called these "automatons." They were initially used as soulless, physical
laborers who did menial or repetitive labor. In a bizarre twist, some
Atlanteans who were losing their way began to use these zombie creatures for sexual gratification, which resulted in births of more zombie
bodies that Cayce called "things." It is unclear if there was any distinction in Cayce's mind between an automaton and a thing. He does say
that later, after the final destruction of Atlantis, the rising leadership in
Egypt convinced the remnant Atlanteans to allow these soulless bodies
to be inhabited by souls seeking to enter this world, and to begin their
own individual journeys through the evolution of matter. Apparently,
Egyptian priests had the ability to transition these zombies into physical bodies appropriated for incarnating souls to use while in this world.
There is not much more on the "things" in the Cayce readings.

Children of Men vs. Children of God

Cayce does make a distinction between men and gods, one that the
Bible also makes. It is a distinction between beings called the "Sons of
God" and the "sons of man" and the "daughters of man." Cayce implies
that the Sons of God were those original, androgynous souls that re-

tained their connection to the Universal Consciousness and the Creative Forces. The sons and daughters of man were those souls who had become so physical, so terrestrial as to have lost their awareness of this initial connection and their celestial nature. In another bizarre twist in Cayce's story, and in the Bible story as well, some of the Sons of God began to breed with the earthly daughters of man, creating creatures that were half god–like in their size and power and half–human. The Bible records this time as follows:

"And it came to pass, when men began to multiply on the face of the ground, and daughters were born unto them, that the sons of God saw the daughters of men that they were fair; and they took them wives of all that they chose. And God said, 'My spirit shall not strive with man forever, for he also is flesh; yet shall his days be a hundred and twenty years. The Nephilim were in the earth in those days, and also after that, when the sons of God came unto the daughters of men, and they bare children to them; the same were the mighty men that were of old, the men of renown. And God saw that the wickedness of man was great in the earth, and that every imagination of the thoughts of his heart was only evil continually. And God repented that he had made man on the earth, and it grieved him at his heart." (Genesis 6:1–6)

There are tales among the ancient Incas of how a band of these gi-

gantic and powerful Nephilim came upon their shores and caused all manner of trouble and evil for the Incas, until, as the Incas tell it, the forces of Nature rose up and killed the Nephilim. The Bible says that the earth was cleansed of all these monsters and misfits by the Great Flood that God sent to cleanse the earth, excepting Noah and his crowded ark. We'll review the Noah story in another chapter.

Sumerian sculptures known to be more than 4,000 years old depict strange beings that are part human and part reptilian. Are these examples of the Nephilim? Source— *Wonders of the Past* (1923).

The Five Projections

As we learned in earlier chapters, the soul group of humanity decided to divide into five distinct groups. The following is a paraphrasing of one of Cayce's readings on the event. In this story he tells how the souls entering earth separated into five projected groups, matching what we eventually have come to know as the five races.

Here's the story Cayce told:

He said that these projections upon this plane were of man's making, not God's will. As these projections began to multiply and to attach themselves to the activities that made for sustaining physical creatures—that of self-preservation and propagation—there developed the self, the ego, the I Am. The growth of ego began the developments towards gratifying material senses and sensory amusement. This in turn built materialistic desires. The more they played out their desires, memories were formed that built repetitive re-experiencing of these gratifications. Rather than the soul's continuing their associations with their celestial Creator and the Cosmos, they sought more and more the terrestrial life and physical stimulation.

Given the early conditions on the planet, the first physical people became "dwellers in the rocks, in the caves, and those that made their homes in nests in the trees" and in the various things that surrounded their environs. "Then began the coordinating of combined forces of a household, which made for the building up of that as became the clans. Together they developed in a manner that their environment suggested."

As the souls became increasingly physical, they spent more thought and effort seeking to supply food, protection, activities for amusement, for material developments, procreation, and other associations one with another. They grew in selfishness and the desire to excel, the desire to place self in control of or the supervision of others. Gradually, tribes, clans, and nations developed. As different groups developed and created their singular identity, there came a need for protection from other groups, so fortresses, weapons, and warfare developed. This further focused their celestial minds on the terrestrial activities of cutting and fitting stone, making iron, brass, copper, and the like for better weapons and buildings. There also arose a need to build and preserve large numbers of laborers and trained armies.

When security was established, their consciousnesses turned toward material ornamentation of the body, ornamentation of the abode, ornamentation of the various surroundings that had to do with the individuals in their various sets, classes, and groups. Groups diversified into those that lived and worked in fields and agriculture, those that were hunters and gatherers, those that lived with and managed animal herds, and those that lived in buildings and cities. Each group developed their own specific interests and activities. As souls impressed themselves further into matter, some souls were attracted to one or more of these groups and activities. Of all the many groups of souls incarnating into the ancient world, the Atlanteans were the least warlike and were peaceful, at least for their first 100,000 years. Later, as their consciousnesses became increasingly selfish, they developed weapons and warfare. Initially, their continent provided them a safe, isolated environment. (E.C. 364-12) But eventually, it was fraught with earthquakes, inundations, wars, and invading beasts.

Before 50,000 B.C. there was a decision to create a division of labor in order to make the transition through matter easier. As described in chapter four, they divided into five groups, associated with the five senses, five races, and five initial locations on the planet:

RED
Sense: feeling and touch.
Location: Atlantis and Eastern America [South, Central, and North];

BLACK
Sense: taste and appetite.
Location: Nubia, Sudan, and the plains of Africa;

YELLOW
Sense: hearing and sound.
Location: Gobi. Cayce said: "The desert in the Mongolian land was then the fertile portion";

WHITE
Sense: sight and vision.
Location: Caucasian and Carpathian Mountains, then, after the pole shift, moved into Egypt, India, Persia, and Arabia;

BROWN
Sense: smell and olfactory.
Location: The Andean, or the Pacific coast of South America, occupied then the extreme western portion of Lemuria (poles were reversed back then, so it would be the eastern portion today) and the western plains of America today.

Reincarnating Atlanteans Today

When Cayce read the Akashic Records, he gave the most marvelous descriptions of souls' abilities in Atlantis. The Atlanteans were an amazing people, despite their eventual demise. Interestingly, from Cayce perspective, they have been and are reincarnating today! Many of the people who requested readings were interested in why they had the interests and abilities they possessed. Cayce told many of these people that they were interested in some things, like metals, engineering, art, and music because these had been interests and abilities they developed on Atlantis. Cayce mentioned metal workers, farmers, decorators, and a host of other occupations in his readings, but the most important details were related in readings involving the long-term development of souls. Here are just some of the stories Cayce read from the Akashic Record for Atlantean souls reincarnated during his time.

In reading 823-1, for a soul that he said would be better named "Alyne," he gave this information:

"She was in Atlantis where she oft laid aside the physical body to become regenerated. She was among the priestesses of the Law of One, serving in the temples where there was the raising of the light in which the universal forces gave expression and brought for the body and mind the impelling influences. She was not only the priestess but also the physician, doctor for those peoples. The entity lived in Poseidia, in the temple, in the spirit influences of the material activities for some six thousand years—if counted as time now."

She could rejuvenate herself so well that she lived for 6000 years! Cayce continues with this:

"With the last of the destructions that were brought about by the Sons of Belial through the activities of Beelzebub, the entity journeyed with those people to the Yucatan land, establishing the temple there. But with those inroads from the children of Om and the peoples from the Lemurian land, or Mu, the entity withdrew into itself; taking, as it were, its own flight into the lands of Jupiter."

Notice how casually Cayce speaks of the activities of Beelzebub! It's as if the Devil were an actual person, a being leading a band of bad guys, the Sons of Belial. Apparently, they drove out our light-bearing priestess to Yucatan. Eventually, even Yucatan became a negative place, so she took flight to Jupiter! How cool is that! How often have you wanted to take flight out of here?

In reading the soul record for another amazing Atlantean, Ms. 3004-1, Cayce gave the following description:

✳✳✳

"The entity was in the Atlantean land, before there were the second of the upheavals, when there was the dividing of the islands [the continent of Atlantis broke into five islands]. The entity was among those that interpreted the messages that were received through the crystals and the fires that were to be the eternal fires of nature, and made for helpful forces in the experience of groups during that period.

"When the destructions came, the entity chose rather to stay with the groups than to flee to other lands.

"The unusual activities that may come with today's new developments in air and water travel, are not new to the entity; none of these are as surprises to the entity. For, these were the beginning of the developments at that period for the escape."

This lady then asked Cayce three very strange questions, but Cayce replied to each one with astonishing answers. These were her actual questions, as strange as they may be.

✳✳✳

"Q: What is the meaning of 532, the number on my forehead?
"A: The number as indicated in self in the Atlantean experience, and that to which each of these numbers may attain.
"Q: The Mene [a count of numbers, found in the Bible, such as "a time, times, and half time"] which is clearly written on my left eye?
"A: This is as a part of the experience in the Yucatan activity as the priestess. Some call it the evil eye. Some call it the surety. What make ye of it? According to that for which ye may use same is the deeper meaning found in thine own self.
"Q: And the double triangle between my eyes, just at the top of my nose?
"A: This is a part of the experience to which the entity attained in the building, during the period of the Mound Builders."

What a soul journey this lady had prior to her present incarnation. Here's the strangest part of this: in her present life she was a housewife in Pennsylvania—the great priestess of the Mound Builders, Yucatan, and Atlantis!

Let's do one more.

When Cayce reviewed the records of 2464-2, a female art student at the time of the reading, he calmly gave this description:

✳✳✳

"In giving the interpretation of the records of the entity during the Atlantean sojourn, something of the history and something of conditions at the time should be comprehended—if the interpretation is to be in the consciousness of the present day experiences.

"Through that particular period of experiences in Atlantis, the children of the Law of One—including this entity, Rhea, as the high priestess—were giving periods to the concentration of thought for the use of the universal forces, through the guidance or direction of the saints (as would be termed today)."

Does this mean that the High Priestess was channeling the universal forces and the guidance from the Saints in higher dimensions? It sure seems to be what Cayce is saying. He continued with her reading:

✳ ✳ ✳

"There are few terms in the present that would indicate the state of consciousness; save that, through the concentration of the group mind of the children of the Law of One. They entered into a fourth-dimensional consciousness—or were absent from the body. Thus they were able to have that experience of crystallizing, through the Light, the speech from what might well be termed the saint realm, to impart understanding and knowledge to the group thus gathered."

No doubt now, the high priestess and her group were tuned to the higher, saintly realms and channeling guidance, understanding, and knowledge into this realm.

We could go on and on with Cayce readings like these, but now it is time to ask ourselves, What has happened to us? How have we fallen from such heights? How long will it be before we regain some of these abilities and awarenesses?

Actually, it's not as bad as it appears to be. Certainly, Cayce doesn't see our situation as poorly as we do. To Ms. 823-1, the 6000-year-old Atlantean priestess, he gave much hope and opportunity in this present incarnation and said that her activities in Atlantis and Yucatan were a part of her present-day abilities: "As a result of this incarnation [in

Atlantis], she can create within herself the higher energies that are stored up from the emotional forces of the body to find regenerations in the lower form of electrical vibrations." Our priestess still had her regeneration powers within her.

One interesting point: Cayce connected her powers with "the emotional forces of the body." That is very interesting because in other readings, Cayce says that our past earth-life memories are in our emotions, while our past non-earth-life memories and influences are in our urges and dispositions. If we have an emotional reaction to someone or something, then it is likely a past-life connection. If we have an innate urge toward certain perspectives, activities, and interests, then it is likely that we have sojourned in dimensions associated with them. For example, our priestess flew to the "lands of Jupiter" after her Atlantean/Yucatan incarnation; therefore, she is likely to have innate urges toward large groups (the masses), expansiveness, high ideals, benevolent activities and perspectives, optimism, generosity, education, and so on—all astrological influences associated with the realms of Jupiter.

Let's return to Ms. 3004-1, who used the sacred fires and crystals to channel guidance into this physical world in Atlantis, Yucatan, and in Ohio as the leader of some Mound Builders. To her, in this present incarnation, Cayce gave the following guidance and identified her present-day abilities.

✳✳✳

"As the tenets of old, all the principles of the divine that are manifested in the material man are found deep within self. And all that we may know of a universal consciousness is already within self. But know thy ideal, that has been, that may be manifested in the material plane—spiritually, mentally, materially; and, most of all, know the Author of such ideas and ideals. Then, study to show thyself approved unto that chosen ideal; condemning none, but living, manifesting that ye profess to believe.

"In the organizations, in groups, in activities that have to do with historical facts, with legends, with

> ancient data, ye find the outlet for thy greater contri-
> bution to others. Thy greater help will be in aiding
> others to find themselves, not finding themselves
> through what any group or individual may believe but
> through what responds to themselves."

Because of her diverse experiences and attunements in ancient times, she became a rare teacher and helper to those seeking to find themselves.

A fascinating astrological influence in her present incarnation was identified by Cayce as being Uranus. Here's what he said about the effects of her sojourn in the nonphysical realms of Uranus between incarnations:

✳ ✳ ✳

> "Uranus makes for the interests in all matters per-
> taining to the occult, to the metaphysical, to the cos-
> mos, to the universal consciousness, to that having
> to do with the basic cause or the reasoning of things.
> Thus not merely from the three-dimensional and that
> of lesson, or karma, but rather the cosmic conscious-
> ness becomes a part—as will be seen from the so-
> journs in the earth of this entity in those periods of
> activity in which there were undertakings that were
> to be a part of a universal consciousness of a
> peoples."

Fascinating, isn't it? As related earlier, in this present life she was a housewife, but beneath her exterior lay the great high priestess of the Atlantean crystal and fire altars, still able to reach into the realms of the saints and awaken within others their personal connection to the divine within. She even lifted them out of their karma into the higher perspectives of the universal consciousness.

Finally, let's look at what Cayce told Ms. 2464, the young art student who was once able to attune with her group of light-bearers to the "realms of the saints." To her, Cayce gave this present-life ability: "As the entity in the future opens (as it has done in the past) those connections between the soul force and the spiritual force, the influences and activities in other than the three dimensions of materiality will become a part of the entity's experience. As we find, then, the entity is one very intuitive; easily separating self from itself—which so few may do; or, as it were, the ability to stand aside and watch self pass by. This is an experience that may be made to be most helpful, if there is first the determining within self as to what is thy ideal—spiritually, mentally, morally, socially or materially."

She was still powerful in her present life! She had within her all the powers she had back in Atlantis, and they would open again. She might not have retained the title of High Priestess, but in this present life, she was still able to give the guidance and insight she did in those glorious times.

As a weakness that she took from Atlantis, Cayce warned that she developed quite a temper toward the Sons of Belial. He suggested that she be careful about reacting too negatively, even to evil. "In other words, with what spirit do ye declare thyself? That in conformity with the universal consciousness, the law of love? Or that of hate, dissension, contention—which brings or produces burdens upon thy fellow associates? For, the law of love is unchangeable; in that as ye do it to the least of thy fellows, ye do it to thy Maker." Sounds like the Master's guidance about loving even our enemies.

As to her present abilities with art (being an art student), Cayce gave the following: "Thus we find a highly emotional entity, one needing to keep itself literally—in body and mind—close to nature, close to the earth. Not as of the earth earthy, but as of the constant rebirth of those influences that so significantly indicate the closeness to God—and creative forces that are manifested in things, conditions arising from nature itself. For, the artistic temperament—with those abilities to draw on nature, as it were—brings the greater harmony, the greater balance within the experiences of the entity in its activity with things, conditions and people."

As for her present astrological influences (from sojourns in these nonphysical realms), Cayce gave these intriguing insights: "In Mercury and Venus we find those activities in which there is a high perception of ideals or tenets or ideas. Hence the artistic temperament towards the depicting of nature, or figures presented in nature; those things as would be of stone or plaster, or murals—as of decorations, should be a part of the entity's activities in the material associations with others. With Jupiter as well as Neptune, we find that these will bring the greater opportunities not only for self-expression but for giving ideas to others that may become helpful, hopeful influences in their experiences."

Obviously, from these three examples, you and I are probably better off than we realize. We have more power and wondrous capabilities than we realize. It's just that the physical world and life are often so mundane and fatiguing that we sink into the blues over our limited powers and boring lives. We must shake this off, because latent within each of us is the ability to journey to the higher realms of consciousness and catch the energy and motivations that come with higher purposes!

How do we do this? First, we have to set aside some time in our lives for such activities and attunements. Now we might say that the high priestess didn't have to wash clothes, clean dishes, make meals, mow lawns, drive the kids to activities, and so on; and we'd be right. Today we are all our own servants. In this respect, life in Atlantis was different. We might also say that we do not live for 6000 years any longer and 80 years goes by fast; and we'd be right. Life today is not like those ancient times in the temples and gardens. But Cayce is clearly calling us to awaken to the power and awareness latent within us and to our important purposes for incarnating today, as indicated in his readings for these three Atlantean priestesses.

6

Atlantis and the Legend of Lilith

As Moses raised the serpent in the desert, so must the son
of man be raised up to eternal life.   Jesus of Nazareth

As mentioned in the previous chapters, Lilith was a key person in Cayce's story of Atlantis. In fact, she is so important, that the entire story needs to be told. The legend of Lilith, the first women, is found in Jewish mysticism, specifically in *The Alphabet of Ben Sira*, written sometime between 700 and 900 A.D. The manuscript recounts a tale that dates back to the time of the Babylonian king Nebuchadnezzar (*circa* 604–562 B.C.). In this account Lilith is Adam's first wife, before the more docile Eve. Add Edgar Cayce's reading of the Akashic Records to this tale and we know that the first Adam was Amilius in Atlantis and Lilith was the first female, also in Atlantis.

According to the Jewish mystical traditions, Lilith considered herself an equal of Adam (called Amilius in Atlantis), made in the image of God (Genesis 1:26–27). Therefore, she would not subordinate herself to this first Adam and his wishes.

According to *The Alphabet of Ben Sira*, this was especially the case with sexual activity; Lilith refused to lie under Adam during sex. She insisted that if anyone was going under someone it was to be him, not her. But

Adam wanted her to be subservient to him. It all ended by Lilith invoking the name of the "Ineffable One," which was thought to be impossible to invoke since the name was inexpressible; but she speaks it and thereby flies away. Adam/Amilius, disheartened by her leaving, calls upon the Creator, "Sovereign of the Universe," to bring her back or give him another, for he had already looked among all the creatures of the earth and found none to be his companion (Genesis 2:18–20). A female godling was the only one who could be a true companion to the male godling.

According to Ben Sira, the Creator then instructs three of his angels to go after Lilith and insist that she return to Adam. The angels were instructed to tell her that if she is determined to remain apart, then she must allow death to exist among her children. It may seem like a harsh demand but her children were then immortals, immortals who had lost touch with God and the purpose of their very existence. In order to insure they did not live forever as terrestrial beings on this little blue planet, the Creator wanted them to experience death, which is only an intermission from physical manifestation. It was hoped that during this intermission the lost souls might recall their original state and seek to regain it.

Amazingly, Lilith agrees to God's terms—not to return to Adam/Amilius, but to accept death among her children! One hundred of her children will die every day. Returning to Adam was not an option for her. "Leave me!" she said to the angels. "I was created only to cause sickness to infants." The angels, still concerned for Lilith, told her that if she did not return with them, then *she* would die. Lilith, not one to be tricked, simply asked them how she could die since "God has ordered me to take charge of all newborn children: males up to eight days, females up to twenty days?" When their trick didn't work, the angels reverted to pleading with her. But she would not go. Yet, because of their loving concern for her, she swore to them by the name of the living and eternal God: "Whenever I see you or your names or your forms in an amulet, I will have no power over that infant." The names of these three angels became powerful shields on amulets worn around the necks of infants. Their names are, in Hebrew: *Snvi, Snsvi,* and *Smnglof,* sometimes written as *Senoy, Sansenoy,* and *Semangelof* (the addition of vowels helps us pronounce them but ancient Hebrew used no vowels).

Ben Sira recounts this legend to King Nebuchadnezzar when the king asks Ben Sira to heal his young son. Ben Sira writes the angels' names on an amulet and puts it around the neck of the king's son, who subsequently recovers his health.

Some Hebrew legends hold that because Lilith left Adam before the Fall in the Garden, having not eaten of the apple, she is immortal and has no part in the curse that later fell upon Adam and Eve. Nevertheless, most Hebrew tales portray Lilith as a demon who seduces men in their dreams. It is said that she lives by the Red Sea, where lascivious demons abide. (Jews have a tradition that water attracts demons.) If Lilith approached a child and fondled him, he would laugh in his sleep; striking the sleeping child's lips with one finger would cause her to vanish. As you can imagine, few Jewish children were allowed to laugh in their sleep. After circumcision a male baby was permanently protected against Lilith. This leads one to ask how then did she seduce their men in their dreams?

The ancient Hebrews may have derived the name "Lilith" from *layil*, which means "night."

Some Hebrew traditions hold that one of her incarnations was as the Queen of Sheba who seduced King Solomon. This mainly comes from an account that says that the Queen of Sheba had unshaven, hairy legs, a sure sign of Lilith because in both Hebrew and Arabian folklore, Lilith is a hairy night-monster.

In Babylonian and Assyrian legend she is *Lilitu*, a wind-spirit, one of a triad. But the oldest work in which she appears, under the name *Lillake*, is the Prologue to the Sumerian tablet of Ur, which recounts the exploits of Gilgamesh, *circa* 2000 B.C. The Prologue recounts this creation legend:

✳✳✳

"After heaven and earth had been separated and mankind and the underworld created, the sea ebbed and flowed in honor of its lord, but the south wind blew hard and uprooted a willow tree from its banks on the Euphrates. A goddess saw the poor tree and put it in Princess Inanna's garden in Uruk. Inanna tended

the tree with great care, hoping some day to make a
bed and throne from it. But alas, when the tree ma-
tured she found that a serpent that could not be
charmed had made its nest in the roots, and a Zu-
bird had made its nest in the branches, and the dark
maid Lilith had built her home in the trunk. "

In this tale we find some of the symbols that appear around the
ancient world: tree, serpent, and bird. According to ancient legend, the
Tree of Life is in the midst of the world; its roots descend into the Underworld and its branches upward to the Heavens. In this Sumerian tale
we find the serpent, a symbol of evil, nested in the roots and the bird,
representing higher consciousness, in the branches. This reflects the
greater story of the lower mind descending into the dark Underworld
and the higher mind flying in the heavenly perspective. Lilith, in this
story, abides in between these two states of consciousness.

Lilith also appears in a Bible passage. It is found in Isaiah 34:14–15
which describes the desolate ruins of the Edomite Desert where satyrs,
reems (large, wild oxen), pelicans, owls, jackals, ostriches, arrow–snakes,
and vultures (kites) keep Lilith company. It reads:

> "Wildcats shall meet with hyenas,
>   goat–demons shall call to each other,
> There too Lilith shall repose,
>   and find a place to rest.
> There shall the owl nest
>   and lay and hatch and brood in its shadow."

In some translations of this passage the name *Lilith* is replaced with
"night monster." The reference to an owl in this passage is significant
because it too refers to Lilith. In a Sumerian relief (see illustration) Lilith
is shown with owl's feet, standing on the backs of a pair of lions and
holding in each hand the Sumerian version of the *Shem*, the Egyptian
symbol for the binding together of eternity and temporality, femininity
and masculinity. In Asia the owl is symbolic of wisdom, particularly
wisdom received in the night. We find this pertinent passage in Psalm

19:2: "Day unto day uttereth speech, and night unto night showeth knowledge." In the Roman Catholic edition of the Bible, the Book of Wisdom refers to wisdom using the feminine pronoun "she." An Asian proverb holds that the reason owls are usually seen alone, as is Lilith, is because "wisdom stands alone."

In the Hebrew *Targum Yerushalmi*, the priestly blessing in the biblical book of Numbers (6:26) becomes: "The Lord bless thee in all thy doings, and preserve thee from the Lilim!" Lilim are Lilith's children.

The Greek commentator Hieronymous identified Lilith with the Greek Lamia, a Libyan queen deserted by Zeus, whom his wife Hera robbed of her children. Lilith took revenge for this act by robbing other women of their children.

In Cayce's reading of the Akasha there was not an evil, dark tale of Lilith, simply one of equality and feminine power. In fact, as Cayce reads the Akashic Record, the feminine and masculine portions of the incarnate Logos returned to earth in several incarnations—at least thirty. Cayce lists among the many incarnations these significant ones: Amilius and Lilith, Adam and Eve, Hermes and Maat, and Jesus and Mary. Each was an incarnation of the Logos, the Word, the Messiah: feminine and masculine aspects of the Divine Presence among us.

St. John opens his gospel with a most mystical explanation of this. "In the beginning was the Logos (Word), and the Logos was with God and the Logos was God. The same was in the beginning with God. All things were made through this One. Without this One was not anything made that has been made. In this one was life, and the life was the light of humans. The light shines in the darkness, and the darkness hasn't overcome it. He was in the world, and the world was made through him, and the world didn't recognize him. He came to his own, and those who were his own didn't receive him. But as many as received him, to them he gave the right to become God's children (again consciously), to those who believe in his name: who were born not of blood, nor of the will of the flesh, nor of the will of man, but of God. The Logos (Word) became flesh, and lived among us. We saw this One's glory, such glory as of the one and only Son of the Father, full of grace and truth."

According to Cayce, the Jewish sect of the Essenes had read Genesis carefully and knew that the Logos was both masculine and feminine. They also read that the Lord had turned to Eve as she was leaving the Garden and promised that out of *her* would come the redeemer of the fall from grace and the loss of the Garden. Cayce said that the Essenes were actually looking among the women of the time for the coming of the feminine Messiah, the feminine Christ, through whom the masculine Christ would be conceived and delivered. In the Essene temple at Mt. Carmel, the leaders took in females that showed signs of being spiritually aware. Anne, the mother of Mary, was one such woman. She conceived Mary, who ultimately conceived Jesus. Mary, according to Cayce's readings, was the return of Lilith. Jesus was the return of Amilius. The Cayce readings say that "there never was a time when there was not a Christ" and "Christ is not a man." He explained that Christ is a spirit and a state of consciousness. This consciousness is aware of the infinite Creator, the Life Force, and the oneness of all life. This consciousness is latent within all souls and can be found if one seeks it and makes room for it.

Lilith.

Lilith and Amilius in Atlantis

In Poseidia, one of the five major regions of Atlantis, Lilith and Amilius attempted to establish a new order. They developed principles to live by and designed a plan whereby all could be redeemed and realigned with the original purposes of the Creator and consciousness. Among their plans was a five-point assault upon the dark forces influencing this world and tempting the Children of the Law of One, even the Elect among them. The plan called for five large groups of light bearers to incarnate in five different regions of the world and establish major centers of enlightened culture and education. These would setup a ring of wisdom and light centers around the earth.

Amilius and Lilith established principles that countered those of the Children of Darkness, who now had a new leader. The Children of Darkness became known in Atlantis as the Sons of Baal or Baaliel, or as Cayce so often called them, Sons of Beliel (a term that St. Paul and the poet Milton also used). But they were not necessarily the most dangerous problem. Among the Children of the One, jealousy over the varying degrees of beauty and power began to infest their hearts. Those close to Lilith and Amilius began to argue over who was the more important. The insidious way in which these little spites and jealousies grew within hearts and minds was and remains today a serious danger to harmony and cooperation. Before long, factions developed among the Children of the Law of One, factions that began to plot against one another's interests and influence. The Sons of Beliel only added to this breakdown with ideas of hierarchies and self-gratification—self-glorification. As bad as this was, there was an even worse development.

In the sacred teachings, particularly in the Vedic ones, it was described as reversing the flow of the life force, energy, and the tendency of the mind moving downward, often depicted as a serpent descending down a tree or staff. For example, in the biblical Garden of Eden, the serpent descends from the Tree of the Knowledge of Good and Evil, and eventually ends up crawling upon its belly in the dust of the earth. This is often countered in mystical ceremonies in the ancient world by raising the serpent (the life force, energy, and the mind) to higher levels of life and consciousness. This idea is depicted in the winged-serpent motifs and legends that we find so frequently in Central American and Egyptian art and mythology.

The raised serpent is even found in the Bible. Recall the teaching that Jesus gave to Nicodemus during a secret nighttime visit (John 3:14).

Nicodemus wanted to learn the deepest secrets, so he sought this strange master who was becoming such a problem for the Sanhedrin, of which Nicodemus was a member. Jesus gave Nicodemus three key teachings. The first was that "we must be born again." We have been born physically but we need to give birth to our spiritual self. The second teaching was that no one ascends to heaven but he or she who first descended from it, referring to the involution of mind into matter prior to the current evolution up through matter. All of us, whether we remember it or not, have a soul within us that first descended from heaven. That part of us is familiar with the formless dimensions beyond the physical world. But key to our study is the third teaching, which Jesus stated this way: "As Moses raised the serpent in the desert, so must the son of man be raised up to eternal life." Here Jesus is referring to the time when Moses left the kingdom of Pharaoh (so symbolic of the outer ego—power and worldly possessions) to search for his true self and God in the desert. In his search he comes upon a deep well around which seven virgins are attempting to water their flocks. Seven virgins in the desert; is there some deeper meaning here? Of course there is. These seven virgins, daughters of a high priest, are symbolic of the seven spiritual centers, the seven chakras, and the seven lotuses within each being. Moses waters them and their flocks, ultimately marrying the eldest one. Afterwards, he meets God in a burning bush and for the first time is instructed how to transform his staff into a serpent and raise the serpent up again into a staff (Exodus 2, 3, and 4).

Moses raising the serpent. Source:
The Doré Bible Illustrations **(1865).**

Later, when Moses has all the people out in the desert with him, he is
instructed by God to place a fiery or brazen serpent upon a raised staff
and anyone who looks upon it will be healed (Numbers 21:8-9). The
writer of Exodus is trying to convey more than a literal, physical story
to us. We have to go back to the Garden of Eden to fully understand
this, because Adam and Eve were not the only ones to fall in the Garden; the serpent fell also. The life force and consciousness within the
descending godlings was falling to lower and lower levels. The life force
can be harmful if misused, but raising it is a key to restoring the levels
of energy and consciousness before the world was.

In Patanjali's *Yoga Sutras* (*circa* 300 B.C.), the process of raising the energy begins with an understanding of where the energy is in the body,
how it is raised, and the path it follows through the body. According to
the *Yoga Sutras*, the energy is "coiled up" like a serpent (*kundalini*) in the
lower part of the torso of the body, near the base of the spine. It moves
up the spinal column (*sushumna*) through the spiritual centers—*chakras*
(wheels) or *padmes* (lotuses)—to the base of the brain and over through
the brain to the brow. The path of the kundalini through the body is
represented by a cobra in the striking position or by pharaoh's crook or
a shepherd's crook. (A crook is a staff with a hook on the upper end.
The shepherd's crook is flared at the very tip.) Many books today teach
that the kundalini culminates at the crown of the head, but the more
ancient images and teachings as well as Cayce's always depict it culminating at the forehead, in the same place where pharaoh's brow cobra is
positioned. This will cause some confusion among many who have
studied and practiced for years using the crown chakra as the highest
spiritual center in the body. Cayce insisted that the true path of the
kundalini comes over through the crown chakra and into the third-eye
chakra on the brow. The seven spiritual centers are connected with the
seven endocrine glands within the body: 1) testes or ovaries, 2) cells of
Leydig (named after the doctor who discovered them), 3) adrenals, 4)
thymus, 5) thyroid, 6) pineal, and 7) pituitary. They are also connected
with major nerve ganglia or plexuses along the spine: pelvic or lumbar,
hypogastric or abdominal, epigastric or solar, cardiopulmonary or heart
and lung area, pharyngeal or throat, and the brain itself.

Though Amilius and Lilith's mission was successful in many ways, the declining awareness of those in the earth was evident. Salvation was not at hand, despite all efforts. A new plan had to be made.

Amilius and Lilith withdrew to the deeper realms in the mind and spirit of the Cosmos to prepare themselves for the next great effort. It was clear that the potential companions to the Creator were falling into selfishness and materiality. The plan to reverse this movement before it got out of hand had failed. Now spirit and mind were going to come fully into this world, experiencing every part of it until it no longer held any lure, and they could take it or leave it at will.

The ancient lands of Mu, Oz, Zu, Atlantis, and many others came to an end, forcing huge migrations to new lands for a new way and new experiences. After the cleansing by the Great Flood, the lands of Yucatan, China, India, Persia, Egypt, Scandinavia, and others became the new centers for soul growth. When the first Eden in Poseidia sank, the second Eden between the Tigris and Euphrates began. Amilius and Lilith gave way to Adam and Eve. Masculine energy rose to power while feminine subsided. But, today, the goddess energy is rising once more and a new age is about to begin in which masculine and feminine energies will be reunited in a new balance, a new way. We are coming full circle. Lilith's spirit returns.

7

Atlantis Technology and the Evidence for Ancient Flight

> For the manners of transportation, the manners of communications through the airships of that period were such as Ezekiel described of a much later date.
>
> Edgar Cayce (1939) Reading 1859-1

The details revealed in Plato's story of Atlantis depicted a 10,000 B.C. civilization that had developed technology and capabilities not known in the western world until the 1400s. Of course, civilizations had developed spears, chariots, and most of the war implements Plato described well before Plato related the story. But his description of the maritime culture and naval fleet of Atlantis, consisting of thousands of ships that could reliably travel anywhere in the world, across any oceans, was utterly fantastic until sometime around the New World "discovery" by Columbus. Cayce described an Atlantis with technological ability in some ways surpassing even what is present today. But it's important to understand that according to Cayce's story of Atlantis, that civilization had 200,000 years of history. That's a lot of time for technology to develop. Assuming that our current civilization continues for another 190,000 years or so, can anyone foresee what future technology will be in the year A.D. 192,006?

There is another aspect to the technology aspect of Atlantis that merits mentioning again. Atlantis went through two periods of destruction before the end came. Each time, the survivors faced rebuilding their lives and land. Edgar Evans Cayce states that the peak of Atlantean technology appears to have been reached just before the 28,000 B.C. destruction. What could we expect to find of that technology? And with the final 10,000 B.C. catastrophe, what would remain of the technology? Surprisingly, there is highly suggestive evidence supporting an ancient technology such as that described by Cayce.

The Cayce readings tell us that before each of the three destructions of Atlantis, large numbers of people migrated around the world taking their flying abilities along with them. However, according to our modern perspective, flight was relatively recently discovered in 1903 by the Wright brothers in Kitty Hawk, North Carolina. Over only a few generations it has been transformed into a powerful, daily means for transportation. How could anyone possibly believe that ancient peoples had the technological know–how to fly? Well, if they did not have it, they sure wrote a lot about it. We have hard, physical evidence of their knowledge and tales of space, air, and underwater flight from numerous carvings, drawings, models, and even manuscripts about flying machines. For example, there are literally hundreds of documents in India that date back to ancient times that can only be described as flight manuals for many different aircraft models! Not only that, but evidence of flight is found around the ancient world: India, Chaldea, Babylon, Egypt, Maya, Inca, South America, and Asia.

Evidence for Ancient South American Hot-Air Balloons

According to the French, hot–air balloons were first used in France in 1783. However, according to records in the Vatican, the first hot–air balloon flight took place in 1709 when de Gusmao petitioned the King of Portugal for permission to launch a hot–air balloon in Brazil. The petition was granted and reports of the effort were sent to the Vatican where they remained unknown until the 1970s when The International Explorers Society of New York rediscovered them. The Explorers first came across a Swiss pamphlet dated to 1917 telling about the flight and revealing that reports had been sent to the Vatican. Their search eventually led to an old French text confirming that when de Gusmao returned to Brazil, he flew his balloon to a height of 60 feet.

The Explorers had originally become interested in the history of hot-air balloon technology because of compelling evidence they had found at Nazca, Peru—burials containing what appeared to be ancient balloons! They also uncovered several Inca legends relating aerial flight in what seemed to be balloons or blimp-like craft. This began to make more sense when they made the connection with the famous lines of Nazca that have to be observed from the air to be clearly distinguished. The Explorers subsequently excavated a host of burn pits on the Nazca Plains that they believe were used to create heat for the balloons. They also found linens that had been stitched together into balloon-like enclosures. The Explorers obtained permission from Brazilian authorities to sew together identical linens in order to attempt a recreation of ancient Nazca flight. In 1973, they successfully launched two of their members to a height of 400 feet in the Condor I balloon using a burn pit identical to those found at Nazca. The balloon remained in the air for 10 minutes, although when the two members got out of the basket, it immediately took off again tearing away its ground tethers. Amazingly, the balloon reached a height of 1200 feet and was carried away by the wind for several miles. It was eventually recovered and is today in the Lima Museum. Over 1000 people witnessed the event along with extensive media personnel. The leader of the Explorers inaugurated their flight by quoting from a Viracocha legend to the media: "He ascended into the sky after having finished making all that is in the land."

Cayce's story of ancient flight seems to be supported by the research of the Explorers who are now firmly convinced that the construction of the Nazca lines was controlled from the air. Their investigations provide especially compelling evidence since they were able to reproduce their balloons using only the materials that would have been present in those times. This may be some of the most definitive scientific evidence supporting Cayce, but it by no means the only evidence.

Ancient Indian Flight

Some of the oldest literature on flying vehicles is found in India. In the classic epic poem *Ramayana* (comparable to Homer's *Iliad* and *Odyssey*) flying ships are presented as a natural part of the story, as if they were commonly understood and used by the people. Determining the origin of the *Ramayana* has been difficult; scholars have dated it from as early as 400 B.C. to as late as 6000 B.C.! Most date the poem to around 1500 B.C. In this epic narrative, two types of flying vehicles appear. The first is called a "Puspaka car." It is described as resembling the Sun and belonging to Rama's brother Raghira, who purchased it from the powerful Lord Ravan. It is an aerial car that goes "everywhere one wills it to go." It is said to resemble a bright cloud in the sky. Consider this passage: "King Rama got in, and the excellent car, at the command of Raghira, rose up into the higher atmosphere." The other type of car is called *Vimana*, which is one of the most common terms used for flying vehicles in ancient Indian texts. A Vimana is described in the *Ramayana* as a "double-deck, cylindrical aircraft with portholes and a dome." (See diagram) It was said to fly at the speed of the wind and had a melodious sound as it flew. In some ancient Indian texts, Vimanas were said to have been so numerous in design and style that it would have taken several books to describe them all. Among the many ancient texts of Indian literature, there are manuscripts that can

Hindu temples typically include a narrow, high roof termed a *sikhara*. The apex of the roof included what many believe is a replica of a *vimana*, a flying saucer-like object. The top left *vimana* at this temple complex at Khajuro, India, is strikingly similar to modern UFO reports and photos depicting flying disks. These structures were built following directions in an ancient Sandscrit text. Source—*Wonders of the Past* (1923).

only be described as "flight manuals" that provide instruction regarding the control of each of the various types of Vimanas!

Another Indian aircraft is described as looking "like a great bird with a durable and well–formed body having mercury heated by fire underneath it. It had two resplendent wings, and is propelled by air. It flies in the atmospheric regions for great distances and carries several people. The inside construction resembles heaven created by Brahma himself," (from Chapter 31 of *Samarangana Sutradhara*—literally, "Battlefield Commander"). King Bhoja wrote this in the 11th Century A.D. However, King Bhoja claims his knowledge was based on Hindu manuscripts that were considered to be ancient even in his time. Some of the manufacturing techniques described in his book have been used by British and American aircraft companies since World War I. Surprisingly they have been found to contain sound aeronautical principles, even though described nearly a thousand years earlier in this old Sanskrit work. King Bhoja writes, "By means of the power latent in the mercury which sets the driving whirlwind in motion, a man sitting inside may travel a great distance in the sky."

The ancient Indian literature contains many varied forms of aerial acrobatics, such as *Dayana* (coming down), *Uddayana* (flying above), *Sundhara* (hitting the target with high speed), *Kanda* (rising suddenly), *Vyanda* (coming down quickly), *Karpostika* (flying still or hovering), and *Smasrina mandala vartina* (spiral or circling flight). The ancient Indian sage Bharadwaja explains the multiple types of Vimanas (flying crafts), such as *áakuna Sundara*, *Rukma*, *Tripura*, *Vairajika*, *Garuda*, and many others. He also gives detailed descriptions of different parts and mechanisms, two of which are *Suryasaktya-Karsanadarpana* and *Souramani*, which literally mean, respectively: solar mirror and solar cell!

Many of the Indian texts describe terrible battles in the sky using these flying machines. Some even describe what may have been the end of this wondrous flying age, the dropping of a terrible bomb: "Gurkha flying in his swift and powerful Vimana hurled against the three cities of the Vrishis and Andhakas a single projectile charged with all the power of the Universe. An incandescent column of smoke and fire, as brilliant as ten thousand suns, rose in all its splendor. It was the unknown weapon, the Iron Thunderbolt, a gigantic messenger of death which reduced to ashes the entire race of the Vrishnis and Andhakas." Does this passage record an ancient mistake with the hydrogen or atomic bomb, which our generation also struggles to avoid?

Some Indian flying vehicles were said to be able to "mount up to *Surya mandala*," meaning the solar region—the planets! And still others could go to the *Naksatra mandala*, which is the stellar region—the galaxy!

One of the palm leaf manuscripts found in India is the *Amsu Bodhini*, contains information about the planets, very detailed information, which seemingly only someone who actually traveled to them or sent flying machines to them could know. The different kinds of light, heat, color, and electromagnetic fields of the various planets, including earth are listed. The manuscript also contains information about methods used to construct machines capable of attracting solar rays and separating this energy into its components. In addition there are instructions for the manufacture of machines to transport people to other planets! Amazingly, it details unknown alloys that the ancients used to construct flying crafts, even ones that cannot be seen by the human eye.

Chaldean and Babylonian Flight

Indian texts are not the only ancient texts to purport the knowledge and use of flight. In the ancient Chaldean work *The Sifrala* there are over one hundred pages of technical details on building a flying machine! It contains words that are best translated as "graphite rod," "copper coils," "crystal indicator," "vibrating spheres," "stable angles," and the like. *The Hakatha* (Laws of the Babylonians) states: "The privilege of operating a flying machine is great. The knowledge of flight is among the most ancient of our inheritances. A gift from those from on high. We received it from them as a means of saving many lives." A variety of Babylonian and Sumerian reliefs depict images of flight. Who were these beings from "on high"? Some quickly answer, Aliens! But ancient literature, including the Bible and its book of Genesis, would indicate otherwise. Chapter six of Genesis clearly describes three types of beings on the earth in ancient times: humans, Nephilim, and the Sons of God. Edgar Cayce's readings indicate that those were times when many souls were still so attuned to the Cosmic Forces as to be like gods or aliens to everyday humans. Atlantis contained many of these highly attuned souls and had also developed an advanced technology that included various types of flying machines. Could they be the beings from "on high?"

Illustration of 10 feet high by 18 feet long Persian rock panel found on a 100 feet high stone cliff 240 miles east of Baghdad, Iraq. The carving depicts Darius (the tall man in the lower left) thanking the flying god Auramazda, who is shown in his flying disk. Source— *Wonders of the Past* (1923).

Maya and Inca Flying Evidence

The Maya and Incas also contribute to the mystery of ancient flight. As mentioned earlier in this chapter, the Nazca Plains in Peru, with their magnificent and enormous land drawings that can only been seen from the air, add to the growing evidence that the ancient ones must have had the ability to fly. In Central and South America, archaeologists have found pre–Columbian models of what are strikingly similar to modern swept wing airplanes! The scientists have dismissed them as merely toys, but this seems like an oversimplification! What were they really, and what did they depict? Why were ancient Inca parents giving their children toy flying machines if the idea hadn't even been conceived until our times?

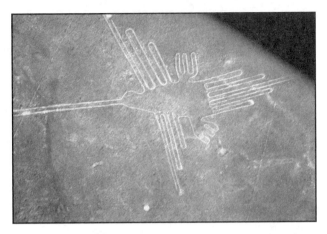

Hummingbird effigy on the Nazca plains. Source—*Greg Little* from © *Philip Baird, anthroarcheart.org.*

Ancient Chinese Flying "Birds"

Ancient Chinese texts describe how a Chinese craftsman named Lu Ban created flying machines between 770–475 B.C. In *Hongshu* Lu Ban even constructs a passenger plane! According to *Youyang Zazu* (a collection of essays from Youyang) of the Tang Dynasty, Lu Ban once worked in a place very far away from his hometown. He missed his wife very much, so he made a wooden bird. After being redesigned several times, the wooden bird kite could fly. Lu Ban went home on the kite to meet his wife and returned to work in the faraway land the next day!

Ancient Egyptian Flying Machines

Ancient Egypt also contributes to the mystery of ancient flight. In 1898, French archaeologist Lauret unearthed a wooden bird from an ancient Egyptian tomb in Sakkara. It was dated at around 200 B.C. The wooden bird is now in the Egyptian Museum in Cairo. Because the archaeologists believed that the ancient people had no concept of flying at that time, it was labeled "wooden bird" and had gathered dust for more than 70 years in a museum in Cairo. In 1969, Khalil Messiha, an

Egyptian doctor who likes making models, happened to see it. This "wooden bird" reminded Messiha of his earlier experience of making model planes. He thought it was not just a bird, since it had *no claws, no feathers*, and *no horizontal tail feathers*. Surprisingly, its tail was *vertical*, and it had *an airfoil cross-section*, which qualified it to be a model airplane. He then made a replica of the model. Although he didn't know how ancient Egyptians flew it, when he threw the model, he found it could glide. Further testing showed it was not only able to glide, but was also on a scale similar to modern gliders.

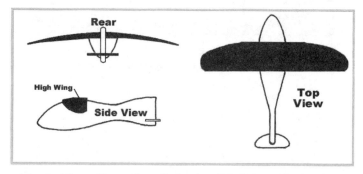

Adapted from illustration of wooden "bird" found in Egyptian Museum in Cairo.

Aeronautical specialists have found that this model was very similar to modern propelled gliders. With a small engine, they can fly at a speed of 45–65 miles per hour, and can even carry considerable cargo. Since ancient Egyptian artisans used to build models *before* constructing real objects, it is possible that this kind of bird–plane was a model by which a real plane would have been constructed. This could have been the flying "bird kite" that Lu Ban made to, perhaps, fly from Egypt to his home in China and back again the next day!

Depictions of flying machines can also be found carved in the stone of one Egyptian temple that is at least 3,250 years old. This temple is located in what many agree is the most sacred ancient city in Egypt: Abydos. Abydos is the Mecca, the Jerusalem of the ancient Egyptians. As you can see in the accompanying photo, the stone clearing contains the glyphs of a helicopter, a rocket ship, and an airplane. Above the rocket ship you can see another craft that some believe is a submarine.

Carvings at Abydos depicting what appear to be a helicopter and other craft. Source—*Ahmed Fayed*.

Archaeologists claim that this particular piece of stone is just a *palimpsest*, meaning: "A manuscript, typically of papyrus or parchment, that has been written on more than once, with the earlier writing incompletely erased and often legible." Of course, this palimpsest is not a manuscript and is in stone, not papyrus or parchment, and would have had to have been the result of some very strange rewriting over incompletely "erased" glyphs in the stone. But this is their answer, and they're sticking with it! As we shall see in a later chapter, there is also evidence that another type of "flight" technology may have been used in ancient Egypt to move the huge stones of the pyramids and erect obelisks.

Alexander the Great's Journal of Attacks by Air

Around 326 B.C. Alexander the Great invaded India. To his surprise and the surprise of his men, they were initially repelled by an aerial attack of "flying fiery shields." Is it possible that some Indians still possessed flying crafts as late as this date? Whatever the case, the Indians were unable to sustain them and were ultimately defeated. Apparently, they also did not still possess the ancient bombs described in the *Ramayana*, or simply did not choose to use them because of the horrible suffering that resulted from their initial use. But there are also numerous other accounts between 500 B.C. to the A.D. 1600s of flying shields and floating rods that, at face value, appear to be similar to both craft and blimps.

Ezekiel's Flying Wheel

Around 525 B.C. Ezekiel described seeing flaming wheels in the sky, which moved as the spirit within them desired or willed. "The four wheels had rims and they had spokes; and their rims were full of eyes round about. And when the living creatures went, the wheels went beside them; and when the living creatures rose from the earth, the wheels rose. Wherever the spirit would go, they went, and the wheels rose along with them; for the spirit of the living creatures was in the wheels. When those went, these went; and when those stood, these stood; and when those rose from the earth, the wheels rose along with them; for the spirit of the living creatures was in the wheels. Over the heads of the living creatures there was the likeness of a firmament, shining like crystal, spread out above their heads. And under the firmament their wings were stretched out straight, one toward another; and each creature had two wings covering its body. And when they went, I heard the sound of their wings like the sound of many waters, like the thunder of the Almighty, a sound of tumult like the sound of a host; when they stood still, they let down their wings." Ezekiel 1:18–24.

During one of Edgar Cayce's readings of the Akashic Record for a soul who flew to several ancient lands during one of his prior incarnations, Cayce explained that this strange passage of Ezekiel's was describing an Atlantean flying ship! Here's that reading: "Before that we find the entity was in the Atlantean land, during those periods particularly when there was the exodus from Atlantis owing to those activities which were bringing about the destructive forces. There we find the entity was among those who were not only in what is now known as the Yucatan land, but also the Pyrenees and the Egyptian. For the manners of transportation, the manners of communications through the airships of that period were such as Ezekiel described of a much later date." (E.C. 1859–1) "Airships"!

Edgar Cayce's Insights into Ancient Flight

During Edgar Cayce's deep trances, in which he was capable of connecting with the Akashic Records and the Universal Consciousness, he explained that ancient peoples were indeed, for a time, much more evolved technologically, possessing the legendary powers so often attributed to the Atlanteans, including flight through air and space. He also explained that they gradually lost this wisdom and ability as they became more self-centered and earthly. This wisdom and ability required one to maintain a oneness, an attunement with the Cosmic Forces. Cayce indicates that we are now in a new era in which all the old attunements and powers will be coming back. The question of how we use these powers today remains to be seen. But so far, we are doing pretty well, having so far avoided the expected nuclear war and stopped the arms race—a feat that once appeared impossible.

Cayce's first description of Atlantean flight seems to indicate that it was done by psychic means. This was because the people were initially so at one with the Cosmos and Cosmic energy and dimensions that they "transposed" themselves from one part of the Universal to the other—body, mind, and soul! But as they became more physically confined and focused, they began to develop low-tech, Nature-compatible physical devices to transport themselves around the planet. These were those pachyderm skins filled with gases that we mentioned in an earlier chapter. Simple, clean, and environmentally harmless. Later, as they became more physical and also more desperate for physical superiority, they developed high-tech machines that harnessed the radiation of the Sun and stars through their tuning crystals for driving the space, air, and underwater flying machines.

It's important to keep in mind that Cayce saw all of us as reincarnated souls from those ancient times. Therefore, the wisdom is latent within us and within the *collective* human consciousness. Flight to the stars may come faster than we currently imagine. Once the understanding comes through the veil separating deeper consciousness from daily consciousness, we could be building and flying further than we ever imagined. When asked if we would ever travel through space at the speed of light, Cayce replied that we'd someday be traveling at the speed of *thought*—the only speed capable of traversing the distances in space. Recall how he said that the earliest Atlanteans were able to "transpose" themselves from one end of the universe to the other. Our great break-through may not be a new alloy or composite, but a new level of con-sciousness.

8

Reincarnated Atlanteans in
the Cayce Readings

What makes the Atlantis readings special? Like all life readings, they were given to help individuals understand and
answer the questions and problems they might have in their
present lifetimes.
Edgar Evans Cayce, Gail Cayce Schwartzer, and
Douglas G. Richards (1997) *Mysteries of Atlantis Revisited*

Edgar Cayce gave over 500 past–life readings for souls who had an incarnation in Atlantis. This was out of a total of 14,306 readings. And since this ancient land lasted some 200,000 years, many of these souls had more than one incarnation in Atlantis.

Additionally, our early incarnations created profound impressions within the soul's psyche that remains with us throughout all of our incarnations. These become innate urges, likes and dislikes, talents, faults, vulnerabilities, and strengths. Innate influences, according to Cayce, are *latent* within the deeper self. They can be accessed consciously and unconsciously, intentionally and unintentionally. When we add in the forces known as *karma*, we can see how these influences affect the soul's disposition and life circumstances today. Cayce often told rein- carnated souls that they could awaken to their latent talents and skills if they would allow some time for intuition, meditation, and dreams in their busy physical lives, because the influences are within the deeper self and the subconscious mind.

These 500+ past–life readings for reincarnated Atlanteans run the gamut from common people to high priestesses, from good people to very bad ones. However, few Atlanteans were what we would consider today to be basic laborers, because in the early periods of Atlantis they did not need materiality or material sustenance in order to survive and in the later periods they had automatons to do their menial labor. For much of the history of Atlantis, Atlanteans were more mental people than physical. They were more minds using bodies to manifest them-selves in the physical, three–dimensional world, than physical bodies with minds. Today, many of us have become mostly physical beings with minds. But back then, we were mental beings using bodies to manifest in the three–dimensional world. This is a very significant dif-ference that clouds our understanding of Atlantis, Atlanteans, and their lives.

Let's look at a few of Cayce's past–life readings for reincarnated Atlanteans.

The House of Ode

Families, as we know them today, did not exist in remote times. In-carnate souls lived in groups. Children were not raised by their genetic parents in a small family unit, as we have today. Children were raised in a group setting by select members of the community who were drawn to the joys and challenges of training and raising children. Adults lived in community with one another, arranged by their natural interests and activities. There was a developing division of talents and a hierarchy that drew souls into positions and activities that naturally determined their immediate soul group. For example, those souls who were drawn to temple work lived together—priest and priestesses, counselors, heal-ers, astrologers, seers, ceremonial facilitators, and so on. On the other hand, administrators of the community's lands, buildings, infrastruc-ture, and resources lived in a different area. Here were the managers, overseers, lawmakers, and the like.

The House of Ode was composed of souls who, according to Cayce, innately understood "the universal forces as may be applied in the way of mechanical construction in a physical plane." They were engineers and builders. A soul called *Ode* (487 in the Cayce numbering system) was the head of one of these engineering households. He and others of this house trained and developed souls skilled in the laws and forces affecting physical construction of buildings, power plants, airports, cities, and the like. It was common for the Ode name to become a part of the name of each individual that belonged to this household. However, according to Cayce, individuality was not as pronounced as it is today. Souls were more group conscious than individually conscious. Soul groups were the dominant arrangement in those times. Even the leader Ode would have had a consciousness of his collective participation with the members of the House of Ode. His role was leader, but his perspective would have been collective and participative.

As souls continued to leave (die to) this world and then reincarnate, they became increasingly individualistic, even to the point of traveling by themselves. Today, in the Western world, we think of each soul as a distinct individual, separate from their parents, family, and community. However, when Cayce was giving a reading for a soul, he often saw them as a member of a soul group, especially as he went back in time to those early incarnations on earth.

As Ode continued on the reincarnation journey, he too became increasingly individualized. In most of his incarnations he was a natural engineer and made his living from engineering, though in different stages of technology, such as a steam engineer in 19th century Germany to an electrical engineer in 20th century America.

The soul Ode did not have just one incarnation in Atlantis. He also reincarnated in the later periods of Atlantean activity under the name *Ajax* (not related to the Ajax of the Trojan Wars). He still had many of the same understandings and skills he had had as Ode.

In his incarnation as Ajax, he and his fellow engineering souls, especially Ajax-ol and Asphar, turn their skills away from building cities and toward designing and building machines that helped heal human bodies that were contaminated with animal's influences. They also developed machines for mining and transforming metals into useful forms that helped civilization grow.

Cayce explained that Asphar and Ajax-ol "made the application or use of the abilities in engineering, and the building of machines for the application of these to the bodies of individuals—where there were [animal] appurtenances to be left off, where there was blood to be changed, or where the vibratory forces were to be set so as to remove those [animal] influences of possessions; and where there were those activities in which with the combination of sodas the bodily forces were enabled to reproduce in a manner as cross to that to which had been set" (E.C. 470-22).

This was also a time when Atlanteans were migrating to new lands. Ajax, Ajax-ol, Asphar, and many others of their group finally gave up their lands and buildings in Atlantis. For safety, they journeyed to Egypt, setting up new operations there and contributing to the growth of the Egyptian civilization.

The reincarnated Asphar asked Cayce to describe in detail "the construction and purpose of the more important machines used by me then." Cayce answered: "The machine in which there was the combining of metals in those periods of fusing or smelting—that combined them in such ways that they might be used in forms not used today. Especially the use of electrical forces with the character of instruments in operations, as well as the fusion of such metals indicated." Asphar asked: "Considering the work in Egypt with electrical forces, explain just how I should apply those talents now." Cayce replied, "In conducting experimentations, by passing a great current through certain compounds or mixtures of metals, that would produce—in smeltering—a different metal. The combinations of iron, copper, of course impregnated with the various forms, which heretofore and in the present have been unable to be used in the forms of smeltering that are the experience of man today" (E.C. 470-22).

Apparently, latent within the reincarnated Asphar was a form of smelting that was not known today, but he could access this as he experimented.

A fascinating twist on this past-life story is that Cayce identified the reincarnation of Ajax-ol as the renowned Henry Ford of our times, the inventor of the assembly line and mass-production of automobiles.

According to Cayce's reading for Henry Ford, his soul helped build the Great Pyramid in Giza and the lost Hall of Records in Egypt.

In another curious twist, Cayce teaches that Atlanteans did not only migrate to other lands, they *intentionally* died to their bodies while in Atlantis, sojourned briefly in the heavens, regaining enlightenment and celestial energies, and then reincarnated into the new lands. One of the most common new lands was Egypt. A soul named Ptel-in was one of these. Here's a bit of his story. He, too, was among the soul group of engineers but made a significant change during his incarnation in Egypt.

Cayce was asked to "give an account of the electrical and mechanical knowledge of the entity as Ptel-in, in Egypt." He answered: "The entity was among those that had laid aside their physical self in destructive forces in Atlantis and picked them up again in the periods of the Egyptian development that followed the closer after the Atlantean destructive forces, or overlapped somewhat.

✳ ✳ ✳

"In that experience not so much of the electrical or mechanical appliances were the activities of the entity, save in the assisting of the preservation of the records and the *mental* distribution of that designed to be for the betterment and the purifying of those peoples of that age, period or land. It must be remembered, as indicated through these sources respecting the peoples of that time, much of the animals—that had been fully cleansed in Atlantis—remained with the peoples in the Egyptian development. But the entity, or Ptel-in, worked with the priest of that age in giving to the people the knowledge of the relationships of the Creator to the created, in the way of preparing the body physical for the receptivity or as a receptacle that might attune its inner self to the divine forces in that particular period of development.

"The activities of the entity in the electrical or mechanical were not so active in the Egyptian as they had been in the Atlantean. And the offices or activities pertained more to the assisting of individuals that sought to cleanse themselves, and were used by the fires in the cleansing temple, and the activities in the Temple Beautiful. For, the entity was then among those that aided the priest in *setting* the individuals so purifying themselves, so making themselves the channels or the receptive channels for the spiritual enlightenment that came through not only those that had sojourned in the earth as constructive forces but through those of the spiritual realm that thought and directed and aided the individuals in their activity, that had purified, had cleansed themselves."

E.C. 440-5

It was a time of establishing a human physical form, especially one that could attune itself to the celestial influences and manifest those into this world.

The Journey of Ikunle

As more Atlanteans understood the fate of Atlantis, many missions were developed to move Atlantean operations and knowledge to new lands. One such missionary was a soul and soul group known as *Ikunle* (likely pronounced *ike'-un-ul*). Cayce gave this reincarnated Atlantean soul a reading when he was only eleven years of age in this incarnation, explaining his soul's past this way:

***

"The entity was in the Atlantean land during those periods when there were the journeyings to many another land. The entity was among those who were sent as the directors to what became the Yucatan land, and in the setting up of the temple and the temple service, the temple of worship, the temple of differentiation in the laborer and the ruler. Then in

the name Ikunle, the entity made for a great service
to a great people; that made for the bringing about of
the preservation of much that may some day make
for a unifying of the understandings as to the relationships of man to the Creative Forces.

"As to the abilities of the entity in the present, then,
and that to which it may attain, and how: These, as
has been indicated, are only limited to the *will* of the
entity; and this dependent much upon the manner of
guiding or counseling during these years of forma-
tive activity—for either the constructive teacher, the
liberator; or the wanderer, with help here, there, everywhere, without any particular purpose. In the preparing, then, follow close with that which has been
indicated. These urges are, as we find, innate—and
are manifesting themselves. Then, study the mind,
the abilities; and guide them aright."   E.C. 1426-1

The ancient world was better developed than we believe today. It
was also much less populated and less physical than we understand life
today. Fortunately, the Cayce readings insist that we will eventually find
records, structures, and artifacts from these very ancient times that will
surprise and excite us. Here's an example of how developed and organized the ancient world was. It is a reading for an ancient Egyptian
priest (294).

* * *

"There were also established storehouses, that would
be called banks in the present, or places of exchange,
that there might be the communications with individuals in varied lands; for even in this period
(though much had been lost even by these peoples)
was there the exchange of ideas with other lands, as
of the Poseidian and Og [South America], as well as
the Pyrenean and Sicilian, and those that would now
be known as Norway, China, India, Peru, and Ameri-

can. These were not their names in that particular
period, but from whence there were being gathered a
portion of the recreations of the peoples; for the understandings were of one tongue! There had not been
as yet the divisions of tongues.

"With the gathering of these people and places,
there began the erecting of the edifices that were to
house not only the peoples, but the temple of sacrifice, the temple of beauty—that *glorified* the activities of individuals, groups or masses, who had
cleansed themselves for service. Also the storehouses
for the commodities of exchange, as well as that gathered by the peoples to match—as it were, still—one
against the other. Hence we find the activities of the
priest, or seer, as really a busy life—yet much time
was given in keeping self in communion with those
that brought the knowledge of that progress made in
the spiritual sense in other lands, especially so from
Poseida and Og."   E.C. 294-148

The Journey of Iltar

Another great Atlantean who had a mission to save the records of
Atlantis was a soul named Iltar. He and a little band of Atlanteans set
out from the great temple of Atlan in Poseidia, Atlantis, for the Yucatan
Peninsula to build new temples and a Hall of Records. Their journeys
and establishments had far-reaching impact on these new lands and
subsequent generations. Here's a portion of Cayce's story about them:

✳ ✳ ✳

"Then, with the leavings of the civilization in
Atlantis (in Poseidia, more specific), Iltar—with a
group of followers that had been of the household
of Atlan, the followers of the worship of the *one*
with some ten individuals—left this land Poseidia,
and came westward, entering what would now be

a portion of Yucatan . . .

"The first temples that were erected by Iltar and his followers were destroyed at the period of change physically in the contours of the land. That now being found, and a portion already discovered that has laid in waste for many centuries, was then a combination of those peoples from Mu, Oz and Atlantis.

"Hence, these places partook of the earlier portions of that peoples called the Incal; though the Incals were themselves the successors of those of Oz, or Og, in the Peruvian land, and Mu in the southern portions of that now called California and Mexico and southern New Mexico in the United States."

E.C. 5750-1

It is fascinating to review the legends of the Maya, Aztecs, and Toltecs and find stories of ancient "Paddler gods" who came from the East, landed on the Yucatan Peninsula, and went about building temples, changing landscapes, teaching the people, and had mighty powers never before seen by the natives. Could Iltar and his ten Atlanteans have been those ancient paddler gods? According to the Cayce readings, they did leave Atlantis in boats, they had great power and knowledge, and they were escaping the sinking lands while establishing new ones. A Mayan ancient stone carving depicts a volcano exploding, a temple falling into the sea, a woman drowning, and a strange man in a canoe attempting to paddle away from the destruction. Could this be the Atlantean Iltar? The natives of Yucatan have a legend about a paddler god named Itzamna in their language. Could this have been Iltar in the Atlantean language? Could Iltar be the parallel legend of Votan, as Andrew Collins suggests?

The Journey of Areil

Areil (pronounced *Ar-E'-il*) was another of those migrating Atlanteans, and one of the engineer-types as well, but more of a designer and decorator. Here's a portion of what Cayce said about his soul journey.

✳ ✳ ✳

"The entity was in that now known as the Egyptian or the Atlantean land, for the entity was among the Atlanteans who first came to Egypt. With the establishing of the varied groups for the expression and manifestation of what would be termed the arts in the present, the entity accepted same and aided in making the correlations of the teachings during the experience.

"So the entity journeyed then to what is now a portion of Portugal, or in the Pyrenees, where a portion of its own groups from the Atlantean land set up a form of worship and a temple activity. And the entity aided in those things pertaining to the particular decorations in the temple. Hence as we will find in the present experience or present emotional forces, there are the innate abilities pertaining to the exterior decorations, to friezes, to interior decorations; so that these may also in the present become a portion of the entity's experience.

"Then the name was Areil.

"As to the abilities of the entity in the present, we find: There is much, as indicated, that is of a high SENSITIVE nature; much that pertains to what many call ethereal or dreamy or not practical.

"But with an ideal the entity may go far. It may be set in the study of those things pertaining to the manner of presenting the beauties in decorations and architectural forces within and without. Or it may be set in the study of the WHY of those things presented in Exodus or Leviticus, as to the manner of building the covenant—ark of the covenant, or the tabernacle, and especially as to the manner of decorations; also the manner of decoration in the temple first built by Solomon and then that represented especially by that written in Hebrews, as to how all of these are but the patterns, the expressions of the emotions from the body of man himself, and how that ONE represents an ideal to the world, to the earth in all forms. For He was the architect, the builder, the maker of all things that were made. Call HIM thy ideal, and study those things not only in sacred history but profane also that pertain to the beautifying of the body within and without, and how that—in their representations to man of the glories that may be his—they may bring to the entity the understandings that it, too, may be a channel, an expression of that which will make for the glorifying of the real Creative Forces in the hearts and minds of men everywhere."   E.C. 1123-1

His mother got this reading for him when he was only 12, but later wrote that he had gone into the engineering corps of the military. She had asked Cayce to identify what specific line of work should he take up, to which Cayce had replied "either interior or exterior decorating, or an artist." Perhaps he got into this line of work after WWII.

The Journey of Altza

Another interesting Atlantean is Altza. She is a soul that is the epitome of "the assistant" or "right-hand man"—a true helper to leaders and authorities in several lifetimes.

At the risk of losing you in the unusual language and complex syntax of the Edgar Cayce readings, I'm going to share her entire life reading with you. Read slowly and you'll get the gist of this remarkable soul and her journey from Atlantis to today.

✳✳✳

TEXT OF READING 1187-2 F 46 (Widowed [eight months ago] Methodist Background)
1. GC: You will give the relation of this entity and the Universe, and the Universal Forces, giving the conditions that are as personalities, latent and exhibited,

in the present life. Also the former appearances in
the earth's plane, giving time, place, and the name,
and that in that life which built or retarded the development for the entity, giving the abilities of the
present entity and to that which it may attain, and
how.

2. EC: (While going back over the dates Cayce said in
an aside: "Henry the 8th, August 1, 1890.") [GD's
note: No questions were asked in regard to Mr. Cayce
saying "Henry the 8th, August 1, 1890", for fear of
interrupting Mrs. 1187's reading.]

3. Yes, we have the entity here, and those relations
with the Universal Forces as are latent and manifest
in the present earth's existence, with those conditions
as do appear as personalities and individualities in
the present earth's plane, and those Universal Forces
as bring such urges and such conditions as show how
such relations are reached in the present plane and
from which these emanate.

4. In the taking then of the present position in the
earth's plane, we find the entity came from that of
Venus, with Mars, Neptune, Jupiter, and with the influences in Saturn and in Moon's forces. Hence we
find one with many of the cares of earth's influence
and these conditions that do bring those of the
earthly influences in the life of the present entity.

5. One slow of wrath.

6. One that is ever forgiving and forgetting those conditions that would be the detrimental forces towards
self in connection with any action of others toward
self.

7. One whose greater ruling passion is love for those
whom the entity may assist, whether of the physical,
mental or spiritual forces of self.

8. One we find who gives much to the assistance of
those whom it contacts, through the ever willingness

to be subservient, in a manner, to the will of others. This has often, as we see, brought much of the disconsolation and of the trouble and worry, physically and mentally, to the body.

9. One whose higher urges lies in that of the educational nature, and the entity, with the taking of the conditions as first presented, would have made a wonderful success for self in that of an educator. One who would have been able, through such forces, to have brought much of the higher forces in the educational field to self and those dependent upon same. One whose endeavors should have been in the Eastern portion of the country (United States). One who would, when the opportunity was offered to have traveled to the East, have been much benefited by same. One whose greater influence now lies in the abilities as that of dietetics and of aid to those pertaining to those conditions about hospital, or of such culinary operations as regarding same.

10. Then, as to how these urges are received, and the elements that have brought the changes in the life's work and endeavors, we see come much from planetary effects through sojourn in same, with environmental force as has played and given its part.

11. In the one, then, before this, we find the entity in the days of Louis the 16th. Was the sister to that ruler and the attendant in the last days of that ruler's life to that body, and the entity in the later days of that existence gained much of the fortitude as is manifested in the present sphere, and through which the entity fought and found much development. In the earlier portions, we find this not so used, which became the drudge to the individual in that plane. Then in the name of Angelica.

12. In the one before this we find in the days of the Roman rule, when in the name then of Octaviao. The

entity then in the Courts of the ruler in that land, and
in the house of the first in command of the soldiers
when the expulsions of the peoples were demanded
for those that rebelled against the then authority. The
entity then did not develop in the plane, for it rebelled
against the dictates of the then force over same.
Hence the urge as we find in the present of seeking to
aid others in their endeavors, whether of mental,
moral or physical, yet looking ever on that side
wherein the best is thought of the conditions attending same. This becomes questionable to others at
times, see?

13. In the one before this we find in the days of the
rule when the Persian forces were being separated by
the warring of the Arabians (now), or the Nomads
then, and the entity then in the tents of the Nomads,
and the name Idoah, being then an assistant to the
second in command of the forces then making war
on the now Persian rule.

14. In the one before this, we find in the days of the
second rule in the Egyptian forces, when the laws
were being given to the peoples as pertaining to the
worship of the spiritual forces manifested in earth's
plane, and the temples being reared or prepared. The
entity then in the household of the ruler in Iconium,
and in the name of Ousou. The entity then we find
followed much in that way of the educational teachers of the day. Hence the urge for all about the entity
to acquire knowledge and power, and the urge as is,
and has been, to become the instructor in such elements. The entity both developed and retarded, for
in the days when the banishment of the Priest, the
entity sided with the Priest forces and this became
detrimental, in the binding and imprisonment of the
entity.

15. In the one before this, we find in the days when

the rule in the land of the Atlantean forces. The entity then the one that served the foods to the high priests of that day. Then in the name of Altza, and the entity seeks, then, in the urge as is seen in present, towards those things pertaining to preparations of various characters for the use in the service of the inner man and the sustenances of the physical. This, then, as we find, coming in the urge wherein through and with the use of the mental forces and will in the present sphere, may become that element to which the entity may at the present bring its highest development in that of the dietetics, or of the assistant to those who prepare such for those who would gain in physical in health-giving flow to the body.

16. Then, in using these, for the entity may prepare self, through will's forces, in assistance, as has been given and as is given, to others through the endeavors of the entity, and about which the entity has drawn those influences for self, apply same in the manner that will ever be first and foremost well pleasing to Him, the Giver of all good and perfect Gifts, for the will must be made One with His, would the Spirit of the Father be manifest through His creatures.

17. We are through for the present.

Notice how she was always the caregiver, teacher, supporter, and assistant, and always in the household or service of the authorities or rulers. In Atlantis she was nourisher of high priests. In Egypt she was in the household of the ruler and was a teacher. In Arabia, among the Nomads, and was the assistant of the second in command of the Arabian forces. In Rome she was in the courts of the ruler. In France she was the sister and caretaker of the ruler, Louis the 16th.

In her recent incarnation in America, her daughter wrote these words to the Edgar Cayce Foundation, describing her mother:

✳ ✳ ✳

"The Life Reading was wonderfully descriptive of my
mother. She had lived a completely selfless life, always putting her children first, or friends for that
matter; never pushing or taking the lead. Her greatest love has been the 'doing' for others. She's a marvelous cook and has been very diet conscious. The
part about the educational influences is true, too. Although orphaned young in life and not having an education, she always studied and learned and instilled
in her children the desire to learn. In late years she
has had a tremendous influence and joy in seeing her
grandchildren educated."

The Journey of Iel

Iel (pronounced *i-el'*) was an Atlantean who designed and wove gar-
ments for her people and the Egyptians, and for their decorations and
ceremonies. She had many varied incarnations, even changing gender
once. Hers is a fascinating story, and one that we hope you can enjoy by
reading her entire life reading. Again, the phrasing can be difficult at
times, but read slowly and get the gist of her soul's journey.

✳ ✳ ✳

TEXT OF READING 504-3 F 52 (Housewife, Protes-
tant, German Parentage)
(Life Reading Suggestion)
1. EC: Yes, we have the entity and those relations with
the universe and universal forces, that are latent and
manifested in the personality of the present entity,
[504].
2. In entering the present experience the entity from
the astrological aspects is very much from the mental approach under the influence of sojourns in the
planetary influences, rather than from purely astrological aspects at time of birth or during period of

gestation. For, if it were considered from the purely astrological given by most of the sages or seers of old, with this particular body the period of gestation would be more the influence in the present sojourn than from the position of the planets or any of the astrological influences, either as to the square of those arising or those setting or in the zodiacal influences of the planets being in their varied aspects during that period.

3. But, as we find, it is as to that which may be most helpful to the entity in applying same in the experience. For knowledge or intellect or understanding without the ability or the desire to apply same becomes stumbling blocks in the experiences of every soul. We seek to give that which the entity in its soul application may use in this material world in this period, in this experience, to aid self and help self in understanding self, self's desires, self's innate influences, and come to make—most of all, for this particular entity—that knowledge, that understanding, a more *vital* thing in this present experience.

4. From the astrological sojourn or planetary influence, then, we find:

5. The Mercurian influence shows a high-minded individual; one capable of analyzing that which may be data or truth, and to a great extent *feel* the application of such understanding *better* than able to give expression to same. Yet as the soul's development has been, it has made this very fact in the body's experience often cause periods when loneliness in the mental forces of the body has been overpowering in many respects. And without those saving graces as may be said to be from the influence of the entity's sojourn in Venus and Jupiter, these lonely periods would have been rather for destructive than constructive forces in the entity's experience.

6. But with Venus and Jupiter also influencing the entity from the innate or mental forces of the soul's experience, duty and vision and the grasp of the broader vision of why and what experiences may mean, has buoyed up the entity in its inner self at such periods and thus brought oft to the entity those strengthening influences, through its turning within itself for counsel with the spiritual influences that are of the soul's development with that whereunto there have been associations in the sojourns in the beyond or the inter-between. If these are raised rather to an experience in the entity's sojourn in the earth, as to where and when there were the counselings with those that had been and were very close to that consciousness which should be the ideal of every soul in this mundane sphere, then may indeed there come even in the present experience that ability whereunto the body may in its associations and within itself, not unto vainglory, not unto selfish purposes but to, make its influence *felt* and more far-reaching in the application of the knowledge and understanding that is innate within the entity's inner self; and not feel so easily sat upon, or so easily bewildered by the bombastic talk of individuals who would reason rather from the material aspects than the spiritual. Indeed very oft does it not do to multiply words with unbelievers, nor does it make for any better thought of self to make for crosses in the application of words or experiences in the souls of any; yet to know whereunto thou hast believed and to be able to be strengthened even as He, from the very spirit of truth itself that is indeed the very breath of life, and makes for the abilities in self's own application of the truth to become more harmonious, more peaceful from within; which of itself when allowed to manifest itself in the countenance even of the brightness of the

glory of the sun itself may bring a more powerful influence upon those whom the entity contacts day by day.

7. As to the appearances and their influence in the activities of the entity in the present sojourn, as we find, many have been the disappointments in the experiences with individuals, in the experiences in the earth. And this has made for a tendency for the entity to oft appear timid or shy, or nonplused at any overpowering influence in those who appear to be very worldly-wise or very expressive of the wisdom that they feel within themselves. Yet these have been in the greater part for developments for the entity, and in the present should be united in the spiritual influences and the strength that may be maintained and gained by the turning within and drawing upon the spirit of the truth as given in Him that has promised to be with thee always even unto the end of the world, of the earth, of the earth's experience.

8. Before this we find the entity was in the land of the present nativity, during those periods when there were the settlings of the land, yet when it was rather taken by the English in exchange for those portions of the land in the northern portion of South America.

9. The entity then, in the name Heidenbergher (Lillian), gained and lost; for it was with those—with whom the entity was associated in that period—that brought about much of the political and material change in the associations of the land known as Manhattan and New England and those portions that had been settled by a Dutch and German peoples that were as the forefathers in the flesh of the entity. Yet the necessity of making changes, in the sojourns and the returnings to the other lands for all of the various changes that were necessitated by the exchange in the material way, brought disappointments—and

physical sufferings from the disappointments, and
made for those experiences in self when fear of what
may happen, of voyages, of wars, of exchange in properties, of those things that deal with law or those
things that deal with international questions, make
for—as it were—tiny shivers in the body itself, as they
move along those of the pineal that make for the
awakening that is in the real heart and *soul* of the
entity. For, its psychic forces—from its developments
through many sojourns—have made for one that is
VERY sensitive; yet, as has been indicated, the
greater portion of this has been subjugated. And were
an analysis made from the standpoint of the psycho-
analyst, it would be said that there has been something in the experience of the entity that has made
for subjugating of many faculties and many of the
conditions in the direction of making itself more *vital* in the groups or periods of association in groups
and associations of the entity itself.

10. Before that we find the entity was in the land now
known as the Fatherland, or in the Nordic land, during those periods when there were the gatherings of
many that went as in defense of an ideal, or rather as
an idea that went to seed in what was supposed to
have been an ideal; for the Father hath said, "Not by
might nor by power, but by my word saith the Lord of
hosts" shall there be brought into the experience of
everyone the proper way of a manifestation of the
Father and His love in and among men.

11. Yet, during the associations of the entity in that
experience of the second Crusade into the Holy Land,
men had—being fraught with words that had fired
the very souls and the minds of men to defend an
idea, defend an ideal in the flesh—made for rather
making might as being right, power as in men's hands
rather than that that comes from listening to the

still small voice from within.

12. The entity in the experience was, as it were, caught between the nether millstone; for neither did the entity in self desire to join into the Crusader's activity nor in the flesh desire to leave its surroundings, for many were the things that were pleasant from the material standpoint during that sojourn, yet for the fear of what was said and would be said by those in the associations the entity SUBJUGATED its own material and better mental abilities for the following in those activities in the experience.

13. Then in the name Heidellenbeucher (the man), for it changed in its sex in that, for the desire that came afterwards from those experiences brought turmoils and strife yet inner soul developments for the entity.

14. In the present experience there is much of the fear of those things that were characterized by the activities during such sojourns, and such activities during that sojourn influence innately the entity's thought and activity. Yet, as seen and as given from the intimations as to the application of self, will is that factor that is the pivot upon which the soul of man may make his body-soul one with the Father or turn into self-indulgences, self-aggrandizements that bring detrimental forces in the experience.

15. Then, with the sources of supply, through the spiritual developments and that which has come and may come as the promise from Him who is the Lord, the ruler of all, will thine self more vital, more powerful in the activities thou mayest join in; whether of mental, of material or of spiritual. For:

16. Before that we find the entity was in that land where there were those that were called upon to give of their body those that were of age, when there had gone out the decree from Herod that all males from

the suckling to two years old should come under the power of that edict.

17. The entity then was a neighbor to Mary, the mother of the Lord, and to Joseph. And the husband of the entity was then a carpenter also, and an aide to Joseph, in the name Cleoapas. Hence the entity knew much of those things that have remained to the WORLD a mystery, and oft in the quietness of the hours of the early morn, when as during that period, the entity suffered in the body as for the loss of the offspring, and as has been given that the cry of Rachel went out to the Father for the deeds done in the body of those that professed to be the followers of the living God. Hence doubts and fears arose during the entity's sojourn in that experience, yet when there again arose those in the activities of the forerunner and later when the Son of Mary had again gathered at Cana in Galilee, the entity was among those present and as an intimate friend of the mother of the Lord, and saw the first of the miracles of the Lord in Cana of Galilee! And these experiences through that sojourn, as indicated in the early morning hours, have often come; sometimes as beautiful visions, at others—when turmoil and strife arose within the experiences of the day—they have come rather as beating upon the mind that made for the influences of those that would hinder, the influences of the evil that would make of these as nightmares—and there has been in the experience often as one torn from the very breast in the destructive forces. This has made for a quieting within and at others a turmoil and strife within the self. Yet, if these will be turned and viewed from those experiences in that sojourn, there may be built that strength; for His promises ever remain, "Whom I WILL raise up—he that loveth the Lord's ways and hateth or careth not for what may be said

in ridicule," for he that will not abase his own personality for the love of the Christ child is not worthy
of His love.

18. Before that we find the entity was in that land
now known as the Egyptian, among those that came
from what is known as the Atlantean land and with
the Atlantean, when there were the incoming of many
that dealt much with the building up of those experiences in spreading the truths that had been set as tenets for the lands of many.

19. The entity was among those that made for the
instructions to the young and to the old, not only in
the art of weaving and making of heavier than the
linens in the land but the coarser and heavier and
finer arts of not only the decorations of the body but
the weaving of the materials and the styles that took
on the representation of the various stations in life.

20. From that experience, in the present the entity
finds that there is a peculiar innate feeling when certain dress or certain type of dress is seen, and that
colors and odors have a peculiar effect upon the entity. And when there are the lotus and the sandalwood
with cedar they become almost, even yet to the inner
senses, overpowering.

21. The name then was Iel, and Iel made for developments in the experience; and her daughters became
those that aided much in preserving—for those even
in this day—that which made for the putting together
of the finery or the GOODS of each individual, as they
were in the material sense put away.

22. As to the abilities in the present of the entity, and
that to which it may attain, and how, in the present:

23. As has been indicated, make the self more in attune to those still small voices that come from within,
from the sojourn in the Promised Land; for promise
and fulfillment promises to the entity have meant, do

mean, much—yet in the material sense have often
been so disappointing to the entity. Turn rather, then,
to those that are safe in Him that is able to fulfill all
that has ever been given to the sons of men, if they
will but attune themselves to His laws, His ways. Just
being kind, just being gentle, but being *powerful* in
same, may the entity make through the considering
of all in self—the more joyous life, the more joyous
experience, throughout this sojourn.
24. We are through for the present.

What an amazingly dynamic series of incarnations. She wrote to
Edgar Cayce and told him that she would not have survived this incarnation without having her life reading to inspire her during the hard
times.

The Journey of Ax-El-Tan

One of the most fascinating souls to reincarnate today was the
Atlantean Ax–El–Tan. (This was not his Atlantean name, but what the
ancient Egyptians called him.) This soul has so many typical features of
ancient Atlanteans that he is a good example for us to review.

In giving the first reading for this soul, Cayce began by noting that
none of his several incarnations in the earth were as powerful an influence upon him today as his incarnation in ancient Atlantis, and that he
"may mean much to the earth in the present, in a constructive or a very
destructive manner, dependent upon the application of the entity and
its abilities." Cayce explained to him that even though he may not be
conscious of the ancient activities and their influence upon him today,
these influences were nonetheless there and affecting him. "Very definite urges are INNATE. And through the very POWER, as it were, of the
entity's manifesting in varied and diverse fields of activity, these urges
have been *buided* that so oft in the present find or seek a manner of
expression. And there be those immutable laws that the entity knows
innately, yet is hardly aware or conscious of same save under those pres-
sures or experiences when there is the arousing as from within those

things that harken to something that is as AFAR OFF. Yet these become more and more desirous of expression" (E.C. 1066–1).

Like so many of Cayce's readings for reincarnated Atlanteans, Mr. 1066 (names were replaced with numbers to maintain privacy) was among those that needed cleansing from animal influences. He went through the purification process in an Atlantean temple, not the Egyptian Temple of Sacrifice that Cayce so often mentioned. Ax–El–Tan was among those Atlanteans that struggled, even fought against the negative, self–gratifying influences and ideals of the Sons of Belial. For a time in Atlantis he was a warrior, then he became interested in machines of convenience, and finally in helping very large groups of people. Here's a portion of Cayce's reading on this matter:

✳ ✳ ✳

"The entity was in the Atlantean land during those periods when there were those activities that brought destruction upon the land—by those who had turned, did turn, the advanced activities into destructive forces. The entity was among the children of the Law of One; those that were the sons of men, yet of the daughters of the Lord or those who had become purified of those entanglements in the animal forces that became manifest among many. Then in its activity, as Ax-El-Tan, the entity made those attempts to curb the activities of the Sons of Belial and Beelzebub. [Beelzebub—Mat. 10:25, etc.] Hence it rose to those positions as the warrior among the Atlanteans; and turned to the use of destructive forces with that expression which finds itself in the entity's activity in dealing with things to 'fight the devil with his own fire.' These became the law of the entity. Yet when these things arose more and more to the force of the Law of One, from the spiritual import, they made for the turning to those things that we know in the present as *conveniences* for man.

"Hence those things that pertain to machinery and

its activities are of interest; locomotion, whether in the airplane, in the gas bags, or the motorbike, or the like—all find a close association with the entity; yet there is a dislike for all. For these brought in the experience that of being carried away from the purpose of *freedom* of activity, *freedom* of speech, freedom to act as the promptings of the conscience of the individual might dictate the expression of itself.

"These, as the entity experienced in the earth, as the entity experienced in those sojourns in the environs about the earth, are well if they are kept in check. But these running riot for self-indulgence, for self-gratification, for selfish interests, become in the end those things that turn and *rend* the very heart of the body itself."   E.C. 1066-1

Another portion of his reading indicated that he had helped large groups of Atlanteans migrate to new lands in order to survive the destruction of Atlantis.

Amazingly, he was 25-years-old when this reading was given in 1935, and at that time he was living in Detroit selling cars (machines of convenience and locomotion). Later, in 1957, he wrote a letter to Gladys Davis Turner, Edgar Cayce's longtime secretary and stenographer, telling how he had moved to D.C. from 1936 to 1940 to help manage the Resettlement Association—this work dealt with the migration of large numbers of people from Oklahoma to California during the Dust Bowl (helping large groups migrate to new lands because their homeland was being destroyed). Then, he was called into the Army for World War II (1940) and then again for the Korean War (1950)—a warrior again. His letter said, "I like the army. I had to get out this time because of my age. I started out as a Lt. and ended up as a Major." In-between these two wars he managed the AAA Traffic Club (60,000 members) out of D.C. from 1948 to 1950 (machines of convenience and large, traveling groups).

It is fascinating how his Atlantean activities dovetailed with his most recent incarnation in America.

Atlantis Rising Again Through
The Souls Who Lived There

Past lives are not a part of Western culture and belief systems, but that has been changing. Many people today, even high school kids, readily understand the concepts and forces of karma. ("What goes around, comes around.") Many now consider reincarnation to be a possibility, even though past–life memories are not common. The important aspect of this concept is to understand that our soul's experiences beyond this incarnation affect us and those around us, whether we are conscious of them or not. Also, reincarnating Atlanteans are affecting our world, whether we are conscious of it or not.

In 1932, Cayce stated that Atlantean souls were once again incarnating into the earth and "are wielding and are to wield an influence upon the happenings of the present day world." Cayce taught that in a rapidly coming new age, all the powers and awarenesses known in Atlantis would return to us. These powers and awarenesses brought destruction back then. How will we use them this time around? Cayce explained that we will regain our ability "to have conscious awareness of our oneness with the forces of Nature and the Cosmic Forces and will be able to use this awareness to care for our material needs." But we will have to be careful to use such awareness and power in combination with a healthy concern for the effect on the whole of life. Atlantis and all its good and bad are rising again. How will we handle their wonders and magic this time around is a question only we can answer through guiding our desires, ambitions, thoughts, and actions.

9

Hidden Records of Atlantis: The Three Halls of Records

> Yet, as time draws nigh when changes are to come about, there may be the opening of those three places where the records are one, to those that are the initiates in the knowledge of the One God.
>
> Edgar Cayce (1933) Reading 5750-1

One of the most interesting pieces of information to come through Edgar Cayce's visions is the existence of ancient Halls of Records. In these Halls are stored the records of a prehistoric descent into matter of the souls who inhabit the earth today. The records document millions of years of activity in the legendary lands of Mu, Lemuria, Atlantis, and others. Cayce said that there are three of these record halls. One is under the waters near the Bahamian island of Bimini, another is underground near the Sphinx in Giza, Egypt, and the third is beneath a temple in the Mayan lands.

According to Cayce, the three record caches are identical and contain stone tablets, linens, gold, musical instruments, and artifacts of import to the cultures that created them. He also indicated that mummified bodies are buried with the records in Egypt. As to the question about what language the historical records may be in, Cayce did not answer directly, only saying that there was a time when the world spoke one language, a time prior to the Tower of Babel legend in the Bible. Therefore, we could assume that the records at each site are in the same language. In one reading he indicated that the Atlanteans had a slightly different dialect or perhaps a differing pronunciation of the worldwide language than the rest of the world. In another reading (2329-3) he actually stated that there are exactly thirty-two tablets or plates in the Egyptian hall of records. He said that these tablets would require interpretation, and this interpretation would take some time. Let's hope it does not take as long as the interpretation of the Dead Sea Scrolls of the Qumran caves.

The Cayce readings also tell us that the tablets in the Halls contain information about the ancient practice of building pyramids including the "pyramid of initiation" otherwise known as the Great Pyramid of Giza. It may therefore be no coincidence that pyramids are found all around the globe, from China to the Americas, in Europe as well as Egypt. The records are also said to describe the construction of the Atlantean power producing Firestone. The records even include a prophecy regarding their opening identifying when and who will discover them. Cayce stated, "as time draws nigh when changes are to come about, there may be the opening of those three places where the records are one, to those that are the initiates in the knowledge of the One God . . . " However, he also warned that they would not be opened until mankind was ready to accept them—"until the time has been fulfilled when the changes must be active in this sphere of man's experience." (Reading 378-16) "This may not be entered without an understanding, for those that were left as guards may NOT be passed until after a period of their regeneration in the Mount, or the fifth root race begins." (Reading 5748-6) In this same reading and others he indicates that the fifth root race would begin to manifest somewhere around the end of the 20th century and the beginning of the 21st century. In other words, the opening of the Hall of Records may be coming soon.

The Records in Egypt

The temple of records in Egypt is entered via a hall or passageway that begins at or near the Sphinx, according to Cayce. He referred to this in one reading as "the chambers of the way between the Sphinx and the pyramid of records." (Reading 1486–1) Cayce's description of this hall of records varied somewhat. He referred to it as a "pyramid of records," a "temple or hall of records," and on some occasions called it "the house or tomb of records." In another reading he clearly states that the records are not located in the Great Pyramid although both projects (the pyramid and Hall of Records) were planned during the same era. In fact the readings indicate that the records are underground as one person was told he had been "a supervisor of the excavations—in studying old records and in preparing and in building the house of records for the Atlanteans as well as part of the house initiate—or the Great Pyramid." (Reading 2462–2) He also describes another person's activities with the building of tombs in conjunction with the construction of the Hall of Records "yet to be uncovered."

Aerial view of Giza Plateau showing location of Sphinx, Great Pyramid, 2nd Pyramid (Khafre) and 3rd Pyramid (Menkaure). Source—*Richard Halliburton's Second Book of Marvels* (1938).

In some discourses Cayce described its location as being off the right front paw of the Sphinx in line with the Great Pyramid. He mentioned the Temple of Isis as a key to locating this hall or pyramid of records. Remnants of the Isis Temple still stand between the Sphinx and the Great Pyramid. In another discourse he clearly stated that the Egyptian record cache is between the Nile and the Sphinx, off its right front paw in line with the Great Pyramid. On one occasion he said the shadow of the Sphinx points to the cache although it seems impossible to cast a shadow across the right front paw since the sun never gets behind the Sphinx's head from the northwest.

The Cayce readings further state that the base of the Sphinx was "laid out in channels," and in the left rear corner of the Sphinx, which is facing the Great Pyramid, one can find the wording of how the Sphinx was "founded giving the history of the first invading ruler [Arart] and the ascension of Araaraart to that position." (Reading 195–14)

A 1933 reading (378–16) describes an elaborate ceremony that was held in 10,500 B.C. for the dedication of the record vault. It was led by King Araaraart, the priest Ra Ta, and a relocated Atlantean named Hept-supht ("he that keeps the records, that keeps shut") who was responsible for the actual "sealing" of the Egyptian Hall of Records. The event was said to have transpired "in the grounds about this tomb or temple of records." Also present were all of the Egyptian and Atlantean officials and others associated with the Law of One who had worked to create the records. The sacred festivities included purification and celebratory rituals performed by those who served in the Egyptian institutions of healing known as the Temple Beautiful and the Temple of Sacrifice. This event was so important to the people of that time that there were more ceremonies and activities associated with it than with the completion of the Great Pyramid. In fact it was indicated that a metal apex on the Great Pyramid was placed there to symbolize and commemorate the earlier sealing of the records.

In the above reading, given for a 56–year–old man who had been identified as a reincarnation of Hept–supt, the recipient asked whether he would receive instructions about the specific location of the records in Egypt. He was told that he was one of a threesome that would be involved in finding the records. The other two were identified as the reincarnations of Atlan and an entity possibly once known as El–ka, although the spelling of this last name is noted as being uncertain. Atlan, who had also had a reading from Cayce in this lifetime, had already returned and was 27 years of age in 1933. During his lifetime he was a long–time A.R.E. member even serving on several occasions on the board of trustees. He died in 1985. There are no other readings for an El-ka. Since Hept-supt and Atlan were each leaders of the effort to place records in Egypt and Atlantis, it would seem logical that the third person that will someday discover the records might be a reincarnation of Iltar who was the leader of the Yucatan record placement. Perhaps, since the spelling is uncertain for El-ka, Cayce actually said Iltar. Or perhaps, El-ka is the name of someone who was with Iltar in the Yucatan. Unlike with Atlan and Hept-supt there were no past life readings given that we could find for someone who had been Iltar. The 1933 reading goes on to say that the other two entities (Atlan and El-ka) "will appear." Since the records have not been opened as of this writing, it seems possible that the reading might have been referring to a collaboration of the three in some future lifetime.

According to the archives of the Edgar Cayce Foundation #378 (Hept-supt) was Ernest Zentgraf, Sr. He and his wife Helene were long-time Cayce friends from New York and served on the board of trustees for the Cayce organization. He was the person who requested the information related to the origins of the Maya in reading 5750-1 (reprinted in the next section). Beginning in April of 1934 he was the subject of a series of readings related to his disappearance from home due to depression from a mishandled financial dealing. The readings indicated that he was contemplating suicide but that he should not be forced to return because that would interfere with his free will. Instead a group close to him began a prayer group on his behalf. He returned home 3 months later a spiritually transformed man. He and his wife, who were also associated with the theosophy movement, migrated to Germany in the 1930s in some sympathy with the Nazis. They returned home after the start of WWII. Zentgraf discontinued contact with the Cayce organization after 1939 although the reason is unknown. He is most likely is no longer living given his age (56) at the time of his 1933 reading.

A later reading in 1934 more directly asks the question of who would uncover the hall of records in Egypt. The answer given was, "As was set in those records of the law of One in Atlantis, that there would come three that would make of the perfect way of life. And as there is found those that have made, in their experience from their sojourn in the earth, a balance in their spiritual, their mental, their material experiences or existences, so may they become those channels through which there may be proclaimed to a seeking, a waiting, a desirous body, those things that proclaim how there has been preserved in the earth (that as is a shadow of the mental and the spiritual reservation of God to His children) those truths that have been so long proclaimed. Those, then, that make themselves that channel. For, as He has given, who is to proclaim is not mine to give, but they that have made of themselves such a measure of their experiences as to be worthy of proclaiming." (Reading 3976–15)

Depiction of Atlantean Hall of Records in Yucatan as described in the Cayce readings. Source—*Dee Turman*, courtesy of Eagle Wing Books, Inc.

The Yucatan Hall of Records

The records hidden in the Mayan lands belonged to a fleeing Atlantean priest named Iltar. Iltar, according to Cayce, was a high priest migrating with his people from the legendary lands of Atlantis to the new "Aryan or Yucatan land" and there built a temple of records. Here is one of the most detailed of Cayce's readings on the Atlantis migration to other continents and the setting up of temples and record caches. His syntax can be difficult, so take your time, read slowly, deliberately.

✳ ✳ ✳

TEXT OF READING 5750-1

This psychic reading given by Edgar Cayce at the home of Mr. and Mrs. Ernest W. Zentgraf, 400 St. Paul's Ave,, Stapleton, Staten Island, N.Y., this 12th day of November, 1933, in accordance with request made by Mrs. Ernest W. Zentgraf, Active Member of the Ass'n for Research & Enlightenment, Inc.

1. HLC: You will give an historical treatise on the origin and development of the Mayan civilization, answering questions.

2. EC: Yes. In giving a record of the civilization in this particular portion of the world, it should be remembered that more than one has been and will be found as research progresses.

3. That which we find would be of particular interest would be that which superseded the Aztec civilization, which was so ruthlessly destroyed or interrupted by Cortez.

4. In that preceding this we had rather a combination of sources, or a high civilization that was influenced by injection of forces from other channels, other sources, as will be seen or may be determined by that which may be given.

5. From time as counted in the present we would turn back to 10,600 years before the Prince of Peace came into the land of promise, and find a civilization being disturbed by corruption from within to such measures that the elements join in bringing devastation to a stiff-necked and adulterous people.

6. With the second and third upheavals in Atlantis, there were individuals who left those lands and came to this particular portion then visible.

7. But, understand, the surface [of Yucatan] was quite different from that which would be viewed in the present. For, rather than being a tropical area it

was more of the temperate, and quite varied in the conditions and positions of the face of the areas themselves.

8. In following such a civilization as a historical presentation, it may be better understood by taking into consideration the activities of an individual or group—or their contribution to such a civilization. This of necessity, then, would not make for a complete historical fact, but rather the activities of an individual and the followers, or those that chose one of their own as leader.

9. Then, with the leavings of the civilization in Atlantis (in Poseidia, more specific), Iltar—with a group of followers that had been of the household of Atlan, the followers of the worship of the ONE with some ten individuals—left this land Poseidia, and came westward, entering what would now be a portion of Yucatan. And there began, with the activities of the peoples there, the development into a civilization that rose much in the same matter as that which had been in the Atlantean land. Others had left the land later. Others had left earlier. There had been the upheavals also from the land of Mu, or Lemuria, [in the Pacific] and these had their part in the changing, or there was the injection of their tenets in the varied portions of the land—which was much greater in extent until the final upheaval of Atlantis, or the islands that were later upheaved, when much of the contour of the land in Central America and Mexico was changed to that similar in outline to that which may be seen in the present.

10. The first temples that were erected by Iltar and his followers were destroyed at the period of change physically in the contours of the land. That now being found, and a portion already discovered that has laid in waste for many centuries, was then a combi-

nation of those peoples from Mu, Oz and Atlantis.

11. Hence, these places partook of the earlier portions of that peoples called the Incal; though the Incals were themselves the successors of those of Oz, or Og, in the Peruvian land, and Mu in the southern portions of that now called California and Mexico and southern New Mexico in the United States.

12. This again found a change when there were the injections from those peoples that came with the division of those peoples in that called the promise land [Israelites: The Lost Tribes]. Hence we may find in these ruins that which partakes of the Egyptian, Lemurian and Oz civilizations, and the later activities partaking even of the Mosaic activities [i.e. activities of the people of Moses].

13. Hence each would ask, what specific thing is there that we may designate as being a portion of the varied civilizations that formed the earlier civilization of this particular land?

14. The stones that are circular, that were of the magnetized influence upon which the Spirit of the One spoke to those peoples as they gathered in their service, are of the earliest Atlantean activities in religious service, we would be called today.

15. The altars upon which there were the cleansings of the bodies of individuals (not human sacrifice; for this came much later with the injection of the Mosaic, and those activities of that area), these were later the altars upon which individual activities—that would today be termed hate, malice, selfishness, self-indulgence—were cleansed from the body through the ceremony, through the rise of initiates from the sources of light, that came from the stones upon which the angels of light during the periods gave their expression to the peoples.

16. The pyramid, the altars before the doors of the

varied temple activities, was an injection from the people of Oz [Peru] and Mu [Pacific Islands]; and will be found to be separate portions, and that referred to in the Scripture as high places of family altars, family gods, that in many portions of the world became again the injection into the activities of groups in various portions, as gradually there were the turnings of the people to the satisfying and gratifying of self's desires, or as the Baal or Baalilal activities again entered the peoples respecting their associations with those truths of light that came from the gods to the peoples, to mankind, in the earth.

17. With the injection of those of greater power in their activity in the land, during that period as would be called 3,000 years before the Prince of Peace came, those peoples that were of the Lost Tribes [of Israel], a portion came into the land; infusing their activities upon the peoples from Mu in the southernmost portion of that called America or United States, and then moved on to the activities in Mexico, Yucatan, centralizing that now about the spots where the central of Mexico now stands, or Mexico City. Hence there arose through the age a different civilization, a MIXTURE again.

18. Those in Yucatan, those in the adjoining lands [e.g. Guatemala and Honduras] as begun by Iltar, gradually lost in their activities; and came to be that people termed, in other portions of America, the Mound Builders.

19. Ready for questions.

20. Q: How did the Lost Tribe reach this country?
A: In boats.

21. Q: Have the most important temples and pyramids been discovered?
A: Those of the first civilization have been discovered, and have not all been opened; but their associations,

their connections, are being replaced—or attempting to be rebuilt. Many of the second and third civilization may *never* be discovered, for these would destroy the present civilization in Mexico to uncover same!

22. Q: By what power or powers were these early pyramids and temples constructed?

A: By the lifting forces of those gases that are being used gradually in the present civilization, and by the fine work or activities of those versed in that pertaining to the source from which all power comes.

For, as long as there remains those pure in body, in mind, in activity, to the law of the One God, there is the continued resource for meeting the needs, or for commanding the elements and their activities in the supply of that necessary in such relations.

23. Q: In which pyramid or temple are the records mentioned in the readings given through this channel on Atlantis, in April 1932? [364 series]

A: As given, that temple was destroyed at the time there was the last destruction in Atlantis.

Yet, as time draws nigh when changes are to come about, there may be the opening of those three places where the records are one, to those that are the initiates in the knowledge of the One God:

The temple by Iltar will then rise again. Also there will be the opening of the temple or hall of records in Egypt, and those records that were put into the heart of the Atlantean land may also be found there—that have been kept, for those that are of that group.

The *records* are *one.*

24. We are through for the present.

Let's summarize some important parts of the story in this Cayce reading:

Sometime before the final destruction of Atlantis (other readings indicate during the 50,722 B.C. and 28–22,000 B.C. destructions), the great landmasses of Mu were broken up and great numbers of Lemurians migrated to the Americas. By 10,600 B.C. Atlantis was in the beginning stages of its final destruction; remnant islands were all that was left of its original greatness. Poseidia was the last island of the Atlantean continent. Iltar and Atlan were high priests in the worship of the One God, in a world distracted by many gods. In other readings Cayce called these worshipers the "Children of the Law of One."

Mexican codex of migration of ancient ancestors across the ocean from a country located to the east. People emerge from a cave and ride upon the back of turtles to Vera Cruz. *Lienzo de Jucutacato* 1 and 2. Source—*The Lost Hall of Records* (1999).

The Yucatan peninsula appeared to be a good land to migrate to and establish a new community. Iltar and his ten followers did just that. They traveled to these new lands, built temples and altars. According to Cayce's reading, on their altars they did not sacrifice humans, they sacrificed their weaknesses, attempting to make themselves spiritually stronger and purer, their minds more cosmically aware. They did this by altering their consciousnesses using circular magnetic stones and evoking the spiritual influences from the One Source. But more earth changes occurred, and Iltar's initial Yucatan temples and altars appear to have been destroyed, as was Atlan's in Atlantis. Iltar seems to have journeyed further inland and built new temples.

Yucatan, Central Mexico, Southern California, Arizona, and New Mexico were fast becoming lands of mixed peoples from around the world. The ancestors of the Incas of Peru who were a mixture of previous Lemurian and Atlantean migrations were also on the move, journeying north to the areas we currently identify as Mayan. Eventually, according to Cayce, around 3000 B.C. a group he called "Lost Tribes," came to the southern area of America and then to Yucatan. The descendants of Iltar's initial group joined with these Lost Tribes and journeyed north to become the Mound Builders in the United States along the Mississippi and Ohio valleys.

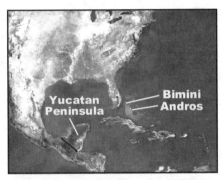

Satellite image of Eastern United States showing locations of Bimini, Andros, and Yucatan Peninsula. The Yucatan Peninsula encompasses the entire Maya lands. The dark line across the Yucatan shows the traditional boundaries of Yucatan. Source—NASA.

The cause underlying much of the final destruction was that the high level of spiritual attunement and worship had slipped into self-gratification and glorification, leading to the worship of Baal, which was a self-gratifying approach to life rather than a oneness with Nature and the Cosmic Forces. Cayce explained that using the same powers and methods, one could create a god or a Frankenstein, and it all depended upon the ideals and purposes motivating the effort. Apparently, all the best of intentions slipped into darkness and selfishness, and the higher attunement was lost. Thus, human sacrifice crept into once pure rituals. The records of this ancient world and its activities remain in Yucatan in one of Iltar's covered temples, in Atlan's cache under the waters of the Bahamas, and under the ground near the Sphinx in Egypt.

Cayce's assertion that remnants of Lost Tribes entered the scene around 3,000 B.C. indicates that new ideas were added to the mixture of cultures in Yucatan, Mexico, and the southern U.S. Some of these new practices were good and some bad. This sounds ridiculous since the Israel you and I know today did not exist in 3000 B.C. You have to know that Cayce's readings stated that the real Israel was and remains "the seekers," not simply a select group of people descended from Isaac and Abraham. Here is Cayce's reading on this: "Thus let there be the study, the closer study of the promises which are made in the Book . . . who is Israel? . . . Israel is the seeker after truth. Who may this be? Those who put and hold trust in the fact that they, as individuals, are children of the universal consciousness of God!" (Reading 5377-1) We provide a more detailed historical analysis of Cayce's assertion about the 3000 B.C. migration of the Lost Tribes to the Americas in our 2001 book, *Mound Builders: Edgar Cayce's Forgotten Record of Ancient America.*

In addition to the previous reading there are several others that provide clues as to the location of the Yucatan records. For example, we are told that Iltar's records are in a temple that is "overshadowed" by another temple that "overhangs" or is built over it. The records in Yucatan may very likely be laid out in underground chambers, since we now know that both Mayan and Aztec temple complexes often had underground tunnels, chambers, and passageways. Cayce also said that Iltar's record cache would "rise again" and that its contents are in the remains of "the temple by Iltar" near where the University of Pennsylvania (Penn) was excavating in 1933. The only location Penn was excavating in Central America in 1933 was Piedras Negras, Guatemala.

At this same location the readings indicated that an "emblem" of the Atlantean Firestone would be found and that "portions" of this emblem would be taken to museums in Pennsylvania, Chicago, and Washington sometime after December 1933. This emblem is further identified not only as consisting of "stones" (note plural form is used) but also as related in some way to a stone altar. "This altar or stone, then in Yucatan . . . is the nearest and closest one to being found." (Reading 440-5) One person asked if he might learn to use the Firestone and was told those who "gained the knowledge" and were properly purified in body and purpose for "the entering into the chambers where these might be found . . . In '38 [1938 or 2038?] it should come about, should the entity [the person receiving the reading]—or others may be raised" in consciousness. (Reading 440-5) Interestingly the Penn expedition was not present at Piedras Negras during 1938 although they occupied the site both the year prior and the year following. The Firestone and/or the Hall of Records may be near a sundial that the readings said would be uncovered after January 1934 by the University of Pennsylvania where it would be found lying between a temple and "the chambers or the opposite temple where sacrifices were made." This would occur "where temples are being uncovered or reconstructed." (Reading 440-12)

Drawing by Tatiana Proskouriakoff of Pyramid K-5 at Mayan ruins at Piedras Negras, Guatemala, showing burning of offerings at altar in front of the temple. Source—*Carnegie Institute* (1946).

The readings also claimed that the remains of the Atlantean immigrants and their settlements in Central America would be hard to locate because they routinely performed cremations and possibly burned their settlements. It was noted that ashes from their cremation ceremonies would be found in "one of those temples" that was prepared for this use—possibly a mortuary temple.

The Bimini Hall of Records

Records in the waters of the Bahamas are in a submerged temple belonging to an Atlantean named Atlan. Cayce said that this temple also "will rise and is rising again." Like Iltar, Atlan was a high priest who attempted to preserve the records of Atlantis, but his temple collapsed and sank during a series of earthquakes and inundations that finally sank Poseidia, the largest of the remaining islands of Atlantis. As related in later chapters, the Cayce readings point to the island of Bimini in the Bahamas as a clue to the location of this sunken temple. The readings relate that Bimini was once a part of the island of Poseidia. Cayce also hinted that following the Gulf Stream to the west and south could lead to evidence of Atlantis.

While the Cayce readings seem to relate less information on the Bimini Hall of Records than the other two, there has been a sustained and prolonged research effort by various people and organizations to discover the submerged temple and other ruins. The results of these controversial efforts are detailed in two later chapters.

Have the Records Been Found?

When people asked Edgar Cayce if they could be a part of the discovery and interpretation of these records, he answered yes, but his reply indicated that it was not necessarily the physical records. As strange as this may seem, according to Cayce, the records are also recorded in consciousness, in the deeper Collective Mind of humanity, and therefore one could open and study the records anytime! Here is an excerpt from one of these strange readings:

✳ ✳ ✳

"Q: How may I now find those records, or should I wait—or must I wait?

"A: You will find the records by that channel as indicated, as these may be obtained *mentally.* As for the physical records,—it will be necessary to wait until the full time has come for the breaking up of much

> that has been in the nature of selfish motives in the
> world. For, remember, these records were made from
> the angle of *world* movements. So must thy activities
> be in the present of the universal approach, but as
> applied to the individual. Keep the faith. Know that
> the ability lies within self."   (Reading 2329-3)

From the perspective that Cayce gained in his deep, hypnotic "sleep," all time is one. There is no space, no time. These are only characteristics of the limited dimension of physical, terrestrial life. Within us is a gateway to oneness, timelessness. The records may be reached by journeying within consciousness and through dimensions of consciousness, as Cayce did. He himself never physically went to Egypt, Bimini, or Yucatan. But he so set aside his terrestrial, outer self, so he could journey through dimensions of consciousness to the Akasha, the mental hall of record.

According to Cayce's readings, each of the record halls will eventually be found and opened. There have been many attempts to locate the records in Mayan lands, the Bahamas, and Giza. There have also been discoveries that indicate that the dating of the Great Pyramid and the Sphinx may be too young, and that these monuments may well have been constructed closer to the dates that Cayce gave, 10,600 to 10,500 B.C. The past and present progress of this research will be reviewed in the following chapters.

10

Research on the
Giza Hall of Records

> . . . there is a chamber or passage from the right forepaw
> to this entrance of the record chamber, or record tomb. It
> lies between - or along that entrance from the Sphinx to
> the temple - or the pyramid; in a pyramid, of course, of its
> own.   Edgar Cayce (1941) Reading 2329-3

For over 30 years, the A.R.E. has been actively investigating the Giza Plateau area of Egypt, near Cairo. Since the Cayce readings repeatedly identify an area near the Sphinx as the location of the Hall of Records, A.R.E. researchers have been especially focused on locating subterranean chambers in that portion of the plateau. Attention has also been paid to new discoveries related to other monuments on the Giza Plateau such as the Great Pyramid since the readings also indicated that they were designed during the same era as the Hall of Records. Thanks to the excellent diplomatic groundwork laid by Hugh Lynn Cayce in the 1970s, this research was allowed to proceed in spite of the skepticism of mainstream Egyptologists who have, so far, been unconvinced of the existence of a high Egyptian civilization dating back to 10,000 B.C.

In an interview in the December/January 1996 issue of *The New Millennium* (an A.R.E. publication), Zahi Hawass, Secretary General of the

Supreme Council of Antiquities, stated that he is unable to support the Cayce information based on the fact that all the artifacts and sites uncovered to date in Egypt provide no evidence of "a great civilization in Egypt before 3,200 B.C." He admits that there are many sites still unexcavated which might provide this data, but until they do, as a scientist he cannot support a theory without evidence. Dr. Hawass also denies accusations that he is blocking further research. He cites an Egyptian law passed in 1983 that requires all researchers to be affiliated with a research institute or a genuine professional scholar as opposed to an amateur archaeologist. He asserts that applications for research are reviewed by a 22-member committee of scholars and no one person makes the final decision.

Giza Plateau showing Sphinx with stones of Sphinx Temple in front (left foreground), Second Pyramid (left background) and Great Pyramid (right background). Source—*Lora Little.*

Dr. Mark Lehner, an American archaeologist specializing in the Giza Plateau, is an interesting character in the conflict between mainstream and alternative views of the age of the Giza monuments. He openly admits to beginning his career in archaeology as a result of his belief in the Cayce information. In fact, he was supported in his studies by Edgar Cayce's son, Hugh Lynn Cayce, in the hopes that he would eventually direct the A.R.E.'s search for the Egyptian Hall of Records. His research over the years has not provided him with any proof of the accuracy of the Cayce information and, in fact, seems to Lehner to overwhelmingly support the orthodox view. In the 1996 *The New Millennium* interview he was critical of the media's coverage of "misinformation" which he viewed as "based on only several weeks of field work . . . .but they will not follow a story derived from decades of field work . . . " He admitted, however, to a continued interest in the Edgar Cayce material as a "social, psychological, and literary phenomenon."

Despite the reluctance of mainstream Egyptologists to accept Cayce's story there has been much research done that relates to the Giza Hall of Records—stimulated by many tantalizing leads. From 1957 until 1979, the Edgar Cayce Foundation (a sister organization of the A.R.E.) worked closely with various organizations, such as the National Science Foundation and Stanford Research Institute (SRI), to try to locate hidden chambers near the Sphinx and the Great Pyramid. Although the capability of the remote sensing technologies such as ground penetrating radar (GPR), magnetometry and resistivity surveys, and acoustic sounding, steadily improved during that time period, all of the anomalies drilled prior to 1979 were determined to be natural formations in the bedrock. However, it must be noted that each of these technologies has its limitations. Since moisture content greatly alters the returning signal, the high humidity and an underground water table relatively near the surface of the Giza Plateau, makes GPR nearly useless. Magnetometry is only useful in detecting metal or areas that have been burned indicating possible ancient settlements. Resistivity can pick up subsurface structures such as walls, building foundations, or ditches 35 to 45 feet below the surface. Resistivity is an active method where probes are placed into the ground. An electric current is passed through them and measured. Some materials allow electricity to pass easily but others are very resistant. The best technology developed so far for finding underground caverns, tunnels, or chambers is acoustic sounding and seismic resistivity. Although these techniques have been used successfully in many areas of Egypt they also have limitations.

Interestingly, the Giza Plateau presents some special challenges for all of these new sensing technologies because of its unique geological makeup. It is a flat-topped hill formed by ancient sea sediments (limestone) with layers of gravel and sand in between. Because the water table is so high under the plateau there are natural caverns and openings as well as fault lines in the bedrock. Determining which of these openings in the rock might be a manmade tunnel or chamber is very difficult.

A 1977 SRI project partially funded by the Edgar Cayce Foundation performed an instrument test by first doing scans of previously excavated underground tombs and passages west of the Great Pyramid. They used electrical resistivity and acoustical instruments. Interestingly, they were unable to clearly differentiate between natural and manmade cavities even when scanning a known target. While this aspect of the plateau can make the search for hidden records frustrating, it also seems at the same time strangely encouraging. What better place to hide the records than in an area full of decoy natural caverns and ancient manmade tombs carved during more recent (*circa* 2500 B.C.) Egyptian history?

The Search for Hidden Chambers In the Giza Pyramids

One of the ongoing mysteries of the Pyramids of Giza is that although they are believed to have been the tombs of the Pharaohs, no burials or funerary artifacts have ever been found within them. As a result, many different groups have come together over the years to examine the Giza monuments in hopes of finding hidden tombs containing valuable artifacts. However, as tourism has become more important to the Egyptian government, so has protecting the ancient monuments that are the main attraction. Beginning in the middle of the 20th century the search for hidden treasures was greatly aided by the introduction of the new remote sensing technologies described in the prior section. They allow analysis without destructive excavation. The earliest attempt to use these noninvasive technologies to look for secret chambers in Giza was called the *Joint Pyramid Project*. It was headed by famed physicist Louis Alvarez and involved not only the Egyptian Antiquities Organization, but also the University of California, National Geographic, IBM, and Hewlett Packard. The goal of the project was to measure cosmic ray penetration within the bodies of the so–called second and third pyramids (Khafre and Menkaure) to see if they contained undiscovered chambers similar to the Grand Gallery in the Great Pyramid.

When first analyzed, the results obtained were initially termed "scientifically impossible" since each time the data was run through the computer a different result was obtained. One of the chief scientists on the team, Dr. Amr Goneid, was quoted as saying that the results, "defied the known laws of physics." Some writers, such as Eric Von Daniken in his book *Return of the Gods* focused on this mysterious result concluding that the pyramids contained some special unknown quality that was confounding the scientist's instruments. The scans were eventually repeated over a period of years and it was determined that the geometry of the pyramids had been miscalculated causing the data collection devices to be positioned incorrectly. By 1970 adjustments had been made in subsequent scans. The results yielded no evidence of hidden chambers in the pyramids of Khafre and Menkaure.

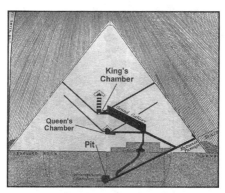

The corridors and shafts within the Great Pyramid. Source—adapted from Smyth *Our Inheritance in the Great Pyramid* (1880).

In 1985 two Frenchmen, Gilles Dormion and Jean Patrice Goidin, an architect, made a visual inspection of the Great Pyramid's interior and concluded that the tomb of Khufu was most likely in an area adjacent to the relieving chambers above the King's Chamber. They also noticed that the stones lining the passage to the Queen's Chamber were arranged in an unusual cross shaped formation unlike any found in the rest of the Pyramid. They theorized that this wall concealed a hidden chamber. They obtained support from the French government and the Egyptian authorities and were allowed to conduct several different types of remote sensing that confirmed the presence of a cavity just where they had suspected it would be. They were given permission to drill three small holes in the passage wall. One of these holes, when drilled to a depth of 8 feet, resulted in a deluge of fine sand pouring out into the passage. Concerned that the movement of the sand might jeopardize the integrity of the pyramid structure, the holes were quickly closed with metal plugs that can still be seen today.

Before the French investigators could return, a Japanese group from the Egyptian Culture Center at the Tokyo-based Waseda University surveyed the floor and walls of the Queens Chamber using GPR and found evidence of a cavity 9 feet behind the north wall of the chamber. They also studied the west passage wall and concluded that the cavity they found could be a concealed, parallel passageway that connected to the cavity they had found in the north wall of the Queen's Chamber. They found yet another hollow space underneath the floor of the passageway and determined that it must be the one filled with sand. But what was most mysterious was their analysis of the sand from the French drilling. It did not match the sand found at Giza or Saqqara meaning that it had to have been brought in from some distance. They had no theory as to why someone would have gone to the trouble of bringing sand from another location when there is no shortage of sand on the Giza Plateau. Strangely, no further follow-up on these cavities has been done.

**Passageway to the Subterranean
Chamber ("The Pit") in Great Pyramid
of Giza. Source—G. Little.**

In 1992 a French engineer used GPR and a micro-gravimeter to survey the descending passage leading to the subterranean chamber nicknamed "the pit." His goal was to verify Herodotus' story of an underground canal leading under the Great Pyramid since evidence for an ancient canal has been found in areas outside of the Giza Plateau. GPR indicated an anomaly that he believed could represent the roof of a SSE by NNW oriented passage. Subsequent micro-gravimeter examination did not confirm a cavity but did find a vertically oriented passage located near the west wall. Strangely, despite these findings they concluded that they were probably just picking up natural underground cavities.

During the summer of 2001, two French archaeologists claimed to have located entrances to hidden chambers in the Great Pyramid. Their discoveries were reported by *ABC Online News Service.* The French researchers used computerized architectural data from Egyptian funeral designs as well as a technique called macrophotography to analyze hundreds of meters of walls within the pyramid. Although the two men called for a joint French-Egyptian effort to uncover the chambers, the response from other Egyptologists, both French and Egyptian, was less enthusiastic.

**Queen's Chamber Passageway
in Great Pyramid of Giza.
Source—*L. Little.***

**Opening to Queen's Chamber airshaft.
Source—*L. Little.***

In 1993, German engineer Rudolph Gantenbrink discovered what appeared to be a small 8 by 8 inch door, or plug, at the far end of one of the airshafts leading from the Queen's chamber in the Great Pyramid. A follow-up study performed in September 2002 (involving the insertion of a fiber optic camera through a hole drilled through the plug) revealed another similar door about eight inches further up the shaft. The second airshaft in the Queen's chamber was also explored and found to contain a duplicate door/plug with two totally intact brass handles. The purpose of the plugs remains a mystery. Some, including Dr. Zahi Hawass, have speculated that they might be related to concealed passages and chambers long suspected to be in the Great Pyramid. At that time Dr. Hawass claimed "it is impossible that these doors are only symbolic." He announced in early October of 2005 that he expected to make a third attempt to penetrate behind the plugs in both shafts sometime that month with a robot designed by scientists from the University of Singapore. Unlike the last attempt, this one would not be televised to avoid the disappointment experienced in 2002. Dr. Hawass promised to issue a press release noting "if something interesting is discovered, we're going to show it to people all over the world." In a 2005 *Reuters* press release, Dr. Hawass speculated, "I believe that these doors are hiding something . . . It could be, and this is a theory, that maybe Khufu's chamber is still hidden in the pyramid."

In summary, the search for hidden chambers in the Great Pyramid has turned up a great deal of supporting evidence. Even so the authorities, with the exception of the Queen's Chamber airshafts, oddly enough seem to have become increasingly reluctant to take the next step of allowing actual excavations in the major monuments. Preservation is said to be the top priority for the Giza monuments. While that is probably true, it has had the unintended consequence of leading many to speculate that more is known than is being revealed to the public.

Dating the Giza Monuments

In 1982 Mark Lehner presented a research proposal to the American Research Center in Egypt (A.R.C.E.) to be funded by the Edgar Cayce Foundation. The project involved carbon dating material from the major monuments located on the Giza Plateau. Subsequently, in 1983 and 1984 the A.R.C.E. team collected 71 samples from the Great Pyramid as well as several other smaller pyramids, tombs, and the Sphinx Temple. Sampling from the earliest levels of the Sphinx was also originally planned but were not obtained since that site was in the midst of a major renovation and mapping project (described later). Although attempts were made to obtain mortar samples from the inner areas of the Great Pyramid, the space between stones was so narrow that no mortar could be removed. Also, some areas had to be eliminated due to contamination by soot from the torches of the early explorers. Interestingly, the group was unable to get permission to sample in the relieving chambers area above the King's chamber. As a result, almost all of the samples were taken from the outer stones.

**Outer stones of the Great Pyramid
showing close fit of stones and little
mortar. Source—G. Little.**

As outlined in detail in Edgar Evans Cayce's book *Mysteries of Atlantis Revisited*, the fourteen samples taken at the Great Pyramid did not yield any dates close to Cayce's 10,500 B.C. era. However, the dates were also not in line with the mainstream chronology. In fact, the dates on average were 374 years *older* than the time of Khufu, the supposed builder/ occupant of the Great Pyramid. The samples ranged from 3100 B.C. to 2850 B.C. Even more interesting is the fact that the samples taken at the top tiers ended up being at least two hundred years *older* than the bottom tiers of the pyramid. Some people asked, was the pyramid built from the top down? Since the mortar yields a date based on the charcoal used in its creation, Egyptologist have tried to explain the discrepancy by asserting that the dates reflect the age of the wood used by the workers at the time of Khufu. If this were true then, for some reason, older wood must have been used to create mortar for the upper levels of the structure. It is equally possible that the mortar in the samples could have been placed there by Egyptians of different generations renovating the ancient structure even before the time of Khufu. But one thing is certain—the true age of the Great Pyramid remains a mystery.

Another date-changing piece of evidence comes from the work of Adrian Gilbert and Robert Bauval, detailed in their best-selling book *The Orion Mystery*. Actually, the initial ideas about Giza star alignments came from Edgar Cayce who stated from his trance state in the 1920s that Giza was laid out according to the stars above it. In 1964 Egyptologist Alexander Badawy and astronomer Virginia Trimble published their findings on how the airshafts and passageways in the Great Pyramid aligned with important stars in both the northern and southern heavens. Then, in 1994, Gilbert and Bauval published their findings, identifying many correlations between the stars and structures on the Plateau:

1. The three great pyramids of Giza—Menkaure, Khafre, and Khufu—match the stars Mintaka, Al Nilam, and Al Nitak (*delta, epsilon,* and *zeta Orionis*) located in the Belt of Orion, noting that the third pyramid (Menkaure) is set off from the other two pyramids just as the third star in the belt (*delta Orionis*) is set off from the other two stars;

2. The alignment is most exact in the year 10,500 B.C., the date Edgar Cayce gave for the construction of the Great Pyramid;

3. The star Saiph is over the pyramid of Djedefre, to the north of Abu Ruwash, and the star Bellatrix is over the "Unfinished Pyramid" at Zawyat Al Aryan to the south. When Orion is on the meridian, the star cluster *lambra Orionis* representing the Head of Orion is over the Dashur pyramids;

4. When Taurus is on the morning horizon, the two pyramids of Dashur, known as the "Red" and the "Bent" pyramids, match the stars Aldebaran and *epsilon Tauri,* the two "eyes" of the bull in the constellation Taurus;

5. The hieroglyphic texts inscribed in the pyramids of Unas (2356-

2323 B.C.) and Pepi II (2246–2152 B.C.) refer to the deceased king ascending into the southern skies in the region of the constellation of *Sahu*, which Gilbert and Bauval identify with the constellation Orion. The authors believe that these texts support the idea that there had been some kind of spiritual relationship intended between the Khufu pyramid (the Great Pyramid) and the Orion constellation.

Of all these correlations, the most provocative argument is the curious and inexplicable "misalignment" of the smaller Menkaure pyramid with the bigger Khufu and Khafre pyramids—exactly matching the arrangement of the third star in Orion's Belt (*delta Orionis*). If this isn't evidence that the designers, impeccable in every other dimension of their work, purposefully offset the Menkaure pyramid because they were laying out the plateau according to the stars above, then what is the explanation for offsetting the third pyramid? Bauval and Gilbert's star alignment information has caused many, including some archaeologists who had their dates so well set, to reconsider the age of the Giza monuments. However, nothing that has been carbon dated on the Giza plateau gives a dating older than roughly 3100 B.C., causing most to be careful about jumping on this 10,500 B.C. bandwagon too soon. The investigation goes on.

Researching the Sphinx

The Cayce readings give some fairly specific directions for the location and make up of the Egyptian Hall of Records. "With the storehouse, or record house (where the records are still to be uncovered), there is a chamber or passage from the right forepaw to this entrance of the record chamber, or record tomb." "It lies between—or along that entrance from the Sphinx to the temple—or the pyramid; in a pyramid, of course, of its own." (E.C. 2329-3)

The Sphinx is a 66-foot high, 240-foot long sculpture with the face of a man and the body of a lion. Located just west of the Great Pyramid, it is sculpted from a single piece of limestone bedrock so that the body of the Sphinx lies below the top of the Giza Plateau. The Cayce readings indicate that the Sphinx was built around 10,500 B.C. during the time of the great priest Ra Ta. However, mainstream archaeology has dated it to the around 2500 B.C. and has stated that the face depicts the Pharaoh Khafre. A thousand years later Pharaoh Thutmosis IV had a stone tablet installed between the paws of the Sphinx telling of a prophetic dream he had while sleeping under the head of the Sphinx. Although the inscription is no longer visible, the tablet is reported to have included one syllable of the name of Khafre providing the mainstream camp with evidence, albeit tenuous, for its 2500 B.C. construction.

The exact age of the Sphinx has been a continuing source of controversy. In 1958 Auguste Mariette found an inscribed tablet in the small Isis Temple located near the Great Pyramid. This tablet, known as the "Inventory Stella," states that both the Sphinx and the Isis Temple were already in ruins during the time of the Pharaoh Khufu and that he was only involved in renovating them. Some have argued that the stela is a forgery. However this is an interesting piece of evidence since, as was noted in the previous chapter, a Cayce reading stated that the Egyptian Hall of Records was laid out near the location of the current Temple of Isis.

**Sphinx with Dream Stela
between its paws.
Source—L. Little.**

In 1992 Boston University geologist Dr. Robert Schoch and amateur Egyptologist John Anthony West, author of *Serpent in the Sky*, announced to the world press that the Sphinx was much older than originally thought. This revelation sent a shockwave through the international community of professional Egyptologists. In the spring of 1996 in a letter to the Egyptology journal *KMT* (pronounced *k-met*; it is the ancient name for Egypt and means, "The Black Land," owing to the rich, black silt left by the Nile after flooding season) John Anthony West outlined his and Dr. Schoch's points:

"1. The Sphinx is not wind-weathered as most Egyptologists think, but water weathered, and by rain;

"2. No rain capable of producing such weathering has fallen since dynastic times;

"3. If it had, other undeniably Old Kingdom tombs on the Giza Plateau cut of the same rock would show similar weathering patterns; they do not; (*KMT*, Summer 1992, p. 53)

"Ergo, 4 The Sphinx predates the other Old Kingdom tombs at Giza. Simple as that."

In his book *Voyages of the Pyramid Builders*, Schoch is willing to take the dates back even further. "The possibility of nonlinear weathering suggests that the very earliest portion of the Sphinx dates to *before 7,000 B.C.*" However, he softens that interpretation of the data to allow for "a rough linear interpretation" of 5000 to 7000 B.C. He also believes that "the current head of the figure—which everyone agrees is a dynastic head— is almost surely the result of recarving." (*KMT*, Summer 1992, p. 53)

While not as old a date range as the Cayce readings give for the Sphinx, this new revelation certainly places its construction much closer to the 10,500 B.C. date than to mainstream estimates. However, other geologists have come forward with contradictory views saying that Schoch has misinterpreted the evidence. For example, a University of Louisville geologist, K. Lal Gauri, believes that a natural chemical process that causes limestone to flake created the weathering found on the Sphinx. Geologist James Harrell attributes the erosion to sand that remained piled up around the Sphinx for centuries. Farouk El-Baz, a geology colleague from Boston University, argues that the rock from which the Sphinx is carved was already weathered at the time it was created. However, Schoch counters that the limestone used for the Sphinx is of a type that does not weather easily. In fact, he notes that the limestone quarried from around the Sphinx and used in the nearby Valley Temple does not show a similar level of weathering. Other geologists such as David Coxill and Colin Reader support the majority of Schoch's analysis although they are not as eager to push the dates back as far as he has. Reader believes that Khafre's Causeway connecting the Sphinx and the Mortuary Temple also predates Khafre.

In their book, *The Message of the Sphinx*, Graham Hancock and Robert Bauval have also found evidence to support the 10,500 B.C. date for the construction of the Sphinx. Their theories derive from a study of the astronomical and astrological based religion of the ancient Egyptians. For example, among much other evidence, they note that a very important aspect of the Egyptian religion involved the continually changing constellations that appeared in the eastern sky at dawn due to the precession of the equinoxes. The star groupings which can be seen rising in the east at dawn indicates which of the 2,200 year long "ages" is currently in effect. They point out that the Sphinx was built facing exactly true east and was probably closely connected to this ongoing astronomical ritual. They further reasoned that since the Sphinx is built partly in the shape of a lion that it would most likely have been built when the constellation of Leo was rising at dawn. To their initial surprise, the astronomy program in their computer identified that the last time Leo would have been rising was in 10,500 B.C. There was Cayce's date again!

Evidence for Hidden Chambers Under the Sphinx

In an attempt to generate a comprehensive and systematic modern survey of the Sphinx and the Sphinx Temple, Mark Lehner submitted a proposal to the A.R.C.E. resulting in the completion of the Sphinx Mapping Project in 1982. The work was done using conventional on-site archaeological survey techniques and hundreds of photographs taken during the 1926 renovation and excavation done by Emile Baraize, an engineer for the Egyptian Antiquities Service. Lehner's mapping project results were subsequently used in the 1990s by the Egyptian Antiquities authorities to perform the most recent renovation of the aging Sphinx structure.

Periodic conservation efforts have been carried out on the Sphinx at least since Roman times. Baraize did the most thorough dismantling of the structure in 1926. During his work he found evidence of several openings along the sides and top of the Sphinx—all but one of which were excavated by Egyptian authorities during the 1990s. One is a recent opening behind the head created in 1837. The second is a 27-foot passage near the tail that splits into two parts, one of which dead ends 14 feet below floor level. The other branch ends at the level of the water table. In a 1997 *Nova Online* interview, Dr. Hawass noted that "the passage is crudely cut, its sides are not straight, but there are cup-shaped foot-holds along the sides." He describes it as being "like an exploratory shaft."

The third opening, a recessed area on the north side first photographed during the 1926 restorations, is more mysterious. In the 1996 *The New Millennium* interview, Dr. Hawass described this third opening as a "sealed door-like area on the north side of the Sphinx's body which was already opened (in 1926) and we'll open it again soon. But I don't expect to find anything in there." In the 1997 *Nova Online* interview, he speculated that "this recess may be nothing more than the over-hanging natural rock which erodes into great recesses and projecting layers."

Aerial photo from Baraize's restoration efforts in 1926 showing several cavities in the body of the Sphinx. *Keystone, circa* 1926.

In the same interview Dr. Mark Lehner noted the presence of "a very large fissure (that) cuts through the entire Sphinx body, running down through the floor around the Sphinx and up through the southern wall of the Sphinx ditch (which is the foundation of the Khafre Causeway)." The 1926 workers noticed this same fissure underneath the masonry on both the north and south hind paws. Baraise installed an iron trap door over the portion of it that opens up around the middle waist area of the Sphinx. Lehner believes that the 1987 Waseda University (Tokyo) electromagnetic sounding survey picked up this fissure, which they reported as a north–south, oriented tunnel running under the Sphinx. The Japanese study also reported finding a "water pocket" at the 7 and 9 feet levels near the south hind paw and a cavity near the north hind paw. In the *Nova Online* interview, Dr. Hawass provided information about the bedrock under the Sphinx. He reports that a 1992 study by the Egyptian National Research Institute of Astronomy and Geophysics using "shallow" seismic refraction "indicated the subsurface rock is composed of four layers and no faulting. They report no evidence of cavities." If that is so, then what is the nature of Lehner's fissure if it is not a cavity or a fault in the rock?

Opening to chamber at rear of Sphinx originally discovered during 1926 excavations. It was recently explored and splits off into two directions one of which ends at 14 feet. Source—L. *Little*.

Regardless of the orthodox clarifications for some of the subterranean anomalies, there remain a few mysterious discoveries that have
not been fully explained. In the 1996 *The New Millennium* article Dr.
Hawass referred to evidence of tunnels in the so-called harbor area in
front of the Valley Temple located directly in front of the paws of the
Sphinx. In addition, in 1980, Dr. Hawass oversaw a project that required
drilling into the ground in an area 165 feet from the front paws of the
Sphinx. The drilling team mysteriously hit bedrock at a depth of only 6
feet. Shortly thereafter, in an area approximately 100 feet away from
that drilling site, a group of Egyptian irrigation specialists were checking groundwater levels and hit red granite at a depth of 50 feet. They
were unable to drill further. Granite is not found naturally in the Giza
Plateau. It is known that red granite was often used to build tombs and
other special structures within some of the major Giza monuments.
However all of this granite had to be transported from a site 600 miles
to the south.

Evidence from earlier research seems to deepen the mystery of the
red granite. The 1977 SRI remote sensing project uncovered three
anomalies under the Sphinx and the Sphinx Temple using electrical
resistivity and acoustic surveys. Two additional anomalies were found
in front of the Sphinx paws including one that gave readings suggesting
it could be as deep as 30 feet. Although the report recommended a
more detailed survey, all of the anomalies were determined to most
likely be natural cavities after they were drilled and probed with micro
cameras. However, the one in the southeast corner of the Sphinx ditch
created a great deal of excitement when it was first discovered and was
described by Lehner in the *Nova* article as being a place "where two
major geological units, one very hard and one very soft meet in a very
irregular interface." Could this be a red granite lined corner of a passage
leading to the Hall of Records or perhaps of the record room itself?

In the early 1990s professional geophysicist, Dr. Thomas Dobecki,
performed seismographic analysis (seismic refraction, refraction tomog-
raphy, and seismic reflection) of the Sphinx and picked up signs of what
could be a large rectangular chamber near the front paws of the Sphinx.
Throughout the 1990s and early 2000s, Dr. Joseph Schor of the Schor
Foundation and a Life Member of the A.R.E., in connection with Florida

State University, led research on the Giza Plateau using GPR to locate underground passageways, halls, and chambers. His efforts resulted in some successes and some failures, as this type of investigation usually does. Their most intriguing success was in 1997. Using GPR, Schor and colleague Joe Jahoda discovered a 25 x 40 foot underground cavern near the Sphinx. After having the data analyzed and confirmed by the National Aeronautics and Space Agency (NASA), Egyptian officials allowed Schor and Jahoda to do limited drilling in order to drop fiber optic cameras down for a better look. Although the cavity appeared to be a natural formation, resembling a cave, it made what seemed to be an unnatural, 90–degree turn. Tentative approval was given for a more sophisticated radar analysis. Complications then arose at Giza, which have, to this writing, essentially stopped Schor's search.

However, the search at Giza may be picking back up. In the 1980s Lehner extended his Sphinx mapping project to the entire Giza Plateau this time employing a computerized 3–dimensional modeling software package called the Geographic Information System (GIS). Calling the effort the Giza Plateau Mapping Project (GPMP) Lehner's goal is to input all data from the last 15 years of excavation in the Giza Plateau and create a mapping tool that will allow scientists and others to visualize the entire Plateau layer by layer. Their results are due to be published sometime in the next year or so. Included will be data from the excavations of the so-called worker's settlement and worker's cemetery that he and Dr. Zahi Hawass began excavating in 1988. It is in an area 1100 feet south of the Sphinx and has been hailed by both as the answer to the question of who built the pyramids. Interestingly, a recent report given by Lehner on May 23, 2005 revealed that the workmen's cemetery dates to a period *after* the pyramids were built. However, there are tombs located underneath this layer being currently excavated that may be found to match the 2500 B.C. time frame.

The ruins of the workers settlement and cemetery on the Giza Plateau as of 1996. Source—L. Little.

In 2004, Dr. Zahi Hawass, longtime chief archaeologist for all the pyramids in Egypt, the Giza Plateau, and Saqqara, now also the Secretary General of the Supreme Council of Antiquities, announced that he had contracted with Birmingham University (UK) to map the entire subterrain of the Giza Plateau using the latest remote sensing technology. This effort appears to be in conjunction with Lehner's ongoing Giza Plateau Mapping Project. As of this writing few results have been released, but both mainstream and alternative Egyptian enthusiasts are anxiously anticipating these findings.

One related report that came out recently seems very intriguing due to its location and the presence of granite. In September 2004 Dr. Hawass announced the unearthing of a subterranean granite shaft discovered in an area somewhere between the Sphinx and the Pyramid of Khafre (the second pyramid). Dated to 2500 B.C. the 33 foot deep tomb contained a wooden coffin and 400 turquoise colored ceramic figurines. The tiny statues were each the size of a man's pinkie finger and are believed to have functioned as afterlife servants for the dead. The figurines were found in six coffin–sized niches that had been carved out of the granite. Hawass told the *Associated Press* that he planned to dig down another 33 feet where he expected to find more artifacts and possibly a granite sarcophagus. In a July 2005 press release primarily describing the discovery of artifacts at Mataryia in northeastern Cairo, Dr. Hawass noted that Supreme Council of Antiquities officials would be "exploring the earth under the Great Pyramid by the end of this year (2005)." No further reports have been released as of the completion of this manuscript.

In summary many have gone searching for hidden record caches, or for *any* records that may shed light upon the great stone builders of the ancient world. The Director of the Giza Plateau has often said that much of ancient Egypt is yet uncovered. Excavations are turning up new artifacts all the time. But there is no indication by anything that has been found so far that there is a record cache of a civilization dating back to 10,500 B.C. Other than the tantalizing clues given by the dates of certain astronomical alignments of the Sphinx and pyramids, there is no specific indication that such records exist. And, unless we are misinterpreting the hieroglyphic records that have already been discovered in Egypt, there is no report of a sophisticated ancient civilization predating the pharaohic period, of which we have so much evidence. However, the hieroglyphic records do tell that the great Egyptian god Hermes (Thoth) hid *his* records in the earth. This is an important message and has driven many to search for the hidden records of Hermes. Since according to the ancient Egyptian religion he was a god from the original creation time, his records could well tell of pre–pharaohic ages. His cache may even have artifacts from pre-pharaohic times. In Edgar Cayce's discourses, Hermes is identified as one of the architects of the Great Pyramid and a key influence in the development of the impressive Egyptian civilization. Even the mainstream Egyptologists are aware of the Hermetic texts and consider that they may indeed exist. Perhaps they are one and the same as Cayce's ancient records. If so, then perhaps the mainstream and alternative researchers will find a place where their interests can converge.

11

The Search for the Yucatan Hall of Records

. . . as time draws nigh when changes are to come about, there may be the opening of those three places where the records are one ... The temple by Iltar will then rise again.
Edgar Cayce (1933) Reading 5750-1

In a series of readings for a 23–year–old electrical engineering student Cayce gave several clues that indicate that the Yucatan records are in a place that was being explored by the University of Pennsylvania (Penn) in 1933. The young man was told that he had had a past life in Atlantis and had been in charge of the power producing Firestone. He subsequently asked many questions that resulted in the most detailed description we have of the Firestone. He was told that an emblem of the Firestone could be found in a place in the Yucatan near the location of the Hall of Records where Penn was excavating in 1933. Cayce officials followed up on that shortly thereafter and discovered that the only place Penn was excavating in 1933 in the area of the Yucatan Peninsula was Piedras Negras, Guatemala. Here are some excerpts from two of these readings.

The first (440-5) was given in December of 1933:

✳ ✳ ✳

3. . . . As indicated the records of the manners of construction of same are in three places in the earth, as it stands today: In the sunken portions of Atlantis, or Poseidia, where a portion of the temples may yet be discovered, under the slime of ages of sea water—near what is known as Bimini, off the coast of Florida. And in the temple records that were in Egypt, where the entity later acted in cooperation with others in preserving the records that came from the land where these had been kept. Also the records that were carried to what is now Yucatan in America, where these stones (that they know so little about) are now—during the last few months—BEING uncovered.

4. Ready for questions.

5. (Q) Is it for this entity to again learn the use of these stones?

(A) When there have come those individuals who will purify themselves in the manner necessary for the gaining of the knowledge and the entering into the chambers where these may be found; yes—if the body will purify itself. In '38 it should come about, should the entity—or others may—be raised.

In Yucatan there is the emblem of same. Let's clarify this, for it may be the more easily found—for they will be brought to this America, these United States. A portion is to be carried, as we find, to the Pennsylvania State Museum. A portion is to be carried to the Washington preservations of such findings, or to Chicago.

The stones that are set in the front of the temple, between the service temple and the outer court temple—or the priest activity, for later there arose (which may give a better idea of what is meant) the activities of the Hebrews from this—in the altar that

stood before the door of the tabernacle. This altar or
stone, then, in Yucatan, stands between the activities
of the priest (for, of course, this is degenerated from
the original use and purpose, but is the nearest and
closest one to being found) . . .
7. (Q) Who is conducting this work in Yucatan?
(A) Would it be sent to any other place than to those
who were carrying on same?
9. (Q) How many facets did the crystals previously
referred to have?
(A) Would be better were these taken from that pattern of same that will be put in the museum in Pennsylvania. For, as given, do not confuse self in the
attempt to use something without having prepared
self to know what to do with same—and bring, unintentionally as before, destructive forces in the experience of self and those about self. Not that this should
not be sought. Not that information may not be asked
for, but be sure that the records are read—and those
that have been given may ONLY be read by those who
have cleansed themselves, or purified themselves!

Another reading (440-12) given in January of 1934 for this same
young man further touches on both the Firestone emblem and the location of the records in the Yucatan. It also seems to confirm that it was
the Penn expedition to which Cayce had been referring in the earlier
reading.

※ ※ ※

28. (Q) Do you think it wise to write the Pennsylvania
State Museum, or called University of Pennsylvania,
telling them of the crystals they will uncover in
Yucatan in order that later they may be interested in
an expedition to Bimini?
(A) This would be well. Seek to find, through not
divers [diverse] channels but through a regular chan-

nel from the university, as to who has led the expeditions in their uncovering and restoration in part (for the better comprehension of that which took place) in Yucatan, and then communicate directly with that leader.

29. (Q) Would you tell us of more that may be uncovered, that we can tell him?

(A) Rather sufficient would it be that there be particular precaution in the uncovering of the stone, or what may appear in the uncovering of what might be termed the sun dial that lies between the temple and the chambers, or OPPOSITE temple—where sacrifices were made. For this is the place, IS the stone— though erosion has made an effect upon same—in which the body will be particularly interested as related to the other forces or expeditions.

Map (1923) of Yucatan Peninsula showing Piedras Negras located toward the lower left center. Until the 1940s, most maps labeled the entire peninsula as Yucatan. Source—*Wonders of the Past* (1923).

30. (Q) In what particular locality in Yucatan is this stone, or these stones?
(A) Where the temples are being uncovered or reconstructed. This has been given, you see.

As can be seen the above readings repeatedly connect the locations of both the Yucatan Hall of Records and the Firestone emblem ("these stones") with a Pennsylvania museum and Penn itself. For this reason inquiries were made many years ago to the Pennsylvania State Museum who directed the researchers to the University of Pennsylvania Museum of Archaeology and Anthropology. Penn was questioned as to the specific sites they were excavating in the Yucatan in 1933. The answer was none in the Yucatan, but they were doing work nearby at the Classic era Mayan site of Piedras Negras, Guatemala during 1933. Although Guatemala is not in the Yucatan as it is defined presently as a "state" of Mexico, at one time the Yucatan encompassed a much larger area—the Yucatan Peninsula. Prior to the finalization of the borders between Guatemala and Mexico the site of Piedras Negras would have been considered part of the Yucatan. It was certainly closely connected to other Mayan sites that are still today considered part of the Yucatan.

Research at Piedras Negras

The Mayan ruins at Piedras Negras were built on a series of rugged mountain foothills and ridges next to where the Usumacinta River marks the present boundary between Guatemala and Mexico. During its height as a Classic Mayan site it was a large complex extending almost a mile from North to South and a third of a mile from East to West in its central ceremonial area. It was the seat of power for a much larger region and included smaller Mayan cities within its rule. It is thought to have had a population of 20,000 at its height. The ceremonial center contains 13 pyramids, 2 ball courts, and multiple temples, residences and steam baths. The oldest pyramids are in the southern part of the site nearest the river and have been dated to several hundred years before the time of Christ. At its center is a large temple complex complete with pyramids built into the side and on top of the highest hill.

Called the *Acropolis*, it is considered a masterpiece of ancient architecture. Piedras Negras is also famous for the large number of hieroglyphic stele found there which figured significantly in the effort to decipher the Mayan writing system. Although the site contains some enigmatic carvings (spirals by the river and Lintel #6), none of its remaining structures or recovered artifacts can be dated to the time of Atlantis. But much of the site remains unexplored.

Artistic reconstruction of the Acropolis at Piedras Negras by Tatiana Proskouriakoff. Reprinted from: *An Album of Maya Architecture,* Carnegie Institution of Washington Publication 558, 1946.

Three-dimensional model of the Acropolis at Piedras Negras at National Museum at Guatemala City, Guatemala. Source—*L. Little.*

Site Map of Mayan ruins at Piedras Negras adapted from *The Inscriptions of Peten* by S. Morley (1938), Carnegie Institution of Washington publication.

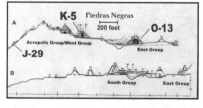

Side view of Piedras Negras showing continuing increase in elevations from south to north and west portions of the site.

Located deep within the Guatemalan jungle, Piedras Negras can only be accessed by travel via rugged mountain "roads" then by canoe or narrow boats over white water rapids. Because the site is located in a rainforest, it is only feasible to work there in the dry seasons — roughly March through June. Even then, the weather is hot and humid and the remoteness of the site requires the most primitive camping conditions. This, along with the nearby guerilla camps occupied during the Guatemalan civil war of the 1980s and early '90s, has helped to protect the site from widespread looting.

Teobert Maler made the first exploratory visits to Piedras Negras in 1895 and 1899. Herbert Spinden, Sylvanus Morley and other Carnegie Institute researchers visited in 1914, 1921, and in 1931 during the first of eight seasons of investigation of the site by Penn. Penn abandoned Piedras Negras in 1939 so that research at the site remained at a standstill until the Brigham Young University (BYU) expeditions of 1997–2000. The fact that BYU, a Mormon affiliated institution has been studying Piedras Negras is an interesting turn of events in itself, given the founding of that particular Christian denomination also known as the Church of Jesus Christ of Latter Day Saints.

The Mormon religion is based on a narrative (published as *The Book of Mormon*) carved on a set of gold plates discovered by Joseph Smith in 1827 under a stone in an earthen mound in rural New York State. According to Smith the plates told the story of three different transoceanic migrations by Semitic peoples to a promised land which Mormon scholars identify as Central America. The first migration is said to have occurred after the fall of the biblical Tower of Babel roughly around 3300—2800 B.C. The other two are believed to have taken place around the time of the traditional Lost Tribes of Israel related to the captivity of the Hebrews in Babylon *ca.* 600 B.C. Descendants of these groups are said to have later migrated to North America where around A.D. 421 they buried a record of their history subsequently unearthed by Joseph Smith.

This history correlates closely with Cayce's 5750-1 reading that appears in Chapter 9. The reading mentions lost tribes coming by boat to southern America and then to the Yucatan around 3000 B.C. and that they were part of a group that eventually migrated to North America to become the Mound Builders. Although Cayce never mentioned the

Mormon religion in his readings he did comment about it in a letter to a friend in 1938 (five years after the 5750-1 reading). In the letter he stated that he was very familiar with the Mormon literature. He had read many of their books and had even heard them preach. He said that he thought the Mormons " . . . have a great deal of truth—but feel sure the founders were a part of the lost tribes—when some of those tribes went to England—others came here to America."

What the University of Pennsylvania Found

Our earlier book, *The Lost Hall of Records*, documents in detail the results of our efforts to determine what Penn found in 1933. During 1999 and 2000 a thorough review of the archival records of the 1931-39 Penn expeditions was accomplished at the Penn Museum of Archaeology and Anthropology. The 1933 expedition received particular attention. There was no evidence that Penn had uncovered Cayce's Hall of Records and none of the artifacts they found were dated earlier than 600 B.C. However, our research led us to believe that the artifact the readings referred to as an emblem of the Atlantean Firestone may be magnetic polished stones, several of which were found at the site by Penn. These stones are known among archaeologists to have been sacred objects used in Mayan ceremonies. This aspect as well as their geologic makeup (hematite/pyrite) fit some of the descriptive qualities of the Firestone given by Cayce. They are also found at other Mayan and Olmec sites therefore explaining Cayce's statement that portions of them were sent to at least three different museums.

Statue from Olmec site of LaVenta *circa* 1500 B.C. of woman with a polished hematite pendant fastened to her chest. Reprinted from *BAE Bulletin*, 153, 1952.

In addition, there are two locations at the site that could be the temples Cayce described as "overshadowing" an underground hall of records, since these areas were especially focused on during the 1933 season. These are the Acropolis (including the northeast ridge area) and the older South Group of pyramids. The 440-5 reading notes that in December of 1933 the records were near "where these stones (that they know so little about) are now—during the last few months—BEING uncovered." This is interesting given that the 1933 season was extended an extra 2 weeks into the rainy season of July in order to excavate a 9 foot jaguar ceremonial mask that had just been uncovered on the side of Pyramid K-5. Located at the foot of the Acropolis hill, K-5's lower foundation is built into the side of a ridge that extends east forming the northeastern boundary of the ceremonial center. In addition, Burial #6 was discovered in 1933 in a shallow cave near the top of the northeastern ridge behind Pyramids K-5 and O-13. Bone fragments from this burial were sent to the Penn Museum as were two polished pieces of pyrite/hematite found at one of the lower temples of the Acropolis in 1933. Interestingly, Penn reported collecting two stalactite fragments that did not come from the Burial #6 cave. Unfortunately, they, along with some inscribed bone tubes, were accidentally burned in a campfire at the site during the 1933 season.

Pyramid K-5 at Piedras Negras
showing giant mask discovered by
Penn at the end of the 1933 season
(Greg Little shown to right).
Source—L. Little.

What Brigham Young University Discovered

By 2001, after 4 seasons of exploration, BYU decided not to return, although they are continuing to perform laboratory analysis of the materials they uncovered there. During their final season (Spring 2000), BYU excavated some of the oldest pyramids located at the site. One of these appears to have a sublevel completed during the Late Pre–Classic Maya era—around 400–600 B.C. Due to the unstable nature of the construction materials, they were unable to completely penetrate to the core of the building. This portion of the site (South Group) and the Acropolis area are the most likely locations for the Hall of Records according to clues given by Cayce in the readings. Additional excavations were performed during 2000 within the Acropolis and, as in the past, were hampered by large piles of debris left at the site by the Penn expeditions.

BYU's most outstanding discovery was during the 2000 season. A 3,000 lb. carved stone panel, which at one time had been attached to a large pyramid, was uncovered on the Acropolis steps where it had fallen hundreds of years earlier. Although some of the carvings are eroded, archaeologists skilled in interpreting the hieroglyphs have determined that it contains the life story of Piedras Negras' Ruler 2. A member of the Turtle Clan, this ruler was named after the founding Father god of the Maya, Itzamna, who was said to have arrived by boat from the east. This is especially interesting since the Cayce readings state that the records were taken to the Yucatan by an Atlantean named Iltar who most likely came by boat from the east. Although the panel was carved well after 10,000 B.C. (it is dated to around A.D. 600), it does contain a reference to the Maya sacred creation date for the "Fourth World" (3114 B.C.) linking some of the events of the life of Ruler 2 to that time frame. Given that Ruler 2 also carries the name of Itzamna, there may be more to the purpose of the panel than the archaeologists are able to determine at this time.

Despite abandoning their on–site excavations, BYU concedes that there is still much that is not understood about the site and that more excavation needs to be done. In the summer of 2002 the chief BYU researcher at Piedras Negras, Stephen Houston, issued an international alert protesting a plan by the Mexican government to build a dam on the Usumacinta River that would flood, and essentially destroy, Piedras Negras. As a result, the initial dam project was scaled down saving the ruins—for now. However, the Mexican government hopes to construct six additional dam sites on the river at some future date. Although excavation has all but halted at Piedras Negras, translation of the many hieroglyphs carved on monuments throughout the site is an ongoing process. In addition archaeologists' understanding of ancient Mayan culture continues to grow.

One intriguing recent finding involves the interpretation of the inscriptions carved on Altar 1, a monument originally uncovered in the 1800s by Teobert Maler in front of the Acropolis at Piedras Negras. The translation revealed a proclamation that a very ancient "Divine Piedras Negras Lord" witnessed some important event that occurred on August 1, 4691 B.C.! The event is related to the Mayan Paddler gods who, like Itzamna, are said to have traveled to the Yucatan from the east over the ocean. This information is especially relevant to the Cayce material since it is the same altar under which a polished hematite disc was unearthed by Penn in 1931 and taken to the Penn Museum.

Altar 1 in front of Acropolis at Piedras Negras as it lies as of 2004. Source—*G. Little*.

Photograph by Maler in 1895 of Altar 1. Source—*Memoirs of the Peabody Museum, Harvard University*, Vol. 2, No. 1, 1901.

In addition, this altar seems to be related to another of Cayce's Yucatan clues referred to in reading 440-12: " . . . particular precaution in the uncovering of the stone, or what may appear in the uncovering of what might be termed the sun dial that lies between the temple and the chambers, or OPPOSITE temple—where sacrifices were made. For this is the place, IS the stone—though erosion has made an effect upon same—in which the body will be particularly interested as related to the other forces or expeditions."

Altar 1 somewhat resembles a sundial in that it has a round top and is supported by 3 rectangular legs. In addition the center of its top is carved with a scene very similar to another carved stone near the river. This large stone, called the Sacrificial Rock, is round and has a pointed side also resembling a sun dial. Of the two stones, only Altar 1 is near temples. In fact it is in the middle of several pyramids in its position in the courtyard at the bottom of the Acropolis. The only other large circular pedestal altar, Altar 5, was found directly in front of Pyramid O-13 and figures significantly in information about a cave at Piedras Negras that will be discussed later.

Lora and Greg Little at Sacrificial Rock by Usumacinta River near entrance to Piedras Negras ceremonial center.

Altar 1 for some unknown reason is inscribed with five ancient dates including the Mayan creation date of 3114 B.C. It is the only monument at Piedras Negras with these ancient dates. Mainstream archaeology has found only a few of these so-called "distance dates" carved on monuments at various Mayan sites. At the Mayan ruins of Quirigua, for example, there are stele that contain the dates 90 and 400 million B.C. The ruins at Palenque contain inscriptions that link the rulers there to ancestor gods who are said to have lived 1 million years ago. The experts are at a loss to explain them since Mayan civilization supposedly only rose shortly before the time of Christ.

The study of Mayan hieroglyphics is still in its infancy but even now it is becoming obvious that the ancient Mayan writing style was very sophisticated and carried multiple levels of meaning. In another possible Atlantean connection, Mayan legends tell us that the god Itzamna originally taught the people to write. Painted Mayan murals accidentally discovered in a looters tunnel at San Bartolo, Guatemala in 2001 have now been dated to the Pre-Classic Mayan era (1000–2000 B.C.). Until this discovery it was believed that the Pre-Classic Maya were primitive and yet these paintings are as sophisticated as those of the more recent Classic Maya. The murals depict the ancient Maya Creation story. In addition, they contain an earlier form of writing that, while resembling the Classic Maya hieroglyphs, obviously predates them. As continues to happen in most all areas of the world, the time frame for the existence of complex civilizations is being pushed back earlier and earlier.

A.R.E.'s 2004 Expedition to Piedras Negras

In April 2004 Greg and Lora Little had the privilege of visiting Piedras Negras, Guatemala in an A.R.E.-affiliated research expedition. This trip was the first A.R.E. sponsored inspection of the site since Scott Milburn's one-man investigation in 1998. On our trip we spent 4 days and 3 nights camping on the Usumacinta River. This allowed us to have two and a half days to explore the site. Our primary goal was to get a firsthand view of this ancient Mayan city that seems to be referred to in the Cayce readings as one of the locations of the three Atlantean Halls of Records. Since the Mayan name for Piedras Negras, *Yokibi*, means "entrance," we were especially interested in finding evidence for caves or underground caverns that might serve as a hiding place for records deposited 12,000 years ago. Interestingly, the hieroglyphic symbol that the Maya used to identify Piedras Negras includes a logograph meaning *cave* and a burial symbol called a *quincunx*. This latter symbol is also connected to the emergence of the Father God Itzamna from the back of a turtle at the time of Creation. Mayan researcher, James Brady, has recently concluded that tunneling was common under the structures of the Mayan center cities. In addition, Piedras Negras is very near the largest cenote (a sinkhole caused by the collapse of underground rivers) ever found in Guatemala.

The Emblem Glyph used by the Classic Era Maya to denote the city of Piedras Negras. Quincunx burial symbol in lower right hand corner. Source—*Adapted from Berlin.*

Another goal was to determine the current status of archaeological research at the site since the close of the Brigham Young University (BYU) expeditions in 2000. We were aware that Charles Golden of the University of Pennsylvania had received funding to do further investigation of the greater Piedras Negras area because of the potential threat of flooding from a proposed Mexican dam site. The World Heritage Fund organization also had recently set aside $100,000 for reconstructive work in the ceremonial center. We wanted to get some information on the nature of the planned work or how much additional excavation might be done at the site.

Ernesto Arredondo, one of the principle Guatemalan archaeologists who worked at Piedras Negras during the BYU expeditions, guided us on the initial part of our visit that involved a tour of the National Museum of Archaeology in Guatemala City. Many of the stele and larger artifacts removed from Piedras Negras by Penn and BYU are housed there. Arredondo had been responsible for overseeing excavations done on the huge hillside palace complex known as the Acropolis. This was especially exciting to us since this is one the areas at the site of interest to us. During our time with him he provided us with some valuable information and made several important points related to the search for the Yucatan Hall of Records:

1. One of the carved hieroglyphic altars in front of Pyramid O-13—Altar 5—indicates that there is a cave located under or behind that pyramid. Penn described this pyramid as "a 'false pyramid' since it is built against the steeply sloping hill, standing free from it only at the top. It attains full height only at the front." The O-13 pyramid is built into the side of the northeastern ridge and BYU has tried repeatedly to tunnel underneath it without success. Unfortunately, the Classic Maya in this part of Guatemala often used large amounts of loose stone rubble between each new construction level making safe tunnel construction all but impossible. However, after one of the attempts BYU noticed a small opening from which cool air was escaping. We were able to locate this opening once we got to the site and indeed the airflow was unmistakable indicating the presence of not only a cave, but most likely some sort of underground cavern leading to another opening. Burial 6 was discovered in 1933 by Penn nearby in a shallow cave located higher up on the ridge behind Pyramid O-13. Interestingly this pyramid is built along the same ridge as Pyramid K-5 where the jaguar mask was uncovered at the end of Penn's 1933 season. If a cave or tunnel does exist under O-13 then it is likely to be connected to K-5 and may even extend under the Acropolis. Some of the tunnels at the nearby Mayan site of Dos Pilas run for miles between and under the major structures.

2. Arredondo agreed that it is quite possible that there are caves or tunnels under the Acropolis and that an unusual, lone pyramid (J-29) built into the backside of the Acropolis hill could be covering the opening to just such a cave. He pointed out, however, that all of the natural caves he had explored in the area were quite shallow.

3. When asked about Charles Golden's recent report of uncovering an abyss accessed by a stairway in Court 3 of the Acropolis, Arredondo

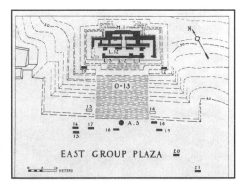

Drawing of Pyramid O-13 built into the side of a ridge showing layout of temple at the top and the round Altar 5 (A.5) as well as the large number of carved stele (12-21) found in front and on top of it. Source—*The Inscriptions of Peten* by S. Morley (1938), Carnegie Institution of Washington publication.

Inside view of possible cave opening at foundation at Pyramid O-13. Source—*L. Little.*

Possible cave opening at foundation of Pyramid O-13 where cool air can be felt escaping. Source—*L. Little.*

Still from video showing the structure J-29 on the back of the Acropolis. Source—*Greg Little.*

J-29 reconstruction with possible entrance into tunnel system. Source—*Dee Turman, courtesy of Eagle Wing Books, Inc.*

noted that he remembered seeing an outcropping of rock that had a natural break in it. They believe that this outcropping had been preserved by the earliest occupants of the site and used for private ceremonies probably related to the ancient Creation story. The abyss did not lead to a cavern as far as he knew. Unfortunately our guides were unable to locate the outcropping while we were at Piedras Negras.

4. He noted that visiting Mormons are very interested to see the six-pointed star intricately carved out of seashell on display in the Tikal section of the Museum. They are also very interested in all Pre–Classic discoveries that cover the period of 1000 B.C. until 200 A.D. We had the same interest since the Cayce readings not only mention the migration of the lost tribes, but also state that an emblem of the Firestone (an object that he says takes the form of a six–sided figure in reading 2072–10) would be found at Piedras Negras and elsewhere.

5. Currently the Guatemalan government's plans for Piedras Negras conflict with those of the archaeologists. The government would like to develop more tourism at the site requiring more restorative work. The archaeologists hope to maintain the site in its natural state so that sci-

entific study is not contaminated by the destructive nature of building reconstruction.

Some other information related to the search for the Yucatan Hall of Records came to our attention during this trip:

•   Mayan security patrols at Piedras Negras were preparing for the return of Stephen Houston in early May of 2004. Original plans were for additional excavations of Pyramid R-1 in the South Court area of PN, but funding limits caused the plan to change to restoration of the giant jaguar mask on Pyramid K-5.

•   Records at our campsite at El Provenir showed that Charles Golden had been in the area as recently as January 2004. He has been involved in mapping the smaller settlements in the greater Piedras Negras area.

•   One of our tour guides had just completed a trip with professional mappers who were investigating the locations of mooring stones along the Usumacinta River in the vicinity of Piedras Negras. Arredondo noted that in some locations these may have even been used by the Maya to anchor bridge structures over the river. While traveling down river to Piedras Negras we came upon some of these stones near the entrance to the most treacherous stretch of rapids on the river.

•   While at Piedras Negras we hiked to the edge of the large dry cenote just southeast of the site. It is 200 feet wide and 200 feet deep. Mayan cave expert James Brady did a preliminary investigation of it and concluded that although artifacts are most likely present at the bottom of the cenote, they are buried beneath a large amount of rubble caused by the repeated collapse of the surrounding edge. The existence of underground caverns or cave structures connecting the cenote to the central city area of PN cannot be ruled out. Excavation within the cenote would be highly productive.

•   After great effort we located Pyramid J-29 that is built into the backside of the Acropolis Hill. It is mostly rubble, almost completely covered by dense jungle foliage, and appears to have had very little excavation. From our external investigation, we concluded that it could certainly be the hiding place of an entrance to underground tunnels. No one has done any work on it since Penn was there in the 1930s. They described it in reports as "a pyramid of major proportions . . . built against a hill, with a large high front terrace at the base." They noted that a sculptured stone (#13) was found there. It was similar to other pyramids at Piedras Negras in that a single-room temple built to house a cylindrical column altar topped it. However, J-29 was unusual in that it was the only one that included "a thick mass of fill between vertical retaining walls, in lieu of a rear wall of solid masonry of ordinary thickness." It had the heaviest outer rear wall thickness of any structure at the site. We wondered if this might be related to its serving as a cover for a tunnel entrance.

All of these findings were reported to the A.R.E. and submitted to the Edgar Cayce Foundation with recommendations for funding future excavations and micro camera explorations of the O-13 and J-29 pyramids to search for underground chambers. Tentative plans include funding a Guatemalan archaeologist through the appropriate authorities to supervise these excavations in 2006. In mid-2005, however, a complicating factor arose. Reports from the region indicated that Piedras Negras had been taken over by heavily armed South American drug runners using the river to move cocaine north. Direct communication with tour operators revealed that near the end of 2005, the drug runners had left the area.

A DVD detailing the 2004 journey to Piedras Negras, *The Yucatan Hall of Records*, is available through A.R.E. Each year new explorations are made in the continuing hunt for these ancient Atlantean tablets. A.R.E. reports on the progress of these explorations in their membership newsletter *Ancient Mysteries* and on their web site. The reports of all of these investigations can also be found in the library at the headquarters of the Association for Research and Enlightenment in Virginia Beach, Virginia U.S.A.

12

The Search for Atlantis in the Bahamas Leads to a Stalemate

> I do not think that the scientists have either proved that it [the Bimini Road] *is* a natural formation or proved that it is definitely not a man-made formation—which would amount to the same thing.　　　　　Graham Hancock (2002)
> *Underworld: The Mysterious Origins of Civilization*

One of the most controversial and bitterly debated aspects of the Cayce readings on Atlantis was the link between the Bahamas' island of Bimini and Atlantis. Bimini is actually composed of two small islands and is located about 50 miles east of Miami. The Cayce readings are very clear on three aspects regarding Bimini's relationship to Atlantis. First, the island was once a portion of Atlantis, specifically part of the island of Poseidia. Second, a temple of the Atlanteans, which Cayce stated was one of the three Halls of Records, was placed near Bimini–but Cayce related that it now lies underwater. Third, Cayce predicted in 1940 that a portion of Atlantis–part of the island of Poseidia–would rise in 1968 and 1969. But the readings involving Bimini were actually obtained for a far different purpose.

In 1926, Cayce began a series of readings for businessmen who were initially interested in whether or not oil could be found by drilling on

Bimini. The first reading indicated that there were no significant amounts of oil present on the island. During the reading, Cayce stated, "but this is the highest portion left above the waves of a once great continent, upon which the civilization as now exists in the world's history found much of that as would be used as a means for attaining that civilization" (996-1). The businessmen apparently had no interest whatsoever in Atlantis at that time, and ignored the Atlantis hint. They next asked Cayce about possible treasure on the island and Cayce replied: "among those larger buried treasures—that consists of gold, bullion, silver, and of plate ware, or beaten ware . . . " Among the treasure that had been buried at Bimini, Cayce specifically mentioned 120,000 gold coins. Six more readings were conducted on Bimini between August and December 1926 (readings 996-2 through 7). Other than the time, date, and place of these readings, no other information is available on them. A note in A.R.E. files relates that Hugh Lynn Cayce loaned the written readings to the people involved at their request. Although repeated efforts were made to obtain them, they were never returned. All of these readings apparently concerned detailed instructions for finding the treasure of gold buried at Bimini.

A fruitless search of the island took place in late 1926 or early 1927 based on information given in the readings. In February 1927, a follow-up reading was conducted (996-8). The first question posed to Cayce was "Will you please explain to us NOW why we were unable to locate this."

Cayce's reply indicated that the information was correct and the search had been conducted with due diligence. The problem, according to the reading, was within Edgar Cayce himself and the motives underlying the quest for gold: "the trouble lies within that of the one [Edgar Cayce — [294]] through whom information is given; for these sources from which the information comes to the material world are from a universal and infinite source, but the channel of same of the carnal or material plane. Hence we know sin lies at the door, and in that information as has been given respecting same, that the house must be set in order."

In a March 1927 reading (996-12) Cayce was asked about how a resort could be set up at Bimini, where the businessmen could obtain sufficient financial resources, and whether water and minerals were to be found on the island. But one of the first questions posed to him was: "Is this the continent known as Alta or Poseidia? [Atlantis]." Cayce replied, "A temple of the Poseidians was in a portion of this land." No other questions on Atlantis were asked during the reading and Cayce also related that a gold vein was located on South Bimini at a depth of 12 to 15 feet. Two more subsequent readings on Bimini were made, but neither of these have any details recorded. These were also lent to the businessmen—but were never returned.

The Bimini Hall of Records and The Famous Atlantis Prediction

In 1933 (440-5) the sleeping Cayce described the locations of the three record halls of the Atlanteans, which were established just before the final destruction around 10,000 B.C. In the reading Cayce mentioned both Yucatan and Egypt. With regard to Bimini, Cayce stated, "In the sunken portions of Atlantis, or Poseidia, where a portion of the temples may yet be discovered, under the slime of ages of seawater—near what is known as Bimini, off the coast of Florida."

Thus, Cayce clearly related that Bimini was once a portion of Poseidia and that a temple containing a Hall of Records was underwater somewhere near Bimini. Since the 1933 reading (440-5) used the plural "temples," it is also clear that more than one temple is there. The specific description he used about what may be discovered ("portion of the temples") implies that ruins could be found.

A 1935 reading (587-4) clearly hinted about a future event that would take place near Bimini. During a life reading for a female pilot, Cayce was asked about a water well that had been found at Bimini, which confirmed some of his statements in prior readings. The well was surrounded by stones with curious markings. Cayce recommended that the well be developed for its healing properties. Then he stated, "And, as may be known, when the changes begin, these portions will rise among the first." What is perhaps the most controversial and famous Cayce reading on Atlantis was given in 1940. During a past life reading, Cayce stated, "And Poseidia will be among the first portions of Atlantis to rise again. Expect it in sixty-eight and sixty-nine ('68 and '69); not so far away!" (Reading 958-3) Strangely, in the follow-up questions that came after this portion of the reading, not a single question was asked about this prediction.

Two aspects of this prediction merit brief discussion. Some people have suggested that Cayce could possibly have been referring to 2068 or 2069. That is very unlikely. The use of the abbreviated years '68 and '69 as well as the statement that it's "not so far away" clearly point to 1968 and 1969. Second, the area of Atlantis Cayce stated would "rise again," was a portion of Poseidia. Since Bimini was linked to Poseidia in several readings, it has been assumed that the Bimini area would be where the prediction was to be fulfilled. But in 10,000 B.C., as we shall later see, the sea levels were actually about 110-feet lower than today. Bimini was then the northwest corner of a massive island that stretched several hundred miles to the southern end of Andros Island. The area between Bimini and Andros is today generally between two to 20-feet deep and is called the Great Bahama Bank.

In 11,000 B.C., the sea levels were over 110 feet lower than today. Cayce's island of Poseidia (a massive island shown in white outlined with black) would have been formed by Bimini (A), Andros (B), the entire Great Bahama Bank, and New Providence Island (Nassau). The overall dimensions of this island fit Plato's measurements. Florida is to the left of Bimini. C is an island that would have been formed by the Little Bahama Bank. D is Cay Sal Bank. Source—*Greg Little.*

The Bimini Search Begins

Skeptics have claimed that the A.R.E. began the search around Bimini in 1968 to make the prediction come true. However, this was not the case. In 1957, Hugh Lynn Cayce, Edgar's oldest son who was the head of the A.R.E., provided assistance to an A.R.E. expedition to Bimini. The group included numerous people, but pilot Joe Gouveia and Dr. William Bell were the best-known members. The primary impetus of the expedition were several reports that granite and stone columns had been found near the Bimini harbor entrance, which divides North and South Bimini islands. The group found the columns, but wasn't prepared to do any study on them. They could not determine if the columns were of recent or ancient origin. Nothing else of consequence was found except one item. As related in *Mysteries of Atlantis Revisited*, Bell found a curious "pillar" somewhere off South Bimini, but in 40-feet of water. The pillar was 4-inches in diameter and extended several feet vertically from the bottom. Bell found that under a layer of mud, the pillar extended into a two-foot diameter "gear-shape." Stone blocks encircled the pillar. Bell took 5 photographs of the mysterious column and numerous people have attempted to refind it—without success. It is possible that the "pillar" may be part of a boat mast or deck equipment of a buried ship.

The A.R.E. also sponsored geological work on the island in 1965–68, and it is likely that various people have searched for the elusive gold vein and the treasure many times. William Hutton, a.k.a. the geologist, examined material dredged from the area of the gold vein and took a few core samples, but no evidence of the gold vein was found. In addition, several commercial pilots took every opportunity to examine the Bahamas waters as they made flights from the Miami area to the Caribbean. But virtually nothing else was reported until 1968.

The First 1968 Discovery—
The Andros "Temple"

In July 1968, commercial pilots Robert Brush and 25-year old Trigg Adams, both of whom had strong links to the A.R.E., were returning to Miami from a flight that took them over extreme northwest Andros. Andros, the largest of the Bahama Islands, lies just over 100 miles to the east-southeast of Bimini. In the shallow water off Andros, they spotted a rectangular enclosure, which appeared to be formed from stone. Upon their return to Miami, they notified Dr. Dimitri Rebikoff, a highly respected French underwater engineer who operated a school for underwater archaeology training focusing on underwater filming and photography. Rebikoff, in turn, notified a Miami–based biologist, Dr. J. Manson Valentine, who taught in Rebikoff's school. In August 1968, Valentine and Rebikoff visited Andros and inspected the rectangular enclosure. After returning to Miami, Valentine issued a press release on the find. Newspapers reported that the site was an underwater temple made from large, smooth blocks of limestone extending many feet into the bottom, relating that it had the same dimensions as some Mayan ruins. (The formation measured 60 feet by 100 feet.) But the articles also speculated that the site might be related to Atlantis. Since the discovery was reported as a temple, obviously A.R.E. members became interested.

Sponge pens in shallow water off Northwestern Andros in 2003. The largest one is identical to the one photographed by Valentine in 1968, which he called the Andros temple. Photo—G. Little.

Valentine, who had a great interest in Atlantis, then mounted several aerial searches along the coast of Andros with Rebikoff. They photographed numerous circular formations and an unusual underwater formation shaped like the letter "e," which came to be known as "Rebikoff's e." Another very unusual formation was found (and photographed) off extreme southwest Andros by Brush and Adams in 1969 when they returned to Miami after making a cargo flight to Puerto Rico. In a 2003 interview with Trigg Adams, he related that Brush wanted to look at southern Andros, which was about 100 miles south of their normal flight path. Because higher altitudes in the area are in Cuban airspace, actually under control by the Havana airport, they flew their massive Constellation at only 500 feet. Brush spotted two massive circular formations just offshore. With Adams at the controls while they circled the formations, Brush opened the pilot's window and took a photo of one of the circles with a Brownie camera. It was a complex circular formation about 500–feet in diameter, which appeared to have three concentric rings of standing stones around it. The other circle wasn't photographed, but they described it as being at least 1000–feet in diameter. Over the years, the strange formations off Andros have been publicized in documentaries and as photos and descriptions in many books, including several by Charles Berlitz. But none of them were visited on-site until an A.R.E. team managed to locate them from the air and then visit each one in 2003. The next chapter contains those details.

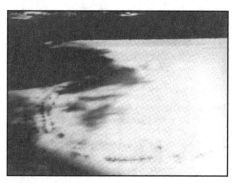

Robert Brush's 1969 photo of large circular formation off extreme Southwest Andros. The formation was long believed to be made from concentric rings of standing stones. Source—*Robert Brush*.

Discovery of the Bimini Road

After the Andros finds, Valentine continued to search various places in the Bahamas, but generally those closer to Florida. While examining the area around Bimini, on September 2, 1968, Valentine finally asked two local fishing guides if they knew of any underwater stones in the area. They immediately took him about a mile off North Bimini, in water about 15 to 20 feet deep. Valentine could see stone forms on the bottom through the water. When he began snorkeling over the area, he was astonished. The bottom contained a massive formation made from what appeared to be huge, consistently placed stone blocks. It was over 1600-feet long and formed an inverted "J" shape. Valentine immediately thought that the formation may have been a collapsed wall or a road, and ever since the formation has been known as the "Bimini Road" or "Bimini Wall." To say that the "discovery" was thrilling for Valentine has to be an understatement. Valentine wasted no time in making an announcement to the press. On September 3, 1968, a Florida newspaper announced the discovery. The Bimini Road immediately became a sensation.

Between the end of 1968 and 1971 newspapers and popular magazines ran countless stories about the ruins of Atlantis at Bimini. During this time, the columns that had been found in the 1950s near the harbor entrance were incorporated into the reports. Valentine and Rebikoff joined forces with an A.R.E.-affiliated group that included pilots Adams and Brush and found additional formations where straight rows of uniform stones essentially parallel the J-shaped formation. An odd twist to this story is that Valentine maintained throughout his life that he had been unaware of the prediction made by Edgar Cayce in 1940.

**Blocks on the Bimini Road.
Source—G. Little.**

In late 1969 another discovery was made by Pino Turolla. Turolla reported discovering 44 "pillars" some distance *west* of the Bimini Road arranged into a circle. The water depth over these pillars was said to be 15-feet. They measured three to five-feet long and were over two feet in diameter. While many people have assumed these columns were the same ones near the harbor entrance to the east, the description of them varies drastically with the ones in shallow water by the shore. These have never been reported again.

The first person to assert that the stones comprising the Bimini Road were primarily beachrock was Valentine himself. In a 1969 article in *MUSE News*, Valentine asserted that since it was readily available and was easy to quarry, beachrock was a likely building construction stone. Beachrock is simply a type of coarse limestone that forms on a beach. The idea that beachrock was a construction stone probably originated from Rebikoff. Rebikoff was involved in surveying and photographing many ancient Mediterranean harbors, virtually all of which were constructed from beachrock. In the same article Valentine described the Andros "temple" as comprised of small oolithic stones covered with sponge—a description that varies quite a bit from the information given to the press in 1968. Strangely, the Andros "temple" was seemingly ignored by nearly everyone. The Hall of Records in the Bahamas was described as in a now sunken temple, and the Bimini Road did not seem to fit that description as well as Andros did. But Andros was remote while the Bimini Road was close and easy to visit.

Rebikoff, who shunned the limelight, differed from Valentine on the origin and purpose of the Bimini Road. European textbooks describe Rebikoff as a "brilliant marine engineer." A quiet, methodical, and deliberate man, Rebikoff wrote that the Bimini Road was the remains of an ancient harbor similar to those he had surveyed in the Mediterranean. A theory that is only now being reconsidered.

Meanwhile, the A.R.E. sponsored a series of expeditions to the Bimini site and countless others went to Bimini to examine it for themselves. One archaeologist, William Donato, of California, made a total of 17 trips there, starting in the 1970s with his last trip (as of this writing) in May 2005. Donato wrote a series of long reports on his finds, many of which are on file in the A.R.E. library. The next chapter goes into more detail on those.

Beginning in 1974, the A.R.E. sponsored and helped to fund a series of expeditions at Bimini by Dr. David Zink, an English professor. Zink made the first reliable map of the Bimini Road and discovered a host of artifactual items. Marble, obvious manmade building blocks, and standing "columns" were among some of the items documented by Zink. Zink also reported seeing another line of stones from the air, closer to the shoreline, but never investigated them. He later visited the Andros "temple" site and discovered it was a sponge pen, which is built to hold collected sponge for cleaning. The same conclusion was reached during A.R.E.'s 2003 expeditions. Zink's 1978 book, *The Stones of Atlantis*, told the story of his Bimini expeditions. Although he had very thoroughly documented his findings, unfortunately, the conclusion of his book focused on a theory that was proposed by a psychic who eventually went to Bimini with him. The formation was, according to Zink, a megalithic site erected by extraterrestrials from the Pleiades. It was a conclusion that was met with skepticism from all sides of the controversy and overshadowed the many years of valuable work he had done. Zink's expeditions to Bimini apparently ended in 1980.

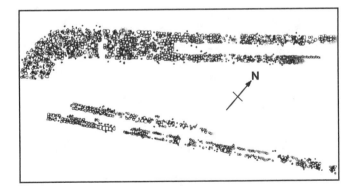

Zink's map of the Bimini Road was made under ARE sponsorship. The drawing shows only the largest blocks. Countless other stones are present around and under the larger blocks. The drawing has been updated; the far ends of the formation extend under sand. Source—*Adapted from Zink*.

During Zink's expeditions, many A.R.E.–affiliated researchers participated for the first time in underwater research. Dr. Douglas Richards, a
biologist, began his Bimini research in 1976 with Zink. Bill Donato began somewhat earlier. Another explorer, Richard Wingate started exploring around Bimini in 1970. Another team was comprised of Talbot
Lindstrom, Stephen Proctor, and others. Proctor was apparently the first
person to explore the mysterious mile–long line of stones found closer
to shore, and he named the site "Proctor's Road." He described the stones
as passing over ancient shorelines and found piles of stones arranged at
regular intervals. Curiously, it was forgotten.

In the 1980s and '90s, many other A.R.E.–affiliated individuals became involved in Bimini research. Dr. Joan Hanley, Vanda Osmond, Ann
and Stan Jaffin, Donnie Fields, Jonathan Eagle, Steve Smith, Ann Smith,
and Jon Holden were among those. In the late 1980s, what appear to be
effigy mounds in an uninhabited part of Bimini were reported for the
first time by participants in Bimini research. Among the effigy mounds
are a fish, a seahorse, whale, and a panther. Archaeologist Gypsy Graves
performed some test work at the mounds, but was unable to determine
whether they were manmade or natural.

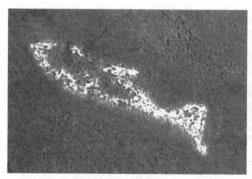

**The "fish" or "shark" mound at Bimini.
Source—G. _Little_.**

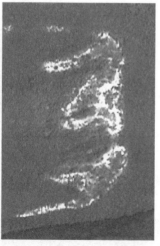

**The "sea horse" mound at
Bimini. Source—G. _Little_.**

In 1980, Zink used side-scan sonar for the first time at Bimini near the shore. In the mid-1990s more sophisticated side-scan sonar was used by Joan Hanley and Bill Donato. In 1996, an A.R.E. sponsored project performed side-scan sonar on a 20-mile long trek down the edge of the Gulf Stream off Bimini. The sonar detected some unusual forms near the top of the drop-off and a few divers, including Doug Richards, went to 130-feet to inspect. But diving at that depth presents problems for sport divers. As related by Dr. Doug Richards in the 2003 book, *The ARE's Search for Atlantis*, "It was hard to even agree on what we had seen."

In 1998 and 1999, Don Dickinson's Law of One Foundation sponsored the most sophisticated search done in deep water at Bimini. The research was conducted under the assumption that ancient sea levels during the last Ice Age were about 300-feet lower at the height of the glacial maximum. Utilizing deep-water tech divers, an area of the Gulf Stream was examined at a depth of about 300 feet by a group led by Dr. Joan Hanley. The divers reported caves, strange looking rock formations, and terraces. Mini-submarines were first used at Bimini by archaeologist William Donato in 1998. During several expeditions near the Gulf Stream, those who submerged in the sub to a depth of 300 feet and over reported seeing unusual formations. In 1999, Joan Hanley's group utilized a 3-person sub and inspected areas along the Gulf Stream during 10 separate dives to 300 feet. Dr. Doug Richards and others participated in this complex operation. While all these efforts reported intriguing observations, nothing definitive was found. During this time period, many other anomalous underwater formations were found around Bimini. These included pentagonal-shaped areas and strange circular and eye-shaped formations all in shallow water.

During a trip to Bimini in 1999 with Trigg Adams, author Graham Hancock inspected the Bimini Road and summarized his thoughts in his massive 2002 book, *Underworld*: "I do not think that the scientists have either proved that it *is* a natural formation or proved that it is definitely not a man-made formation—which would amount to the same thing." At Bimini, Hancock's wife, Santha Faiia, took two photographs of stone circles found not too far from the Bimini Road. Hancock looked under many of the stone blocks and found prop stones, an observation made also by Rebikoff and Valentine. As we shall see shortly, skeptics assert there are no prop stones under the massive blocks.

In 2001, the Edgar Cayce Foundation received funding from Don Dickinson's Law of One Foundation to perform an IKONOS high-resolution satellite–imaging project around Bimini. The images were taken of a 243 square mile area. The satellite photos revealed what appeared to be relatively straight lines in water off northeast Bimini and about a dozen circular formations off South Bimini. One of the circles was 200-feet in diameter and was close to shore at South Bimini. According to Doug Richards's chapter in *The ARE's Search for Atlantis* (2003), Jonathan Eagle processed the images and shared them with a Virginia Beach geologist. The satellite photo of the area where Cayce stated a gold vein was located showed that dredging was occurring. In 2002 Eagle and the geologist went to Bimini and examined the area where the dredging was taking place. They took some cores and samples. While gold wasn't found at the site, the geologist reported that other mineral results pointed toward the gold vein being there.

IKONOS satellite image of the "straight lines" off NE North Bimini. It has been speculated by others that they are somehow related to the gold vein Cayce stated was at Bimini. The IKONOS images also showed numerous identical lines further to the NE. In 2003, Greg and Lora Little found they were natural sand channels. Source—ECF.

Beginning in 2003, Greg and Lora Little (coauthors of this book) began a series of expeditions to Bimini, Andros, and other locations. They began by focusing on the reported enigmatic circles and formations off Andros. Since no one had examined the circles and lines that the IKONOS satellite–imaging project found, they also visited Bimini. In May 2005 the Little's joined forces with archaeologist Bill Donato and made a startling discovery at Bimini. These explorations are detailed in the next chapter, however, a summary of skeptical research at Bimini must first be presented.

The Skeptical Geologists

Not long after the discovery of the Bimini Road, a Virginia Beach, Virginia geologist, Wyman Harrison, sampled two stones of the formation and visually observed the site reporting that all the blocks were limestone that had fractured in place. According to Harrison's 1971 *Nature* article, the site was completely natural adding, "at no place are blocks found to be resting on a similar set beneath."

Harrison also examined 30 cylinder–like columns found near the harbor entrance between North and South Bimini (east of the Bimini Road), but wrote that these were the ones found by Turolla. Turolla, however, reported he found 44 pillars, much larger than the ones Harrison investigated, in 15–feet of water *west* of the Bimini Road. Harrison found that two of the columns were fluted marble and noted they were not from the Bahamas. He wrote that "Georgia is probably not the source and there is only a small chance it could have come from Vermont." The remaining cylinders Harrison asserted were cement noting, "The cement cylinders are also composed of material which is not indigenous to the Bahamas." Samples of the cement were evaluated by several others. One researcher stated that the cement seemed to be a high-temperature product resembling the over–burnt product of limekilns. The other researcher reported that a chemical analysis found quartz and coal particles suggesting that it was probably made sometime after 1800—because that was when the fire limekiln process was first used in America. Harrison reasoned that the cylinder–like columns were probably dumped or lost by modern or historic ships, but made no attempt to compare the columns to similar artifacts that had been discovered at ancient harbors in the Mediterranean or to ancient cements.

Two of the many cylindrical columns in shallow water near the main harbor entrance. Source—*2005 photo by G. Little.*

A master's level geology student, John Gifford, performed work at Bimini for his thesis. With support from the *National Geographic*, Ball and Gifford published a report in 1980 in *National Geographic Research Reports*. They began by relating that Harrison had shown the formation was completely natural, based on Harrison's examination of the two small stone pieces and his visual observations. Ball and Gifford also observed that no blocks on the formation rested squarely on other blocks and that no regular prop stones were present under any of the large blocks. In essence, they asserted that all of the blocks were either lying on bottom sand or on the solid limestone foundation forming the seabed. In an area of the J-formation of the Bimini Road, Ball and Gifford took a sample from the bottom and performed uranium–thorium testing on it to determine its date. It dated to 15,000 years ago. Carbon dating of material (such as shell) from several stone blocks at the site and nearby yielded dates ranging from approximately 3000 to 6800 years ago.

Another geologist, who had a bachelor's degree in biology, published the most damaging findings and asserted that his research had essentially proven that the Bimini Road was natural. Eugene Shinn had worked a few years for the U.S. Geological Survey's new field office in

Miami when he performed the study in 1977. Shinn published findings from 17 stone block cores he allegedly made at the formation with the results detailed in 1978 in the obscure journal *Sea Frontiers*. Shinn later published a summary of his 1978 results with archaeologist Marshall McKusick in a 1980 article in *Nature*. In 2004 Shinn again published a summary of his 1978 findings in the *Skeptical Inquirer*. In the 1980 and 2004 articles, Shinn claimed that all 17 cores showed "constant dip direction from one block to the next" and that all 17 cores "tilted toward deep water" essentially proving that the formation began as a single piece of limestone that formed on an ancient beach. Shinn initially presented one carbon date obtained from shell in a core and two years later, with archaeologist Marshall McKusick, reported more carbon dates. These ranged from 2000 to 3500 years ago. The post–1978 articles related that the cylinders examined by Harrison in 1971 were all cement, and in 2004 they became "Portland" cement.

The Natural Beachrock Hypothesis

To understand the geologists' position on the Bimini formation—that it is a slab of natural limestone beachrock that fractured in place—it's necessary to briefly describe how beachrock forms. Beachrock forms rapidly in the Bahamas where constant wave motion and tidal flows push

Bimini beachrock. Note how the limestone is tilted toward the water. Source— G. Little.

sand and small pebbles onto the gradually rising beach. The water has a high concentration of carbonate material in it some of which settles onto the sand and pebbles that are accumulating on the shore. The shores of Bimini have numerous examples of beachrock.

In the simplest of terms, the carbonate material chemically fuses with the sand and pebbles creating a cemented stone that gets, as Shinn related in 1978, as hard as iron. The stone is actually coarse limestone, but on a beach it's commonly referred to as *beachrock*. Because the motion of the waves pushes the sand and pebbles upward onto a beach line, the forming beachrock almost always tilts toward the water. If the rock is cut, the interior of beachrock often shows a distinctive bedding pattern of visible layers that tilt toward the deep water. Consistent internal bedding of the layers of sand and pebbles and the tilt of the internal layers toward deep water are the critical factors that are used to determine if a beachrock formation is in its natural location or was moved. *Shinn's assertion that all 17 of his cores tilted toward deep water is the critical point in the geologists' belief about the Bimini formation.* Shinn stated that the Bimini Road began as a massive slab of beachrock that formed on a deep layer of sand that once extended above the surface. The sand washed away, gradually settling the slab to the bottom. Over time, the slab fractured into rectangular and square blocks resulting in the formation seen there today. If Shinn's results actually did show that all 17 cores dipped or

tilted toward deep water, it would be a powerful argument that the Bimini formation is completely natural. The assertion that there are no blocks set on top of each other and that there are no regular prop stones under any blocks only serve to support the natural beachrock idea. However, even if multiple tiers and prop stones were present at the site, the issue of all 17 of Shinn's cores "dipping toward deep water" would still prevail.

In essence, by the year 2000, a stalemate had occurred be-

Limestone beachrock slab at Bimini shoreline. The three arrows point to discernable internal bedding layers as well as showing how the stone tilts toward the water. This was what Shinn hoped to find in his cores. Source—*G. Little.*

tween Bimini proponents and skeptics. While many people who personally examined the site were convinced that it was manmade, the assertions from the skeptics made Bimini a pariah to academic research-

ers. Only one archaeologist, Bill Donato, openly asserted that the skeptics were wrong, but efforts to disprove the skeptics' claims were in
vain. Results were suggestive and intriguing, but insufficient. The academic community has accepted the natural beachrock idea as correct.
Kenneth Feder's 2006 archaeology textbook, *Frauds, Myths and Mysteries*
states as a fact the Bimini Road is the product of "natural erosion processes," and that all the columns at Bimini are cement. Shinn and
McKusick were the most skeptical, asserting that the entire Bimini affair
was a hoax designed to promote tourism at Bimini and promote Edgar
Cayce. But, as we shall see in the next chapter, scientists can greatly
stretch the truth and ignore contradictory facts to maintain their own
belief systems.

13

From Andros to Bimini–
The Skeptics' Claims Collapse:
But Proof of Atlantis Still Lacking

> You must realize that because of all the craziness surrounding the Bimini site and the unusual people, it was hard to take the exercise with the same seriousness we would have employed with our regular research. We did it for fun. There was not the peer review usually associated with our real jobs. The details you have pointed out are evidence of minimal peer review. I got a little carried away to make a good story...
> Eugene Shinn (2005) U.S. Geological Survey official e-mail

As related in the last chapter, in 2003 a series of expeditions began a new chapter in the *A.R.E.'s Search for Atlantis*. One major cause for the turn of events was British author Andrew Collins appearance at the A.R.E.'s 2002 *Annual Ancient Mysteries Conference*. Collins' 2000 book, *Gateway to Atlantis* was a serious and meticulous examination of the evidence of Atlantis and included Edgar Cayce's readings. Collins detailed the Bimini research and noted an important 1927 Cayce reading that pointed toward making a search to the west and south of the Bahamas: "[evidence] of the first highest civilization [i.e. Poseidia] . . . will be uncovered in some of the adjacent lands to the west and south of the isles [i.e. the Bahamas]" (996–12). Collins proposed that Cayce's statement of looking to the west and south led to Cuba. Cuba, according to Collins, was the most likely spot of the main island of Atlantis. A 2001 announcement by Canadian researchers doing side-scan sonar work for the Cuba government thrust Collins into the media limelight. Canada-based Paulina Zelitsky and her husband were contracted to find Spanish galleons that were known to have sunk in Cuban waters. The financially strapped Cuban government hoped to salvage some of the incredible amounts of gold held as cargo on these ships. While performing their side-scan sonar in 2,200-feet of water off the extreme southwest tip of Cuba, they detected a massive flat area that seemed to be littered with stone structures. Their announcement created great excitement, and they began seeking funds for an exploration of the area. The Appendix at the end of this book contains a review of the current status of this discovery as well as other Atlantis claims.

Collins' book included some aerial photos that had been taken of the enigmatic circular formations off western Andros. These caught the attention of the Little's, who believed that the never-explained formations could be found and investigated first-hand. Since a Cuba expedition was out of the question (because of American travel restrictions), it was decided to begin by investigating Andros. This seemed logical given two Cayce readings. One of these was the previously mentioned Cayce reading pointing to the south and west. The other Cayce reading (364-3) recommended surveying the Gulf Stream beginning at Bimini. If the Gulf Stream is followed to the south and west, it leads to western Andros. Two underwater formations that had only been seen from the air became the first primary targets, the three-ringed circle photographed by Brush and Adams back in 1969 and Rebikoff's e.

The details of the 2003 expeditions were presented in a late 2003 book, *The ARE's Search for Atlantis*, and readers are referred there for complete explanations. A DVD documentary of the same name was made from video taken during the many expeditions. It should be noted that none of the expeditions to Andros or Bimini were funded by the A.R.E., the Edgar Cayce Foundation, or any other outside sources.

The initial investigation began with an interview with Trigg Adams to identify the exact location of the enigmatic triple-ringed circle. While Valentine widely circulated the photo Brush took, strangely, when

Adams was given the photo, he claimed that it was the first time he had seen it. He said that Brush had given the photo to Valentine. Various books assert that the circle was anywhere from 3000-feet in diameter to 1000-feet in diameter. Adams explained that the triple-ringed circle was perhaps 500-feet in diameter, but a nearby circle was 1000-feet in diameter. While efforts had been made by others to find the enigmatic formation based on the various descriptions given in books, no one had ever found it. Adams pulled maps and showed us precisely where it was—at extreme southwest Andros, not far off shore. He stated that no one had ever asked him where it was!

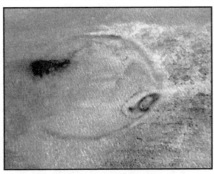

Aerial photo of 325-foot circle off SW Andros. It is completely natural—formed from huge sponge and a small coral head in its middle. Computer comparisons indicated that this was the same formation photographed by Brush in 1969. Source—G. Little.

On February 4, 2003, the Little's made a 4-hour aerial survey of western Andros starting at 900-1000 feet. The first underwater formations found were numerous square and rectangular enclosures near the town of Red Bay, located at extreme northwest Andros. Rebikoff's e formation was easily found following GPS coordinates contained in Bill Donato's many reports. Beginning in the middle of Andros, about halfway down the island, circles appeared in the shallow water. The GPS coordinates of these were taken and the flight continued. As they approached southwest Andros, they descended to 500 feet to stay under the Havana Cuba ADZ. A 400 to 500 foot white circle, outlined by several black bands, was found at the location specified by Trigg Adams. The formation looked strikingly similar to the Brush photo. The only thing left was to identify the second, larger circle found by Brush and Adams nearby. Three miles further south, it was found.

The trip to the circles at southwest was done over two days. All the formations proved to be completely natural. Incredibly, the "standing

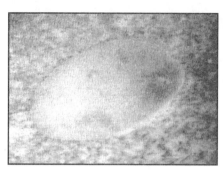

About three mile south of the 325-foot circle a 1000-ft circle was found precisely matching what Trigg Adams stated. This circle was also natural, but very impressive. Source—*G. Little.*

stones" that ringed the large circle Brush photographed, turned out to be gigantic sponge. At low tide, many of the sponge stick out of the water. Even close-up, they looked like stones. It was a major disappointment, but it solved one of the most persistent enigmas of Andros.

In March 2003, the Little's returned to Andros with the intention of visiting Rebikoff's e. Even with GPS coordinates, the unusual formation was difficult to find on water. Compounding the problem was the presence of several small circular forms in the area. But Rebikoff's e was eventually found. From the surface, essentially right on top of it, the unusual shape was visible. It too turned out to be natural. Then the underwater rectangular formations were visited. There were so many present in the area that determining which one was the "temple" site described by

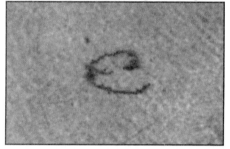

Rebikoff's "e" shown from the air. It is located off NW Andros—it is completely natural. Source—*G. Little.*

Valentine was difficult. One of these, however, was identical in size to the "temple" and also had smaller "inner rooms" as shown in the 1968 aerial photo taken by Valentine. All of the formations are sponge pens formed by piling large stones into square formations with subdivided areas. Vertical sticks are embedded into the stones and bottom to allow collected sponge to wash out as the tides constantly flush through the area.

The night before the Little's returned to the states, a local named

Dino Keller, a former dive operator, told them of a nearby underwater stone formation that looked like the Bimini Road. According to Keller, the formation was uncovered by Hurricane Andrew in 1992. The next morning the Little's went to Nicholls Town Bay where they eventually found it several hundred yards off the shore. It was a three-tiered stone formation enclosing a natural harbor area. It was about 150-feet wide and 900-feet in length. The blocks comprising the formation appeared strikingly similar to the stones of the Bimini Road. They subsequently made a series of trips to the formation with the last trip in May 2005 with Bill Donato. The formation was called the "Andros Platform" to avoid the confusion that came with the term "road."

The Andros Platform has characteristics similar to the Bimini Road, however, the lowest tier toward the shore has a long row of massive blocks extending its entire length. Source—*L. Little.*

Turning their attention to the Bimini circles and the straight lines that had been identified by the IKONOS satellite project, they discovered that most of the circles were natural. The large 200-foot circle off South Bimini, however turned out to be formed by modern dumping. The "straight lines" were simple sand channels formed by the constant currents at the northeast end of Bimini. Though the results were disappointing, they eliminated these sites as needing further examination.

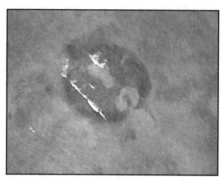

Aerial image of a 200-foot circle—just off South Bimini—discovered by the ARE IKONOS satellite project. The formation is an underwater "mound" caused by construction dumping—probably from the 1950s. The light areas inside the circle were created by modern barges removing sand and debris to use as landfill. Source—*G. Little*.

Cayce's Prediction of Atlantis Rising Again—The Bimini Road

While the 2003 expeditions to both Bimini and Andros were disappointing, the discovery of the Andros Platform was an unexpected surprise. A University of Leiden physics department computer expert, Dr. Rudolph Zweistra, found numerous tool marks in the Littles' video of the Andros Platform. One tool mark had already been identified, but Zweistra found several more. He asserted that the formation was probably manmade.

But one nagging thought entered the picture. Since all the formations at Andros that had been reported in 1968 and 1969 turned out to be natural, what conclusion could be reached about Cayce's 1940 prediction that a portion of Poseidia would "rise again" in 1968 and 1969? The answer had to be at Bimini.

During trips to Andros in 2004 with production crews from *The History Channel* and the *National Geographic*, the Littles made detours to Bimini and took several hours of surface video of the Bimini Road. While they

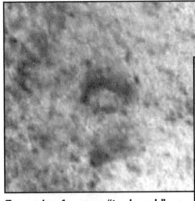

Example of square "toolmark" on stone block of the Andros Platform. The indentation is about 4-inches square and is deep, but generally filled with sand. Source—*L. Little*.

A trip to Andros during a 2004 documentary with the *History Channel* revealed this intriguing area of the Andros Platform. An underwater cameraman was sitting on a huge block next to one with a mortise in the midst of an unusual circular formation with stone slabs. Source—*L. Little*.

had accepted that not much more could be done there, careful examination of the Bimini Road video showed that some areas of the formation seemed to vary greatly from the skeptical geologists' claims. If Cayce's prediction was correct, the Bimini Road had to be it. Archaeologist Bill Donato's reports were then examined. Donato had found numerous mortises on Bimini Road stones, several artifacts, and found an intriguing limestone wedge under a massive block in 1998. Extensive discussion took place with Donato on all of these finds. In addition, Graham Hancock's stone circles discovered near the Road brought up the issue of the essentially unexamined line of stones called "Proctor's Road." Piles of stones were said to be there, but no one had ever performed a full examination of the site.

Gradually, a plan evolved. The precise location of Proctor's Road had to be identified from the air and then the formation had to be examined in the water. Next, at the Bimini Road, a concerted effort had to made to look under stone blocks to find the wedge Donato reported in 1998. The entire formation had to be carefully examined for any evidence that could determine if the formation was artificial or natural. As time permitted, a trip to Andros, passing over the Great Bahama Bank would be made and the Andros Platform would be examined for the first time by an archaeologist.

A decision was made to do whatever was necessary to document all the activities as well as provide sufficient resources. Dr. Lora Little took the role of videotaping all of the underwater activities as well as photographing as necessary. She also directed the boat directly over significant areas so that GPS coordinates could be taken for future reference. Doris Van Auken assisted with photographing as well as serving as a go-between the boat and water investigators. Bill Donato and Greg Little performed the dives. Eslie Brown of Bimini's KnB EZ Dive served as boat captain and Krista Brown recorded GPS coordinates and occasionally marked significant finds with drop buoys. The boat provided essentially unlimited dive tanks to allow for near continual diving in the relatively shallow areas. The expedition took place over an 8-day period in May 2005.

Proctor's Road—Stone Anchors, Stone Circles, Mortise Cut Stones

The May 2005 trip began with an aerial survey to identify the exact location of Proctor's Road. The area is not on the regular flight paths to the Bimini airport and while it has been noticed and mentioned previously, virtually no systematic investigation has been conducted. Surprisingly, the weather conditions were perfect, and all of Proctor's Road was clearly visible from an altitude of 500 feet. Using digital video and a zoom lens, five large stone circles were clearly visible in the shallow water as well as many other partial circles.

Diving at the site the next day, the entire formation was filmed underwater. What appear to be numerous ancient shorelines were clearly visible, and the mile-long line of stones comprising the formation passed directly over many of these. The stone circles were easily found. There are two distinct types there. Some of them consisted of large stone

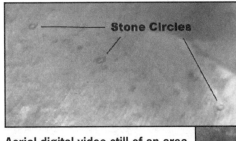

Aerial digital video still of an area of Proctor's Road showing several underwater stone circles. The Bimini Road is located just a half-mile away, toward deeper water. Source—G. Little.

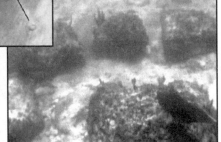

Video image of a portion of one of the stone circles at Proctor's Road. The blocks are generally 3-4 feet square and over a foot thick. Source—L. Little.

blocks simply piled into a rounded heap. The most curious circles consisted of large rectangular blocks arranged into a circle, where the middle of the circle was the seabed. These are clearly anomalous. The circles are located at fairly spaced intervals and between them thousands of smaller, flat stones cover the bottom. The large blocks forming the circles stand out in stark contrast to the smaller stones on the bottom. Several other "partial" circles were found and occasionally one of the large blocks sits alone among the smaller flat stones. Wedged under some of the large blocks associated with the stone circles are several eroded wooden beams and planks. The dive operators, who have operated there for many years, were not aware of these formations and were surprised by the discovery.

Associated with the stone circles were artifacts that were not anticipated, and it took some time to understand them. Numerous stone anchors, varying from round stones with a large hole drilled in the middle to large, wedge–shaped anchors with multiple holes were found. The anchors are identical to ancient Roman, Phoenician, Greek, and Egyptian anchors recovered at numerous ancient Mediterranean harbors.

All of these were left in place. Several large blocks showed what appear to be mortise cuts and grooves.

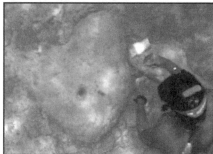

Krista Brown by one of the stone anchors at Proctor's Road. Source—*L. Little.*

Block at Proctor's Road with what appears to be a mortise cut. Source—*Bill Donato.*

Several ancient Mediterranean harbors, especially one at Cosa, Italy, utilized "mooring circles," constructed by forming circles of piled stone. These mooring areas were generally built outside of the main harbor area for ships that were only making a brief stop or for those that were not allowed in the main harbor. Cosa had five of these and they appear similar to the ones at Proctor's Road.

Interestingly, at Cosa, the main harbor is formed by a 330–foot long breakwater that still exists. Dozens of columns are scattered on the breakwater. They are virtually identical in appearance to those at the Bimini harbor entrance, which is not too far from the end of Proctor's Road. The Cosa cylinders—or columns—are of two types. They are either fluted marble or cement—precisely the same kind at Bimini that were described by Harrison in 1971. Modern chemical analysis of the hydrated cement used by the ancient Romans has shown that they used fires to heat limestone and added a host of other minerals, including sandy quartz from sandstone. In addition, ancient Greek cement has been extensively analyzed and is surprisingly similar to modern cement. The presence of the anomalous stone circles and the stone anchors are highly suggestive that the area served as a harbor at some point in the past. The area is under about eight feet of water, less than half the depth of the main Bimini formation. Thus, its possible use for mooring is probably more recent than the main Bimini formation.

Bimini Road Findings Confirm It Is Manmade

Over 14 hours of scuba diving was done by both Greg Little and Bill Donato to examine various portions of the Bimini Road and other areas. At least a dozen sites on the road, each containing multiple tiers of stone blocks, were easily found in direct contradiction to the claims of Harrison, and Ball and Gifford. Several of these were set "squarely" on top of an underlying block, but the top blocks generally showed substantial erosion. These were found primarily in an area of the formation (to the north) that has a large amount of coral and plant growth. The formation at that point extends into sand for an unknown distance. Massive schools of fish were present in this area to such a degree that it was difficult to actually see through them. Sharks are often present in this area of the formation, and it can be speculated that the skeptics may have avoided this area or primarily viewed it from the surface. Bimini is an area with numerous sharks and a *Shark Lab* is operated on the island.

**One example of at least a dozen multiple
tiers of blocks at the Bimini Road.
Source—*Bill Donato.***

Curiously, the multiple tiers of stone in this area cannot usually be discerned from the surface because of sand and plant growth. Indeed, from the surface all of the blocks appear to be resting on the sandy bottom. However, while scuba diving on the bottom, these are very visible and were actually easy to find. In many places on the Bimini Road, it is apparent that large underlying stone blocks are present just under the sand that covers the bottom edges of the blocks seen from the surface. In general, it appears that very little of the Bimini Road is actually sitting on the limestone bedrock or on bottom sand. At other locations, especially in the middle of the "J," some blocks appear to be heaped on top of others in a haphazard, jumbled manner. While some would argue this is the result of dumping, it also has the same appearance as ancient Mediterranean breakwaters where stone is simply piled and allowed to fall into place.

This video still from the surface shows how large squared blocks are buried by sand under many of the large blocks seen from the surface. Source—L. Little.

One intriguing set of blocks that was found was three tiers high. The bottom block rested on a large heap of rubble, which again, directly contradicts skeptics' claims. The top block of the three tiers showed a distinct U–shaped channel cut across its entire bottom. Groove marks were also visible along the ends of this block. It is approximately 5–feet in length and nearly two feet thick.

Triple tier of stone blocks at Bimini Road. Note the U-shaped channel on the underside of the top block. On its left end, groove marks can be seen. Source—G. *Little*.

In addition, numerous cube–like prop stones were regularly found under many blocks. This finding also directly contradicts skeptics' claims about the formation and confirms the assertions of both Rebikoff and Graham Hancock. Without external lights or a flash, it's impossible to see anything clearly under the blocks. It is reasonable to assume that the observations made by Harrison, and Ball and Gifford were primarily made from the surface or without the aid of underwater lights. It is estimated that the underside of less than 10 percent of the blocks on this end of the Bimini Road were examined, but those that were not covered by

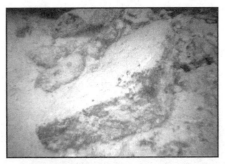

Example of an angular, smooth rectangular block found all over the Bimini Road site. Source—G. *Little*.

sand showed either prop stones or a far more intriguing leveling stone under them.

Scattered around the Bimini Road are numerous smooth, angular, cut rectangular stone slabs averaging about 3 feet in length, by 2 feet in width, and 8–inches thick. Inspection of the extensive underwater video has revealed several dozen of these in various places. When these blocks were first encoun-

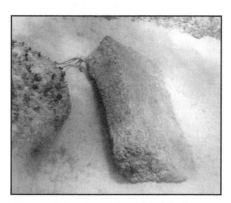

Some of these rectangular blocks are embedded into the bottom. Source—Bill Donato.

tered during the 2005 expedition, they were intriguing, but it was realized there was no proof where they came from or when they were placed there. In brief, the idea that they were dumped was initially the most logical explanation. However, during the time the underside of many massive blocks was inspected, many of these rectangular slabs were discovered *under* the larger stones. In all these examples, the massive blocks visible from the surface were literally resting on top of the smaller rectangular slabs. In several cases, the rectangular slabs were discovered to be literally stacked on top of each other essentially leveling the massive block on top of them. There is no way that these slabs could have been dumped from ships. It was one of the most important discoveries and it can be asserted that it constitutes definitive proof that the hand of humans was involved in altering the formation. To our knowledge, these rectangular blocks serving as leveling stones have never before been reported. This may be because it took considerable effort to get under some of the stone blocks to access the underside.

A bottom surface search yielded several artifactual finds. For ex-

Many cut rectangular slabs were found under several huge blocks seen from the surface. This is the most impressive photo of them. The underside of a massive block is at the top of the photo. A large rectangular slab is directly underneath it as a leveling support stone. Under this slab, portions of two more rectangular slabs can be seen. Source—G. Little.

ample, a unique "u-shaped" mortise cut into a 3-foot square stone was discovered. It is possible it could be natural, but a few ancient stone anchors found in the Mediterranean are identical to it.

The view from the bottom (while scuba diving) is very different from the surface view. The simultaneous presence of both views enabled the team to discover several other important artifacts. While snorkeling and filming from the surface, Lora Little saw a strange looking stone with a plum-bob like shape. After gaining the divers' attention, she directed them to it. The stone, about 3-feet long, had a large hole bored through its middle. On both ends groove marks were clearly discernible where a rope had been attached. This unique stone anchor is identical to several ancient Greek stone anchors that have been recovered at Thera. It was covered with a deep layer of coral and carbonate crust on the exposed side and was found just to the outside of the main J-shape, toward land. Lora also filmed another stone anchor within the main J-shaped formation. It was a large circular stone about 4-feet in diameter with a large hole drilled through the middle. Lora spent about 25 hours snorkeling, all the while videotaping and photographing.

One of the objectives of the expedition was to attempt to find a spe-

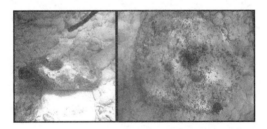

Two stone anchors found by Lora Little at the Bimini Road. The one on the left is identical to ancient Greek anchors recovered at Thera. Source—L. Little.

cific stone block that Bill Donato photographed in 1998. The stone Donato photographed in 1998 wasn't found due to the presence of vast amounts of sand, but the search led the divers to brush sand from the sides of several blocks.

While brushing sand from around one particular block, several smaller and unusual stones became visible under a corner. As these stones were removed, more and more stones were visible. From deep under this block, over two-dozen black, cut stones were recovered. These varied in size from irregularly shaped brick-like stones to highly angular triangular shapes. They appeared to be granite and a group of geology students from an Ohio college performing a field practicum at Bimini agreed the stones were probably granite. In the States, the stones were sent to two independent commercial geology labs. An SEM with elemental X-ray analysis revealed that the stones lacked one element to actually be granite. The stones were identified as "contact metamorphic stones" (fossilized limestone and clay combined under heat and pressure). In essence, they are a type of gray marble. Interestingly, Harrison had identified the marble columns he examined in 1971 as "contact metamorphic stones." According to the geology labs' analysis, this particular type of stone is indigenous to the Bahamas, but not to Bimini. According to one lab, this stone was a highly desirable building material. The lab believes that these stones were perhaps dumped ballast. A more likely alternative is that they were discarded because they were too small for construction. But because they were found wedged under a large block, the possibility they were dumped from a passing ship as ballast is improbable.

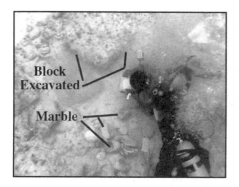

Video frame from surface of where the cut marble was recovered from under a block. Source—*L. Little*.

Several pieces of the cut marble recovered from under a block. Source—*Bill Donato*.

The results of the May 2005 expedition point to the Bimini formation as once serving as an ancient harbor. Stone anchors, quite dissimilar to historic-type anchors, are present at both the Bimini Road and nearby Proctor's Road. The main J-shaped formation appears to have been constructed as a breakwater utilizing the same techniques that were used by Phoenicians and others in the ancient Mediterranean. Harbors were often made at convenient shore locations where natural beachrock had accumulated on sand bars and ridges that jutted into the water forming natural harbor areas. Some beachrock slabs were cut and placed in areas that needed additional support and height. Prop stones were placed under many large beachrock slabs to level the top of the break-water. In key areas, flat, rectangular slabs, called ashlar blocks, were placed on the top of the breakwater to form unloading platforms. The rectangular slabs scattered across the Bimini site are identical to ashlar blocks. In fact, several virtually identical J-shaped breakwater, formed from beachrock, are at Dor, Atlit, and several other harbors in the Mediterranean. At Bimini, the long double line of uniform stones, located about 100 feet from the J-shape toward the present shore of Bimini, appears to have been a quay, a paved cargo staging area that was constructed along the shoreline. The Phoenician harbor at Atlit, has a similar quay still in existence.

Photomosaic of three video frames from what would have been a quay at the Bimini Road. Source— *G. Little*.

Many of the first discoveries at Mediterranean harbors were stone anchors lying on the bottom. Subsequent excavations into the silted harbor areas yielded maritime artifacts. When they were initially found, virtually all of the ancient Mediterranean harbors were silted. Due to annual hurricanes that hit Bimini, small surface artifacts would have been covered or swept away. The area that would have formed the harbor at Bimini has an easily penetrated, silted, sandy bottom. No excavation has ever been done there.

While skeptics have made much over the inaccurate "fact" that there are no multiple tiers of stones at Bimini, the results from this report show that their assertions are untrue. There are numerous double tiers of stones at Bimini. Only *one* of these is needed to invalidate their claim. The one three-tiered formation that was found shows what seems to be a silt-flushing channel cut across the bottom of the top block. However, there is one other aspect to the ancient harbor theory that skeptics have avoided mentioning. Many of the Mediterranean harbors had only one or two layers of stone blocks forming a breakwater, for the simple reason that breakwaters were often built on the top of natural ridges jutting into the water. One layer of stones was all that was often needed. For those interested, the European Commission maintains a large and detailed website on research on ancient Mediterranean harbors that includes the history of research at each as well as photos. It can be accessed at: http://www2.rgzm.de/Navis2/Home/Frames.htm

The possibility that the Bimini formation was an ancient harbor is intriguing. The enclosure is similar in size, shape, and construction techniques to many Mediterranean harbors. The stone circles at Bimini are similar to those at Cosa, where similar marble and cement columns have also been found.

The main Bimini formation is under 15–20 feet of water while the stone circles are under eight to ten feet. Current sea level estimates for the Bahamas produced by the former head of Florida State University's underwater archaeology program, Dr. Michael Faught, indicate that modern sea levels were reached as early as 5,000 B. C. and no later than 3,000 B. C., implying that the use of the Bimini formation as a harbor would have been somewhat earlier. But this is definitely inconsistent with currently accepted archaeology timetables for the Bahamas. Nevertheless, the main Bimini harbor, formed by what is commonly known as the Bimini Road, may have been utilized before 5,000 B.C.–perhaps 6–8,000 B. C.–the time when sea levels in the Bahamas were about 15–feet lower.

Faught has found that in 10,000 B.C., the Bahamas sea levels were no more than 90 to 110 feet lower than today. A.R.E. researchers, looking at 300-foot-deep areas near the Gulf Stream, were investigating shorelines that were present far earlier. Faught's research indicates that around 17,000 B.C. the sea levels were 300 feet lower than today.

Indications are that the stone circles at Proctor's Road may have been utilized as mooring areas when the sea level was perhaps 7–8 feet lower than today. This would have been sometime around 5000 B.C. While this scenario is certainly speculative, it seems possible, based on the evidence, that the main Bimini harbor was utilized until rising sea levels made it unusable—*circa* 5000 B.C. Then, the mooring circles were constructed until they too became unusable by rising sea levels, perhaps between 4000 and 3000 B.C. In fact, that was the same time period when the Great Bahama Bank, stretching from Bimini to Andros, 100 miles away, was submerged by rising waters. For whatever reason, the maritime culture that utilized Bimini as a port was abandoned and probably forgotten. Over the centuries of increasingly warm weather, hurricanes probably increased in frequency and ferocity, and with the majority of the prior land mass submerged under the rising seas, the area was completely abandoned by this unknown maritime culture.

While these findings do not support the idea that the "modern" Bimini Road was Atlantean, there is an intriguing possibility that merits mention. First, it has to be mentioned that the large island formed during the last Ice Age by the combination of Bimini, the Great Bahama Bank, and Andros matches the general description and size mentioned by Plato for the main island of Atlantis. As demonstrated in several photos taken from the bottom, the Bimini Road is actually elevated off the bottom. In addition, almost everywhere under the blocks that are easily viewed from the surface, there are more stones. In most cases, these appear larger than the surface blocks. This idea is also supported by the discovery of smooth slabs of rectangular stones underneath many of the huge surface blocks. In brief, it appears that there is more of the formation underneath what is today called the "Bimini Road." Precisely what is there isn't known, but it raises many possibilities. But the overall finding from the 2005 Bimini expedition was definitive proof showing the skeptics' claims about the site are completely inaccurate.

The Bimini Road may well have been a complex harbor in 6,000 B.C. to 8,000 B.C. when sea levels were 15 feet lower. Source—Dee Turman, courtesy of ATA Productions.

The Primary Skeptics Crumble Under Scrutiny

It should be mentioned that the Bimini skeptics have invested themselves into their assertions for nearly 35 years. All contradictions to their beliefs are probably perceived as a direct threat to them professionally and psychologically. The long history of science has countless examples of widely held beliefs that were proven wrong by research. But even in the face of incontrovertible proof that these beliefs were wrong, many scientists refused to accept the new evidence. Most people are aware of such examples, and it is not necessary to detail them here.

Because the findings of the May 2005 Bimini expedition were completely contrary to the skeptics' claims, Greg Little engaged in a series of e-mail exchanges with Eugene Shinn and a brief exchange with John Gifford. This came after the Little's obtained a copy of Shinn's 1978 article. In spite of the discoveries that were made at Bimini, the fundamental beachrock hypothesis stemming from Shinn's core research wasn't countered by the May findings. In both 1980 and 2004, Shinn

claimed that all the core results were totally consistent, in essence asserting that all 17 cores dipped toward deep water. A careful examination of Shinn's actual results revealed that was not at all the case.

In his 1978 *Sea Frontiers'* article, Shinn explained that he did two separate sets of cores at two different sites on the Bimini Road. He wrote,
*"The purpose of this was to determine if the bedding in **all** the blocks dips uniformly
toward the sea (to the west of Bimini). If it does, then it is highly unlikely that the
blocks had ever been transported."* [All emphasis added to this and subsequent quotes.] One area on the site had 8 cores performed and the other
area had 9. *He actually reported that at the site with eight cores, no internal strata—
no dipping—was visible or present.* He wrote: "Beach bedding was not readily
visible in these cores," relating that no dipping was found.

In his results on the area with 9 cores, *Shinn simply reported that "many"
of these nine cores were horizontal while the others dipped toward deep water.* The
two sentences Shinn used to describe his findings on these 9 cores was:
"Bedding in all the cores from this area was either horizontal or dipping
predominantly toward the sea. No blocks were found that dipped predominantly away from the sea or parallel to the shore."

Shinn's results did *not* report that none of the blocks dipped toward
the shore (away from the sea), they relate none of them dipped *predominantly* toward shore, implying something else. He describes them as
horizontal—meaning level or flat with no dip present. He strangely reported no actual numbers on how many of these 9 cores were horizontal versus dipping toward sea or land. The fact that the journal would
publish the paper without having any actual numbers cited in the results is puzzling, but in his e-mails, Shinn wrote that the Editor of the
journal "was pleased to publish the geological explanation" of the site.

Because Shinn specifically wrote that "many" of the set of 9 cores
were horizontal and not dipping, it's reasonable to assume that more
than half of them (5 or more) were horizontal. And it is also likely, based
on Shinn's descriptions, that some of them had some tilt toward land,
though not what he describes as *predominantly*. In sum, *of Shinn's 17 cores,
he reported that the first set of 8 showed no internal bedding planes and no dip. Of
the other 9, a reasonable guess is that at least 5 were horizontal. Thus, it is likely that
at least 13 of 17 cores (or 76.5 percent) showed no dip toward deep water while 23.5
percent or less actually dipped toward deep water.*

There are three possible outcomes in the internal strata of the cores: 1) a dip to deep water; 2) a dip toward land; 3) no dipping present or visible. Thus, by chance alone, one would expect to find about 33.3 percent that dipped to the deep water. *Shinn's reported outcome was actually less than what would be expected by chance.* In all three of Shinn's articles, the decision between the two explanative alternatives for the Bimini Road—natural *versus* manmade—was stated to be determined by the outcome of the dip shown in the cores. As related previously, Shinn wrote in 1978 that, "The purpose of this (the coring) was to determine if the bedding in *all* the blocks dips uniformly to the sea (to the west of Bimini)." Shinn's core results showed that the vast majority of the stones did not dip toward the sea. This fact actually argues for the artifactual nature of the formation.

The most influential archaeology article on Bimini is the 1980 *Nature* article Shinn published with Marshall McKusick only two years after the *Sea Frontiers* article came out. McKusick is, of course, held in high esteem in the archaeological community. In the 1980 *Nature* article, the only new data that was reported were a few carbon dates, which are addressed later. The major point in the article was the summary of what Shinn found in 1978. Here is the exact quote from *Nature* (1980) that resummarizes Shinn's 1978 findings: "Two areas of the formation were studied, and *both show slope and uniform particle size, bedding planes and constant dip direction from one block to the next.*" (p. 287) That sentence in the article is the foundation of Shinn and McKusick's natural beachrock hypothesis. In his 2004 article in the *Skeptical Inquirer*, Shinn related a much shorter assertion about his 17 cores writing: *"all the cores dipped toward deep water."*

But in Shinn's 1978 article, he reported that less than 25 percent of the cores actually dipped toward deep water. There was no "constant dip direction from one block to the next." Nor did all the cores show "a uniform slope." The 2004 assertion that "all the cores dipped toward deep water" wasn't, in any manner, the actual case.

Extensive details of Shinn's responses to numerous questions are contained in a 2004 DVD documentary, *The Ancient Bimini Harbor: Uncovering the Great Bimini Hoax* as well as a 29-page report. Many of these details concern a series of factual errors included in some of Shinn's articles. These are intriguing from a scientific accuracy perspective, but the present discussion will be limited to his assertions about the cores.

In response to questions about the 8 cores he reported with no internal strata—and no dipping, Shinn replied, "You can not see bedding/layers in a core only 4 inches in diameter." That was confusing because all of Shinn's cores were 4-inch cores. If you can't see bedding in 4-inch cores, why did he do them, and how did he then discern bedding in the other 9 cores? He never addressed this issue, nor did he specifically address why his 1980 and 2004 articles related that all 17 of the 1978 cores showed an internal strata dipping toward deep water.

With respect to the other 9 cores—many of which were horizontal—he was asked why he later wrote that they all "dipped toward deep water"? He replied: "the critical point was that none dipped toward land." But that was not what he asserted in 1980 or 2004. He was also asked about the discrepancy between his actual 1978 results and what he wrote in 1980 with McKusick, where they wrote: "Two areas of the formation were studied, and both show slope and uniform particle size, bedding planes and constant dip direction from one block to the next."

Shinn replied, "You are very astute to note that statement. I should have said only at the south site." But even at Shinn's south site, less than half of his cores actually dipped toward deep water. When asked about the *Skeptical Inquirer* article where he wrote, "Sure enough, all the cores showed consistent dipping of strata toward the deep water . . . " he replied, "It had been almost 30 years since the first study when I wrote the *Skeptical Inquirer* article. I suppose I could have been a little more precise."

As an explanation, Shinn wrote: "You must realize that because of all the craziness surrounding the Bimini site and the unusual people, it was hard to take the exercise with the same seriousness we would have employed with our regular research. We did it for fun. There was not the peer review usually associated with our real jobs. The details you have pointed out are evidence of minimal peer review. I got a little carried away to make a good story . . . "

In 1978, Shinn briefly discussed the columns at Bimini—investigated earlier by Harrison—writing that they "turned out to be cement barrels . . . " He described the two marble pillars Harrison found as "lengths of marble." In McKusick and Shinn's 1980 *Nature* article, they began by describing Harrison's 1971 observations about Bimini. When summarizing the cylinders Harrison investigated, they stated, "some submarine structures described as pillars were hardened concrete originally stored in wooden barrels and dumped overboard in recent times at the harbor entrance." There was no mention of the marble columns. In McKusick's 1984 article discussing Bimini, all he wrote about the columns was, "temple pillars are merely hardened cement in discarded barrels." In Shinn's 2004 article, he wrote, "(Harrison) showed that so-called columns on a site about two miles from the stones were made of Portland cement."

It can be reasonably concluded that the presence of the marble cylinders—reported by Harrison as not from the Bahamas nor probably from America—created a complication in the skeptics' arguments about Bimini. To make the arguments against Bimini unequivocal, the marble had to be ignored until it "disappeared." The same idea can be suggested about the core results. In brief, they didn't support the contention that the formation was natural. The core results needed to unequivocal, so they were described as "consistent" in 1980 culminating with Shinn's 2004 claim that *all the cores dipped toward deep water.*

Another area of interest were the carbon dates Shinn and McKusick reported. All of Shinn's articles cite carbon dates ranging from about 2000 to 3000 years ago. An e-mail to Shinn mentioned that a recent *Marine Geology* article about Florida beachrock stated that carbon dating of beachrock using what's called a *bulk dating method* was unreliable because of contamination from recent carbonate material. Shinn wanted to know who wrote the article and where it was published.

Strangely, the article was made more intriguing because of one of the authors' names. It was Eugene Shinnu. Shinnu had the same snail mail USGS address and title as Eugene Shinn. The article had direct implications on the reliability of the Bimini carbon dating Shinn performed, but Bimini wasn't mentioned in it. The article clearly reported that utilizing the bulk carbon dating method on beachrock tended to result in dates that are often too recent. This is due to the constant contamination created by carbonate in the seawater. The reply to Shinn cited the source and mentioned that he was one of the authors of it.

Shinn explained how the study took place and related, "you are right, dating of beachrock is not very precise especially if it is a bulk sample.

The dates listed in the nature article were bulk dates done at a later date by a student learning the carbon 14 method."

John Gifford, now at the University of Miami, was also contacted. Gifford sent a copy of his 1980 article with Ball and related that he was open to new findings. Gifford also wrote that he taught a course in pseudoscience in archaeology. These courses usually utilize Kenneth Feder's text wherein Gifford's Bimini research is cited. A summary of the findings was sent to Gifford, along with a few questions. At issue were Gifford's assertions that no prop stones were present at Bimini nor were there any multiple tiers of stones. Among the questions, he was asked if lights were used to look under stones and if the observations were made mainly from the surface. He did not respond again.

Conclusion

An article detailing the Bimini discoveries from the May 2005 trip—as well as the interactions with Shinn and Gifford—was released in November 2005 (http://www.mysterious-america.net/biminihoax.html) with a brief press release going out on newswires. The report was widely cited on the Internet, including on archaeology news services. The subsequent response was unexpected. While many skeptics indicated that they would not read any of the report, many did so within a week. All but a few grudgingly admitted that the Bimini Road may well have been a harbor. The stone circles, anchors, and slabs of stone under the large blocks were the strongest evidence, in their opinion. Surprisingly, positive responses came from archaeology students and even a few archaeologists at major universities. Some skeptical message boards on the Internet posted links to Shinn's 2004 *Skeptical Inquirer* article on the Bimini Road and asserted that looking at anything else was a waste of time.

The May 2005 findings at the Andros Platform were somewhat disappointing. Large areas of the platform were covered with sand but other areas were very clear of sand. Bill Donato, the first archaeologist who has examined the site, concurs with the idea that it was a harbor breakwater. The formation appears to have been made in a manner similar to Mediterranean harbors. Beachrock blocks were placed on the top of a natural ridge that jutted into the water off a point enclosing a natural harbor area. The top tier may have had a flat area, with a quay on it. A large corner from a top block (carbonate limestone under eight feet of water) was removed and taken onto the boat. A piece from the middle of the block was removed. The sample was sent to Beta Analytic Labs in Miami, Fl. The lab prepared the sample for carbon dating by removing the exterior layers and removal of contamination. The resulting carbon date showed that the stone formed in 4480 B.C. +/- 140 years. Thus, the Andros Platform may well have been utilized around the same time as the Bimini harbor.

The evidence from May 2005 is clear-cut and definitive. The Bimini site has many artifacts, including numerous stone anchors, multiple tiers, prop stones, and many cut rectangular slabs of stone under large blocks to level them. The assertions of Harrison, and Ball and Gifford (that no prop stones are present and not one example of a multiple tier of stones is there), were easily discredited. Using the criteria Shinn proposed (that all the stones should tilt toward deep water if it is natural), his actual findings indicate that the formation is not natural. In short, the Bimini Road is clearly an ancient harbor, utilized at a remote time when no maritime cultures were supposedly in the region. Whether or not the site will eventually be related to Atlantis or not remains to be seen. From the perspective of ascertaining whether Cayce's 1940 prediction was true, the answer is clear: We don't know yet. Cayce stated that a portion of Atlantis would rise in 1968 and 1969 near Bimini. He didn't say that it would be recognized as such.

The Andros Platform would have been a harbor perhaps around 4,000 B.C. Source—*Dee Turman, courtesy of ATA Productions.*

14

Assessing Cayce's Most Important Atlantis Statements–Conclusion

> Cayce did not claim infallibility. In fact, he said that under some circumstances, a "reading" could be influenced by the intentions and mindset of those asking him the questions.
> Little, Van Auken, and Little (2001)
> *Mound Builders: Edgar Cayce's Forgotten Record of Ancient America*

Cayce's story of Atlantis actually contains numerous specific statements that are amenable to validation. That is, Cayce's assertions can be compared to current scientific knowledge. Our previous books have evaluated Cayce's assertions about Central America, the Mound Builders, and South America. In general, Cayce appears to have been 73 to 90 percent correct in his specific statements regarding the history he relates in those areas.

In addition, prior chapters have looked at research on Cayce's three Halls of Records, and this, the final chapter, evaluates some of Cayce's other important assertions about Atlantis. There are several ways this information can be presented, but perhaps the most logical way to begin is to examine Cayce's statements chronologically.

10 Million Years Ago

In 1925, Cayce revealed that the first souls entered into primitive life forms with limited consciousness sometime prior to 10 million years ago. At an unknown time after this appearance, the souls entered into various animal forms, which include descriptions by Cayce that are similar to early primates and hominids. According to the readings, their bodies were not the more "perfected bodies" that appeared in Atlantis around 210,000 years ago. In one description of these post-10 million-year ago creatures, Cayce stated that some were very small, like midgets while others were gigantic, up to 10 or 12-feet tall (364-11). In a 1932 reading (364-12) Cayce related that these first became dwellers in caves and nested in trees. At the time Cayce gave these startling readings, they were considered to be preposterous and impossible by known science. For example, a 1922 textbook, *The Outline of Science*, related that the first primates appeared 1.2 million years ago and the first upright-walking hominids appeared only 500,000 years ago.

In July 2002, a 40-member research team confirmed the discovery of an eight million year old hominid in Chad, Africa. Their results were published in *Nature*. In a 2001 interview of paleontologist Dr. Bridgette Senut, who was asked about the ongoing research looking for the first hominid, Senut asserted that they probably appeared sometime between nine to ten million years ago and that they nested in trees—precisely as Cayce related in 1925 and 1932. The idea that many early hominids were very small, like pygmies—or "midgets" as Cayce described them—is fully accepted.

Another discovery confirming one of Cayce's more fantastic claims was reported November 7, 2005. In 1932, Cayce related that some of the early humanlike forms (emerging after the pre-10 million year ago influx of souls) stood 10 to 12 feet tall. This idea has also been considered to be fantastic and highly improbable. But in 2005 McMaster University earth scientist Jack Rink reported on new data on *Gigantopithecus blacki*, a giant ape that measured an astonishing 10-feet tall. The first evidence of *Gigantopithecus* was a single tooth found in a Hong Kong apothecary shop in 1935. Gradually, paleontologists found more pieces of the huge ape and were able to reconstruct its complete size. *Gigantopithecus* has now been found in the fossil record as long ago as 6.3 million years.

210,000 B.C.—A New Human Form Appears on Atlantis

It would not be possible to confirm that any life forms appeared on Atlantis for a simple reason. Atlantis no longer exists. But if evidence showed that a new type of human—approaching the characteristics of modern *Homo sapiens*—suddenly appeared around 210,000 years ago, it would lend support to Cayce's contention. As Cayce described this new human, it was not quite the fully modern human body, but was a vast improvement over the prior primitive forms. In 1992, a relatively new type of genetic research on ancient remains pointed to a common human ancestor (a female) who is believed to have first appeared in Africa about 200,000 years ago. This woman was dubbed "Eve" by the researchers. There is no basis to link this genetic information to Cayce except for the startling correspondence between the date Cayce cited and the date the geneticists cite. But the 200,000 B.C. date for the appearance of Eve is now accepted by geneticists. In addition, it is not believed that Eve was fully a modern human—a *Homo sapien*. More information on this type of testing is found later in this chapter.

106,000 B.C.—Perfected Human Bodies Appear

Cayce's Story of Amilius and Lilith relates that perfected human bodies (*Homo sapiens*) first appeared in Atlantis in 106,000 B.C. An assessment of this assertion is difficult, again, because Atlantis no longer exists. But also, the current genetic and archaeological evidence is unclear and sometimes contradictory. In a 2001 paper published by the *American Institute of Biological Sciences*, geneticist Donald Johanson relates that 100,000 years ago the Old World was occupied by a diverse group of near-modern hominids including *Neanderthals* and *Homo erectus*. The origin of modern humans, *Homo sapiens*, is generally believed to be Africa. While early forms of hominids migrated from Africa to other parts of the world, the current theory asserts that *Homo sapiens* developed in Africa around 100,000 years ago and then migrated to areas where other hominids already lived. Some evidence of these first *Homo sapiens* has been found in several non–African locations. The 100,000 year ago date is generally consistent with Cayce's 106,000 B.C. date. Most geneticists accepting this idea assert that there was a second wave of *Homo sapiens* migrated out of Africa around 50,000 B.C.—because that's when they started appearing in larger numbers in various areas of the world. The other hominid forms living in areas of the world (such as Neanderthal) were gradually replaced by the more advanced *Homo sapiens*. This theory is called the *Out of Africa Model*. A competing theory asserts that the early hominids that left Africa around 100,000 years ago in small numbers gradually evolved into modern humans (*Homo sapiens*) in different regions of the world simultaneously. This theory is called the *Multiregional Continuity Model*. Evidence from the Multiregional Continuity Model is consistent with Cayce's assertions.

In general, Africa is pinpointed as the site of human emergence for two reasons. First, the majority of truly ancient hominid remains have been discovered in Africa partly due to an ideal climate that preserves bones. Second, the oldest type of mtDNA is known to be of African lineage. But neither theory has gained complete acceptance and researchers have a great deal of work left to clarify the origin of modern humans.

Pre-50,722 B.C.—Five Races-Five Projections

Sometime before the first destruction of Atlantis, which occurred after the 50,722 B.C. meeting to discuss the problem of the large animals, Cayce relates that five races developed simultaneously in five different places. Cayce's descriptions of these races were based on a division of the five senses and color, but he asserted that the races were equal. Human DNA research comparing different racial and ethnic groups shows an astonishing similarity in DNA. Geneticists have found that the DNA differences between modern human populations from Europe, Africa, or Asia are almost nonexistent. In contrast, the closest living relative to humans, the chimpanzee, shows large variations in DNA even between chimps compared from the same living group. Cayce's assertion that separate races, each race essentially identical to the others, developed 50,000 years ago does have some strong support in research. The Multiregional Continuity Model supports it as well as new DNA testing. But a full understanding of this requires that the type of DNA testing performed in this research be explained.

Mitochondrial DNA

In *The Lost Hall of Records* (2000), by John Van Auken and Lora Little, a somewhat startling proposal was made by Greg Little in a brief Afterword. Little speculated that a genetic trace of Atlantean migrations to various parts of the world may well have been discovered. The idea was expanded in the subsequent books *Mound Builders* (2001), *Ancient South America* (2002), *Secrets of the Ancient World* (2003), and in several articles in the A.R.E.'s monthly membership publication *Ancient Mysteries*.

The type of genetic research that may have uncovered Atlantean migrations is conducted on mitochondrial DNA, or *mtDNA*, for short. The mitochondria are small organelles found by the thousands in nearly every human cell. Their function is to convert sugar (glucose) into a usable form of energy for the body's life processes. The mitochondria are a type of ancient bacteria existing in a symbiotic relationship with cells. As bacteria, they carry their own DNA and replicate on their own. In contrast to human DNA's massive 3 billion bits of information, mtDNA has only 16,569 bits of information, encoded in links between pairs of amino acids. But mtDNA is far easier to test than is human DNA and it is now routinely done by many labs around the world.

The mtDNA found in humans is passed along only through the female side. That is, your mtDNA came from your mother, who got it from her mother, and so on, back to the first human female. This first modern female carrying the original version of mitochondria is referred to as *Mitochondrial Eve*. She is believed (by archaeologists and geneticists) to have existed in Africa sometime around 200,000 B.C., but as related earlier, this is partially speculation based on the current theories and knowledge.

The initial research on human mtDNA was conducted in the 1980s on Native American tribes by geneticists from Atlanta's Emory University, during efforts to track down genetic diseases specific to Native

Americans. The geneticists were mainly interested in human DNA (*nDNA*) when they began the research, but they wanted to use another form of DNA to calibrate possible mutations found in human DNA. Because all humans carry the mitochondria they obtained from their mother, mitochondrial DNA was seen as the ideal comparison. They expected all the mtDNA they tested from the Native Americans to be identical because it was assumed that the simple one-celled mitochondria wouldn't mutate.

Samples of mtDNA are typically obtained from hair roots in living subjects. When the geneticists began comparing the amino acid sequences they obtained from the Native Americans' mtDNA, they were astonished to discover that four different variations of it were present. The four variations found in the mtDNA of the tested Native Americans were termed *Haplogroups* and were labeled A, B, C, and D, for the sake of simplicity.

The variations—the four haplogroups—had developed as a result of mutations in the mtDNA amino acid sequence. A mutation is essentially the substitution of a different amino acid in the normal links between two amino acids. Most of these mutations are trivial but some of them are the cause of diseases.

The way the different mtDNA haplogroups formed from mutations isn't as difficult to understand as one might think. Mitochondrial Eve, the first female, had the original form of mtDNA. Her offspring were all given her mtDNA in the fertilized egg. Their offspring were given the same mtDNA, and so on. But in nature, things are seldom perfect. Somewhere down the line of female descendants, the mtDNA that was passed on to a daughter had an imperfect duplication of the mtDNA in the egg—a mutation occurred. As mentioned in the prior paragraph, a mutation in mtDNA is the substitution of one amino acid for another. But when the mutation in mtDNA appeared in this female, her subsequent offspring were given her mutation. Their offspring, in turn, had the same mutation passed on to them, and so on. Over the past 200,000 years, there have been at least 42 major mutations that occurred, and several subsequent minor mutations within the 42 major ones. Each of the 42 major mutations are called *haplogroups*, and alphabet letters were assigned to each as they were discovered. When the alphabet was ex-

hausted, numbers were added. The first female who had a new mutation is called a *mini-Eve* by geneticists. Strangely, Cayce's idea of many
Adam and Eves has found support in this research.

The reasons for the mutations are varied, but they include a sort of
random chance factor that happens when DNA replicates itself through
RNA. Across the billions of replications, errors can and do occur. But
environmental factors are also involved. Take for example, a tribe who
has always lived in a region of the world where sunlight exposure is
very low. If a small group of these people migrated to areas near the
equator, they would be exposed to sunlight and radiation levels never
before experienced by their tribe. Over time, the exposure to the higher
radiation levels would increase the chance of a mutation occurring. The
same idea applies to other aspects of the environment, such as chemi-
cals and minerals in water or food. While many people interpret the
idea of mutation as something bad, that's only sometimes the case.
Mutations can also provide adaptations to new conditions. Most of the
time, mutations have no discernable effect, but they can be detected
through DNA analysis.

When haplogroups A, B, C, and D were discovered in Native Americans, geneticists soon tested the mtDNA of modern Siberian tribes, finding that they also had the A, C, and D haplogroups present in them. Not
long afterward, the B haplogroup was found in the South Pacific and
parts of Southeast Asia. The results were immediately hailed by archaeologists as confirmation that all the Native Americans had come from
Siberian Asia into Alaska over the land bridge that had formed during
the last Ice Age. These people are termed "Clovis" by archaeologists, and
since the late 1930s the idea that all the ancestors of Native American
tribes came from Siberian Asia in 9500 B.C. has been the dominant idea.

In 1997, however, this "Holy Writ" of American archaeology collapsed
from three independent findings: First, a site in extreme southern Chile
was confirmed to have been settled long before the Siberian migration
occurred. This meant that someone had entered the Americas before
Clovis. Second, the genetic research on mtDNA had progressed to the
astonishing extent that geneticists could determine *when* ancient migrations had occurred and *where* the migrating groups came from. This
unexpected development came from research showing that mtDNA

mutates fairly quickly and at a steady, predictable rate. This mutational rate has enabled geneticists to calculate the dates of the first appearance of each different haplogroup (or the first development of a major mutation) as well as smaller mutations within each haplogroup (generally called *haplotypes*). Thus, mtDNA became a time machine that allowed geneticists to calculate, within limits, when particular haplogroups and haplotypes emerged. Then, by comparing the variations of mtDNA found in different populations around the world, the time each haplogroup migrated to a particular area could be calculated. This development was greatly aided by an avalanche of mtDNA research conducted on ancient remains.

Surprisingly, the first results from using mtDNA as a time machine showed that people probably entered the Americas as early as 47,000 years ago. Although the initial research was ridiculed by many archaeologists, it has been confirmed repeatedly by both genetic research and actual excavations at sites. But the third and biggest blow to the "Clovis-first" idea came when it was announced that an unknown mtDNA Haplogroup (labeled "X") was discovered in about three percent of living Native Americans.

Haplogroup X was soon found in small numbers in Finnish populations (less than one percent), and it was immediately speculated that X *had* to be European in origin. To maintain the idea that all Native Americans came from Asia, archaeologists asserted that historic Europeans (perhaps the Norse) had obviously inbred with some Native Americans leading to the small presence of Haplogroup X in some tribes. But by late 1997, geneticists were extensively testing ancient remains for mtDNA, which had been recovered from mounds and burials. Samples of mtDNA obtained from teeth and bones were found to have perfectly preserved samples of mtDNA. What was found in North America was astonishing. Haplogroup X was found in high numbers in burial mounds located in the lands traditionally known as Iroquois. Up to half of the remains taken from some mounds showed the presence of haplogroup X. The implication was clear: Haplogroup X had been in America in truly ancient times. It was a disturbing finding to many archaeologists. But what has since followed borders on incredible.

Atlantis and the Iroquois

Today, there are 42 major haplogroups that have been identified in living populations as well as several extinct versions discovered in South America. Most of these modern haplogroups have now had their origin identified, but haplogroup X remains a mystery. Many people assert that it is Caucasian in origin, but this is mere speculation that emerged when it was found in Finland. Cayce, in fact, stated that the Atlanteans were a "red" race, and that many Atlanteans migrated to the Iroquois lands and merged with the people already there. The presence of high levels of haplogroup X in mounds located in the traditional Iroquois land led the present authors to carefully examine other populations where haplogroup X has been found.

Atlantean Migrations to America, Egypt, the Pyrenees, the Gobi, Yucatan, and Peru

Edgar Cayce's chronology of Atlantis relates that a wave of migration occurred after the first destruction (*circa* 50,000 B.C.) and also at the time of the second destruction (28,000–22006 B.C.). The largest migration occurred just before the final destruction of Atlantis (10,000 B.C.). In brief, these were primarily to Egypt, the Pyrenees Mountains, the Gobi area, northeast and southwest America, the Yucatan and other parts of Mexico, and Peru. Current genetic research on mtDNA samples removed from ancient remains has identified the presence of haplogroup X in Egypt and Israel, the Pyrenees Mountains, northeast and southwest America, portions of Mexico, and Peru—as well as in ancient remains found in Florida. Haplogroup X has also been confirmed to be present in a small tribe in the Altaic Mountains of the Gobi. The tribe is of ancient origins. What is perhaps most amazing is that the estimates made by geneticists—of when haplogroup X entered key areas—closely match Cayce's chronology. Emory University researchers have shown haplogroup X first entered the Americas perhaps as early as 36,000 years ago, but the period around 24,000–28,000 B.C. is the center point of their estimate.

A 2003 study in the *American Journal of Human Genetics*, coauthored by

43 geneticists, provides the most up-to-date information on the dispersion of haplogroup X throughout the world. The largest migration of haplogroup X into America occurred around the center point date of 10,400 B.C. Astonishingly, that is almost the precise date Cayce gave for the preparations to preserve the Atlantean records and when a large migration from Atlantis occurred.

The 2003 study mentioned in the prior paragraph confirmed observations that have been consistently made since the discovery of haplogroup X in 1997—only 9 years ago. "Haplogroup X is an exception to this pattern of limited geographical distribution" that has been found with all other mtDNA haplogroups. Wherever haplogroup X originated, it has found its way to many places, but it is primarily found in relatively large numbers in regional pockets across the globe. These pockets are the traditional Iroquois lands, in a small region of the Gobi, Egypt and Israel, ancient cemeteries in the Pyrenees, and in ancient remains in Peru.

The geneticists' estimates of the first appearance of haplogroup X centers on 50,000 years ago, the approximate date given by Cayce for the appearances of the "Five Races." But where it actually originated isn't known. For that reason, most geneticists simply assume it must have been in North Africa. Haplogroup X itself shows a sub-mutation (called $X1$), which occurred when an influx of people came into the Mediterranean and Red Sea areas at a date coinciding with Cayce's timetable of the beginning of the second destruction of Atlantis. The center point of the geneticists' estimate for the appearance of X1 is 28,500 B.C.—just before the second destruction began. Combined with the evidence indicating the largest influx of haplogroup X into the Americas came in 10,400 B.C., the implications are increasingly obvious—haplogroup X may well be Atlantean. These developments are clearly astonishing and may eventually provide solid proof that the essence of Cayce's story of Atlantis is true.

Second Haplogroup X Mutation, the Flood, and the Incredible Druze

The 2003 study mentioned in the prior paragraphs also contained data on the distribution of haplogroup X in living populations from everywhere in the world except the Americas and South Pacific. (Data on the Americas and South Pacific areas were included in prior reports.) The 2003 study included 13,589 individuals from 100 distinct ethnic groups or localized regions. A second mutation of haplogroup X (called X2) was identified. The appearance of X2 was found to center around the date 21,000 B.C., which according to Cayce was just after the end of the second destruction of Atlantis—and the biblical Flood.

In general, the highest percentages of X2 were found in groups living near the Mediterranean, as would be expected if a migration to the Mediterranean was made by a maritime-oriented culture in 21,000 B.C. Current populations residing in the Caucasus Mountain regions, long believed to be the home of the "white race," (an assertion by many scholars as well as Cayce) showed a zero percent of the X1 variation and only two percent of X2. Thus, haplogroup X cannot be considered to be a white race. Except for the one aforementioned tribe in the Gobi, all other Siberia locations showed zero percent as did all of India, and the Urals, and all of Western and Southern Africa. In all the other locations—*with one notable exception*—the X1 haplogroup (the oldest dated to 28,500 B.C.) essentially showed zero percent.

Of all 100 groups included in the massive 2003 study, one highly distinct group showed a remarkably high percentage of both X1 and X2. The Druze located in Israel and Egypt, showed nearly 27 percent of their population has the X haplogroup. This is the highest percentage of haplogroup X found in any current population in the world, and is generally 10 times higher than the incidence of Haplogroup X in any other populations. It is a curious finding, made even more incredible by the beliefs of the Druze.

The Druze are a mysterious, closed social sect and faith, not a racial identity per se. It is estimated that worldwide there are about one million Druze, with over 100,000 in Israel, a quarter million in Lebanon, and another quarter million in Syria. There are traditions of the group extending into remote times, but since the formal founding of the Islamic sect around a thousand years ago, it is known that they have carefully managed to marry only within their own sect. They have their own civil laws and courts and the Israeli government officially recognizes the Druze. The Druze society does not accept converts, does no missionizing, nor does it share its religious materials or history with outsiders. The symbol of the Druze is the five-pointed star, because it is the natural number of man. They combine core Islamic spiritual beliefs with Judaism, Christianity, and Gnostic ideas. Most Moslem groups assert that the Druze are not Islamic. The Druze assert that the story of creation is a parable about the one true God. Monotheism is the pivotal ideology of the Druze and some sects are known as The Order of O:N:E:, an interesting parallel to Cayce's Children of the Law of ONE, an assertion that will become clearer shortly.

Official Druze organizations assert that many of the beliefs various people attribute to the Druze are inaccurate. The Druze themselves consist of two distinguishable groups within the faith. A priestly group, consisting of a small percentage of all Druze, are the keepers of the deep secrets. It is said that the large bulk of Druze populations live their entire lives without knowing the most closely guarded secrets. In the United States, there are several small and active Druze communities. The most famous American member of the Druze is the radio and music personality, Casey Kasem. The Druze are devoted to the Seven Commandments of the Universal Mind: 1) A truthful tongue is the first and greatest virtue; 2) Cultivation and protection of other Druze brethren; 3) Excision of fallacies and falsehoods; 4) Rejection of villains and aggressors; 5) Adoration of the Lord; 6) Cheerful acceptance of all that comes from God; 7) Spontaneous acceptance of God's will.

The Druze believe that the rituals and ceremonies that have developed in organized religion have misled people from the "pure faith" of attunement with the one God and also believe that God has manifested as a human several times—including as the Christ.

The reason why the Druze neither evangelize nor accept converts is startling. The starting point of this practice is that the idea of reincarnation is completely accepted by them. They believe that the way to escape the entrapments of the physical earth was shown to every living person in past lives. If individuals chose to reject the idea of the ONE in the past, the Druze assert that they should not be allowed into the sect today. Rather, the individual must transform him- or herself in ways that lead to the correct path to escape physicality. In short, in order to be a Druze, one must be born into the faith. The ancient traditions that the Druze teach among themselves is a complete mystery to outsiders but there are hints about their history that have been derived in scholarly translations of ancient Druze manuscripts.

In a brief, seven-sentence Druze manuscript titled *Behold, the Battle Lies Within You*, the last sentence reads, "So beware, every spiritual battle ever spoken of between Existence and Non-existence, Knowledge and Ignorance, Good and Evil, Light and Darkness has always taken form on earth, if only you could remember the legendary events that took place in the lost continents of Atlantis and Gemorah and that characterized the spiritual tendencies of the Children of Light and the Children of Darkness for tens of thousands of years." Another brief Druze manuscript is titled *Survivors of the Ancient Battle*. The brief story mentions the Children of Light and Hermes and asserts that the ancient language was encoded into the memory of the Druze. The manuscript asserts, "They spoke the Language of Light in Atlantis through forms of communication that no technology has in this age yet recovered." A core Druze belief is that they are the reincarnated souls of the Children of Light—the followers of the Law of One—from Atlantis.

As discussed several times in this book, Cayce's story of Atlantis relates that an ongoing struggle occurred among the Atlanteans. The Children of the Law of One seemingly were constantly pressured by the Sons of Belial—those who rejected the way of the one God. Cayce's story tells us that some followers of the Law of One went to Egypt to escape the oppression and practice their beliefs without interference. The high levels of haplogroup X found in the Druze, combined with their religious and spiritual beliefs (which are strikingly similar to those of the Atlantean Children of the Law of One), lead to an amazing conclusion. The Druze may well be the direct descendants of the Atlantean Law of One group, who initially migrated to Egypt, as well as Atlanteans reincarnating today. It is a truly amazing assertion, but it is an assertion that the Druze themselves appear to make.

Back to the Five Racial Projections

Cayce's story of a separate racial appearance in Atlantis sometime around 50,000 B.C. is certainly supported by the mtDNA evidence. Haplogroup X perfectly fits Cayce's scenario. But what about the other races he mentioned? According to Cayce, the same time the red Atlantean race developed, the Black race appeared in Southern Africa, the Yellow race appeared in Mongolia, the White race appeared in the Caucasus and Carpathian Mountains, and the Brown race developed in South America and Lemuria—in the South Pacific.

Mitochondrial DNA evidence gives no clues about the color of races, but it does provide evidence of when and where major haplogroups appeared. Geneticists have broadly combined the known haplogroups into meaningful categories based on regional areas where each first appeared as well as evidence showing that specific haplogroup mutations are related. For example, the L (L1, L2, and L3) haplogroup is considered a southern African lineage. Eight groups (H, I, J, K, T, U, V, and W) contain the vast majority of mtDNAs from European, North African, and Western Asia Caucasians. Haplogroups A, C, D, E, F, G, and M embrace the majority of the lineages found in Siberian Asia and Native Americans. Oceania, the broad area of the South Pacific, and portions of Southeastern Asia have a high incidence of haplogroups B, P, and Q. Haplogroups M and R (and haplotypes M2, M2a, R1–5) are generally restricted to India. Haplogroup X was actually given that letter (X) because when it was found, it was truly a mystery.

In *Mound Builders* (2001), *Ancient South America* (2002), and *Secrets of the Ancient World* (2003) the present authors showed that Haplogroup B had been found in large numbers in tribes in America's southwest and in Central and South America—especially along the Pacific coast and Peru. But geneticists' estimates of Haplogroup B's first entrance into the Americas center on 33,000 B.C. On the other hand, Haplogroup B was in the South Pacific, the center of Mu, at least 50,000 years ago. And there is clear evidence that an event in the South Pacific led to a large movement of haplogroup B to Melanesia in 28,000 B.C., a date coinciding with the beginning of the second destruction of Atlantis. A 2005 study in *Molecular Biology and Evolution*, coauthored by 13 geneticists, now indicates that the other major haplogroups found in the South Pacific (P and Q) also emerged there around 50,000 B.C. In 2001 we speculated that haplogroup B may well be the genetic trace of ancient Mu, but haplogroups P and Q also appear to be the same. As to Cayce's assertion that the "brown" race emerged in South America as well as in the South Pacific, the evidence supporting the South America contention is missing.

Geneticists have traced the eight European haplogroups by comparing North African mtDNA to the mtDNA obtained from populations in the Caucasus Mountains. A 1999 study in the *American Journal of Human Genetics*, with 10 coauthors, found that the European Haplogroups emerged at a date centering on 50,000 B.C. in the wide region of the Caucasus.

Research on Siberian–Asian haplogroups (A, C, D, etc.) indicates these first emerged in about 62,000 B.C., a date somewhat older than Cayce's. The Indian haplogroups (M and R) are considered a mystery, but geneticists assert they appeared sometime between 50,000 and 70,000 years ago. The Southern African haplogroup L is the oldest known, but other more modern versions, L1 and L2, appeared in central Africa as early as 100,000 B.C. There are more African–based haplogroups that appeared at later dates, generally further north. But identifying those that may be the ones referenced by Cayce's idea is currently impossible.

In sum, support for Cayce's contention of five races appearing simultaneously sometime prior to 50,000 B.C. appears strong, but it does have some discrepancies in the mtDNA evidence. The strongest evidence, nearly perfectly matching all the details provided about Atlantis, comes with haplogroup X. Cayce's assertion of two races appearing in the South Pacific and Caucasus Mountains in 50,000 B.C. is almost completely supported. The dates of the emergence of the Siberian–Asian race is close, given the time frame involved: 62,000 B.C., but the African appearance at the same time can't be resolved from what is presently known.

Evidence For the Final Destruction— The Carolina Bays Event

Cayce's date for the final destruction of Atlantis (10,000 B.C.) is clearly in line with the date given by Plato (9,600 B.C.). Various proposals have been made to explain the destruction, and most people agree that the rising waters at the end of the Ice Age played some role. In his book *Gateway to Atlantis*, Andrew Collins cited strong evidence that an impact from a fragmenting comet was the deathblow to Atlantis.

A similar idea was proposed by a German scientist, Otto Muck, in his 1978 book, *The Secret of Atlantis*. By studying undersea charts, Muck (pronounced mook) came to believe that the 9000–foot–high ridge that divides the Atlantic, called the Mid–Atlantic Ridge, was the location of Atlantis. Muck asserted that a catastrophic event caused the Mid–Atlantic Ridge to volcanically erupt about 11,600 years ago. From aerial photos taken over the Charleston, South Carolina area in 1930, Muck found his evidence. Thousands of identically oriented oval craters were found. As Andrew Collins relates in his book, these have become known as the *Carolina Bays*. These oriented craters are actually found all the way down Florida. Muck asserted that a six–mile–wide asteroid came out of the sky from the northwest and broke into two major pieces and millions of smaller fragments. The two largest fragments struck the Atlantic Ocean, creating the Puerto Rican Trench. The smaller fragments struck the eastern half of America, creating what we know today to be over a half million craters—the Carolina Bays. According to Muck, the impact caused volcanoes to erupt on a large island that is now the Mid–Atlantic Ridge. The island was literally split apart and sank.

The Mid–Atlantic Ridge—and the Azores—have been linked to Atlantis by many researchers. Cayce's statement that in 210,000 B.C. Atlantis stretched from the Mediterranean to the Gulf of Mexico would certainly incorporate the Azores and the Mid–Atlantic Ridge. But Cayce never mentioned the Azores. In 2000 and 2005, a huge research team studied incredible undersea volcanic vents only a few miles from the Mid–Atlantic Ridge. The area is under 2,100 feet of seawater and was dubbed the "Lost City" because of the unusual life found near the heated vents. Claims have been made that earlier research found evidence that indicated the entire Mid–Atlantic Ridge was once above water, and while that may be true, there is simply no definitive proof. Nevertheless, both Plato and Cayce made statements that would indicate the Azores were a part of the Atlantis Empire.

The Carolina Bays event remains moderately controversial and Collins agrees with newer interpretations of the Carolina Bays impact—

a fragmenting comet was the cause. Most experts who continue to investigate the causes of the event are convinced that either a comet or meteor caused it, but newer investigations propose different solutions leading to the same catastrophe.

In the March 2001 issue of *Mammoth Trumpet*, Richard Firestone (of the Lawrence Berkeley National Laboratory) and consultant William Topping outlined the results from their 10-year study of the Carolina Bays event and technical research on artifacts and radiocarbon date analyses that were affected by the event. The scientists' research was supported by a grant from the National Science Foundation. They discovered that "chert artifacts obtained from several widely separated Paleoindian locations in North America revealed a high density of entrance wounds and particles at depths that are evidence of high-velocity particle bombardment." They also discovered that the particles showed evidence of great heating apparently caused by a high-speed particle entry into the atmosphere. In addition, surface artifacts that were subjected to the bombardment showed substantial depletion of ^{235}U, proving that thermal neutrons impacted the artifacts and the surrounding landscape. After adjusting for the influence of nuclear fallout resulting from modern nuclear testing, the authors concluded that the earth had been struck by some sort of "nuclear catastrophe" coming from the sky. The area where this event was focused was the eastern half of America and portions of Central America.

Because of the depletion in radiocarbon caused by the event, Firestone and Topping concluded that the date most people cite for the Carolina Bays event (9,000 B.C.) is too recent. The date of this catastrophic event, according to the authors' calculations, was *circa* 10,450 B.C. (give or take a few hundred years)—closely matching Cayce's 10,000 B.C. date for the destruction of Atlantis. They calculate that the disaster heated portions of the atmosphere to over 1000^{0} C and that it may well have been responsible for the final mass extinction of large animals in North America in 10,000 B.C.—an event that has long perplexed archaeologists. Flash fires were instantly created by the widely dispersed sudden impacts. Firestone and Topping have suggested that a supernova, a cosmic-ray jet, or some sort of explosion in the galaxy caused the Carolina Bays and the disaster that happened *circa* 10,000 B.C.

While there now is scientific consensus that a catastrophic event occurred sometime around 10,000 B.C., the evidence for this event had
been scant in the region of the Bahamas and the Caribbean. Since the
region is mainly water, that should be expected. Recent research, however, has confirmed that massive flash fires occurred throughout the
region at the same time the Carolina Bays event occurred.

One of the most curious mysteries that has long baffled geologists
working in the Caribbean and Bahamas is the presence of small, blackened pebbles embedded into limestone formations, dated to the late
Pleistocene period (*circa* 10,000 B.C.). Scientists studying the black pebbles
for the U.S. Geological Survey wrote: "The blackened pebbles generally
are composed of soilstone crust, lightly lithified grainstone, or multi-
component limestones. . . . in karst potholes, which are abundant
throughout the Caribbean."

While there have been several ideas proposed by geologists about
the source of the enigmatic blackened pebbles found throughout the
Caribbean and in Florida, no one discovered the solution until 1988.
Performing actual direct experimentation on soil, the researchers found
the cause of the black pebbles: the entire region had been subjected to
a sudden heating to at least 400^0 C. In brief, they believe that massive
flash fires swept through the entire region sometime toward the end of
the Pleistocene epoch—around 10,000 B.C. But when the geologists published the study, it was 13 years before the Carolina Bays event had
been confirmed. So the study, curious as it was, was inexplicable.

A fascinating discovery made by underwater archaeologists in November 2002 supports the conclusion that a massive flash fire swept
through the Gulf and Caribbean in around 10,000 B.C. Archaeologists,
looking for a slave ship that sank in 1700 off the coast of Florida, made
an unexpected find (quoting here from the *Ancient Mysteries* newsletter
account): "About 35 miles south of Key West, Florida, electronic equipment on a research vessel identified anomalies on the seafloor at a depth
of 40 feet. Dives revealed nothing but sand on the ocean floor, but the
divers believed something was under the sand. After obtaining a permit
from the Keys National Maritime Sanctuary, a 4- by 9-foot area was
excavated. After removing five feet of sand and 10 inches of a thick
mud, black rocks were encountered. (Initially, they believed that the

rocks were ballast for the slave ship.) Beneath the rocks, a piece of burnt pine was found. When it was taken to the surface, the wood 'smelled like pine.' More pine was found and carbon dating showed that the wood had burned 8400 years ago. Additional research showed that the team had found the remains of a pine forest that had been above water for some time after the last Ice Age had ended. A fire had swept through the forest, blackening the limestone rocks."

While the report cited above found the radiocarbon date to be only 8400 years ago, it does not take into account the finds by Firestone and Topping. When the date is adjusted by their recalculations, based on the nuclear event that struck the Americas sometime around 10,000 B.C., the ancient forest fire discovered near Key West appears to have occurred the same time as the Carolina Bays event.

Conclusion

Edgar Cayce's story of Atlantis is a fantastic tale of humanity that detailed individual's lives, the rise and fall of a highly technological civilization, catastrophic disasters, masses of people escaping terrible cataclysms, and an ongoing battle between two clearly defined factions. The same struggles of the Atlanteans have probably been played out in all civilizations in one way or another. The parallels to the situation in ancient Greece was clearly one reason Plato decided to tell it.

Some people ask why Atlantis matters? On one level it matters because it is a lost or forgotten history. The truth, in itself, is important. The truths about the past can help tell us who we are, where we came from, and the struggles our ancestors faced. History can tell us how to avoid mistakes in the present. The saying, "history repeats itself," relates that we seldom heed these lessons. But on a deeply personal level, Atlantis matters to individuals if they perceive a parallel in their own lives. The day-to-day struggles that faced Atlanteans seem to be the same daily struggles we face. Rapid advances in technology, labor saving devices, pleasure producing diversions, wealth, power, and improved weaponry are all goals of modern civilizations and societies—our society. Many people believe our continual increased use of energy resources—whether coal, oil, or nuclear—is setting the stage for an environmental disaster. According to Cayce's story of Atlantis, the disasters that struck Atlantis were due, in part, to the Atlanteans' misuse of their energy–producing devices. Living within our modern world—with the same challenges that were described in Atlantis—all of us have to find our own balance between the requirements of life in our technologically oriented society with personal spirituality and a sense of purpose. Many people find this balance too difficult to achieve, and so their goals increasingly focus on the acquisition of more stuff and the use of ever more clever technology. People either see a need for seeking a deeper spirituality, or they don't. In the same way, people perceive a deeper importance in the story of Atlantis, or they don't.

Perhaps the best way to end this book is with the very beginning as Cayce related it. We started as souls projecting into physical matter to essentially experience the physical realm. As we became more and more enthralled with the experiences in the physical world, we became more and more enmeshed in physical matter. We eventually became trapped, and many souls forgot their source and purpose. More perfected bodies were developed to allow the many trapped souls to experience the type of consciousness that was necessary to see the truth. The perfected bodies also gave us consciousness to perceive the choices we have and the freedom to choose. The story of Atlantis shows us the choices and the consequences of them. All of us have the freedom to choose, and in one way or another, we do so.

Appendix

Other Atlantis Speculations–
Current Status

Since the early 1900s so many researchers, writers, and others have speculated on the location of Atlantis that a complete summary of these is not practical. Many suggestions about the location of Atlantis are made without any evidence whatsoever. Yet, in order to make this book fairly comprehensive, it is important to acknowledge the most important theories as well as provide a current status report on each.

As related several times previously, the most widely held idea by those who dismiss Plato's Atlantis as a fiction is that he had to adapt the story from some historical event. If the Atlantis story was completely fictional, it is unclear why skeptics believe Plato needed an outside inspiration. But the idea Plato used a real event as an inspiration appears to have been made only after archaeologists and geologists confirmed the destruction of a small island off Crete. This island, Santorini—also known as Thera—was destroyed by a volcanic eruption in 1500 B.C. It is with Santorini that we begin.

Santorini—Thera

In 1909 a classical scholar at Belfast University, K.T. Frost, suggested that Plato got his inspiration for Atlantis from the Bronze Age Minoan culture that was then being excavated on Crete in the Aegean. Excavations at the Knossos Temple revealed a startling and previously

unknown maritime culture that worshipped the bull and erected fan-
tastically detailed structures. Evidence that the Minoans had contact
with Egypt was clearly documented in exquisite wall paintings. Frost
made his Atlantis assertion in a letter to the *London Times* that was largely
ignored by scholars. In 1939 however, the Greek archaeologist Spyridon
Marinatos was excavating another Minoan site at Amnisos on Crete.
Marinatos discovered that a layer of volcanic pumice covered all the
walls and structures, which he noticed were all oddly collapsed in the
same general direction. He came to believe that a massive volcanic eruption on the island of Santorini had destroyed the entire Minoan civilization and that a massive tsunami caused by the eruption had collapsed
all the walls. Later excavations on Santorini showed a similar fate fell on
the Minoan towns located there. Marinatos estimated the size of the
eruption to be 300,000 times more powerful than the first nuclear bomb
test explosions conducted by the United States. By 1950, Marinatos
adopted Frost's idea that the Minoan culture had served as Plato's inspiration for Atlantis, noting the circular harbor area on Santorini that
was left after the eruption and collapse of the volcano's cone. In 1967,
extensive excavations at Akrotiri on Santorini revealed a Pompeii–like
city buried in volcanic pumice. In the late 1960s and 1970s, a rash of
books appeared from mainstream academics arguing that Santorini had
been Atlantis. The strongest argument came from the Greek geologist
Angelos Galanopoulos, who claimed that the eruption of Santorini occurred in 1500 B.C. Since Plato related that Solon had first received the
Atlantis story around 600 B.C., Galanopoulos realized that if he added
900 more B.C. years to the 600 B.C. date, it added to 1500 B.C. The conclusion was obvious to him. Plato stated that the story was 9,000 years
old when it was told to Solon, but Galanopoulos reasoned that Plato
added a zero to the actual 900 years, either intentionally or by mistake,
making it 9000. Because Santorini measured roughly 35 by 22 miles
prior to the eruption, Galanopoulos also claimed that Plato exaggerated
the size of the plain surrounding the Center City by roughly the same
factor of 10. The vast majority of academics jumped on the idea and the
mystery of Atlantis, at least to them, was solved.

Nevertheless, many others have pointed out major flaws in this
theory, and it is far from being universally accepted among scholars.

First, Plato's clear description of Atlantis as being some distance into the Atlantic is simply ignored by the theory. Second, even if the size of the plain surrounding the Center City was somewhat exaggerated by Plato, the island surrounding the plain, as described by Plato, was far larger than Santorini. Third, Plato described the mountain in the middle of the Center City as a low hill, not anything remotely resembling a volcanic cone. Fourth, while Atlantis is usually depicted as a "sacrificial bull cult" by those who support Santorini, the fact is that Plato's account of the Atlantis religion specifically stated that a bull was sacrificed only once every five or six years. Plato went into great detail in describing the statues and decorations of the Atlantean temples, and nowhere in these descriptions is bull worship portrayed. Yet, Santorini has numerous examples of such paintings on walls. In the 1978 book, *Atlantis: Fact or Fiction*, a University of Oklahoma historian, Rufus Fears, remarked:

✳ ✳ ✳

It is disturbing that, in the last quarter of the 20th Century, serious scholarship is still called upon to debate the possibility that Plato's Atlantis is a remembrance of Minoan Crete. Even at a superficial glance, the equation of Atlantis with Minoan Crete, is revealed as a tissue work of fabrications, a flimsy house of cards, constructed by plying dubious hypotheses upon pure speculation, cementing them together ' with false and misleading statements and with spurious reasoning.

Current Santorini Research Status—Excavations have been nearly continuous on Santorini, but essentially nothing new has developed since 1967 to further strengthen the case. Most scholars continue to authoritatively cite Santorini as Plato's inspiration for the story. For example, a 2004 *National Geographic Channel* documentary on Atlantis concluded that Santorini was the only real possibility for the mythical land of Atlantis. Many of the skeptics who cite the Bimini discoveries as a ploy to promote tourism in the Bahamas point to Santorini as Plato's Atlantis.

Santorini itself enjoys a heavy tour trade touting itself as being the "official" site of Atlantis.

Antarctica

The theory that Antarctica, located at the South Pole, was Atlantis has numerous proponents. Explorers confirmed the existence of Antarctica in the 1820s. It is the fifth largest continent and is about 1.5 times as large as the lower 48 states of America. The Antarctica–Atlantis link began with a 1950s theory by a professor of science history at New Hampshire's Keene College, Charles H. Hapgood. Hapgood theorized that the massive buildup of the ice caps at the earth's poles created a destabilizing force on the crust. The crust, the generally solid plates of rock on the earth's surface, floats on a molten, liquid core of stone and iron near the middle. Hapgood came to believe that the crust became so out of balance by the ice caps, that it literally slid on the molten core to the extent that the poles were moved close to the equator. Geological evidence has now shown that Hudson Bay was once the North Pole and that the British Isles were once about two thousand miles south of their current location—implying that Antarctica was once the same distance further to the North. The discovery of the 1513 Piri Re'is Map, showing an ice-free Antarctica, was the final link that Hapgood needed. His 1958 book, *Earth's Shifting Crust*, is considered a classic and in his 1966 book, *Maps of the Ancient Sea Kings*, Hapgood asserted that an ancient maritime culture was plying the world's oceans well before civilization supposedly appeared. Several prominent proponents of the theory are Rand and Rose Flem-Ath (authors of the 1995 book *When the Sky Fell: In Search of Atlantis*) and British author Graham Hancock supports it.

In recent years the Antarctic-Atlantis idea has become cloaked in rumors of government conspiracy, UFOs, Nazis, and disappearing maps. In 1996, maps of Antarctica began disappearing from shelves and even the US Geological Survey temporarily ran out. The Hispanic writer Scott Corrales began checking on the rumors and found that the USGS maps of Antarctica had, indeed, ceased being supplied to sellers. Corrales found that the USGS was updating the map. But in 1999 a Russian research station near the South Pole announced that they had found the remains of a massive lake under the ice caps. It was named Lake Vostok and international scientists mounted a series of expeditions to the site to look for microorganisms, possible new enzymes, and substances that could be of interest to the pharmaceutical industry.

The lake was unexpectedly found to be over 2000 feet deep and was warmed by deep geothermal sources. Then the Russian scientist Ian Toskovoi made an astonishing announcement in March 2000. Toskovoi revealed that a powerful magnetic anomaly had been found on one end of the lake. The anomaly was huge—46 by 65 miles in size—and was believed to be caused by the earth's crust being significantly thinner in that area—for unknown reasons. In a 2002 *FATE Magazine* article, Corrales wrote that the rumor mills in the "lunatic fringe" jumped on the discovery asserting that the site was an underground Nazi base holding over two million Nazis and a fortune in gold that had been stolen during World War II. UFOs were also alleged to be there.

Corrales also related that NASA had been involved in research in the Vostok area in the hopes of developing and testing technology that could one day be used on frozen planetary bodies, but NASA suddenly pulled out. Tales of the presence of Navy SEALS, mysterious illnesses plaguing participants, and national security considerations have been widely circulated regarding NASA's withdrawal. All in all, such rumors have stoked the fires of many who consider Antarctica to be the home of Atlantis, an opening to a hollow earth, and a secret Nazi base.

Current Antarctica Research Status—For those who wish to make an expedition to Antarctica, many cruise companies now offer tours there and opportunities to assist in ongoing research are available. Numerous countries maintain research stations in the region. Other than the Lake Vostok discovery, nothing else of substance has been found there that indicates an ancient human occupation. However, given the strength of the evidence, the chances are very high that the continent did lie closer to the equator in the remote past and that it was inhabited.

Cyprus

As related in a previous chapter, the island of Cyprus has some of the most important ancient harbors along its shores. The island today has less than one million inhabitants and is deeply divided between Greek and Turkish loyalties. According to traditional archaeological timelines, "hunter-gatherers" inhabited Cyprus by 8500 B.C. It later developed Copper and Bronze Age cultures and was dominated by Egypt in about 1000 B.C. The Phoenicians established harbors at Cyprus starting around 850 B.C.

A 2003 book by Robert Sarmast, who describes himself as "an Iranian-American born in Iran," declared that a sunken land bridge between Cyprus and Syria was the lost continent of Atlantis. In *Discovery of Atlantis* Sarmast wrote that he "precisely followed Plato's clues," which eventually led him to the area. Maps, charts, and bottom soundings convinced him that the seabed there almost perfectly matched everything Plato said about Atlantis. As to the "few things Plato stated" about Atlantis that don't match Cyprus, Sarmast asserts that bad translations were the primary cause. For example, Sarmast says that Plato could not possibly have mentioned the Atlantic Ocean in his account, despite the fact that all translations of Plato state that Atlantis was in the Atlantic. He also asserts that the "Pillars of Heracles"—interpreted as the Straits of Gibraltar—is an assumption not based on fact. Despite these obvious flaws, Sarmast claims that he obtained 50 clues from Plato's Atlantis story and that the area between Cyprus and Syria fulfills almost all of them. The area lies under 5000-feet of seawater.

In 2004 and 2005 Sarmast mounted expeditions to the area with some funding from the Cyprus Ministry of Tourism. In several widely reported news conferences, Sarmast announced that his research team had found the Center City of Atlantis, identified by the Acropolis surrounded by canals. He claimed to have found "prominent structures" including walls, river paths, the canals, and other formations exactly matching Plato's measurements of various elements of the Center City. He characterized the evidence as providing irrefutable proof that Cyprus was Atlantis. While some news reports stated that photos of buildings and other features were obtained from the bottom and Sarmast related that he "saw" structures on the bottom, only side-scan sonar was employed during the expeditions. The images Sarmast released were computer-generated images of the bottom's contours. The most "convincing" image of the Acropolis is reprinted here courtesy of Sarmast, and readers are encouraged to draw their own conclusions. The outlines of the rectangular temple of Poseidon are supposedly visible at the top of the egg-shaped Acropolis. Not long after the first 2005 press conference, a group of marine geologists stated that they had examined the area several years earlier because it has the remains of ancient "mud volcanoes" on the bottom. Sarmast's Acropolis, they claimed, is simply a mud volcano showing mudslides down the sides of the irregular shaped cone.

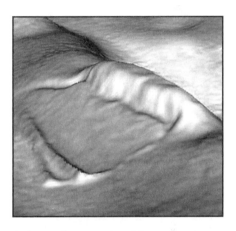

Robert Sarmast's side-scan sonar image of what he states is definitely the Center City of Atlantis in deep water off Cyprus. The center hill (the Acropolis) is, according to Sarmast, the higher elongated "hill" toward the center left. The dark lines are the canals encircling the city. Source—*courtesy of Robert Sarmast.*

Current Cyprus Research Status—In late 2005 Sarmast announced that he had signed a $5 million deal with a U.S. documentary maker to produce a "live" two-hour show where they would send down a submersible with remote cameras to beam the first camera images of Atlantis to the world sometime in 2006. But given prior problems with weather, logistics, and other funding—and previous postponements—it is more likely that the event will take place in 2007.

Spain

A 1928 book, *Atlantis in Spain*, by E. M. Whishaw made what was apparently the first claim that Spain was Atlantis. In the early 1970s, an American educator, Dr. Maxine Asher, mounted expeditions to Bimini and coastal Spain following Edgar Cayce's statement that Atlantis stretched from Gibraltar to the Gulf of Mexico. In an early episode of the popular television series, *In Search Of* . . . Asher related that she had found a variety of structures and stone blocks offshore near Cadiz, Spain. However, Spanish authorities would not allow Asher to take the camera crew to the site and dive for the show. She has made several small clips of underwater film available on her website. The film shows what appear to be well-formed stone blocks lying haphazardly on the bottom. In the late 1990s, Asher's team claimed to discover a half-mile wide city under 200 feet of water not far from Gibraltar, on the Spanish side of the Strait. Several other Spanish investigators have recently claimed that Atlantis lies in the water around Cadiz, but only a few photos of what look like modern stone blocks have been offered as evidence. The area is a major shipping lane and some of the photos that have been offered appear to be the remains of modern dumping. The more recent Spanish investigators appear to be focusing on the area Asher previously identified.

In 2004, the *BBC* issued a story with a provocative and teasing headline: "A scientist says he may have found remains of the lost city of Atlantis." The story implied that ruins were allegedly found at a Spanish National Park near Cadiz. Rainier Kuhne of Germany's University of Wuppertal issued an Internet article relating that he had been given a satellite image of Cadiz. In a marshy area near the southern coast of Spain, Kuhne claimed that he could discern two rectangular forms in the center of what looks like a partial circular line. Kuhne asserts that the two rectangular forms are the remains of the two temples that Plato stated were on the Acropolis in the middle of the Center City of Atlantis. According to Kuhne, the "line" was one of the concentric canals. Kuhne's measurements of the "building structures" showed that they were 20 percent larger than Plato's description, and he believes that the "stade," the ancient Greek unit of measurement, was actually larger than what is usually accepted. Kuhne also argues that when Plato used the word "island" to describe Atlantis, he really meant a "coast" or "region." As to the time of Atlantis' destruction, Kuhne says it took place in 500 B.C. and that a regional flood occurred at that time. Strangely, Kuhne appears to have not asked locals about the area and is awaiting funding to mount an expedition. The satellite image Kuhne used is not the best resolution and a blow-up of the "rectangular structures" shows that they don't seem to actually be rectangular.

Current Spain Research Status—Kuhne's "discovery" appears to be awaiting funding and little information has come from him since his initial announcements. Asher is supposedly releasing a book in 2006 detailing her finds. Several other Spanish researchers have reported that numerous independent researchers have been making exploratory dives along the coast of Spain, especially focusing on the area described by Asher and at Cadiz. Of all the areas where individuals and groups are searching for Atlantis, this is the most confusing, with various individuals claiming to be the first. It is very likely that throughout the next few years, a host of claims will be made. But it does appear that along Spain's coast, ruins will eventually be discovered and verified.

Black Sea/Turkey

Research in the Black Sea has shown that a massive flood did occur in the region sometime around 5500 B.C. In 2000, underwater explorer Robert Ballard confirmed that humans had lived along the ancient shoreline, finding remains 300 feet below the present surface of the sea. Researchers believe that in 5510 B.C. the Bosporus Strait, connecting the Black Sea to the Mediterranean, broke apart apparently because of rising sea levels. The resulting flood apparently drowned countless people. The primary researchers believe that this flood may be the basis of Noah's flood, but others suggest that it may be the inspiration for Plato's Atlantis. According to the proponents of the idea, the ancient Greeks called the Bosporus Strait the Pillars of Heracles. The Black Sea idea is also put forth by a few proponents of ancient Turkey as Atlantis. Turkey certainly has some of the most ancient building structures on earth, but few people accept that Turkey was Atlantis.

Current Black Sea Research Status—In truth, none of the researchers actively searching the bottom of the Black Sea are looking for Atlantis. They have found evidence of human habitation, evidence of a flood, and artifacts such as ancient boats.

Ireland

Lewis Spence actually once suggested that Ireland might have been Atlantis basing the idea on mythology and the size of the island. More recently, Ulf Erlingsson of the University of Uppsala in Sweden, made the same proposal in the book, *Atlantis From a Geographer's Perspective.* According to the book, Plato's story of Atlantis sinking referred to a small portion of Ireland called the Dogger Bank that was submerged around 6000 B.C. It lies in the North Sea at a depth of 165 feet. Erlingsson suggests that Ireland was the main island of Atlantis, close to the size Plato described when giving his measurements, but the center city was supposedly on the Dogger Bank.

Current Ireland Research Status—The UK has been conducting more and more underwater archaeological investigations in recent years. Numerous finds of human habitation have been made, especially in shallow water along the coast. The majority of the artifacts recovered have been stone tools, points, and broken implements. However, in response to Erlingsson's claims, marine archaeologists in the U.K. have stated that the Dogger Bank shoal has been thoroughly investigated and nothing had been found.

Spartel Island

Spartel Island is a small underwater mud shoal located just to the outside of the Straits of Gibraltar. It is about 5 by 2.5 miles in extent and lies in water between 170 to 300 feet deep. During the last Ice Age, Spartel was above the surface, at least until 14,000 B.C. or so. In 2001, a French history professor Jacques Collina-Girard touted the idea that Spartel could have been the basis for Plato's Atlantis and the media widely reported the discovery. Girard announced several planned expeditions to Spartel but none apparently took place and details are sketchy of what actually occurred. UNESCO supposedly granted funding, but the expeditions were apparently delayed several times.

Current Spartel Research Status—According to several unconfirmed reports, the *National Geographic* has funded a future expedition to Spartel with Collina-Girard with the intention of making a documentary. Several others (Spanish researchers) have also related that they intend to make expeditions to the area.

Indonesia—Sundaland

The idea that Atlantis was Indonesia has been touted since 1997 by physicist Arysio Numes dos Santos of Brazil. Santos believes that the Atlantic Ocean was, at the time of Plato, actually the area of the Pacific Ocean between Africa and Asia—the South China Sea. Santos believes that a sunken civilization can be found in the South China Sea between Indochina and Borneo. According to Santos, the Garden of Eden was also in the area. The entire region, including a large sunken plain, is often referred to as *Sundaland* after biologist D.S. Johnson first used the term in 1964.

Curiously, geologist Robert Schoch, who teaches undergraduate science at Boston University, supported Santos' claim in his 2003 book, *Voyages of the Pyramid Builders*. Schoch relates that he is convinced Plato's account of Atlantis is primarily fictional, but it contains elements of a Mediterranean war that took place ten to twelve thousand years ago. Strangely, only a few pages later Schoch states that he agrees that Sundaland is the best fit for Plato's Atlantis arguing that the area may be the home of all the world's languages and human genes. Schoch asserts that when the people of Sundaland began fleeing the area around 10,000 years ago because of rising waters, they migrated to a host of places, carrying civilization with them.

Current Indonesia/Sundaland Research Status—For over 12 years Raimy Che-Ross, once a visiting scholar with the Malaysian Commonwealth Studies Center at Cambridge, has been examining ancient Malaysian manuscripts, examining satellite images, and scouring the Indonesian jungles for a legendary lost city. In February 2005, Che-Ross announced that he had found the lost city of *Kota Gelanggi*, reportedly constructed from black rocks. While the ruins are on land and covered in jungle, speculation has run wild that the site may be related to Atlantis. The Malaysian government has funded a large archaeological project at the city. Virtually no underwater archaeological exploration has been done in the submerged portion of Sundaland and apparently none of the individuals who assert it was Atlantis have announced plans to conduct actual research there.

India/Sri Lanka

India is home to one of the oldest and most advanced civilizations known—the Harappan. Numerous ancient Indian texts relate that this ancient culture built a large number of cities and ports that have apparently vanished. While many early scholars believed that the tales were fictional, gradually many of these cities were found and excavated in the Indus Valley, beginning with railroad construction in the 1800s. Mohenjo–Daro, believed to have been constructed around 2500 B.C. was one of the most important sites found. Gradually, numerous Harappa seaports were discovered and Indian archaeologists, led by S.R. Rao who founded India's marine archaeology program, began searching underwater along the Indian Ocean. Author Graham Hancock played an important role in many of these expeditions and his massive 2002 book, *Underworld*, documents the finds.

Near the ancient seaport of Dwarka, stone ruins were found in 1993 about three miles offshore under 60 feet of water. Massive rectangular stone blocks and a curious U–shaped structure were discovered there. In 1991 more stone ruins were found in the Gulf of Cambay. While some archaeologists scoffed at the idea, Rao recovered hundreds of artifacts from the ruins including pottery, bone, tools, and figurines. Sri Lanka, lying just off the southern coast of India, has also yielded both underwater and numerous land–based ruins. Some people suggest that India may have served as the inspiration for Plato and the underwater discoveries are cited as evidence.

Current India Research Status—Underwater archaeologists continue to search along the coastlines of India and also investigate the finds already made. More discoveries will, no doubt, be made and announced. But it is unlikely that any of these finds will definitively be linked to Atlantis.

Malta

Malta is a small island approximately 14 by 8 miles in size located off Sicily. It is about twice the size of Washington, DC. Two other much smaller islands, Gozo and Comino, are located just off the coast and are considered to be part of Malta. During the last Ice Age, Malta was linked to Sicily by a now submerged land bridge. The island has some of the oldest ruins in the world and is famous for having deep erosion ruts running into the water, apparently for horse–drawn carts. The ruins of a temple at Gigantija are believed to be the oldest temple ruins in the world. In 1854 a Maltese architect, Giorgio Grongnet, claimed that Malta had been Atlantis. Two more recent books, *Malta: Echoes of Plato's Island* and *Malta Fdal Atlantis*, make the same claim. There is no doubt that some ruins have been found in the underwater area between Malta and Sicily. In addition, Malta strongly supports archaeological work and maintains a strong tourist industry partly based on archaeology. The link between Malta and Atlantis, like all the claims of Mediterranean–based lands, relies on Plato being wrong on his most critical points.

Early 1920s photo of the excavated Gigantea Temple site on the small island of Gozo, Malta. This temple is considered by many to be the oldest known in the world, and is one reason that some people assert Malta may have been Atlantis. Source—*Wonders of the Past* (1923).

Current Malta Research Status—Malta has ongoing and continuous archaeological work conducted at several places on the island, which also serve as tourist sites. While discoveries are frequently made as excavations continue, nothing has turned up linking Malta to Atlantis. A recent effort has centered on underwater archaeology and many discoveries will, no doubt, be made in that area. One important difference between Malta's effort to link itself to Atlantis and the many other regions and countries that are working to the same end, is that Malta's media completely support the effort.

Troy

The Preface to Eberhard Zangger's 1992 book, *The Flood From Heaven*, gives the author's rationale for locating Plato's lost Atlantis at an unexpected site—Troy.

✳ ✳ ✳

He argues, first, that the Atlantis story was meant by Plato as an account of something historical . . . Rather than proposing a "correct solution" for the problem of Atlantis, rather than even arguing for the existence of such a solution, it is a plea for freedom to think along new lines. It is in the Bronze Age city of Troy that Dr. Zangger finds the most plausible model for the account of the vanished splendors of Atlantis, but there are no triumphant claims for a total correspondence. Perhaps the greatest attraction of Troy is the clear glimpse that has been given, within the past few years, of the secrets, which it still holds. This is especially true of the Trojan plain around the citadel.

As related above, Zangger was convinced that Plato's inspiration for Atlantis was a historical event. Troy was, as we now know, a historical city that was destroyed. In addition, the city of Troy was surrounded by a plain that bordered the Aegean.

Current Troy Research Status—While excavations at Troy continue sporadically, there is no indication whatsoever that archaeologists working at the site have or will find anything that even remotely links Troy to Atlantis.

Index

Gulf Stream studies, 203, 211
IKONOS imaging project, 204, 214–215
Marble, 201, 205, 225
Mortises, 216, 219, 223–224
Proctor's Road, 202, 216–219, 226, 228
Prop stones, 203–204, 220–224, 226–227, 235
Rectangular slabs, 222–223, 226
Sea level history, 227–228
Straight Lines, 204, 214
U-shaped blocks, 221–222
Black Sea, 8, 265–266
Blavatsky, Helena Petrovna, 25–28
Book of Mormon, 179
Book of the Dead (Egyptian & Tibetan), 62
Brady, James, 186, 190
Brasseur de Bourbourg, Charles, 20
Brigham Young University (BYU), 179, 182–183, 186
British Honduras, 54
British Isles, 12
Brush, Robert, 196–199, 211–213
Bull rituals, 17, 257–258

C

Cabot, John, 22
California, 117, 147
Canary Islands, 54
Carolina Bays Event, 250–254
Caribbean, 22, 54
Carpathian Mountains, 51, 249
Carthaginians, 21, 22
Cataclysms, 5–6, 18–19, 23, 27–28, 30–31, 143
Caucasus Mountains, 51, 61, 246, 249
Cayce's accuracy, 236–255
Cayce Edgar, 35–43
Cayce, Edgar Evans, 25, 40, 43, 97, 109, 161–162
Cayce, Gertrude, 38, 42
Cayce, Hugh Lynn, 40, 153, 154, 193, 195
Cay Sal Bank, 195
Cayuga, 55
Cenote, 186, 190
Center City of Atlantis, 13–16, 55–56
Central America (See also Yucatan), 22, 23, 32, 66, 143, 252
Cerve, Wilshar S, .32
Chakras, 94
Chaldea, 101–102

Charney, Desire, 23
Children of Darkness (see Belial), 92
Children of God, 74–75
Children of Men, 74–75
Chimalpopoca Codex, 23
China (see also Gobi), 103, 115, 137
Christ (see also Logos), 57, 91
Cleito, 13–14
Clovis, 242–243
Collins, Andrew, 1, 10–12, 21, 22, 24, 117, 210–211, 250–251
Columbus, Christopher, 22, 54
Comets, 6, 47
Cosa, Italy, 219
Crantor, 6, 20
Creative Forces, 67
Critia/Critias, 4–18
Crystal of Atlantis (see Firestone, Tuaoi Stone)
Cuba, 22, 24, 32, 198, 211, 212
Cypress, 261–263

D

Daughters of man, 74–75
Death Ray (see Firestone), 58, 61
Dee, Dr. John, 22
Destruction of Atlantis, 18–19, 28, 30, 33–34, 43, 46–47, 50, 51, 58–59, 63–66, 147, 250–254
Dickinson, Don, 203–204
Dobecki, Thomas, 169
Donato, William, 200, 202–203, 205, 209, 212, 214, 216–220, 224–225, 234–235
Donnelly, Ignatius, 24–25
Dropides, 4–5
Dream Stela, 164
Druze, 245–248

E

Eagle, Jonathan, 202, 204
Eddy, Sherwood, 40
Eden, 59, 92, 94–95
Edgar Cayce Foundation, 155, 211
Egypt (see also Giza), 2, 4, 6, 8, 25, 31, 46, 61, 66, 74, 92, 95, 103–105, 106, 112–113, 118
Elephants, 45
El-Ka, 139–140
Esai, 52, 58
Essenes, 90–91
Eve, 56–57, 86, 90, 94, 238, 240, 242

274

A.R.E. PRESS

The A.R.E. Press publishes books, videos, and audiotapes meant to improve the quality of our readers' lives—personally, professionally, and spiritually. We hope our products support your endeavors to realize your career potential, to enhance your relationships, to improve your health, and to encourage you to make the changes necessary to live a loving, joyful, and fulfilling life.

For more information or to receive a free catalog, call:

1–800–723–1112

Or write:

A.R.E. Press
215 67th Street
Virginia Beach, VA 23451–2061

About the Authors

Dr. Greg Little, a nationally certified psychologist, has published several hundred articles in professional journals and magazines. He has an M.A. in psychology and a doctorate in counseling from Memphis State University.

Dr. Lora Little has studied the Cayce material for over twenty years. She writes a column for a nationally syndicated magazine and also volunteers in a music services program that she founded while working in a hospice center.

The Littles reside in Memphis, Tennessee.

John Van Auken is an author and speaker on reincarnation, karma, and higher consciousness. He is considered an authority on the Edgar Cayce material and ancient Egypt. John lives in Virginia Beach, Virginia.